Slowly,
he lowered himself on top of her.

Her body was gloriously hot, flushed with blood and throbbing with a life force that made him tremble with desire.

"Stop wiggling, lass. Have mercy on me."

"Me have mercy? I'm the one who's captured."

"Cease." He pressed more heavily on her.

Her gaze flickered down, then back to his face. "Get off. Now."

"Ye want me to? I'm halfway there already."

She looked at him, her eyes wide. He had a sinking feeling that she thought he was mortal. She wanted him to be mortal. And that meant she knew about Vamps. He studied her lovely face—the high cheekbones, delicate jaw, and beguiling green eyes. Some Vamps claimed mortals had no power whatsoever.

They

By Kerrelyn Sparks

ALL I WANT FOR CHRISTMAS IS A VAMPIRE
THE UNDEAD NEXT DOOR
BE STILL MY VAMPIRE HEART
VAMPS AND THE CITY
HOW TO MARRY A MILLIONAIRE VAMPIRE

KERRELYN SPARKS

ALL I WANT FOR
CHRISTMAS
IS A
VAMPIRE

AVON

An Imprint of HarperCollinsPublishers

This is a work of fiction. Names, characters, places, and incidents are products of the author's imagination or are used fictitiously and are not to be construed as real. Any resemblance to actual events, locales, organizations, or persons, living or dead, is entirely coincidental.

AVON BOOKS
An Imprint of HarperCollins*Publishers*
10 East 53rd Street
New York, New York 10022-5299

*This one is for everyone who reads
the Love at Stake books,
and the booksellers who sell them.
May your love never be at stake!*

Acknowledgments

Ian MacPhie might still be looking for his true love if it wasn't for the support and encouragement of some wonderful people. I'd like to thank my husband and children for enduring the terrors of Deadline Hell with me. My critique partners—Vicky, MJ, Vicky, and Sandy—are always there when I need them. My thanks to the West Houston, Northwest Houston, and PASIC chapters of RWA and the fabulous bookstore Katy Budget Books. My thanks also to my agent, Michelle Grajkowski, and my editor, Erika Tsang, and the whole team of professionals at Avon Books. May you all get what you want for Christmas!

Chapter One

The air hummed with bass guitar and rampant lust. He'd come to the right place.

Ian MacPhie strode across the renovated warehouse, his steps falling into rhythm with the pounding drums. The Horny Devils was the best place he could think of for finding a woman. The nightclub was teeming with them. All lovely and all Vamps.

Bright red and blue laser lights zipped here and there, highlighting the ladies' scantily dressed, bouncing bodies as they danced close to the stage. They surged in time with the pounding music like a wild sea at high tide, and he was sucked toward them in a greedy undertow.

One of the red lights zoomed past him, flashing in his face and blinding him for a few seconds. A burst of panic shot through him. What if none of these ladies found him attractive? What if he'd suffered twelve days of agonizing pain to look older and . . . ugly?

As a Vamp he couldn't see his new face in a mirror. He'd appeared in a few digital photos at

Jean-Luc's wedding, or he thought he had. He hadn't recognized the strange man in the pictures. Heather had assured him he looked good, but she'd been such a happy bride, she'd thought everything was beautiful that day.

As Ian's vision readjusted, he realized his moment of panic didn't matter. None of the ladies were looking at him. They all faced the stage, their gazes riveted on the male dancer who strutted down the runway with an Indian warbonnet on his head. The war paint on his hairless chest depicted an arrow that pointed south where a bunch of strategically placed eagle feathers hid his wampum.

Ian took a deep breath and assessed the situation. True, the ladies hadn't noticed him, but he hadn't really tried to get their attention yet. These lassies were certainly in a lusty mood, so his chances were good. Time to put his new face to the test.

He eased into the crowd. Now what should he say? Jean-Luc had successfully courted Heather using charm and wit. He'd give that a try. "Good evening, ladies."

The roar of the music was so loud, only two lady Vamps heard him. They turned their heads and boldly inspected him.

"Not bad," one of them yelled at the other.

Ian gave them what he hoped was a charming smile, though it faltered a bit when he noticed the second girl was wearing black lipstick. He supposed the modern lassies considered that attractive, but it gave him flashbacks of the bubonic plague.

"Nice kilt," the black-lipped girl yelled. "Cute knees."

"Aren't you a dancer?" the first girl shouted.

"Nay. Allow me to introduce myself. I am Ian Mac—"

"Oh, I thought your kilt was a costume!" The first girl laughed. "Do you seriously dress like that?"

The black-lipped girl joined in on the laughter.

"We need to see more than your cute knees!"

Ian hesitated. He needed a witty, charming response. "I'm sure that could be arranged."

Unfortunately, his attempt at flirtatious banter went unnoticed. A sudden surge of high-pitched screams distracted the two girls, and they turned back to the stage. Feathers were flying, and the crowd of women bounced up and down, determined to catch a feathered souvenir.

"Begging yer pardon." Ian tried to regain the two girls' attention. "Could I buy you a drink?"

"That one's mine!" The black-lipped girl shoved the other girl to the side so she could nab a feather.

Ian stepped back, dismayed at how the ladies were pushing each other. He glanced at the stage and gulped. By all the saints, the women had plucked the dancer like a chicken. These modern lassies were more aggressive than he'd realized. When it came to finding his mate, he had assumed he would do the hunting.

Ian moved back to keep from getting jostled by the frantic feather-grabbing women. Perhaps it was a matter of timing. Aye, timing was very important when hunting prey. He would sit back and wait for the right moment. Sooner or later, the dancers would have to take a break, and maybe then the ladies would be more easily impressed.

And while he waited, he'd fortify his nerves with a stiff drink. He strode toward the bar. He had it all figured out. He was searching for a girl who was honest, loyal, pretty, and intelligent. In that order. And of course she would need to be madly in love with him.

That last part was a little tricky. How did he go about making the perfect girl fall in love with him? He doubted his alleged cute knees would be enough.

The female bartender had a phone to one ear and her hand pressed to the other to muffle the loud music. "Sure, I'll keep talking. So you're from California? Land sakes, that's far away."

Two young ladies materialized beside her. They'd used the sound of the bartender's voice as a beacon to help them teleport to the right location.

"Welcome to the Horny Devils." The bartender smiled as

she hung up her phone. "What would you like to drink?"

"Two Blood Lites," one of the California girls ordered. She snapped her sparkly rhinestone-covered cell phone shut, then dropped it into her shiny handbag.

The second girl pointed toward the stage. "Oh my God, he's so hot!"

The girls forgot all about their drinks as they scampered toward the stage.

Ian lifted a hand in greeting. "Good evening, ladies."

They passed him by, their gazes glued to the dancing Indian, who was down to his last two feathers.

Ian sighed. What was the world coming to when a man with honorable intentions had to compete with a male stripper? How could he impress these modern lassies? Maybe Vanda could advise him. With her purple spiky hair and spandex clothing, she'd become a very modern woman. And a very successful one since Vamps were teleporting from the West Coast to come to her club.

Ian settled on a stool at the bar and received a bright smile from the bartender. Miss Cora Lee Primrose no longer wore hoop skirts and her blonde hair in ringlets, but she still sounded like a Southern belle from the Civil War.

"Hey there," she greeted him. "How'd you like to try the latest thing in Fusion Cuisine?"

"There's something new?" He'd been away for too long.

"Yep. It's called Bleer. Synthetic blood mixed with—"

"Beer?"

Cora Lee looked disappointed. "You've already had it?"

"Nay. Lucky guess. I'll take a glass." Ian removed a fiver from his sporran and set it on the counter while she filled a glass with amber liquid. The aroma of blood and yeast made his mouth water. By all the saints, it had been centuries since he'd tasted beer.

"Here you go." Cora Lee set the glass in front of him.

He took a long drink, then licked the reddish foam off his lips. "Excellent."

She grinned. "Glad you like it. Are you new in town?"

Bloody hell. He had thought her initial smile meant she recognized him, but she hadn't. He took another gulp of Bleer to ease the sting. Cora Lee had been in Roman's harem for fifty years, living in the same house where Ian lived and worked as a guard. Had he changed that much?

"It's me, Ian."

Her blue eyes widened. "Ian?"

"Aye. Ian MacPhie."

"You can't be Ian. He's just a young'un."

He glowered at his glass of Bleer. It was a wonder he hadn't gone crazy from being treated like a child for five centuries. "Ye used to ask me to help tighten yer corset. Ye must have thought I was too young to be eyeing the curve of yer hips or the way the corset pushed yer breasts—"

"Why, I never!" Cora Lee stepped back.

"Nay, no' with me, that's for certain."

She huffed. "I would never bed a child."

"I'm three hundred years older than you," he growled.

She tilted her head to study him. "I do declare, your eyes bear a remarkable resemblance to Ian's."

"That could be because I *am* Ian."

"Are you sure?"

"Of course I'm sure. Who else would I be?"

She gave him a suspicious look. "It's just that . . . I don't recall you being so . . ."

"Charming?"

"Grumpy." She sighed. "Ian was such a well-mannered and friendly boy. I was quite fond of him, really."

"Bloody hell, I dinna die. I just look twelve years older now."

"Land sakes. How did you do that?"

Ian hesitated. Roman's Stay-Awake drug was best kept a secret. "It was something I . . . ate. In Texas."

"Something you *ate*? You *wanted* to look older?"

"Aye."

"But why would you do something so awful?"

He gritted his teeth. Being trapped for centuries with a fifteen-year-old face had been a living hell. If Cora Lee couldn't figure that out, well, he didn't feel obliged to explain. "Maybe I just want to get laid."

She huffed. "And you were such a nice young boy."

"Aye." He gulped down the last of his Bleer.

Cora Lee studied him, frowning. "If you got what you wanted, then why are you so grumpy?"

"I'm no' grumpy!"

Her eyes suddenly widened. "Oh, I get it. You haven't gotten laid yet. Maybe I can help."

Bloody hell, he could do his own hunting. He noticed the music's volume had decreased. The Indian dancer had left the stage, and the female natives were restless. He needed advice quick. "Is Vanda here? I need to see her."

"Just a minute." Cora Lee rushed to a table where a lady Vamp sat, chatting with a few male customers. "Pamela! You'll never guess who that fella is over there."

Was Cora Lee trying to set him up with Lady Pamela Smythe-Worthing? No. Hell, no. The Regency-era viscountess from Britain had also been in Roman's harem, and she'd spent fifty years sneering down her nose at him.

Lady Pamela stood and examined him. Her frilly Regency gown was gone. She'd completely embraced the modern age with a red miniskirt and black leather camisole.

"Oh dear, look at that shabby old kilt." Lady Pamela's snooty accent was still the same. "He must be another barbarian from Scotland. Doesn't anyone from that dreadful country die a natural death anymore?"

Ian arched a brow. She had to know he could hear her.

Cora Lee grinned. "Pamela, that's Ian!"

Pamela's eyes widened. "Surely you jest. I shall be quite overset if you're toying with me."

"It *is* Ian," Cora Lee insisted. "He grew a bunch."

"He certainly did." Pamela's gaze raked over him. "I must

say, this brings to mind a question of the utmost importance."

"You mean how did it happen?" Cora Lee guessed. "He told me it was something he—"

"No." Pamela waved a dismissive hand. "The question is"—she leaned close to Cora Lee—"is he a virgin?"

"Land sakes!" Cora Lee giggled. "He did say he wants to get laid."

"Hmm." Pamela tapped a finger against her cheek as she considered. "A five-hundred-year-old virgin. This could be interesting."

Bugger. Leave it to Lady Pamela to make him feel like a circus freak. Ian turned his back to her and strode toward Vanda's office.

"Whoa there!" Cora Lee zipped over at vampire speed and blocked the door. "Vanda gets all riled up if we interrupt her while she's busy."

"Indeed." Lady Pamela sauntered over. "Vanda is the brains behind this business." She smoothed back her long blonde hair. "We're the beauty."

"We sure are." Cora Lee fluttered her eyelashes.

"Congratulations," Ian grumbled. Did the two ladies realize they'd just admitted to being brainless? He silently raised the attribute of intelligence on his wish list from number four to number three.

Cora Lee cracked the door and peeked in. "Woohoo, Vanda! There's someone here to see you."

"It had better be a sexy new dancer," Vanda growled. "Business is down this month."

"I say, capital idea!" Pamela gave Ian a sly grin.

He strode into the office.

Vanda glanced away from her computer screen. "Nice costume. Let's see what you've got under the kilt."

"Oh goody!" Cora Lee clapped her hands together.

"Indeed." Pamela shut the door behind them.

"I'm no' exposing myself." Ian crossed his arms, frowning. "And this is no' a costume."

"Oh, the girls will love that accent." Vanda stood as she looked him over. She was wearing her usual purple catsuit with a black whip around the waist. "You'll need a plaid thong to match your kilt."

"With a red tassel on the end," Cora Lee added.

"Smashing," Pamela murmured.

"Could you make the tassel twirl?" Vanda circled a forefinger in the air.

What the hell? Ian stepped toward her. "Vanda—"

"Come now, we're embarrassing the poor chap." Pamela sidled up to Vanda and whispered, "We think he's a virgin."

He glared at them. "Vanda, do ye no' recognize me?"

She smirked. "Honey, if I'd met you before, you wouldn't be a virgin."

Pamela laughed. "Now which one of us will have the honor of deflowering him?"

"We could draw straws," Cora Lee suggested.

"I'm no' sleeping with any of you," Ian growled. "Vanda, it's me, Ian."

"What?" Vanda blinked, then she narrowed her eyes. "No, I don't think so."

"Bloody hell." He ran a hand through his long hair and accidentally pulled a strand loose from the tied leather strip in the back. "I thought ye might cut my hair like ye used to. And I—I need to talk."

"Ian?" Vanda walked up to him, looking at him closely. "It's really you? What happened?"

"I know!" Cora Lee waved a hand in the air. "He ate something."

"You *ate* something?" Vanda gave him a dubious look.

"He could eat me," Lady Pamela murmured, casting him a seductive look from under her eyelashes.

Cora Lee pressed her fingers to her mouth and giggled.

"I canna say more on the matter." Ian motioned with his head toward Cora Lee and Lady Pamela. A secret would never be safe with them.

Vanda nodded slowly, then glanced at the two blondes. "You two check on the customers."

"Humph. You just want the virgin to yourself." Lady Pamela strolled from the room, followed by Cora Lee.

Vanda shut the door, then walked back to Ian with a grin spreading across her face. "I can't believe it! You're all grown up." She hugged him. They had once been close in height, but now the top of her head reached his chin. "What on earth did you eat that made you grow older?"

"Doona repeat this, but I drank Roman's Stay-Awake drug. I took it twelve days, so I aged twelve years."

Her eyes narrowed. "But you're so much bigger and taller . . . it must have hurt."

It had. He shrugged. "My hair grew a lot, too. I thought it might need cutting."

She pulled the leather thong free from his ponytail and stood back to study him. "I don't think the short curls suit you anymore. You have a rugged look to you now."

Rugged? As in mountainous terrain? No wonder he was having such a hard time shaving. There'd always been a small dent in his chin, but now it felt more like a bloody crater. Actually, it was bloody half the time. Shaving without a mirror was damned hard.

"I like your hair long." Vanda circled her desk and retrieved a pair of scissors from the top drawer. "But it's a little ragged on the ends, so I'll give you a trim."

"Thank you." Ian sat in a chair facing her desk.

Vanda fetched a hairbrush from her handbag and went to work easing out the tangles. Ian closed his eyes, enjoying her familiar touch. She'd cut his hair for the last fifty years, and in that time, he'd confided more to her than anyone else. Even Connor and Angus.

He couldn't tell another man how frustrated he had been. Connor was his immediate supervisor, and a tough guy who would have interpreted his frustration as childish whining. Angus MacKay was the head of MacKay Security and In-

vestigation and Ian's boss. He was also the one who'd saved
Ian from certain death by transforming him in 1542. But
Angus had struggled with guilt for trapping him with the
body and face of a fifteen-year-old. Nay, he could never let
Angus know how unhappy he'd been. But Vanda had under-
stood and kept his secrets.

The scissors snipped. "When did you get back in town?"
she asked.

"Tonight."

"You teleported here from Texas?"

"Nay. I was in Scotland."

"Oh." She continued cutting. "The last I'd heard you were
in Texas, guarding Jean-Luc."

"I was. Last summer."

The snipping sound ceased for a moment. "I heard Phil
was there, too."

"Aye." Was Vanda interested in Phil? He'd been the daytime guard at Roman's townhouse when the harem lived
there. As far as Ian knew, Phil had kept his distance from
the ladies. It was one of Angus's cardinal rules. A guard
never ever became involved with his charges.

Vanda went back to cutting. "So how is Phil?"

"Fine." Ian wondered if she knew about Phil's secret.

"Is he coming back to New York?"

"Eventually. He's training someone to be Jean-Luc's new
daytime guard." Meanwhile, Connor had hired a new mortal
guard, Tony, to live at the townhouse while they waited for
Phil to return. Ian hadn't met him yet, but he wondered if
Tony was a shape shifter, too.

"What were you doing in Scotland?" Vanda asked.

"Nothing much. After all the growing I did, Angus insisted I take a few months off to . . . recover."

"Then it *was* painful." She leaned over his shoulder to
look at him. "Are you all right now?"

"Aye." That wasn't quite true. Growing five inches in less

than a fortnight had taken some adjustment. He'd had to drink huge amounts of synthetic blood to fill out his bigger body. While in the Highlands, he'd had some major repairs done on his small castle. He'd helped with the construction work at night, and the result had added some muscle to his bigger frame. But still, he tripped over his huge feet and cut his new face when shaving, especially around that damned crater in his chin. "I'm fine."

With a dubious snort, she resumed cutting. "How was Scotland?"

"Fine." He was always elated when he first arrived in the Highlands, for it was home and it filled his soul with peace. But after a few nights, he would always realize that every mortal he knew from his past was dead. And then the loneliness would set in.

Vanda sighed. "I get the feeling there's a lot you're not saying. I thought you wanted to talk."

"I am talking."

"I don't have all night like I used to. I have a business to run."

He paused, listening to the clicking sound of her scissors. How could he just come out and say that he wanted to find true love and be blissfully happy in a marriage that would span the centuries, and yet he wasn't sure how to go about it? "How is yer business?"

"*Fine.*" She tossed her scissors on the desk and brushed out his hair with more force than necessary. "Are you going to talk, or do I need to take my whip to you?"

He grinned. Vanda liked to act tough, but she was all bluster no bite. "All right. I'll talk. With my new, older face, I've been thinking . . ."

"Amazing. Did your brain grow, too?"

"Verra funny. I came here tonight because I'm looking for . . ." He couldn't say the words *a woman*. Vanda would probably laugh at him. "I have a crater in my chin."

She laughed at him. "It's a dimple." She tilted her head, studying him. "Are you worried about your looks?"

"No, of course not." He shifted in his chair.

She perched on the edge of her desk. "No one has told you how you look?"

"Men doona speak of such trivial matters. Jean-Luc's new wife said I looked . . . good."

Vanda snorted.

Bugger. He knew Heather had been lying.

Vanda shook her head. "Good is a huge understatement. You're absolutely gorgeous."

A seed of hope burst in Ian's heart. Maybe the right woman could fall for him. "Ye—ye're no' just being kind?"

"Have you ever known me to be particularly kind?"

"Ye have been to me."

"Well." She adjusted the whip around her waist with an annoyed look. "You remind me of my youngest brother. But I guess I can't treat you like a child anymore."

"Sorry to spoil yer fun," he growled.

She grinned. "I'm really happy for you, Ian. You must be thrilled to be all grown up."

"Aye." He drummed his fingers on the arm of his chair.

Her smile faded. "You don't look very thrilled. What's the matter?"

"Now that I look older . . . I'm looking for . . ."

"Yes?"

"A woman."

Her mouth twitched. "Well, that's a start." Her eyes suddenly widened. "Oh my God, you really are a virgin?"

"Nay! I'm almost five hundred years old. What the hell would I be waiting for?"

"Lady Pamela thinks you are. You didn't deny it."

"It's no' something a man should discuss in public. It's verra private."

Vanda chuckled. "You're so old-fashioned. Sex isn't something to be ashamed of."

"I'm no'—" He couldn't deny it. By all the saints, he was ashamed. "It's no' the sex, ye ken. It's the way I had to go about it. It—it never felt right."

Vanda's face grew serious. "We've all done things we regret in order to survive."

"This was more than regrettable. I dinna behave with honor." He'd never confessed this to anyone before.

"What did you do?"

He gathered his shoulder-length hair in the back and tied the leather thong around it. "After Angus changed me, he told me how to go about feeding. In exchange for blood, I was to give the ladies pleasure and make sure they were satisfied."

Vanda sucked in a deep breath. "Sounds good to me."

Ian looked away, embarrassed. "I dinna know now. I was only fifteen, ye ken, so I frequented some brothels at first so I could learn. I—I was a quick learner."

"That's not so awful."

"It *was* awful once I stopped going to brothels. I had trouble seducing the ladies when they thought I was a child. I was getting verra hungry, so I resorted to using mind control to make them see me as older. I left them happy, but . . ."

"You felt guilty?"

Ian clasped his hands together. "Aye. I deceived them. Every relationship I have ever had was based on trickery and deception. I canna stomach doing that again."

"I see."

He sat up. "Now, for the first time in my life, I can be honest. I can finally find the right woman for me."

Vanda smiled. "Then you've come to the right place. With your handsome face, you'll have no problem getting lucky tonight."

"I'm no' looking for one night. I've had centuries of one-nighters. I want to find my true love. I want the same kind of happiness that Roman, Angus, and Jean-Luc have."

Vanda's smile turned into a grimace. "Then you've come

to the wrong place. The ladies who come here aren't usually interested in commitment."

Ian slouched against the back of his chair. "Then how can I find her?"

"Maybe I can help." Vanda eased off the desk. "I was thinking about finding a nice guy for myself, so I joined a site online." She sat behind her desk, grabbed the mouse, and clicked. "This is the hottest new place for singles."

Ian leaned over the desk so he could see the computer screen. He scanned the site called *Single in the City*. It boasted more than half a million clients, all in the vicinity of New York. "That willna work for me. I canna date a mortal."

"Why not?"

"I told you. I refuse to deceive the woman I'm courting. I would have to lie to a mortal until I knew she could be trusted. And then, when I confessed my true nature, it would destroy her trust in me. It wouldna work."

"I disagree. It worked for Roman and Shanna."

"He was no' courting her from the start. He just wanted a dentist. Their romance happened accidentally. And believe me, she was verra upset when she found out the truth."

Vanda shrugged. "She got over it."

"I willna lie to the woman I'm courting. So she had better be a Vamp. A Vamp would understand all I've been through. A mortal woman would no' take kindly to the way I used other women in the past. And I wouldna blame her."

"If she loved you, she would understand."

"My mind is made up. All I want is a vampire."

Vanda sighed. "Okay, but I think you're limiting yourself."

"And she must be a bottle-drinking Vamp who is honest, loyal, intelligent, and pretty."

"Now you're severely limiting yourself." Vanda frowned at the computer screen. "Luckily for you, there's a way to tell who's a Vamp." She clicked on her profile. "See this?"

Ian read the line she pointed at.

I enjoy life to its fullest. (V)

"All the Vamps slip these *V*s into their profiles," Vanda explained. "It's our secret code to let each other know who we are. If someone asks to meet you, and she doesn't have the *V* in her profile, you simply refuse."

Ian's heart beat faster. This was not how he'd envisioned hunting for his true love, but it was a lot better than nothing. "It might actually work."

"Of course it'll work. I have a digital camera here." Vanda opened a drawer. "We'll take your photo and fill out your profile. It'll take a few hours."

"Hours?"

"The profile is quite extensive. You'll have to write an essay." Her face brightened. "I know! *I'll* do it."

"You? Why?"

"Because I'm a woman, and I know what women want to hear. This is brilliant!" She grabbed a pen and notepad.

Her offer was very appealing since Ian had no idea what he should write in an essay. "Remember, it is important to me that ye be honest."

"Of course. But get real, Ian. We can't say you're five hundred years old in your profile."

"I'm four hundred and eighty."

She tapped the pen on the paper, waiting.

"Fine." He groaned. "Ye can say I'm twenty-seven."

"Great." She wrote the number down. "And how tall are you now?"

"Six foot two." He frowned. "Be sure to say I want an honest and loyal woman. Intelligent and pretty, too."

"No problem. Now smile and show me those dimples." She lifted the camera. "And don't worry about a thing. I'm going to make you irresistible."

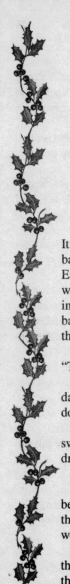

Chapter Two

It was close to dawn when Ian teleported to the back porch of Roman's townhouse on the Upper East Side. He punched the button on his Smart Key wireless remote to disarm the alarm before unlocking the door. The kitchen was dark, except for the backlit digital keypad next to the door. He punched the code to reactivate the alarm.

"Hold it right there," a gruff voice warned him. "Turn around slowly."

Ian turned and spotted the gleam of a Highland dagger, held by a large Scotsman by the kitchen door. "Dougal?"

"Aye." Dougal Kincaid flipped on the light switch. No recognition lit his eyes till his gaze dropped to Ian's kilt. "Is that you, Ian?"

"Aye, it's me. Do ye want to see my ID card?"

"Nay." Dougal smiled as he sheathed his weapon beneath a knee sock. "I recognize yer plaid more than yer face. We dinna expect ye back for another week."

"I was bored." Lonely was more accurate, though Ian didn't want to admit it. "How's everything been?"

"Fairly quiet." Dougal retrieved a bottle of synthetic blood from the refrigerator, then popped it into the microwave. "Are ye coming back to work then?"

"No. I still have a week of vacation." A week when he could concentrate on his search for the perfect mate.

Dougal tilted his head as he studied Ian. "I'd heard ye'd gotten older, but 'tis amazing how different ye look."

"Aye, I can hardly recognize myself." Ian had gazed for five minutes at the photos Vanda had taken. And it wasn't just his face that was different. His body had grown so quickly, he'd barely had time to adjust. He occasionally knocked his hand against things when he overreached with his longer arms, and sometimes he tripped over his bigger, size thirteen feet.

The microwave beeped, and Dougal removed his bedtime snack. "We just had a martial arts practice downstairs." He guzzled down some blood. "Ye should have seen it. Our new guard knocked Phineas off his arse."

"Really?" Ian was impressed. It wasn't often that a mortal could defeat a Vamp in hand-to-hand combat.

Dougal headed out the door. "I'd better get to my shower before the sun rises."

The sun was nearing the horizon. Ian could already feel his metabolism dropping. He followed Dougal down the back stairs to the guardroom in the basement. The pool table had been shoved to the far wall by the sofa to create a large open space for their practice sessions.

Ian picked up a chair that had been knocked over and noticed one of the legs was broken. "That must have been one hell of a fight."

"Aye. A bit embarrassing for Phineas, though." Dougal finished his bottle as he strolled into the dormitory next door. A bathroom door banged shut.

Ian wandered into the dormitory, expecting to see Phineas McKinney, but the young black Vamp wasn't there. The sound of rushing water emanated from both bathrooms, so he was probably taking a shower like Dougal. A lot of

Vamps liked to be clean before succumbing to death-sleep. It helped them feel less like a dead, rotting corpse.

The dormitory was nearly empty now. Ian remembered a time when there'd been ten coffins in the room, one for each Vamp guard to sleep in. Most of the Vamps were gone now, transferred to Eastern Europe to hunt for Casimir.

The floors upstairs were just as vacant. At one time, there'd been Roman, ten harem ladies, and numerous visiting Vamps. It had been an exciting place. But now everyone had moved on.

Roman lived with his mortal wife and child in White Plains, with Connor serving as their bodyguard. The Vamp guards who lived here at Roman's townhouse worked security at Romatech Industries, where synthetic blood and Vampire Fusion Cuisine were manufactured. Connor was head of security there, but he planned to pass the title to Ian so he could concentrate solely on Roman and his family's safety.

Ian was delighted with his upcoming promotion, but annoyed that it hadn't happened until now when he looked older. He'd started working for MacKay Security and Investigation in 1955, and he'd never made it past second-in-command. Even his best friends had found it difficult to treat him as an adult when he had looked fifteen.

He pulled his knitted jumper over his head and tossed it into the laundry hamper. He sauntered over to the coffin he'd slept in for more than fifty years. The pillow and blanket boasted the red and green MacPhie tartan, the same as his kilt. He removed his sporran and the knife from his sock, then deposited them in the small dresser by his coffin. He kicked off his shoes, then halted with a sudden thought. He'd grown five inches.

Bugger. He'd outgrown his coffin.

He climbed inside, and sure enough, his feet hung over the end. There was only one other coffin in the dorm, and it belonged to Dougal. The twin bed was for Phineas. All the other beds were upstairs.

Well, why not? In a few weeks Ian would be in charge here as well as Romatech. He could sleep anywhere he wanted. He strode from the dormitory and up the stairs.

Usually he had a snack before bed, but tonight he was full of Bleer. Vanda had joined him at the bar around four A.M. to announce his profile was complete, and he was officially posted on the *Single in the City* dating service.

A third glass of Bleer had boosted his confidence. He'd talked to a few ladies, and they'd agreed to meet him at the club tomorrow night.

When he reached the ground floor, the alarm went off. He froze a second, then realized what was happening. An intruder! And dammit, his reaction was too slow. He shouldn't have had that fourth glass of Bleer.

He ran into the parlor. Empty. He swiveled, tripped over his feet, and stumbled to the keypad by the front door. He turned off the alarm, so he could hear. He caught a slight noise, emanating from the library. He eased toward the entrance.

A gust of cold air from the open window stirred the curtains. The person who'd opened that window had triggered the alarm, and that person was still in the room.

Female. And mortal. The scent of her blood swirled around him, caressing his skin like the touch of a lover. She was his favorite flavor—Type AB positive.

Thank God Roman had invented synthetic blood in 1987, so Ian and other Vamps were no longer slaves to bloodlust. Even so, his body reacted with the same primeval instinct that had ruled him since his transformation in 1542. His gums tingled. He had enough years of experience to know how to control himself, but it was taking some extra effort tonight. That fifth glass of Bleer had been a bad idea.

Her back was to him as she studied the bookshelves on the far wall. No doubt she was planning to steal the rarest books in Roman's collection. The library contained everything from medieval tomes hand-scribed by monks to first print editions from the nineteenth century.

She hadn't heard him arrive in his stocking feet. And she hadn't heard the alarm since it was set at a frequency only Vamps and dogs could hear. And she certainly didn't sense the reaction she'd ignited in him.

He felt ten degrees hotter in spite of the cold December air that drifted through the open window and over his white undershirt. The lamp between the two wingback chairs was turned on low, and it cast a golden glow across the room to outline her form with a shimmering aura.

She made a stunning cat burglar, dressed entirely in black spandex that molded to her waist and sweetly curved hips. Her golden hair hung in a ponytail down her back. The ends swished gently across her shoulder blades as she moved her head from side to side, scanning the bookshelf.

She stepped to the side, silent in her black socks. She must have left her shoes outside the window, thinking she'd move more quietly without them. He noted her slim ankles, then let his gaze wander back up to golden hair. He would have to be careful capturing her. Like any Vamp, he had super strength, and she looked a bit fragile.

He moved silently past the wingback chairs to the window. It made a swooshing sound as he shut it.

With a gasp, she turned toward him. Her eyes widened. Eyes green as the hills surrounding his home in Scotland.

A surge of desire left him speechless for a moment. She seemed equally speechless. No doubt she was busily contemplating an escape route.

He moved slowly toward her. "Ye willna escape through the window. And ye canna reach the door before me."

She stepped back. "Who are you? Do you live here?"

"I'll be asking the questions, once I have ye restrained." He could hear her heart beating faster. Her face remained expressionless, except for her eyes. They flashed with defiance. They were beautiful.

She plucked a heavy book off a nearby shelf. "Did you come here to test my abilities?"

An odd question. Was he misinterpreting the situation? "Who—" He dodged to the side when she suddenly hurled the book at his face. Bugger, he'd suffered too much to get his older, more manly face, and she'd nearly smacked it.

The book flew past him and knocked over the lamp. The light flickered and went out. With his superior vision, he could see her dark form running for the door.

He zoomed after her. Just before he could grab her, she spun and landed a kick against his chest. He stumbled back. Damn, she was stronger than he'd thought. And he'd suffered too much to get his broader, more manly chest.

She advanced with a series of punches and kicks, and he blocked them all. With a desperate move, she aimed a kick at his groin. Dammit, he'd suffered too much to get his bigger, more manly balls. He jumped back, but her toes caught the hem of his kilt. Without his sporran to weigh the kilt down, it flew up past his waist.

Her gaze flitted south and stuck. Her mouth fell open. Aye, those twelve years of growth had been kind. He lunged forward and slammed her onto the carpet. She punched at him, so he caught her wrists and pinned her to the floor.

She twisted, attempting to knee him. With a growl, he blocked her with his own knee. Then slowly he lowered himself on top of her to keep her still. Her body was gloriously hot, flushed with blood and throbbing with a life force that made his body tremble with desire.

"Stop wiggling, lass." His bigger, more manly groin was reacting in an even bigger way. "Have mercy on me."

"Mercy?" She continued to wriggle beneath him. "I'm the one who's captured."

"Cease." He pressed more heavily on her.

Her eyes widened. He had no doubt she was feeling it.

Her gaze flickered down, then back to his face. "Get off. Now."

"I'm halfway there already," he muttered.

"Let me go!" She strained at his grip on her wrists.

"If I release you, ye'll knee me. And I'm rather fond of my balls."

"The feeling isn't mutual."

He smiled slowly. "Ye took a long look. Ye must have liked what ye saw."

"Ha! You made such a *small* impression on me, I can barely remember."

He chuckled. She was as quick mentally as she was physically.

She looked at him curiously. "You smell like beer."

"I've had a few." He noted her dubious look. "Okay, more than a few, but I was still able to beat you."

"If you drink beer, then that means you're not . . ."

"No' what?"

She looked at him, her eyes wide. He had a sinking feeling that she thought he was mortal. She wanted him to be mortal. And that meant she knew about Vamps.

He studied her lovely face—the high cheekbones, delicate jawline, and beguiling green eyes. Some Vamps claimed mortals had no power whatsoever. They were wrong.

Their eyes met, and he forgot to breathe. There was something hidden in those green depths. A loneliness. A wound that seemed too old for her tender age. For a moment, he felt like he was seeing a reflection of his own soul.

"Ye're no' a thief, are ye?" he whispered.

She shook her head slightly, still trapped in his gaze. Or maybe it was he who was trapped in hers.

"Ian." Footsteps approached them. "Ian, what the hell are you doing?"

He dragged his gaze away from her and saw Phineas standing beside them. "What?"

Phineas gave him a confused look. "Why are you beating up on Toni?"

He blinked and glanced at the woman he'd pinned to the floor. "Ye're . . . *Toni*?" Their new guard was a woman?

"You're Ian?" Disappointment flickered in her eyes before she looked away. "You're one of them."

That hurt. For centuries he'd been judged too young, and now, after all the pain he'd endured, he was still found wanting. His jaw shifted as he ground his teeth. "Ye have something against Vamps?"

Her eyes flared with anger. "Yes. I tend to get really pissed when they attack me."

"She's got a point, bro," Phineas muttered as he adjusted the tie around his purple satin bathrobe. "You shouldn't attack her. She's our friend."

Ian moved his weight off her. "Friendship is earned."

She scooted away from him and sat up. "I'm not here to be your friend. I'm your guard. That's all."

He stared at her. Connor had hired a *woman* to guard *men*? This was unheard of in the vampire world. A mortal woman wouldn't have the strength . . . unless she was a shifter like Phil and Howard. "Are ye—" How could he put this when shape shifters were a secret? "Do ye change a bit at a certain time of the month?"

She gave him an incredulous look. "Are you asking me if I get PMS? Are you serious?"

"Nay! I dinna mean—" Ian stopped, interrupted by Phineas's laughter.

"I know what you're thinking, man, but she's normal."

"Normal?" She glared at Phineas. "I nailed your ass earlier this evening."

Phineas held up his hands in surrender. "Don't hurt me, sweetness. You're a strong, beautiful hunk of woman."

She inclined her head. "Thank you."

"Connor told me on the phone that he'd hired a Tony," Ian muttered. "I thought ye would be a man."

Her eyes narrowed. "I thought you would be somewhat intelligent."

"Snap!" Phineas grinned. "She got you good, bro."

Ian scowled. "It was perfectly logical to assume Tony was a man's name."

She lifted her chin. "Is it logical to attack people without talking to them first?"

"In this case, aye, it was. The window was open—"

"I opened it," she interrupted. "It was as stuffy as a tomb in here, and I was hot."

"Sweetness, you're so hot, you're sizzling." Phineas made some hissing sounds.

Ian shot him an annoyed look, then resumed his explanation. "The window sensor triggered the alarm, and when I investigated the matter, I found you looking at verra expensive books, dressed like a cat burglar."

"Yeah, you do look like a hot and sexy Catwoman." Phineas clawed at the air. "Meow! Hiss!"

Now she gave Phineas an annoyed look. "These are my workout clothes." She switched her green-eyed glare to Ian. "And I never heard an alarm."

"Only Vamps and dogs can hear it."

"Oh. Which one are you?"

"Snap!" Phineas slapped his leg. "She's killing you, man."

"Phineas," Ian growled. "I'm trying to have a conversation here." He turned to Toni. "I'm sorry, lass, but this will never work. Ye canna guard a houseful of men. Ye see how Phineas reacts to you."

"He's a lot nicer than you are!" Her eyes glinted with anger. "And it's not my problem if you're a bunch of sexist pigs. I can do this job, with or without PMS. I beat Phineas earlier, and I would have pinned you down, too, given more time."

"Lass, ye would never pin me." He leaned toward her. "I like to be on top."

Her eyes flashed with green fire.

"Good one!" Phineas shook a fist in the air. "You're making your comeback, bro. You da man!"

"He's a pig," Toni grumbled.

"Oink, oink," Phineas squeaked.

"Enough, Phineas!" Ian glowered at him. "I can see why ye were murdered young."

A laugh escaped from Toni, but she quickly squelched it and frowned at him.

She had a sense of humor? It wasn't all that important in the grand scheme of things, but Ian was suddenly taken with the challenge to make her laugh again, or at least make her smile. Unfortunately he couldn't think of anything amusing to say.

He rose to his feet and executed a gallant bow. "I apologize for attacking you. I hope I dinna hurt you."

Her frown relaxed slightly. "I'm okay."

He offered a hand to help her up.

She regarded him suspiciously. "You're not going to tell Connor to fire me, are you? I really can do this job."

An uneasy feeling settled in his gut. Why on earth would a lovely mortal woman want a job guarding vampires? "I'll let ye stay if ye answer a few questions honestly."

A guarded look flitted over her face, then she smiled brightly and took his hand. "Sure. What do you want to know?" She rose gracefully to her feet.

His hand tightened around hers. The uncertainty in his gut twinged. He knew she wasn't going to be entirely honest. Her smile was too forced, and her heartbeat had just speeded up.

"Why do ye want this job?" he asked quietly.

She pulled her hand from his grasp. "It pays extremely well. And I get free room and board, which is worth a fortune in Manhattan."

"And ye get stuck in a house all day with some dead carcasses."

"No job is perfect." She folded her arms across her chest. "None of you wake up crying or needing a diaper change, so it's easier than the usual babysitting job."

Babysitting? Now that was bloody annoying.

Meanwhile Phineas was snickering. "Yeah, take care of

me, hot mama. I need a sponge bath. And some of that baby oil rubbed all over me. I'm feeling a bit chafed, if you know what I mean."

Her mouth twitched.

Did she find Phineas amusing? That irritated him even more. Ian stepped closer to her, gritting his teeth. "We're no' babies. We're seasoned warriors."

She affected a big shudder. "Ooh, I'm scared."

Did she doubt their prowess? Ian moved closer. "Lass, ye have no idea how fierce we can be."

Her smile withered, and a pained look crossed her face. "I know that too well. There's no need to remind me."

"Were ye attacked?" Ian looked at her neck, but couldn't see any sign of bite marks above the high neck of her black outfit. "Is that how ye found out about us?"

The stubborn lift of her chin indicated her refusal to divulge more information. But she'd mentioned before that she tended to get pissed whenever vampires attacked her. The sun would be rising soon, and Ian and the other Vamps would fall into their death-sleep. All day long they would lie defenseless and vulnerable. And their guard appeared to hold a grudge against them.

"Lass, why should I trust you to watch over us?"

Her brows lifted. "Are you worried about what I might do when you're totally helpless and at my mercy?"

He grabbed her by the shoulders. "Are ye threatening us? I could erase yer memory, and shove you out the door right now."

"No!" Now she looked panicked. "Please. I—I really need this job. I promised Connor that I would never harm any of you. Ask him. He believes me."

Ian released her and stepped back. "I *will* ask him."

She glanced at him nervously. "I need to change into my uniform before my shift starts."

Phineas yawned. "Yeah. I'm getting sleepy. Good night, sweetness." He extended a closed fist toward Toni.

She responded with a smile and a knuckle pound. "See ya tomorrow, Dr. Phang."

Phineas grinned, then sauntered toward the stairs. "Yeah, that's me. Dr. Phang. Long in the tooth, and long in the wang." He descended the stairs to the basement, his voice still drifting toward them. "The doctor is in the house. Oh, baby, I've got the cure."

Ian could feel the pull of death-sleep, too, but as an older Vamp, he was able to resist it better than Phineas.

"Perhaps we should start over." He extended a hand. "I'm Ian MacPhie."

She gave him a wary look. "Toni Davis." She gripped his hand, quickly let go, then headed for the stairs.

He followed her. "I really did think ye were a thief. I doona normally attack women."

"Unless you're hungry." She started up the stairs.

"I doona attack for food. We have evolved past that."

"Yeah, right." She continued up the stairs without looking back.

He climbed the steps after her. "Ye doona believe me?"

She shrugged. "I've seen your kind drink from bottles."

"Then ye know we're different from the Malcontents."

Her knuckles whitened as she suddenly gripped the banister hard. Then she released it and ascended more stairs. "I gather your noble nature is somewhat new. Before the invention of synthetic blood, you must have attacked people for food."

He gritted his teeth. "I never used violence."

She reached the landing and whirled around to glare at him. "Did you use mind control?"

He flinched. "Ye doona understand."

"Oh, I think I do. Mind control made it easy for you to manipulate people." Her eyes narrowed. "But they were still victims, and you were still violating them."

"We were never like the Malcontents. Those bastards are murderers. We never killed for food."

"Okay. You weren't killers. You were just parasites." She turned to continue up the stairs.

He grabbed her arm to stop her. "If ye hate us, why have ye taken a job to protect us?"

She pulled away and started ascending the stairs. "I don't hate you. And I have my reasons."

"What reasons?" He stumbled on a step with his new size thirteen feet.

She glanced back. "Why are you following me? Don't you need to go to the basement and . . . die?"

"I'm no' sleeping there."

"But I've seen your coffin down there." She gave him a wry look. "It looks so cozy."

"Then ye sleep in it."

"Over my dead body. Oh, wait a minute. It's *your* dead body. In about five minutes. So I'd better hurry." She jogged up the rest of the stairs.

Smart ass. His gaze slid down to her round, firm rump, so deliciously defined in black spandex. It was enough to turn him back into a biter. He followed her, watching her hips sway as she strode down the hall. She stopped at a door on the right.

He paused beside her. "I outgrew it."

"What? Your ego?"

"Lass, ye doona need to carry a weapon. Yer tongue can slash a man to shreds."

She smiled. "I'll take that as a compliment."

"I outgrew my coffin. I'm five inches taller than when I was last here."

Her eyes widened. "Connor mentioned that you'd grown, but I didn't quite believe it. I thought vampires were always stuck at the age when they died."

"That is true, normally. But I aged twelve years over the summer."

"Oh." Her mouth quirked. "Welcome to puberty."

He planted a hand on the wall beside her and leaned forward. "Ye saw under my kilt. Ye know I'm a grown man."

She lifted her chin in a defiant gesture, but her cheeks turned a pale pink. "I'm trying very hard to wipe that unfortunate incident from my memory."

He smiled slowly. "Let me know if ye succeed."

Her blush deepened. "Mr. MacPhie, I should remind—"

"Call me Ian. Is Toni yer full name?"

"No. Look, I'm trying to talk to you since I estimate in about three minutes, you'll keel over dead."

"If I do, will ye put me to bed?"

"This sort of talk is not appropriate—"

"Is yer name Antonia?"

Her eyes darkened. "No."

"Tonatella? Tonisha?"

"No."

"Toni Baloney?"

Her mouth twitched. "I'm trying to be serious."

"Me, too." He let his gaze wander over her. "I'm *dead* serious."

She snorted. "Mr. MacPhie, I signed a contract two nights ago, and it clearly stated that I am not to become involved with anyone I'm guarding."

His heart stuttered, and it wasn't caused by the rising sun. "I dinna realize we were involved."

"We're not!" She huffed. "But you are flirting with me, and it has to stop."

He blinked. He was flirting? He'd been more tempted to wring her neck than seduce her. "Ye think I was flirting?"

"Well, yes."

He leaned closer. "Did ye like it?"

"You're still doing it."

He smiled lazily. "Sweetheart, I can do it all night long."

"The night is over." She turned and grabbed the doorknob. "Good night, Mr. MacPhie."

He stepped back. He wouldn't let her rejection bother him. Why should it bother him? "I wasna being serious. Ye need no' worry about me pestering you. I *am* looking for true love, but only with a lady Vamp."

She released the doorknob and turned toward him. "Then you believe dead women are better than live ones?"

"I dinna say that. But I am better suited for a Vamp."

"Really? Are the live ones too hot for you to handle?"

Was she challenging him? "I havena met a woman yet that I couldna handle."

"Right." She eyed him warily. "You probably used vampire mind control on them."

Damn, but she knew exactly where to plunge in the knife. "Aye, I used mind control. And they loved it. It made their orgasms stronger." He arched a brow. "Would ye like a demonstration?"

Her eyes seethed with anger. "I'd like you to go away. And die." She opened her bedroom door.

He stepped closer. "Why do ye guard us when ye doona like us? Why would ye spend yer days trapped in a house with the Undead?"

"Good night, Mr. MacPhie." She shut the door in his face.

"I'll find out about you, Toni," he yelled, then stalked back to the stairs.

The sun was touching the horizon now. He could feel the death-sleep pulling him into oblivion. He gazed up the stairwell to the fifth floor and concentrated hard. In an instant he was there.

He stumbled into Roman's office and shut the door behind him. With the aluminum shutters covering the windows, the room was dark, but no problem for his superior vision. He crossed the office to the bedroom and collapsed on the king-sized bed. By all the saints, this was so much better than a narrow coffin. He stretched out, enjoying the comfort. His breathing slowed as death-sleep stole over him.

Wait. He shook his head. He still needed to find out about Toni. He rolled toward the bedside table and grabbed the cordless phone. His vision blurred as he punched in Connor's cell phone number. Just a few more minutes, that was all he needed.

"Hello?" Connor sounded sleepy.

Ian stretched on his back, holding the phone to his ear. "Tell me about Toni."

"Is that you, Ian?" Connor yawned. "Call me later."

"Tell me about Toni. How did ye find her?"

"I came across her in Central Park." Connor yawned again. "Monday night."

And this was only Wednesday morning. Ian opened his mouth, but no words came out. His eyes flickered shut.

"Three Malcontents," Connor's voice slowed, "attacked her . . . verra vicious . . ."

No wonder she hated vampires. Ian lost his grip on the phone. Was she planning to stake them all in their sleep?

As death-sleep dragged him under, he wondered if he would ever wake again.

Chapter Three

I deserve to be happy.
I will accomplish my goals.
I will achieve something meaningful with
my life.
I am worthy to be loved.

Toni repeated her morning affirmations as hot water sluiced down her body and steam billowed around her. She just needed to believe. Yeah, right. In the last few days, her life had started spiraling down the toilet.

I deserve to be happy. She sighed. Her family didn't believe in her, so why should she? She turned the water off. She needed to toughen up emotionally and not let other people drag her down—people like Ian MacPhie.

How could a dead guy be so handsome? She pulled back the shower curtain. Why couldn't he have been mortal? For one fleeting, wonderful moment, she'd thought he was human. But no. Swish down the toilet. He was one of them.

She stepped out of the shower, scolding herself.

Don't think about him. He has no power over you. Unless . . .

Unless he used vampire mind control. Toni's bare skin prickled with goose bumps, and she shivered in spite of the hot steam surrounding her. She glanced down at the bite marks that covered her chest and torso.

She'd fought those three vampires. She'd thought she might survive until they'd taken over her mind. She'd sat there in the dirty snow, shivering and helpless while their cruel thoughts invaded her head and forced her to remove her shirt. Her bra. A deep shudder racked her body. If Connor hadn't come along when he had . . .

She blinked away tears and grabbed a towel to dry off. She would remain in control and stay focused.

I will accomplish my goals. She had to succeed. Sabrina was counting on her. Already Toni had confirmed the existence of vampires and invaded the good-guy camp.

Good-guy vampires? Who would believe that? But Connor had saved her, and he swore all good Vamps had given up biting. She'd seen them drink from bottles, but still, it was hard to completely trust them. No matter how well these good Vamps behaved, she could still sense the beast lurking just below the surface. She'd felt it even stronger with Ian, but instead of repelling her, it had excited her.

How foolish could she get? Only a complete idiot would challenge a beast that could bite. She would ignore him.

I will achieve something meaningful with my life. This would happen. She and Sabrina had it all planned out.

Toni padded into the bedroom while she towel-dried her hair. Her gaze wandered over the soft, golden walls and large canopy bed hung with blue and gold brocade fabric that matched the curtains and comforter. The two dressers that flanked the bed looked like Louis XVI antiques.

One thing she had to reluctantly admit: the Vamps had excellent taste. Dougal claimed this room once belonged to a Vamp princess who was a member of Roman Draganesti's harem. Apparently Roman had disbanded his harem when

he married. Toni snorted. What a great guy. As far as she
could tell, all the male Vamps were a few centuries behind
on their opinions of women. Ian MacPhie certainly was.

I am worthy to be loved. The last affirmation was the hardest to believe. She tossed her towel into the laundry hamper.
Dammit, she was loved. Grandma had loved her.

And remember what happened to her? You failed her.
Toni quickly squashed the nasty inner voice that kept sabo-
taging her affirmations, telling her she didn't deserve to be
happy, and she wasn't worthy to be loved. She was worthy,
dammit. And she would not fail Sabrina. Even if it meant
living in a house full of blood-drinking creatures.

She popped in her contacts and dressed in her guard
uniform of khaki pants and a navy polo shirt. Connor had
given her small sizes, but still, the men's clothes hung on her
frame like shapeless sacks. Obviously MacKay Security and
Investigation was not accustomed to hiring female guards.
Dougal and Phineas had been surprised, but they'd accepted
her easily enough once they'd seen her fight.

Ian was much more suspicious, but she wouldn't let him
scare her away. She would remain calm and cool. In control.
Nothing was going to faze her.

She jumped when her cell phone blasted forth with loud
music. Damn. Carlos had given her a new ringtone a week
ago, but the sudden explosion of "Cum on Feel the Noize"
by Quiet Riot always gave her a jolt.

The male vocalists screamed while she dug through her
handbag. Hopefully, it was Sabrina calling. Toni had gone to
the hospital last night to see her, but Sabrina had been sleeping so peacefully, Toni hadn't wanted to wake her.

She yanked open the phone. "Hello?"

"Toni?" The gruff voice sounded urgent. "What's going
on there?"

"Howard?" Her supervisor? Howard Barr was in charge
of daytime security, and he monitored Toni from his location at Roman Draganesti's house. Howard was supposed to

call for a morning report at eight A.M., but yesterday morning he'd used the house phone, not her cell phone.

Her gaze flickered to the bedside table where the digital clock glowed 7:26. "Is something wrong?"

"That's what I'm asking you," Howard continued in a rush. "I did my morning rounds here, and Connor had his cell phone open by his ear. Were you talking to him?"

"No. Everything's fine here—"

"I don't think so. Connor's phone was connected to your house phone there. I hung up and tried to call, but your line is still busy."

Toni glanced at the phone on her bedside table. A light indicated it was still in use. Of course. Ian had said he would check up on her. "It must be Ian MacPhie."

"Ian?" There was a pause during which Toni could hear the shuffling of papers. "Are you sure? He's not due back for another week. And his coffin's empty."

"He outgrew it."

"So it's true? The boy doesn't look fifteen anymore?"

She wrinkled her nose. "He looks older than that, but his behavior's not what I would call mature."

Howard chuckled. "Made a good impression, did he? Look, he's not showing up on any of my monitors, so you'll have to find him and make sure he's all right."

"I'm sure he's fine. Where would he go? He's dead. That sorta cuts down on his mobility."

"Yes, but we're responsible for these guys during the day. You can't guard a corpse if you don't know where it is. So find him."

Toni groaned silently. There were five floors in this townhouse, six counting the basement, more than eighteen bedrooms, and a bunch of bathrooms and closets. It would take all morning to search the whole place.

"I'll call back in ten minutes." Howard hung up.

Ten minutes? Toni dropped her phone into the pocket of the men's trousers she was wearing, and still barefoot, she

rushed into the hall. He wasn't conveniently sprawled out
dead in the hallway, so she would have to hunt him down.

She jogged down the stairs to the ground floor. She didn't
expect to see him here, but there were surveillance cameras
in the foyer and the kitchen, and she knew Howard would
expect to see her pass by in her search.

She'd been hired on a probationary status for two weeks,
and Connor had warned her that the cameras in the townhouse were linked to monitors in White Plains. In other
words, she was watched constantly to make sure she could be
trusted. As if she would ever try to harm one of the Vamps.

Connor had stressed the fact that once she took the vow
to protect Vamps, that vow would be sacred. The cost of
betrayal was severe and final. If she incurred their wrath,
there would be no place to hide where they couldn't find her.
Her body would never be found. Then he'd proceeded to tell
her about the great medical/dental plan, high-yield money
market accounts, and vacation opportunities that MacKay
Security and Investigation offered its employees.

Under normal circumstances, she would have chosen
option number one: having her memory erased so she could
return to her normal life. But circumstances weren't normal,
so she'd gritted her teeth and taken the vow.

Ian was not to be found on the ground floor, so she headed
down to the guardroom in the basement. Her gaze flickered
to the couch by the wall. Nope, not there. She glanced up at
the surveillance camera and shook her head.

She paused by the door of the dormitory. She was required
to check this room four times a day, but it still gave her the
chills. Well, not the room so much, but the dead bodies
inside. She took a deep breath and entered.

Dougal was on his back in his coffin, wearing an old-
fashioned nightshirt that reached his knees and looked a bit
like the nightgown her grandma used to wear.

Phineas was sprawled across his twin-sized bed, wearing

nothing but red silk boxer shorts. Toni glanced at the framed photos on his bedside table. An elderly woman and a young girl and boy, most probably the aunt and younger siblings he talked about. She wondered if they knew he'd been transformed into a vampire almost two years ago.

She peeked inside the bathroom and winced at the towels and clothes littering the floor. Thank God she didn't have to clean up after them. There was a Vamp-owned maid service that came in at night. Her gaze landed on a stack of girlie magazines in a basket. Aack! What pigs.

She jogged up the back stairs to the ground floor, then went up another flight on the grand staircase. There were no surveillance cameras on the top four floors, so at least she didn't have the uncomfortable feeling of being watched. She sprinted past her bedroom to check the remaining five bedrooms on the second floor. Then she rushed through all the bedrooms on the third floor. With time running short, she dashed through the rooms on the fourth floor.

Dammit, he wasn't in any of them! She checked the last bedroom with a growing sense of doom. She even looked in the closet. Had she made a mistake by not checking all the closets below?

Cum on feel the noize! She jumped and dug the phone out of her pocket. "Howard?"

"Toni, have you found him yet?"

"No." She was breathing heavily from all the running about. "I've searched every floor. Except the fifth one."

"Check it out."

She blinked. Connor had warned her not to venture into Roman Draganesti's private office and bedroom. Apparently the big kahuna still had some stuff there. Probably a skeleton in the closet. "I thought that floor was off-limits."

"Normally yes, but we can't go all day without knowing where Ian is. So go look around." Howard hung up.

She dropped the phone in her pocket and climbed the

stairs. On the top landing, she discovered two doors that flanked an oil painting of some ruins. She tried the door on the right. It opened.

The room was totally dark. She fumbled along the wall by the doorjamb until she located a light switch. A lone light-bulb turned on, situated over a large desk. Bookcases sat behind it and a red velvet chaise in front. Her heart lurched at the sight of the computer on the desk. It could be the answer to her prayers.

The large room stretched back into shadow. Toni could make out the shape of more chairs, a table, and a wet bar. At the far end of the room, she spotted the dark wooden panel-ing of a set of double doors.

She crossed the room, her bare feet silently cushioned on the thick carpet, her gaze sliding past expensive antiques. So this was the private lair of a powerful vampire coven master? Maybe she should take some photos with her cell phone. No, it wouldn't help Sabrina. The lush decor only proved that the owner was rich, not Undead.

As she approached the double doors, she heard a beeping sound like a phone off the hook. She shoved open the doors. The shadow of a huge bed loomed before her with a darker shadow on top. She skirted the bed to the right and fumbled with the lamp on the bedside table. A dim light, no brighter than a night-light, came on.

There he was on the far side of the king-sized bed, lying on top of a tan suede comforter. His face was turned away from her, so all she could see was his thick black hair and the ponytail that curled on top of the pillow.

Some men might look effeminate with shoulder-length hair and a skirt, but on Ian, the effect was quite the oppo-site. There was something wild and rugged about him, like a Scottish warrior who refused to be civilized. Just the sight of him made her heartbeat quicken and thoughts of rebellion sneak into her head.

He rested on his back, his long length stretching to the foot of the bed. Her gaze wandered over the white T-shirt, tightly molded to a broad chest and muscular abs. His red and green plaid kilt lay rumpled about his legs, the hem rucked up past his knees. It looked like he'd simply fallen onto the bed without caring how he landed.

Toni edged around the bed, passing by his huge feet encased in black socks. The old wives' tale about men with big feet must be true. Her gaze drifted back to his kilt. His legs were spread apart with the plaid fabric draped slightly between them. What a shock it had been to realize the guy didn't wear any underwear. Her face grew warm, remembering the amused tilt of his mouth and the glint in his eyes. No shame whatsoever. No, he'd looked . . . bold, as if he'd enjoyed her surprise inspection.

She tilted her head, focused on the dark, shadowy area between his thighs. Slowly, she leaned to the side.

Cum on feel the noize!

With a gasp, she straightened. What had gotten into her? The man was dead, and she was trying to look up his skirt? Thank God there were no cameras up here.

She opened her phone. "It's okay, Howard. I've got Ian here. He's in bed."

There was a pause.

"Girl, you have a man in your bed?"

Toni winced. "Carlos! I—I wasn't expecting you."

He chuckled. "I realize that, *menina*. So, who is this guy in your bed?"

"He's not in *my* bed, and it's not—"

"Oh, you're at his place?"

"Well, yes, sorta." Toni shoved her damp hair behind her ears. "Look, Carlos, I can't talk right now." At the sound of his suggestive chuckling, she huffed. "It's not what you think. The guy is really . . . dead right now."

"You wore him out? You go, girl."

Toni groaned. Maybe it was his Brazilian heritage, but her next-door neighbor, Carlos Panterra, had a one-track mind. "Carlos, is everything fine at the apartment?"

"Yes, of course. I was just feeding your cat. She says she misses you and Sabrina. I do, too."

"I know. We'll be back soon, I hope. Now I've got to go before Howard calls."

Carlos gasped. "You have *two* men? Girl, you are hot!"

"It's not—never mind. I'll explain later." She moved up the side of the bed.

"It's that new ringtone I put on your phone," Carlos continued. "Now you're rocking the boys big time."

"Yeah, right. Bye, Carlos." Toni snapped her phone shut and dropped it in her pocket. It was a stinking shame she was so inept at modern technology. She had no idea how to remove the ringtone Carlos had cursed her phone with.

Speaking of phones, there was still a beeping one on the bed with Ian. He'd obviously been holding it next to his ear, but now his fingers were relaxed, curling slightly where they rested on the pillow. The receiver must have slid down the pillow, for it was now nestled in the crook of his neck and shoulder. His head was turned toward her, his eyes shut.

She had a creepy feeling his eyes might suddenly open and gaze at her with the blank look of a zombie. With a shudder, she pushed that thought away. She reached for the receiver, but accidentally brushed her hand over his fingers. She jerked her arm back. Shoot, she'd never touched a dead person before. But he hadn't felt cold and stiff as she expected him to.

She slipped her hand between his fingers and his neck and slowly pulled the phone out. Her knuckles grazed the tip of his chin. It was rough with whiskers. She winced, realizing how close she was to touching his mouth. His lips were slightly parted, perfectly shaped.

She stepped back, bringing the phone to her chest. His expression was peaceful, so different from the intense emo-

tions she'd seen earlier. The thick black fringe of his eyelashes cast a shadow on his pale cheeks. Beautiful. A man
shouldn't look that sweet and rugged at the same time.

Her gaze fell to the dimple in his chin. It had been one of
the first things she'd noticed about him. The whole time he'd
been fussing at her, she'd wanted to poke it with her finger.
She reached out her hand, then snatched it back. What was
she thinking? He was one of them.

She dropped the receiver back into the cradle on the bedside table. It immediately rang.

She jumped. Good grief, she needed to get a grip. She
lifted the receiver. "It's okay, Howard. I found him."

There was a feminine giggle. Definitely not Howard,
unless he had a secret she didn't know about. "Hello?"

"Hi!" Another giggle. "Is Ian there?"

Toni hesitated. If this girl knew Ian, wouldn't she know
he was dead at the moment? "He's not able to come to the
phone right now. Can I take a message?"

"Well, I guess so." The caller giggled again.

Toni found a pen and pad of paper in the nightstand
drawer. She waited, but there was silence. "Hello? You'll
need to give me the message."

"Oh, right. Okay. Let me think." Another giggle.

Toni waited while the caller grew silent, apparently attempting to think. Did Ian actually know this girl? Hadn't
he said he was looking for a Vamp woman? This girl had to
be mortal because it was daylight, and she was conscious.
Sorta. "Can you tell me your name?"

"Oh." More giggles. "I'm Mitzi."

Toni wrote on the pad of paper. "And your message?"

"Can you tell Ian I think he's really hot?"

"Sure." Toni glanced at Ian. He looked stone cold to her.
"How did you meet him?"

"I haven't yet. I just found him on *Single in the City*. It's a
dating service, you know?"

"I see." Was that how Ian planned to find his true love? That didn't make sense if he was looking for only Vamp women.

"Yeah, I just saw his profile," Mitzi continued. "And his picture. And I had to call because he's so *hot!*"

"Right. Do you want to leave a number?"

Mitzi recited her number. "Can you tell him I want to go out with him? And he'll probably get lucky, 'cause he's so *hot!*" She giggled, then thankfully hung up.

The second Toni set down the receiver, the phone rang again. This had to be Howard. "Hello?"

"Is Ian MacPhie there?" a throaty female voice asked.

Another woman? At least it wasn't Mitzi. "Ian is unavailable at this time. May I take a message?"

"My name is Lola. I was just reading Ian's profile at *Single in the City*, and I must say, it was fascinating."

"I bet." Toni glanced at the computer in the office next door. She might need to take a look at this profile.

"Yes," Lola continued. "I especially liked the part about Ian's castle in Scotland, and how he's spending some of his vast fortune to renovate it."

Vast fortune? Toni snorted, then covered it with a dainty cough. She seriously doubted Ian had a vast fortune when he was working as a security guard for Romatech Industries. Would he really stoop to telling lies on the Internet in order to get dates? The man was gorgeous. Why would he have to lie about anything, other than the little problem of being dead half the time?

"You see," Lola lowered her voice dramatically, "I was a royal princess in a former life. I belong in a castle."

"Wow."

"I'm also a vegetarian," Lola announced. "I do hope Ian is one, too. He's so hot."

"Right. Well, I can safely say he doesn't eat meat."

"Splendid." Lola recited her phone number. "Ta-ta."

Toni wrote the number down, then she glared at Ian. "Liar. You said you didn't want to date mortals."

Cum on feel the noize! She jumped. Now this had to be

Howard. Or Sabrina. She pulled out her cell phone. "Hello?"

"Toni?" Howard's voice boomed. "What's going on?"

"Everything's fine. Ian's in the bedroom on the fifth floor. The phone was off the hook, but I put it back."

"What was so urgent that he had to call Connor?"

Toni winced. "He was probably calling about me. The concept of a female guard was too bizarre for him."

Howard chuckled. "He'll get used to you. Has he seen you fight yet?"

"Yeah, a little."

"Then he knows how tough you are. He'll learn to trust you in time."

She grimaced. Ian was actually right to suspect her. She did have a hidden agenda, though she certainly didn't mean the Vamps any harm.

"Do you need anything today?" Howard asked. He made sure groceries were delivered to the townhouse, so Toni wouldn't have to leave her charges unprotected.

"I'm fine for now, but I have a final exam Friday at NYU. I'll need to leave around noon."

"I remembered that. We've arranged for me to come to the townhouse so you can go."

"But I thought you had to guard Roman and Connor."

"They're staying at Romatech, so the guards there can keep an eye on them. Don't worry. We've got it covered."

"Thank you." Toni felt relieved, but a bit shocked that the Vamps were willing to change their routine just to help her out. "Just one exam to go, and I'm officially done with my master's."

"Great." Howard paused. "You know, you can probably get a better job than this. It's not very . . . intellectual."

"It's fine. The pay is a lot more than I expected."

"Yeah, well, the Vamps know how important it is to have mortals they can trust."

"I understand." The phone on the nightstand rang. "Oh God, I hope that's not Mitzi or Lola."

"Who?" Howard asked.

"These girls keep calling for Ian. Apparently he signed up with an online dating service."

"You're kidding."

"I wish. I'll call you back for the ten o'clock report." Toni shut her cell phone and answered the house phone. "Hello?"

"Hi," a soft female voice answered. "Is Ian there?"

Toni groaned. "He's . . . meditating right now."

"Cool. I'm Destiny." She gave her phone number. "Ian is just so hot. You know, I'm totally synthesized to the harmonic vibrations of the cosmos, so I can tell that Ian and I belong together."

"I see." And his *vast fortune* had nothing to do with it. "Any message for Ian?"

"Yes. I love to take walks in the rain and sit on the beach to watch the sunrise."

"Great." Toni wrote *Plans to kill you by spontaneous combustion* beneath her name. "Thank you for calling."

She hung up and glared at Ian. "Do you realize my best friend is in the hospital, and instead of being able to call her, I'm stuck talking to your silly girlfriends?" Her voice rose to a shout, but Ian just lay there, oblivious.

"Why are you looking for a woman? Why would a vampire even believe in true love? Do you really think you can be faithful *for centuries?* A few years is too much to ask for these days!"

He didn't answer.

"Well, at least you don't talk back. I'm the boss here during the day, and don't you forget it."

He didn't argue.

She stalked into the adjoining office. She hadn't gone to college just to end up a social secretary for a horny, hot vampire. So much for her third affirmation, *I will achieve something meaningful with my life.*

She needed to talk to Sabrina. That would calm her down.

She opened her cell phone and dialed the hospital. "Sabrina Vanderwerth's room, please?"

"One moment," the operator replied. "Please hold."

Toni sat in the black leather chair behind the desk and booted up the computer. Maybe she could find something useful in the computer files. Her search in the library had yielded nothing. The phone on the desk rang. Great, another woman. Toni quickly took her name and number, then hung up after Britney expounded on ten reasons why Ian was hot.

Meanwhile, the hospital operator came back on her cell phone. "Sabrina Vanderwerth has been released."

A sliver of alarm crept down Toni's spine. "But I just saw her last night. When was she released?"

"I'm not able to give out any personal information."

"Wait," Toni began, but the dial tone signaled she'd been cut off.

The phone on the desk rang. "Arrgh!" Toni quickly took the name and number of another girl who thought Ian was hot. Then she dialed Sabrina's cell phone.

After seven rings, she was transferred to voice mail. "Bri, this is Toni. I just heard you were released from the hospital. Call me." She checked her phone for messages. Zilch. Where was Sabrina?

The phone on the desk rang again. This time it was LaToya who thought Ian was hot. Then Michelle, and then Lauren. Apparently Ian's hotness was becoming legendary.

"This is too much," Toni growled. She used the house phone to call her apartment. Maybe Sabrina had simply gone home, and she was worrying over nothing.

The phone rang until the answering machine picked up. "Bri, are you there? Call me, I'm worried about you."

She called Carlos in the apartment next door. "Have you heard from Sabrina?"

"No, what's wrong?"

"She's been released from the hospital, but I don't know where she is."

There was a pause, then Carlos spoke, his voice deeper than usual. "Toni, you need to tell me what's going on."

"I will, tonight, when I get off work." Toni hung up, then the phone instantly rang.

"Damn!" She grabbed the receiver. "What?"

"Good morning. This is Travis Buckley."

A man's voice. "Yes? What is it?"

"Is Ian MacPhie there?"

Toni blinked. "You . . . want to talk to Ian?"

"Oh yes, honey. I saw his picture on *Single in the City*, and I thought he was so . . ."

"Hot?"

"Exactly." Travis chuckled.

Toni wrote his name down. "I would love to tell him you called."

"Super." Travis gave her his number. "I think he's über-hot."

"Oh, totally." Toni hung up, then rubbed her temples. "This can't be happening to me. I'm stuck in the Twilight Zone." She turned to the computer and clicked on *My Documents*. A security box came on screen, asking for the password.

"Damn." If she wasn't such a techno-moron, she could get around this, but she didn't have a clue. Oh well, even if she found a document where a bunch of Vamps confessed to being real, would it actually prove anything? Anyone could write such nonsense and claim it was true.

Speaking of false claims, she needed to check out Ian's profile on *Single in the City*. It was easy to find. He was on the home page in a list of the ten most popular guys. His photo was great, but his profile sounded like Don Juan on Viagra. The more she read, the more she felt steam coming out of her ears.

The phone rang again. And again. And again. The list of names was now up to thirty-four girls and two guys who all thought Ian was hotter than liquid magma. How would she ever locate Sabrina? Or study for her final?

The phone jangled again. She snatched it up. "Yes, Ian is *hot!* But you'll have to wait your turn."

"Cool." The girl smacked on chewing gum. "I don't mind sharing. Is he into group sex?"

Toni grimaced. "You'll have to ask him about that."

"Okay." She popped her gum. "So who are you?"

"I'm . . . his parole officer."

"Cool. I've got one of those, too. Got busted for solicitation."

"I hate it when that happens."

"Yeah. So this Ian dude, is he really as rich as his profile says?"

Toni gritted her teeth. "Just give me your name and number." She wrote down the information and slammed down the receiver. "I can't take it anymore!"

She fumbled in the desk drawer and found a big, black permanent marker. She stalked into the bedroom and glared down at Ian. "If I fail my final, it'll be your fault!" She smoothed his white T-shirt across his rock-hard chest and abs, then wrote in capital letters HOT, HOT STUDMUFFIN. Beneath that she wrote, *For a good time, call Travis.*

Then she marched downstairs to the ground floor, and turned on the answering machine. The Vamps wouldn't like it, but she was not about to screw up her last exam because of Ian's love life. As she descended into the basement, she heard the phone ringing again. The guys in the cellar were fine, so she called Howard for the ten o'clock report. She explained about the answering machine, and he agreed.

While she ate her lunch in the kitchen, the phone rang twelve more times. It was still ringing when she went upstairs to her bedroom. She disconnected the phone there so she could study in peace. She checked on the guys again at one and four P.M. for her afternoon reports.

She also called the hospital back and talked to a nurse on the floor where Sabrina had stayed. The nurse admitted Sabrina had left with family, but wouldn't say more than that. It had to be Sabrina's aunt and uncle, since they were the only family Sabrina had. Toni couldn't recall their last name. The information would be at the apartment. Meanwhile, Sabrina never called back, so Toni continued to worry about her.

At four-fifteen, Toni changed out of her uniform and descended to the kitchen to make a snack. She would be able to leave after the guys woke up, which was any minute now. Fortunately, the sun set early in December.

"Good evening." Dougal sauntered into the kitchen, followed by Phineas. They headed straight for the refrigerator for some bottles of blood.

"Hey, guys." She finished her salad. "Sleep well?"

The door slammed open, and Ian marched in. He glowered at Toni and slapped a hand against his black-marked T-shirt. "What the hell is this?"

Chapter Four

Ian had forgotten how pretty she was—pretty enough to scramble his thoughts for a second. But it didn't matter how shiny and golden her hair was, or how pink and sweetly curved her mouth was. Or how her green jumper matched the bonnie green of her eyes. Any guard who wrote graffiti on a sleeping Vamp was not a guard who could be trusted.

Phineas took one look at him and spewed his breakfast all over the kitchen counter. Then he started snickering. Dougal, at least, was attempting to stifle his laughter.

"Eeeuww." Toni grimaced at the bloody mess.

"Don't worry, sweetness. I'll clean it up." Phineas grabbed a sponge from the kitchen sink. "You got him good."

"I wouldna call this *good*." Ian glowered at Toni. She hadn't answered his question. She just sat at the table, fiddling with a paper napkin, while a pink blush swept up to her cheeks. The scent of her rushing blood ignited his hunger. His gums tingled. His stomach twinged. He stalked to the refrigerator, grabbed a bottle of synthetic blood, and guzzled it down cold.

She wrinkled her pretty little nose. "You're drinking it cold?"

"Are ye offering me some that's hot?" he growled.

Her cheeks grew a brighter red. "No, of course not."

"Why so pissed, bro?" Phineas wiped up the counter. "I'd be happy if Toni wrote on my shirt. Shit, she could write on me all day long."

"You don't wear a shirt to bed," Toni muttered.

"Aha!" Phineas grinned at her. "You've been admiring my awesome bod while I sleep. I knew it. The ladies can't resist Dr. Phang." He rinsed out his sponge, then went back to work. "You should be writing your love notes on me."

"They're not love notes," Toni protested.

"That's for certain," Ian grumbled. "I'm definitely no' interested in Travis."

Phineas snorted, then took aim and tossed the sponge into the sink. "Two points! Look, I've been telling you guys to stop wearing those skirts. It gives out mixed signals, if you know what I mean."

Dougal frowned. "The kilt is a fine and manly tradition amongst the Scots."

"I kinda like 'em," Toni conceded.

Did she really like his kilt? Ian had always considered the MacPhie tartan one of the best. Or perhaps she had liked what was underneath. He slapped himself mentally. This girl distracted him far too easily. "Ye dinna answer my question." He tapped his chest. "Why the hell did ye do this?"

She lifted her chin. "I will admit now that it was a mistake, but at the time, I was very angry with you."

"Angry?" Ian gave her an incredulous look. "What could I possibly do to make ye angry? I was dead all day."

"You were live on the Internet. People were looking at you on *Single in the City*, and the phone was ringing off the hook. I have problems of my own to deal with, so—"

"Ladies were calling *me?*" Ian interrupted her. He couldn't believe it. Vanda's plan was working.

Toni shot him an annoyed look. "Didn't you see the messages I left for you upstairs? On the nightstand?"

"Nay, I was distracted by this." He pressed a hand against his chest. He wanted to stay angry, but the thought of women actually pursuing him was amazing. "Ladies were calling me?"

Toni groaned, then took her plate to the sink. "Yes, Mr. Super Ego. Forty-three women and two men, to be precise. And that was before ten A.M."

"Two men?" Phineas snickered.

Ian muttered a few words in Gaelic that made Dougal laugh. His initial excitement was wearing off, for he now realized that all the women who had called during the day were mortal. None of them would do.

The phone rang, and Phineas reached for it.

"Don't bother." Toni returned to the table where she'd left some clothes on the back of a chair. She looped a green scarf around her neck. "It's probably another desperate woman. The answering machine's been picking them up since this morning."

"But she might be hot!" Phineas lifted the receiver. "Hello there," he said in a deep, sexy voice. "You have reached the luxurious abode of Dr. Phang, the love doctor. Tell me where it hurts, baby."

"Toni," Dougal spoke quietly. "Ye're supposed to answer the phone during the day. We doona want people thinking the house is vacant."

"I know." She stuffed her arms into a jacket. "But—"

"No, Travis, I'm not interested!" Phineas slammed the phone down. "Shit."

Toni snorted. "See what I mean? That's why Howard agreed to let me use the answering machine." She hitched her handbag over her shoulder. "See you guys later."

"Where are ye going?" Ian asked.

She ignored him and strode from the kitchen, leaving the door swinging in her wake.

"Bloody hell," Ian growled. He gulped down the rest of his cold breakfast, then set the bottle in the sink on his way to the kitchen door.

"Ian." Dougal stopped him. "Doona chase her away. We're in desperate need of mortal guards we can trust."

He pointed at his T-shirt. "What makes ye think we can trust her?"

"She's a good fighter, and she has good reason to hate the Malcontents," Dougal replied.

"And she hasn't killed us in our sleep," Phineas added. "Yet."

"That's reassuring." Ian strode into the foyer and found Toni by the front door, punching buttons on the security panel. "Ye canna leave."

"I don't see why not. I'm off duty." She finished the code to release the alarm, then reached for the doorknob.

"I need to talk to you."

"I don't want to." She motioned to the answering machine. "But there are hundreds of women who do."

"Ye're exaggerating."

She marched across the foyer to the sideboard where the phone and answering machine were located. She punched a button, and a robotic male voice spoke.

"You have three hundred and fourteen messages."

Ian's mouth fell open.

Toni gave him a knowing smirk, then strode back to the front door. "You'd better get busy. It'll take you hours to return all those calls."

"I'll just delete them."

She turned slowly to face him. "You're not going to answer them?"

"They called during the day, so they must be mortal."

"Good grief, you're an arrogant snob!"

He stiffened. "It's no' a matter of arrogance. It's reality."

"*Your* reality! You think you're too good for mere mortals."

"Doona presume to know what I'm thinking."

Her eyes narrowed. "Fine. We'll stick to the facts. Those are real people who called with real feelings. Only a pompous oaf would deny them the courtesy of an answer."

He moved closer to her. "Doona lecture me on courtesy, no' when ye wrote this rubbish on me while I slept."

"I was *angry!*" She stepped toward him, her cheeks growing flushed. "I had to endure hours of people moaning, 'Ooh, Ian is so hot!' You're lucky I only wrote on your T-shirt. I almost puked on it!"

He had trouble concentrating on her words, because her rushing blood filled his nostrils, and her racing heartbeat pounded in his mind. Just gazing into the fiery green depths of her eyes made his hearing grow dull. The scent of her blood combined with the fragrance of her hair and skin, and he'd never breathed in air so sweet.

She stepped back. "Is something wrong? Your eyes look a little weird."

He struggled to think. Why had all those calls made her angry? Then a sudden thought struck him. "Ye were jealous."

"*What?*" she scoffed. "Don't be ridiculous."

He pointed to the words on his chest. "Ye dinna like other ladies saying I was a studmuffin."

"They never called you a—" She winced. "I have to go." She moved toward the door.

He followed her. "The studmuffin part was yer idea?"

"It wasn't meant as a compliment," she muttered.

He smiled. "But it is yer honest opinion, aye?"

She grabbed the doorknob. "I have things to do, places to go."

He planted a hand on the door. "Such as?"

"None of your business."

His smile faded. "Ye never told me yer full name. Or why ye agreed to guard us."

"I told you, good pay and free room and board."

"And I told you I doona trust you. Ye're hiding something."

Her eyes glinted with anger. "I took a vow to protect your egotistical hide."

"Why would ye protect us when ye doona like us?"

She arched a brow. "Maybe it's just *you* I don't like."

His gaze drifted over her face, then down over her hip-length jacket and tight-fitting jeans. "I can tell when ye're lying, lass. I can hear yer heart racing and smell the blood rushing to yer face."

Her cheeks turned pink. "I don't have to explain myself to you."

"Fine. Then I have no choice but to investigate you." The phone rang, distracting him. "Don't leave," he warned her, then headed toward the phone.

Toni made a frustrated noise behind him, and he glanced back. With an impatient gesture, she tugged her hair free from the scarf that had pinned it down. The strands of gold tumbled down around her shoulders. Somehow, she managed to make a simple movement look graceful and beautiful.

The answering machine picked up, and a woman's voice filled the foyer. "Ian, I just read your profile, and I'd love to meet you. Are you there? Pick up!"

He reached for the receiver, then hesitated.

"What's wrong?" Toni asked.

"I doona know what to say."

She snorted. "How about *hello*?"

The caller gave her name and telephone number.

"It's no' that simple." Ian couldn't tell if this woman was a Vamp, and it wasn't something he could just ask. Bugger. He'd have to actually meet all the women who called after dark. The minute he saw them, he'd know if they were alive or Undead. But what if there were hundreds of them?

The woman hung up, then the phone rang again.

He dragged a hand through his hair. "This is too much. I shouldna have let Vanda do this."

"Vanda?" Toni asked. "Is she another girlfriend?"

"A friend. She wrote my profile and put me on the dating site. She only meant to help, but—"

"What?" Toni walked toward him. "You didn't write your own profile?"

Another woman's voice came on the answering machine. Ian turned down the volume so he could talk to Toni. "I let Vanda write it. She said she knew what women wanted to hear. I suppose she does, since so many are calling."

Toni wrinkled her nose. "It's not what I would want to hear. I've never read such hogwash in all my life."

"Ye read my profile?"

She tucked her hair behind an ear. "I was curious. I mean, hundreds of women were calling. I wanted to see what had gotten them all excited."

"And ye thought it was hogwash?"

"Of course. 'My true love will be like a shimmering, star-lit princess in my enchanted Highland castle. And I'll be her devoted love slave, attending to her every waking desire till she's flooded with waves of sensual pleasure.' Oh, the rapture! The ecstasy! The *nausea*!" Toni pointed at her mouth like she wanted to induce vomiting.

Ian winced. Vanda's prose did sound overly dramatic, but then Toni's reaction seemed a bit exaggerated, too. "It's verra interesting that ye would commit the lines to memory. I'm flattered ye studied it so carefully."

Her mouth dropped open, then snapped shut. "You should have Vanda do some serious editing. The way it's worded right now, it doesn't sound very . . . manly."

He arched a brow. Was she challenging him again? "I'll take a look at it tonight."

"You haven't read it yet?"

"Nay." He shrugged one shoulder. "I'm sure Vanda did a better job of it than I ever could."

Toni gave him a suspicious look. "It's not like you to be modest." Her eyes suddenly widened. "Oh my gosh, are you nervous about dating?"

He swallowed hard. She'd hit a bull's-eye. "It's . . . hard to explain."

"How can you be nervous? Haven't you been seducing women for ages, so you could get their . . . blood?"

"That was different. I'm looking for my true love now, the woman I'll marry and spend the rest of my life with. I'm no' really sure how to go about it, or if I'll find the right one. There are so many to choose from."

"Yeah, the dating scene is rough." Her gaze grew sympathetic. "But you shouldn't worry. You'll do fine. You just need some practice. You did really well last night when you flirted with me."

"Ye enjoyed it?"

Her eyes hardened. "I wouldn't say that."

He tilted his head. "Ye're a woman."

"Brilliant, Sherlock. You must be a professional investigator."

He smiled. "I am, actually. That's my area of expertise." He noted the wary look that suddenly appeared in her eyes. Was she worried about what he might find out about her? "Ye said I needed more practice. Would ye let me practice with you?"

She glanced toward the door. "I was just leaving."

"It would only take a few minutes." He gestured toward the parlor. "I would really appreciate it."

He could see the wheels turning behind her lovely green eyes. Perhaps if she was nice and humored him, he would forget to investigate her? Fat chance. She was far too intriguing.

"I could spare a few minutes, I suppose." She wandered slowly toward the parlor.

"Thank you." He waited while she dropped her handbag on the couch, then removed her jacket. When she perched on the edge of the sofa cushion, he sat beside her.

She glanced warily at him. "I'm not sure you really need this. You were flirting like a pro last night."

"I dinna realize what I was doing till ye told me. I must

have been distracted by all the other emotions I was feeling."
Like suspicion. And lust.

"Then you'll probably do fine as long as you don't get self-conscious about it."

"Perhaps. Or it might be easier with you because it doesna matter."

She stiffened. "Because I'm a mortal and beneath you?"

"Nay!" What made her so touchy about that? Had someone slashed her ego in the past? "Toni, I barely know you, but I canna see anything remotely unworthy about you. Any man would be blessed and honored to receive yer love."

Her eyes widened.

"I only meant that we doona have to worry about how we feel about each other. It doesna matter because we canna have a relationship. It's against the rules."

"Right." She leaned back and crossed her arms. "Okay. Since I can't be affected in any way, let's see what you can do. Try your best mojo on me."

Mojo? What the hell was that?

She shifted to face him. "You see me in a bar. I'm a sexy, *Vamp* lady with a gorgeous set of . . . fangs. So you make your move . . ." She watched him expectantly.

Smooth and charming. That had worked for Jean-Luc. "Good evening, miss. Ye're looking quite fetching tonight."

"Thanks." Her eyes narrowed. "Lovely weather we're having."

"Quite so. A bit chilly, perhaps."

"Indeed, Mr. Darcy. I fear the sheep will be shivering on the moor." She made a face at him. "What century did you come from?"

"The sixteenth, but I've adjusted over the centuries."

She scoffed. "Not enough. You're still behind about two hundred years."

"I was trying to sound charming."

"Prince Charming's not a hero anymore. Haven't you watched *Shrek*?"

He didn't know what she was talking about. "I thought charm could never go out of style. It worked for Jean-Luc."

"I don't know him. Look, you've got to sound more modern. More hip. Try again."

He searched his mind for the right words. "Yo, hot mama, let's get down?"

She burst into laughter. "Now you sound like Phineas, except that you just said, 'Let's get *dune*.' Oh God, the accent is so funny."

"Thanks." He gave her a wry look. "Perhaps I can mispronounce myself into a lady's affections."

Toni grinned. "You still sound old-fashioned."

"Is that such a bad thing?"

She tilted her head, considering. "I suppose it depends on the girl. Some girls like having a man open the door for them. But a lot of modern women would interpret chivalrous behavior as rude. We can open the damned door for ourselves. Don't ever consider us the *weaker* sex."

"Then ye're misinterpreting my motives. I would open the door to show respect, no' disrespect."

"But do you really respect women? Haven't we just been your dinner for centuries?"

"Ye've been my salvation. I could never have survived without you."

Her eyes widened. "We see things so differently from each other."

"That only makes you more fascinating to me." He gazed into her eyes and saw a mixture of emotions struggling against one another. She was so beautiful. So determined to be tough and hide her wounds. Would it frighten her if she knew how attracted he was to her? "I would never harm you, lass. I hope ye know that."

She pulled back suddenly and looked away. "Were you using mind control on me?"

"No."

"Then why am I—" She gave him a wary glance. "Never mind."

Was she feeling it, too? This strange pull between them. He stretched an arm along the back of the sofa. "Tell me, Toni, when it comes to dating a modern lass, would it be all right for me to kiss her on the first date?"

She pulled her handbag into her lap. "A peck on the cheek would be fine. Or a quick kiss when you say good-bye."

"What if I want more?"

Her cheeks reddened. "If you want to jump in the sack, that's your choice."

"I was only referring to a deeper, more satisfying kiss. But since ye're in a hurry to get me in bed—"

"I think you've had enough practice." She jumped to her feet and pulled on her coat.

He stood. "Thank you. This was verra educational."

"Right." She swung her handbag onto her shoulder. "Believe me, you'll do fine with the dating." She headed for the front door.

"That's good. I have two dates tonight."

She glanced back. "*Two?*"

Was she jealous? "The nights are long. I'll see you in the morning before sunrise. We still need to talk."

She shook her head as she reached for the doorknob. "There's nothing to talk about."

"I have questions that need answering."

"You're too nosy."

"If ye refuse to talk to me, I'll have to investigate you."

Her eyes flashed with anger. "Why can't you leave me alone?" She left, slamming the door behind her.

That was a good question. He had two dates tonight and plenty of phone calls he could return. But for some reason, he couldn't leave Toni alone. She filled his thoughts. He desired her, but it was more than lust. She was a mystery. A beautiful, clever mystery. And damned fun to flirt with.

He teleported to the fifth floor to shower and change. First
he would go to Romatech to see Connor and begin his investigation. He had a few hours to kill before meeting his dates
at the Horny Devils.

In the bathroom, he yanked the T-shirt off, then stared at
the words Toni had scribbled. Could she really be jealous
that so many women desired him? Or did he just want her to
be jealous? One thing was certain. He was totally intrigued
by their beautiful female guard.

Angus MacKay's cardinal rule repeated in the back of his
mind. *A guard must never become romantically involved
with his charges.* She was forbidden. She was mortal.

"Bloody hell." He tossed the T-shirt in the trash.

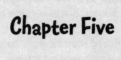

Chapter Five

Jedrek Janow moved slowly across his new office at the Russian-American coven house in Brooklyn. So far, so good. His electronic scanning device wasn't picking up any bugs. When he'd arrived Tuesday night, he'd found a few. He suspected there was a mole in his coven, but until he found the bastard, he'd keep checking the office every night.

Such disloyalty and incompetence would not be tolerated. As the new master, he'd made it clear last night that he expected more from this coven. Any member who wasn't willing to die to achieve his goals might as well die now. He'd punctuated his speech by staking a coven member who hadn't looked properly impressed.

That simple act had done wonders for everyone's motivation. The men had offered to hunt for him. The women had offered to screw him. All except one. The little brunette, Nadia, had looked terrified of him.

So of course he'd selected her. He smiled, re-membering the brutal hour he'd spent with her. When he'd finally let her slink away in tears, he'd relished the certain knowledge that her fear of him had grown. She still had some spirit in her, though. He'd break it soon enough. It was a game he'd enjoyed many times over the centuries.

He finished scanning the room. It was clean, and it would stay that way now that he was in charge. The former coven masters had been idiots. Ivan Petrovsky had ended up betrayed and assassinated by his own coven. Katya Miniskaya had made a ton of money, only to squander it all in a pathetic attempt to kill a former lover who'd jilted her.

Neither Ivan nor Katya had recognized what was truly important. When Roman Draganesti invaded this building during the daytime to rescue one of his minions, Ivan had simply increased the number of day guards. The idiot! Draganesti had been *awake* during the day. The significance of that had completely evaded Ivan. And Katya.

A vampire who could stay awake during the day could rule the world. All vampires would have to bow to him for fear of being slaughtered during their daily death-sleep.

"Master?" Yuri knocked on the door. The door was open, but he was afraid to enter without Jedrek's permission.

Good. They were learning fast. Jedrek sat behind his desk and dropped the bug detector in a drawer. "Enter."

"I have the report and photos you requested."

"Show me."

Yuri set some digital photos on the desk. "This is Romatech and some of the Vamps who work there."

Jedrek recognized the pictures of Draganesti and his bodyguard, Connor Buchanan. "Who is this?"

"Gregori Holstein. A vice president at Romatech."

"Where is the information on Draganesti's home?"

Yuri gulped. "We haven't been able to find it. Yet," he quickly added in response to Jedrek's glare. "Here are some photos of his townhouse in the Upper East Side."

Jedrek looked through them. There was a kilted Scotsman and a young black man in the MacKay uniform.

Yuri pointed at the photo of a third man. "This guy arrived last night. We're not sure who he is. He doesn't match any of our older photos."

Jedrek studied the picture of a young man in a red and green kilt. "Another damned Highlander. I swear MacKay has an endless supply of them." He picked up the last photo of a young blonde woman. "Who is this? Their whore?"

"Perhaps." Yuri shifted his weight. "She's mortal."

"How can you tell?"

"I . . . recognize her. I fed on her Monday night."

Jedrek set her picture down. "Wasn't that the night you let Sashenka get slaughtered?"

"Connor Buchanan killed him," Yuri said quickly. "We had everything under control until he showed up."

Jedrek curled his hands into fists. "It was three against one. You should have killed the damned Scotsman. What did I tell you about incompetence?"

Yuri paled. "It will not be tolerated."

Jedrek stared at the man, allowing Yuri's fear to grow as the seconds ticked by. He breathed deeply. He loved the smell of fear. "You are fortunate the event happened before I became master. I am hungry now. Fetch me a mortal."

"Yes, Master." Yuri bowed. "Right away."

Jedrek smoothed a finger over the face of the girl in the photo. "Bring me a blonde. I hear they're more fun."

After a subway ride and short walk to Washington Square, Toni arrived at the second-floor apartment she shared with Sabrina. She dropped her handbag and keys on the coffee table, then shrugged out of her jacket and tossed it and her scarf on the love seat. Sabrina's cat, Vanderkitty, jumped from the easy chair to weave around Toni's legs.

"Hey, Van." Toni rubbed behind the orange tabby's ears. "Have you seen your mama?"

Van gave her an annoyed look, then marched off to the kitchen area to assume a regal pose by her food bowl.

"Don't give me that. I know Carlos has been feeding you."
Toni peered inside Sabrina's bedroom.

It looked the same as it had last Sunday—discarded jeans
on the floor, textbooks lying open across the purple chenille
bedspread. Before going out Sunday night, Sabrina had
spent most of the day studying for finals this week—finals
she had missed. Toni had visited all of Bri's professors on
Monday to explain why Bri would be absent. She would receive incompletes in all five of her classes.

It was as if Sabrina's life had suddenly frozen in time, and
her room along with her. Toni wondered if their lives would
ever be the same.

She turned on the bedside lamp, then dug through the top
drawer of Bri's bedside table. Her heart squeezed when she
spotted a birthday card Bri had kept. Toni had given it to her
years ago. It was the first time she'd bought a card that was
addressed to "Sister."

As far as Toni was concerned, Bri *was* her sister. They'd
been best friends for ten years. They spent their holidays
and vacations together. God knew their real families didn't
want them.

Which was why it was so weird for Bri to leave the hospital with her aunt and uncle. Toni had heard so little about
this couple over the years, she couldn't even recall their full
names. Joe and Gwen something-or-other who occasionally
remembered to send Bri a Christmas card. Why had they
suddenly developed an interest in their niece?

Toni located a pink fuzzy address book and thumbed
through the pages. It was sad how few names were in the
book. Even sadder how many names had been crossed out
over the years. Poor Bri. It was so hard for her to find people
she could trust.

Toni carried the address book back into the living room
and flopped down on the love seat. Vanderkitty jumped onto
the back of the love seat to perch by Toni's ear.

"You miss your mama?" Toni interpreted the loud purring as a yes. "Yeah, me, too."

She flipped through the pages of the address book. "Aha!" Under the *P*s, she found Dr. Joe Proctor and Gwen, who lived in Westchester. This had to be them, although Toni hadn't known Uncle Joe was a doctor.

She reached over the sofa arm for the cordless phone on the end table and noticed the blinking message light. Four messages. Three were from her, since she'd called three times. Maybe the fourth one was from Bri.

Toni punched the play button and listened to her voice grow increasingly worried with each message. Finally the last message.

"Bri, this is Justin. You gotta forgive me, babe—"

Right. Toni turned the message off. Then she dialed the number for the Proctors. What kind of doctor was he? A proctologist? Her snort was interrupted by a feminine voice with a Hispanic accent.

"Dr. Proctor's residence."

"Hi. Is Sabrina there?" Toni heard muffled voices in the background.

A different voice came on the phone. "Good evening. This is Gwen Proctor."

"I'm Toni, Bri's roommate. I'd like to talk to her."

"I'm afraid that's not possible at the moment. She's sleeping, and we hate to wake her up, the poor dear. She's been through such a terrible ordeal."

Tell me about it. Toni had survived a vampire attack, too. "Is she all right?"

"Yes, of course." A definite chill had crept into Gwen's voice. "Thank you for calling."

"Can you tell her to call me when she wakes up?"

"We don't want to upset her delicate condition."

Was that a *no?* "Bri will want to talk to me."

"Perhaps, but you're not qualified to talk to her properly.

My husband is an excellent psychiatrist, an expert in the type of severe psychosis that Sabrina is exhibiting right now."

Toni's stomach dropped like she'd swallowed a cement brick. "Bri is *not* psychotic."

There was a pause where Toni could hear whispering.

"Ms. Davis?" a brusque male voice came on the phone. "This is Dr. Proctor, Sabrina's uncle. I can assure you she's receiving the best care available."

"I just want to talk to her."

"Under the circumstances, I cannot allow that."

Toni's fist squeezed around the receiver. "Look, she's twenty-three years old. You can't decide whom she talks to."

"You would not be a positive influence on her at this time," he answered calmly. "The poor girl believes she was attacked by vampires."

Toni gritted her teeth. "Yes, I know—"

"And she fears they'll return to harm her again. We are providing her a safe environment for her recovery."

"That's great, but I still want to talk to her."

"The last time she talked to you, she asked you to prove that her attackers were actual vampires," Dr. Proctor continued. "And you agreed."

"She was lying there injured in a hospital room. How could I say no?"

"I cannot allow her to speak to anyone who will encourage her in these paranoid delusions. You would severely jeopardize the progress we've made."

Toni swallowed hard. "What are you doing to her?"

"Giving her expert care. Good night." He hung up.

"Wait!" Toni glared at the receiver. "You asshole!"

"I hope you're not referring to me."

Startled, Toni jumped in her seat, then turned toward the man climbing through the kitchen window.

"Carlos!" she scolded her next-door neighbor. "How long have you been there, listening?"

"Long enough."

"In that case, I *was* referring to you." She hung up the phone. Now that she thought about it, she was glad he had eavesdropped. She needed a friend she could confide in, and with Sabrina gone, Carlos was all she had left.

It wasn't the first time he had snuck up on her. The man moved with a quiet, stealthlike grace. She assumed he'd acquired the skill from his trips into the Amazon jungle, where a person was better off not announcing his presence. With his shoulder-length black hair, black sweater, and black leather pants, Carlos was barely visible on the fire escape landing their two apartments shared.

He straddled the windowsill, his white teeth flashing as he grinned. "Come now, girl, you should be nice to me. It sounds like you might need someone with my talents."

She snorted. "Which talent would that be? The one where you dance the samba, wearing a sequined thong?"

He looked affronted. "I wear a lot more than a thong. I have a hot pink satin cape and a headdress with ostrich feathers. It's enormous." He winked. "Like the rest of me."

Toni laughed. Carlos always went back to Brazil for a few days at carnival time. Since he was working on his master's in anthropology at NYU, he claimed the trip was educational. Toni and Bri had certainly learned some new things from the videos he brought back.

He swung his other leg over the windowsill, then straightened his long, lean frame. He was gorgeous, but more likely to dress Toni and Sabrina than date them. Vanderkitty leaped from the love seat, bounced across the kitchen floor, and landed in his arms.

"She never greets me like that," Toni muttered.

"She knows who's the boss around here. Hello, love." He rubbed the cat's head against his smooth, tanned cheek, then set her on the linoleum. "I was coming over to feed her when I heard you getting all huffy on the phone."

"That was Sabrina's aunt and uncle. They've got her at their house, and they won't let me talk to her."

"Humph. Some people are so rude." Carlos opened the cabinet under the sink and removed Van's bag of kibble. "*Menina*, you said you'd tell me what was going on."

"Yeah, I know." But how could she explain without sounding crazy? "I hardly know where to start."

"Start with the bastards who attacked Sabrina." Carlos poured kibble into Van's bowl. "It was Sunday night, yes?"

"Yes. She went ice skating with Justin in Central Park. They had an argument, and she left on her own."

Carlos put the kibble back under the sink and slammed the cabinet door shut. "*Merda*. She should have called me."

"Or me," Toni agreed. "Unfortunately, Justin upset her so much, she wasn't thinking properly."

Carlos's amber eyes narrowed. "Did he hurt her?"

"Emotionally, yes. He made a comment about how they should spend the money she's going to inherit."

Carlos winced. "I didn't think he knew about that."

"Me, neither. Anyway, Bri felt totally betrayed, and she took off on her own. Then the bad guys attacked her."

"Poor *menina*." Carlos strode into the living room and perched on the arm of the easy chair.

"There were three . . . thugs," Toni explained. "Bri ended up with abrasions and cracked ribs. Some people found her, lying unconscious in the snow, and called 911. The police interviewed her at the hospital, but they thought she was delusional, you know, from all the hypothermia and blood loss. They didn't believe her story."

Carlos made a sound of disgust. "She was obviously attacked. Did they think she injured herself?"

"No, but they thought she was imagining the thugs worse than they really were."

"They beat her up and left her for dead. What could be worse than that?"

Vampires. But no one had believed Bri. Even Toni had thought her friend was conjuring up some imaginary boogey monsters as a response to the trauma she'd endured. "Bri was upset when no one believed her, so she asked me to go to the park and find the guys who attacked her."

Carlos sat back. "Are you crazy, girl? You should have asked me to come with you."

He was right. Carlos was an expert in martial arts. When he had first met Toni and Bri two years ago, he'd insisted they go to classes with him. "I wish I had. But I didn't think anything would happen."

Carlos frowned. "You didn't believe her, either?"

"I believe her now. Monday night, I was alone in the park, and the three . . . guys showed up. I tried fighting them off, but . . ." Toni had done well until they'd started moving super fast. That had been her first clue that the attackers weren't normal. Then a blast of cold air had slammed against her head, and they had invaded her mind. The memory caused a shudder to run down her spine.

"*Menina*." Carlos sat beside her on the love seat. "What are you not telling me?"

"I . . . can't explain. It's too strange."

He gave her an annoyed look. "I spent part of my childhood in the Amazon jungle. I spent last summer in the jungles of Malaysia. I have seen stranger things than you can imagine."

Toni took a deep breath. She wasn't supposed to tell anyone about vampires, but how could she explain Sabrina's dilemma without revealing their existence? "I need your word you won't repeat this to anyone. I'm serious. I'll be in big trouble if the truth gets out because of me."

"I can keep a secret. Tell me."

"The bad guys *bit* Sabrina. Me, too."

Carlos stiffened. "They were like animals? They wanted your . . . flesh?"

"No. They wanted blood. They were . . . vampires." She watched Carlos's face, half afraid he would laugh at her.

He stared blankly at her for a few seconds, then raised his dark eyebrows. "Are you serious?"

"I could show you the bite marks."

"Vampires?"

"Yes. They have nasty, long fangs. They can move super fast, and the worst thing, they can take over your mind."

Carlos dragged a hand through his black hair, pushing it back from his face and revealing a small gold stud in each ear. "My God, *menina*, how did you ever escape?"

"Then you believe me?"

"Yes. I know you wouldn't make something like this up." He took her hand in his. "Tell me everything."

She closed her eyes briefly. "It was terrifying. They were inside my head, ordering me to do things against my will. My mind was screaming no, but I couldn't stop them."

Carlos squeezed her hand. "It's okay, love."

"Then out of nowhere, this big guy in a kilt showed up, brandishing a sword, and yelling at the vampires to leave me alone."

Carlos's amber eyes lit up. "Oh my, a macho hero."

"That's what I thought. He stabbed one of the vampires with his sword, and it turned to dust. The other ones released me, so they could fight him. And that's when I realized my mind was free. So I joined in on the fight."

"Oh, good for you, girl."

"Then the two bad guys vanished, and—"

"Vanished?"

"Yeah. It's another vampire thing. Then the Scotsman grabbed me, and we vanished, too."

Carlos gasped. *"Merda!* Where did you go?" His eyes narrowed. "Are you saying the Scotsman is a vampire, too?"

"Yes, but he's a good one. His name is Connor, and he took me to Romatech Industries."

Carlos nodded slowly. "I've heard of that place. It's run by that famous scientist who invented synthetic blood."

"Roman Draganesti. I met him. He's the leader of the good Vamps."

"Good Vamps?"

"Yeah. Roman gave me a blood transfusion. Then Connor offered to erase my memory of the whole ordeal. They really don't want people to know that they exist."

Carlos gave her a wry look. "I can believe that."

"But I couldn't let them erase my memory, 'cause I needed to tell Sabrina that she was right."

"Claro."

"Luckily, there was another option. Connor knew I could fight, so he offered me a job, guarding the Vamps during the day. You see, they're totally helpless then. And they're in desperate need of mortals they can trust."

"So that's where you've been during the day?" Carlos asked. "You're guarding vampires?"

"Yes. Today was my second day. It's a fairly easy job. They're basically dead during the day, so there's not much going on. But I do have to stay there. I'd be in big trouble if I left them unguarded."

Carlos snorted. "If they're dead, how could they know if you left?"

"I have to call in reports to my mortal supervisor, Howard. And he's watching me on monitors. He's been very understanding. He's taking over for me Friday so I can take my final. And he let me use the answering machine today when every ditzy female in the city was calling for . . . him."

"Him?"

"I don't want to talk about him. I've got enough problems without . . . him."

"Ah." The corners of Carlos's mouth tilted up. "So is this *him* one of them?"

"He's a Vamp, yes. A very annoying one." Of all the Vamps, Ian was the only one who suspected her of a hidden agenda. The fact that he was correct just made it more aggravating.

The man was driving her crazy. Since her attack, she had every reason to hate vampires. The damned monsters deserved to be hated. It was like they'd stripped her humanity by reducing her to nothing but a food source. And when they'd taken over her mind, it had felt like her soul was being squashed. So how the hell could she find Ian so attractive?

For a second, she'd thought he must be controlling her mind. But she'd never felt the jab of cold air on her brow. Nor had she heard his voice in her head. No, her attraction was real. Crazy, but real.

Any man would be blessed and honored to receive yer love. Her heart had almost stopped when he'd said that. It was the loveliest thing anyone had ever told her. It made her feel attractive and . . . worthy. *I am worthy to be loved.*

The way he had looked at her, like he was reaching deep inside her, had made her painfully aware of an emptiness in her soul. He was dangerous. And beautiful.

"*Menina*, it seems to me you have a conflict of interest."

"I'm not going to let him get to me."

Carlos smiled. "I wasn't referring to *him*. Though I suppose he does explain that mushy look on your face."

"Excuse me?"

Carlos chuckled. "I was referring to this new job of yours. You're paid to protect the Vamps, yes?"

"Yes. I took a vow to protect them."

"But at the same time, you want to prove Sabrina's telling the truth about vampires. Seems to me, if you expose the secret about vampires, you will be breaking your vow to protect them."

"I thought about that. You see, if we just let a lawyer or a psychiatrist know the truth, then they'll be bound by client confidentiality. So they'll know Bri isn't crazy, but at the same time, they won't be able to expose the Vamps and hurt them."

"Ah." Carlos nodded. "A tricky plan, but a good one."

"The problem is finding actual proof of their existence. I thought about taking photos of them in their death-sleep, but they look totally normal."

"Like they're asleep?" Carlos asked.

"Exactly. Well, Dougal looks kinda dead, 'cause he sleeps in a coffin, but even so, it would just look like a photo of a dead guy. And people die all the time. It's hardly revolutionary. I looked in their library—"

"They have a library? They're not in a dark, gloomy crypt somewhere in a graveyard?"

"No, they have a luxurious townhouse. Five floors of beautiful antiques and artwork. You wouldn't believe the canopy bed I'm sleeping in."

"Oh God." Carlos pressed a hand against his broad chest. "It sounds fabulous. When can I see it?"

"I can't sneak you in past the surveillance cameras."

He scoffed. "Don't bet on it, girlfriend. So what's the story with Sabrina?"

"Her aunt and uncle checked her out of the hospital and took her to their house in Westchester. Uncle Joe's a psychiatrist, and he says she's suffering from severe psychosis. He won't let me talk to her."

Carlos frowned. "What do you know about this aunt and uncle?"

"Not much. They never showed much interest in Bri before now."

"Yes, but she stands to inherit a lot of money once she graduates, yes?"

"Yep. Eighty-five million."

Carlos's eyes widened. "I had no idea it was so much!"

"Well, she doesn't advertise it, for obvious reasons. Her parents didn't want her to become a useless trust fund baby, so they stipulated in their will that she had to graduate from college before she could inherit the whole amount. She's been getting a yearly allowance since she was fourteen."

"And when does she graduate?"

"Next spring. Well, actually, it'll be longer than that 'cause she's getting incompletes this semester."

Carlos stood and paced across the floor. "She could be in serious trouble."

Toni swallowed hard. "I was afraid of that."

"I need all the information you have on the aunt and uncle."

"This is it." Toni handed him the pink fuzzy address book. "Their last name is Proctor."

He ripped out the page, then folded it. "I'll check them out, especially their financial records."

"How will you do that?"

He slipped the paper into a pocket of his tight leather pants. "I have a computer."

"So do I, but I wouldn't know how to check on someone."

"No offense, love, but it took you months to learn how to download e-mail."

Toni sighed. It was true. She was totally inept when it came to modern technology. She'd lived her first thirteen years at her grandmother's house in rural Alabama, where their one phone had a rotary dial and their one television had four channels and no remote control.

"That reminds me." She dug through her handbag and handed him her cell. "I need a different ringtone."

He grinned. "You don't want to rock the boys?"

"No, I'll leave that to you. I need something less . . . loud, please."

"No problem." He jammed the phone into his pocket. "How long were you planning to stay here?"

"About half an hour. I need to pack some more clothes to take back with me."

"Fine. I'll be right back." Carlos slipped out the kitchen window.

Toni looked in the refrigerator for something to drink, but everything there had caffeine. Not good when she needed to be asleep by ten every night so she could rise early in the morning. She poured herself a glass of ice water, then headed to her bedroom to pack.

Monday night, after she'd survived the attack and accepted employment, she'd been stuffed in the backseat of a sedan, and Dougal had driven her here to pick up some clothes. She'd been in such a state of shock, she'd only grabbed a few things from her bedroom while Dougal had waited in the living room. Then he'd driven her straight to the townhouse, and she'd been there ever since.

She realized now that the Vamps hadn't wanted her to get loose with the knowledge she possessed. The fact that she'd been allowed to go out tonight must mean that they had decided to trust her. How long would she have to live with them? It was hard to say. How could she help Sabrina if she couldn't even talk to her?

"Your phone's ready." Carlos strolled into her bedroom.

She jumped. Good grief, he was too good at sneaking up on people. She dropped the cell phone into her suitcase, next to her box of daily contacts.

Carlos wandered over to inspect her clothes closet. "Hmm, this is too frumpy. Oh my God, I love this black leather vest. What a shame it's too small for me." He took the vest out to admire it.

Toni smiled as she emptied her underwear drawer in the suitcase. She had missed Carlos.

"By the way, I did a quick check on Dr. Proctor's financial records. He's in debt up to his greedy little eyeballs. Been living way beyond his means."

Toni's mouth fell open. "You were gone twenty minutes, and you learned all that?"

Carlos shrugged and hung her vest back in the closet. Then he gasped. "Girlfriend, hasn't anyone ever told you never ever wear horizontal stripes?" He pulled out the offending T-shirt. "This should be burned."

"Thanks. I was looking for that." Toni whipped the T-shirt out of his hand and tossed it in her suitcase.

"Humph." Carlos proceeded to her dresser to check out the rest of her clothes. "Now this is nice. You should take this." He pulled out a skimpy red satin teddy.

"It's December. I'm taking some flannel pajamas."

"But *menina*, don't you want to look sexy for *him*?"

Toni slammed her suitcase shut. "You have definitely gotten the wrong idea about *him*."

Carlos's amber eyes twinkled. "Are you sure? I only need to mention *him*, and your cheeks bloom like a red rose."

"That's irritation, not attraction." Toni pulled her suitcase off the bed and rolled it from the room. "I've got to go, Carlos. Take care of Vanderkitty."

"Will do. And I'll see what else I can find out about Sabrina's uncle."

"Thank you." Toni stopped to give him a hug. "I don't know what I'd do without you."

He grinned. "Now hurry on back to *him*."

"Stuff it, Carlos." She left the apartment to the sound of his chuckling. Hopefully, Ian would be busy all night pursuing Vamp women. If she was really lucky, she'd make it back to the townhouse and her bedroom without having to see *him* at all.

Chapter Six

Ian approached the bed where Toni was sleeping. Her heartbeat was steady, her face calm and peaceful. He hoped she was having sweet dreams. Connor had described the attack on her. She'd be lucky if it wasn't giving her nightmares.

He thought back to the last time he'd had a dream. It was the eve of the Battle of Solway Moss in 1542. He'd slept fitfully the night before his first battle, and he'd dreamed of shallow mountain streams turning red with blood. He fell into the stream, and it suddenly became bottomless, sucking him under, drowning him in blood. The very next night, he'd joined the ranks of the Undead when Angus had found him dying on the battlefield.

Ian snorted. At least in the last four hundred and sixty years, he'd greatly improved his fighting skills. He'd never been seriously injured since that first fateful night. And he was no longer plagued with nightmares before battle. He no longer dreamed at all.

He'd begun his investigation at Romatech by having Connor tell him about the attack Monday night. Connor had overheard the Malcontents' mental voices as they controlled Toni, and he'd used those voices as a beacon to teleport straight to the scene of the crime.

When Ian examined her personnel file, he'd been surprised to learn that she had an apartment in Greenwich Village. He'd also been surprised by the bachelor's degree in general business and a near complete master's in sociology. Why would someone that smart take a dead-end job, guarding the Undead? Was she conducting a study?

Connor didn't believe she was using them for research. After all, she couldn't have known about their existence before the Malcontents had attacked her. He had run a background check, and her only offense was a traffic ticket for speeding. Like Dougal, Connor had asked Ian not to chase her away. Until Phil returned from Texas, they were in desperate need of a day guard.

What Ian hadn't said was that he was in more danger of pulling her close than pushing her away.

"Doona pester her," Connor had ordered. "The lass needs time to recover."

So Ian had gone to the Horny Devils for his two dates. The women had been pleasant enough, but his mind kept returning to Toni, and the inconsistencies between her personnel file and what she'd told him.

He glanced at the digital clock next to her bed. Six-thirty. Thursday morning. Shouldn't she be waking soon? He paced about the room. His gaze continued to wander back to her, all snug and cozy in her bed. With his superior vision, he could still see her well in the dark room. She was lovely, the way her golden hair spilled across the pillow, the way her delicate hands curled close to her face.

Bloody hell. He paced away. He had to stop thinking about her that way. He'd already decided he wanted a Vamp woman who was honest, loyal, intelligent, and pretty. Toni wasn't a Vamp. And he had serious doubts about her honesty and loyalty.

But she was very intelligent and pretty. Not to mention intriguing. She seemed to ignite all his senses at once, and it was such an intoxicating feeling, he found himself looking for any excuse to be with her.

He stopped. Was that why he felt this compulsion to investigate her? He mentally reviewed his suspicions. No, his questions were legit. It was his attraction to her that was way out of line. She was a guard. She was forbidden.

When the alarm went off, he zipped to the bedside table and turned it off.

With a little moan, she stretched. Her eyes opened.

"Good morning, lass."

She gasped and pulled the covers up to her chin. She quickly looked around the room, then focused on him. "What are you doing here?"

"We need to talk."

"Now?" She squinted at her door, still closed and locked. "How did you get in here?"

"I teleported in. Yer door wasna damaged."

"That's not the point. You invaded my privacy."

He shrugged one shoulder. "Do ye no' look at me when I'm in my death-sleep?"

"That's my job."

"And investigation is my job. I have a few questions regarding yer employment application. First off, I noticed ye dinna give yer complete first name."

She gave him an annoyed look. "I have to go to the bathroom. And you need to do your vanishing act." She slipped out of bed and waved a hand at him. "Hocus pocus, disappear."

He stepped back as she strode to the bathroom, and he couldn't help but notice how her breasts jiggled slightly beneath her red T-shirt. No bra. With his superior vision, he could detect the exact location and shape of her nipples. When she passed him, he turned to watch her from behind. Her pajama bottoms were red with little black and white penguins. They fit snugly around her hips and rounded bottom. When she paused at the bathroom door, he quickly lifted his gaze so she wouldn't catch him ogling her.

She glared at him. "Why are you still here?"

"We havena talked yet."

With a groan, she entered the bathroom, then shut the door in his face. He paced about the room. He didn't want to question her through the door. He needed to see her face to help him decide if she was being truthful. He glanced at the clock. He didn't have much time before the sun reached the horizon.

He raised his voice so she could hear him. "I wanted to thank you for the wee practice session. I felt more comfortable talking to my dates."

No answer.

He moved close to the door and heard the water being turned on. "The ladies were verra pleasant to talk to. I enjoyed their company, but . . . it just wasna right. There was something missing, some . . . *je ne sais quoi.*"

"Chemistry," she said, then muttered a curse. "Idiot. Don't talk to him," she whispered to herself.

He grinned. "After my dates, I came back here to go through the phone messages. I found three recordings where the ladies actually admitted to being Vamps. So I called them back and arranged to meet them tonight."

No answer.

There was a brushing sound, followed by some spitting. He figured she was brushing her teeth. "Ye'll be happy to know that I phoned all the mortals who called during the day. I told them I was verra sorry, but I was already taken."

The door opened, and she gazed at him, her pretty green eyes wide with surprise. "You called all of them?"

"Aye. Some of them werena home, so I left a message."

"There were hundreds of them."

"I know. It took me several hours." He rubbed his whiskered chin. "I've been told recently that I'm a rude, arrogant snob, so I'm trying to mend my evil ways."

She snorted. "Too late." She walked past him to the dresser and removed some undies from a drawer.

Blue and lacy, he noted. "I left a new recording on the answering machine, so anyone who calls today will hear that I'm no longer available."

"Oh, that was a good idea."

"Aye." He felt a sudden pull as if a vacuum cleaner was sucking out his energy. The sun must be nearing the horizon. "I'd like to discuss yer employment application."

"I filled it out truthfully." She planted a hand on her hip. "And I'm insulted that you're questioning that."

"I'm no' saying ye lied." He yawned as he moved toward her.

She glanced at the clock. "You're just about out of time, huh? And I need to take my shower, so off you go."

He felt another tug from his death-sleep and grabbed a bedpost to steady himself.

"Aw, feeling a little sleepy, are you? Time to go beddie-bye?"

He steeled himself against the weakness. "I still have some time. Answer my questions, and I'll leave."

She opened the closet and tugged a polo shirt off a hanger. "The way I see it, I only have to avoid you for about two more minutes." She grabbed a pair of pants and turned toward the bathroom.

He zoomed forward and caught her in his arms. She gasped.

He inclined his head closer to hers. "Can ye avoid me now?"

She clasped her clothes to her chest with one hand and pushed at him with the other. "I'm not talking to you."

He noted with great satisfaction that her push had been weak. She didn't object as much as she pretended to. And her body was warm and soft. He splayed his hands across her back and pulled her closer. "We could find other ways to pass the time."

Her eyes flashed with anger. "You—you're a liar!" She shoved harder, and he released her.

"I havena lied to you, lass."

"You said you only wanted Vamp women." She stepped back and hugged her clothes to her chest. "Why should I tell you anything if you're not trustworthy?"

He couldn't believe it. She was turning the tables on him. "It's *you* I doona completely trust."

"You're the one trying to break the rule of noninvolvement."

"Bloody hell, I'm a man! Do ye expect me no' to notice how beautiful ye are?" He swayed on his feet.

She reached out a hand to steady him, then pulled her arm back before making contact. "Don't you dare fall dead in my bedroom. How could I explain that?"

"No one will know I was here. Trust me."

She gave him a sad look. "How could I ever trust a vampire?"

"I'm still a man," he whispered. "And I would never hurt you." With his last ounce of energy, he teleported to the fifth floor, pulled off his jumper, and collapsed on the bed. He'd get his answers tonight.

As death-sleep washed over him, he wished he could dream of lovely girls with golden hair and eyes as green as a Highland meadow in springtime.

I deserve to be happy.
I will accomplish my goals.

Toni began her morning affirmations in the shower. As she soaped up her arms, she recalled how Ian had grabbed her and pulled her close. She'd been too stunned to fight him off. *Yeah, keep telling yourself that.*

*I will achieve something meaningful with my life.
I am worthy to be loved.*

Dammit, she'd liked being in his arms. She was out of her mind. She wouldn't think about him anymore. She rinsed off and started her affirmations again.

*I deserve to be happy.
Do ye expect me no' to notice how beautiful ye are?*

Good grief, now *his* words were repeating in her head. But what nice words. And what had he told her earlier? *Any man would be blessed and honored to receive yer love.* With a sigh, she turned the water off. She'd waited all her life to hear someone tell her the right words. What rotten luck that it was coming from a vampire.

She dressed, popped in her contacts, and pulled her damp hair back into a ponytail. She'd dry it later. For now, she needed to make her rounds and call in her first report. She went to the basement to make sure the little Vamps were all snug in their little Vamp beds. Dougal and Phineas were fine. Time for the long trek upstairs. Of all the floors, Ian had to pick the top one. At least the five flights were good cardio.

She found him on the king-sized bed, stretched out in his kilt, white T-shirt, socks, and shoes. His sweater was on the floor. She picked it up, folded it, and placed it beside him on the bed. His face was peaceful, but rugged with black stubble shading his jaw. She fought an urge to stroke a fingertip down his cheek and poke the dimple in his chin.

She turned away from his face and noted his shoes. That couldn't be comfy. She had one shoe pulled off when she realized it had only been yesterday morning when she'd been afraid to even touch him.

She glanced at his face. He was becoming human to her. And not just human, but attractive. Damn. She dropped his second shoe on the floor and left the room. She needed to quit this job as soon as possible. She just needed to find proof that the Vamps existed. Then she could shove that proof in Dr. Proctor's face and demand he let Sabrina go. And then she would be out of here. She'd never have to see Ian again.

A sudden wave of sadness caught her by surprise. Damn, why couldn't he have been mortal? Why couldn't she have met him at NYU? If he'd approached her there with his gorgeous face and lilting, soft accent, she would have fallen for him in a second. God help her, she wanted to hear him say more lovely things to her. She wanted to know if his thick, black hair felt soft if she raked her fingers through it.

How old was he exactly? He'd mentioned the sixteenth century. It was fascinating once she thought about all the things he must have seen over the centuries. What kind of baggage was he carrying on his broad shoulders? What kept him going night after night through the centuries? Did he really want to share his long life with one special woman?

Stop thinking about him. She strode across the office and sat at the desk. The computer hadn't yielded any proof. Maybe there was something in the drawers. She rummaged through the desk and discovered a thin black book. The title, printed in white, read *The Black Pages.*

As she scanned the first few pages, her heart began to race. This could be it. Proof positive. The advertisements were clearly meant for the Vamp public.

Ace Aluminum Blinds and Shutters. Block out that annoying sunlight and enjoy the dark!

Aerobics and Weight Training. Is your body centuries old? Keep it in great shape with us!

Brooklyn Blood Bank. Catering to Vamp needs. Are you tired of synthetic blood and hankering for the real thing?

This was it!

She was so excited, she called Carlos. "It's called *The Black Pages*. It's perfect!"

"I'm not sure it constitutes proof," Carlos said with a yawn. "Anybody can print anything off a computer."

Toni groaned. "Don't be such a downer."

"I'm sorry, *menina*. I'll be happy to look at it, though. Can you bring it tonight? Let's have dinner at your place. I'll order in Chinese."

"That's sounds wonderful." She would switch to her biggest handbag, so she could sneak the phone book out of the house. "Have you found out anything more about Sabrina's uncle?"

"Not yet. I have a final this afternoon and a paper due tomorrow. But I'll find the time."

"Okay. Good luck with your stuff." Toni hung up.

It was eight A.M. and time for her first report. After she got off the phone with Howard, the phone started ringing constantly. She was relieved Ian had recorded the new message, and she didn't have to deal with all the girls who thought he was hot. Even if they were right.

By four-thirty that evening, she was ready to go. She had hidden *The Black Pages* in a big handbag. The minute Dougal and Phineas arrived in the kitchen, she said her good-byes and headed for the front door. Ian materialized in the foyer just as she was unlocking the door.

"Toni, wait!" He rushed forward and stumbled, nearly falling on his face. He righted himself just in time. "Bugger."

She hesitated before opening the door. "Are you all right?" Good grief, the poor man was blushing.

"My feet grew from a size nine to a thirteen in twelve days," he muttered. "I'm still getting used to it."

His feet weren't the only things that had grown. Toni's face grew hot as she attempted to override that memory. She was being shallow, she chided herself. The man must have suffered while he was growing that fast. "It must have been painful."

He shrugged one shoulder. "It was worth it to finally look like a man."

And what a man. "Well, you certainly got some good results."

His eyes started to twinkle. "Like a hot, hot studmuffin?"

She winced. That line was going to haunt her the rest of her days.

He stepped toward her. "We still need to talk."

Not that again. Maybe she should try a new tactic. "I'd love to talk, but can we do it later? I have to go now. My dinner date is waiting."

His eyes narrowed. "Ye have a date?"

She started to say it was just with an old friend, but why put the guy out of his misery? He looked kinda jealous, and she kinda liked it. "You're not the only one who dates around here, you know."

He frowned. "I have three dates tonight."

Great, studmuffin. Rub it in. "Have fun." *Not.* She marched out the door.

Chapter Seven

Forty-five minutes later, Toni was in her apartment, wolfing down Chinese food and giggling with Carlos over the advertisements in *The Black Pages.*

"Look at this one." He pointed. *"Undead Body Armor. Protect your chest against those pesky wooden stakes."*

She nearly choked on a noodle. "I still like the Fang File the best. Gotta keep those fangs sharp."

Carlos chuckled. "You know what's good, *menina*? You're able to laugh at vampires now."

"Believe me, that awful attack still bothers me. I'm just getting better at not thinking about it." If she did think about it, she'd probably burst into tears. "I have a long history of learning to laugh at pain instead of cry."

He patted her arm. "You're doing fine. How long can you stay tonight? I'd like to do a recon of Dr. Proctor's house in Westchester. We need to know the layout in case we have to extract Sabrina."

"Excuse me?" Sometimes Carlos didn't exactly sound like an anthropology student.

"Never mind. I'll handle the uncle. You keep working on getting proof that these vampires exist."

She sighed. They'd already decided that anyone reading *The Black Pages* would simply think it was a joke book. "I'm totally stumped. I mean, it sounds easy to get proof, but it's not. Even if I videotaped someone admitting he's a vampire, people would just think I had hired an actor."

Carlos stared into space for a moment while he considered. "You need to catch them in the act. Get a recording of them vanishing or their fangs coming out. Go someplace where a lot of them are gathered, and they feel totally free to be themselves."

"A vampire hangout?"

"Exactly." He jumped up and headed to the kitchen window. "I've got something in my apartment you can use."

"A rope of garlic?" There was a loud knock on her door, and she jumped.

Carlos hesitated. "Are you expecting someone?"

"No." She rushed to the door and peered through the peephole. "Oh no!" Oh shoot! With his super hearing, he'd probably heard her.

"What's wrong?" Carlos reversed direction and headed back into the living room.

"Nothing." Damn! How had Ian discovered her address? Her employment application, of course. He'd probably gone back to Romatech to get it. A second knock shook the door, and she scooted away from it.

"You want me to get it?" Carlos asked.

"No, I'll get it," she whispered. It's just . . . him."

"*Him?* The infamous *him* of no name?"

She lifted a finger to her mouth to shush Carlos up. No doubt Super Vamp was listening to them.

Carlos's mouth curled up. "The *him* whose very mention causes your eyes to glaze over with a take-me-I'm-yours look?"

"That's not true!" Toni winced as she looked back at the door. She dashed over to Carlos and hissed quietly, "Go back to your place now. Before I kill you."

"Are you kidding?" Carlos perched on the arm of the easy chair. "I wouldn't miss *him* for anything."

She swatted Carlos on the shoulder, but he didn't budge. It was no use. She leaned close so she could whisper. "Don't say a word about him being a Vamp. You're not supposed to know."

"My lips are sealed." Carlos's eyes twinkled. "Unless he has other plans."

She huffed. "Don't you dare make a move on him."

"Ah. Feeling a bit territorial, are we?"

She glared at Carlos's smirking face.

A third knock banged loudly.

"He's not getting any younger, love," Carlos murmured. "Let the poor man in."

"I *am* going to kill you." She gasped when she realized *The Black Pages* was sitting right there on the coffee table. She stuffed it under the easy chair's seat cushion, then rushed to the door. Vanderkitty followed her. She flipped the lock and opened the door.

"About time." Ian marched in, his kilt swinging about his knees. His gaze flitted past Toni to rest on Carlos. With a lift of his chin, Ian regarded the other man sternly. "I doona believe we have met. Are ye Toni's date?"

Carlos remained sitting while he looked Ian over. "Nice kilt."

Van hissed at Ian, then jumped into Carlos's lap. "Good kitty." He slowly petted the cat.

Ian arched a brow. "Who are you and why are ye here?"

Toni stepped in front of him. "It's none of your business what I do when I'm off duty."

Ian lowered his voice. "Aye, but when ye're on duty, I'm no' in a verra talkative mood. Ye said ye'd love to talk to me later. So I'm here. This is later."

"This is not a good time."

He glanced at their empty plates on the coffee table. "Ye're done with yer dinner, aye?"

Carlos set Van in the easy chair, then approached with a hand extended. "I'm Carlos Panterra, Toni's next-door neighbor."

Ian shook his hand. "Ian MacPhie."

Carlos glanced from Toni to Ian and smiled. "I'll leave you two alone then."

"You don't need to go, Carlos." Toni gave him a pointed look.

"*Menina*, I have a little gift for you, remember? I'll be right back." He sauntered toward the kitchen.

Toni frowned at Ian. "I thought you had three dates tonight."

"No' real dates," Ian muttered. "I'm just meeting them at a nightclub." He lowered his voice, "For my kind."

"A nightclub?" Carlos asked with one foot on the windowsill. "You should take Toni. She loves music and dancing. Don't you, *menina*?"

She stared at Carlos, confused.

"It's no' a suitable place for her," Ian began.

"Too wild?" Carlos asked. "Don't worry. Toni loves to get wild. Don't you, love?" He winked.

"I—I doona think she would like it," Ian insisted, and Toni realized he wasn't able to explain that this was a vampire nightclub.

"Toni just adores places with lots of action." Carlos gave her a pointed look, and it finally clicked.

A vampire hangout! It might be the perfect place to get the proof she needed. "Oh yes! I would love to go."

Ian's eyes widened. "Ye would?"

"Of course." She gave him a dazzling smile. "You will take me, won't you?"

"But ye know what kind of people will be there," he whispered.

"I'd really like to go." Toni made sure that Carlos had disappeared through the kitchen window. "I'm still a bit uncomfortable around vampires. But if I go with you to this club, it might help me get over it. I could see you all in a different light."

Ian nodded. "Connor told me how bad the attack was. I'm verra sorry."

"Oh." Did he really care? "I—I'm okay."

He looked genuinely concerned. "It happened only a few nights ago. Ye havena had time to recover."

"Well . . ." She smoothed a loose tendril of hair back from her brow.

"Connor said ye fought bravely. He was verra impressed."

She drew in a shaky breath. No, dammit, she wasn't over it. This whole conversation was getting on her nerves. And the bite marks on her chest and torso were starting to itch. "I don't know how I would have survived if Connor hadn't come along when he did."

"I understand now why ye hate mind control so much. Connor told me how they forced ye to take—"

"Please stop!" She didn't want the memories crashing over her right now.

"Toni." He touched her shoulder, and she flinched. "Och lass, I would never hurt you."

She blinked, refusing to cry. This would never do. A stubborn, suspicious Ian she could handle, but a sweet, compassionate one? He was melting all her defenses.

She backed away and folded her arms across her bite-marked torso. "So how is the investigation going? Have you decided whether I'm trustworthy yet?"

"I still doona know yer full name. But yer refusal to talk to me is verra understandable after the way ye were attacked."

"True." Or maybe her refusal was a shield to keep her from feeling too attracted to this guy. Not that she would ever admit that.

"I'm still no' certain why ye dinna let Connor erase the memory. It is causing ye pain, lass."

She snorted. "If I had all my bad memories erased, there wouldn't be much left."

Ian frowned. "Surely that canna be so."

Toni thought back. No, there had been happy times. Sweet memories of her grandmother. Fun times with Sabrina. Moments of pride when she'd done well in school.

"My mother didn't want me." With a wince, she pressed a hand against her mouth. Damn. How had that slipped out?

Ian looked stunned. "How could that be?"

"I'm . . . illegitimate."

He shrugged one shoulder. "I dinna think that mattered in modern times."

"It didn't matter to my grandmother. She was happy to raise me. But my mom has always been embarrassed by her big mistake. Me." Toni waved a hand in dismissal. "It's not important. I don't know why I mentioned it."

"Because it causes ye pain. It's the pain we endure that makes us strong. Ye're verra brave no' to run from it."

Toni's gaze was drawn once more to Ian's, and she felt her pulse jump. Her skin tingled with awareness. Her lips went dry. Her mind grew fuzzy, and all she could think about was moving closer to him. When he stepped toward her, she wondered if he was feeling the same compulsion.

"I know the memory causes ye pain, but I'm verra glad ye kept it."

"You want me to suffer?"

"Nay. But if ye hadna kept yer memories, I would have never met you."

"Oh." Her brain grew even foggier, and she couldn't think of anything to say. She licked her lips, then noticed his gaze shifting to her mouth. Oh God.

"I'm back!" Carlos announced at the kitchen window.

Toni jerked back to her senses. Good grief, how long had she and Ian stared at each other? He moved back and folded his arms across his chest.

Carlos sauntered into the living room and gasped. "What are you doing, girl? You haven't changed clothes!"

"Excuse me?"

"You can't go to a nightclub like that." Carlos huffed. "Come on, let's get you ready." He grabbed her arm and dragged her toward her bedroom. "Make yourself comfortable, Ian. We'll just be a moment."

Ian looked confused. "Ye're . . . dressing her?"

"Don't worry. I'll make sure she looks fabulous." Carlos shoved her into the bedroom and shut the door. Then he rushed over to her closet. "You need to show some skin. How about this?" He pulled out a short denim skirt.

"I'll freeze my tail off."

"You're wearing it." Carlos tossed it on the bed, then returned to the closet. "You have to wear this vest. I just love it." He dropped the black leather vest on the bed.

"I'll need a shirt underneath."

"Must you?" Carlos groaned. "If you insist." He grabbed a sleeveless white turtleneck top. "Now you'll need some black boots, more makeup, and God forbid you wear that ponytail."

"You think this club will help?" she whispered.

"Yes, and I have something for you." Carlos pulled something small and metallic from his pants pocket. He attached it to her vest. "It'll send images back to me."

It looked like a spy camera. "Are you sure you're an anthropology student?"

He chuckled. "Some of the jungle tribes I've come across don't like the bigger cameras. They get very nervous when they see themselves shrunk down inside a little box. So I've learned it's better to record them this way."

"Oh." She supposed that made sense.

"You're all set." Carlos patted her shoulder. "Good luck."

Ian listened as he sat on the love seat, but whenever they whispered, he caught only a word or two. Something about nervous jungle tribes? What the hell was Carlos talking about? And why should *he* get to watch Toni dress? Just how close was he to Toni? The man had introduced himself as only a next-door neighbor.

A slight sound drew his attention. Carlos had exited Toni's room, closing the door with a click. He hunched over and shut his eyes, his brow furrowed. Ian opened his mouth to ask what was wrong when Carlos suddenly straightened.

He pressed a hand against his chest. "I swear by all that is holy, if I ever find another scrunchie in this apartment, I will hack it to pieces with a meat cleaver."

Ian wasn't sure what a scrunchie was, but it sounded ominous. "Is Toni all right?"

"Yes. Thank God I was there to save her. You'll just love the outfit I picked out. And I gave her a new do."

A new what? Ian was confused.

"I insisted she wear more makeup." Carlos waved a hand to emphasize his words. "But she's such a natural beauty, she hardly needs any at all. Don't you just hate that?"

Were they speaking the same language? "She's verra pretty."

"She's a nice girl." Carlos's face grew grim. "I'll be very upset if you hurt her."

Now this he understood. "I would never harm her." Ian leaned forward, resting his elbows on his knees. "How long have ye known her?"

"Two years. She and Sabrina are like sisters to me."

"Who's Sabrina?"

"Oh dear, I left a quesadilla in the oven. See you later, Ian." Carlos dashed to the kitchen, scooted through the kitchen window, then shut it behind him.

There was something definitely odd about that man. His scent was off, and his behavior inconsistent. There was a click of stiletto heels against the wooden floor, and Ian's attention snapped back to the bedroom door.

"I'm ready," Toni announced.

He gulped. His brain quickly registered luscious red-painted lips, loose silken hair, a clingy knit top, a tiny skirt, trim golden thighs, and high-heeled black boots. He blinked. She was still there, still stunning.

She walked toward him, her hips swaying just enough to hypnotize. "Will this be okay for your club?"

"Aye," he croaked. Thank God the Horny Devils was mostly full of females. But even a female Vamp could be tempted by Toni. "Ye'd better stay close to me."

"How can I?" She leaned over the coffee table to gather her belongings, and her knit top molded tightly against her breasts. "Don't you have *three* dates?"

"Aye." Her bra must be too tight, for he could swear she was spilling out of it. "They're lovely handfuls."

She shrugged on her jacket. "So you think they're beautiful?"

His gaze dropped to her long, lean thighs. "Aye, slender and golden, kissed by the sun."

"They're *tanned?*" She looped her scarf around her neck. "How did they manage that? Hello?"

He dragged his eyes up to hers. "Yes?"

She gave him an annoyed look. "Let me give you a little dating advice. Look at a woman's face when you talk to her, not her skirt."

"Yer *skirt* invites a man's attention. I've seen handkerchiefs that were bigger."

She swung her handbag over her shoulder. "At least I wear underwear under *my* skirt."

"I hope they're nice since everyone is sure to see them."

Her eyes glinted with challenge. "Not everyone."

He smiled slowly. "We'll see about that."

With blushing cheeks, she turned toward the door. "Let's not keep your dates waiting."

Ian jumped up and hurried past her to open the door.

She stepped into the hall and dug the keys from her handbag. "Where is this club?"

"Hell's Kitchen."

"How appropriate." She locked the door. "Are you going to click your heels and magically poof us over there?"

"No, I'm driving." He escorted her toward the stairs. It would be faster if he teleported them straight to the club, but driving her there would give him more time to talk to her. "I have a car parked nearby."

She started down the stairs. "You know how to drive?"

"I've been driving since 1913."

"Good grief. I hope you traded in for a newer model."

He grinned. "Actually, I still have my first car, a 1913 Rolls-Royce. I've kept my favorites over the years—a '38 Bentley, a '59 Morgan, and a '69 MGB Roadster. My latest purchase is a 2005 Aston Martin."

She halted halfway down the stairs with a stunned look on her face. "You really do collect expensive cars? Don't tell me the other stuff in your profile is true."

"What other stuff?"

She continued down the stairs. "Stuff like your *enchanted* castle in the Highlands."

He chuckled. "I wouldna call it enchanted, unless ye're entranced by the notion of mildew."

"Then you really do have a castle?"

"It's no' nearly as huge as Angus's castle. I would describe it as more of a large manor house."

"Oh. How . . . cozy." With an irritated look, she crossed the foyer to the entrance door, her high-heeled boots clicking on the marble floor. "Since you didn't even write your profile, I'm sure all those sappy promises are false."

He reached the door first. "What promises?"

She snorted. "You still haven't read it, have you?"

"I've been busy returning hundreds of phone calls. And investigating you. What promises?"

She shrugged like she didn't care. "There was one about remaining faithful to your wife *forever*. Like that could happen."

"It would happen."

She looked doubtful. "And then there was a promise to keep your shimmering, starlit princess in a state of orgasmic ecstasy *forever.*" She rolled her eyes. "Like that could happen, too."

His mouth twitched. "I could certainly try. I do want my wife to feel well pleasured."

She bit her lip and looked away. "You really intend to get married then?"

"Yes." He opened the door, and a blast of cold air knocked her back a step.

She tugged her scarf up over her ears and mouth so her voice sounded muffled. "God, I'm gonna freeze my ass off."

And such a lovely ass. He stepped in front of her to block the wind. "This way. It's no' far." He led her down the street and glared at the men who passed them by and stared at Toni's exposed legs.

"How could someone in your situation take wedding vows seriously?" she mumbled from under her scarf. "You can't honestly claim that you'll stay faithful for centuries."

"Doona accuse me of dishonesty."

"I'm sorry, but some of the stuff in your profile doesn't make sense to me."

There was stuff about her that didn't make sense, either. And he still didn't know her full name. Ian fumbled in his sporran for the car keys. He'd driven one of Roman's cars here, a black Lexus.

"For instance," she continued, "you claim you want to lavish tons of money on your princess. If you're so rich, how come you're working as a security guard?"

"My specialty is investigation. I've broken into Langley twice, undetected."

"Sneaky rascal, aren't you?"

He grinned. "As for the money, I doona have nearly as much as Roman or Angus. They have billions." He punched a button on the keypad, then opened the car door. "I only have a few million."

She gave him a wry look. "You should be ashamed. What have you been doing all these centuries—goofing off?"

With a chuckle, he motioned to the open door. "Are ye no' cold?"

"I'm confused. Why work at all? Why not stay in Scotland and drive your fancy cars all night?" She hunched over to climb into the car.

"I did that for several decades, but it got old." He enjoyed the view as she separated her legs to get into the front seat. Her tiny skirt hitched up dangerously high. "I wanted more excitement in my life."

"I guess you're getting it." She frowned as she tugged at the hem of her skirt.

"Aye, that I am." He smiled as he shut her door. Then he circled the vehicle and slid behind the steering wheel.

He drove to the West Side Highway, then turned north, headed toward Hell's Kitchen. Whenever he glanced to the right, his gaze gravitated to her legs. Slim and muscular, they could squeeze a man tight around his waist. He inhaled sharply when she rubbed her hands up and down her thighs.

"Do you mind if I turn up the heat? It's a little chilly in here."

He held on to the steering wheel with a death grip. "It seems quite warm to me, but go ahead."

"Thanks." She leaned toward the center of the car to fiddle with the temperature control.

Unfortunately, the air vents blew her sweet scent straight into his face. A wave of desire cascaded from his nostrils to his groin. Spending time alone with her had been a bad idea. Instead of getting answers, he was getting a hard-on. "What is yer full name, Toni?"

She waved a hand, dismissing his question. "I met Roman last Monday. He told me his wife, Shanna, is mortal, and that some other guy has a mortal wife, too."

"Jean-Luc, aye. I attended his wedding in September."

"If these other Vamps are marrying mortals, how come you're too prejudiced to even date them?"

"I'm no' prejudiced." His gaze drifted to the bare, golden skin of her luscious thighs. "I find some mortal women verra attractive." Dear Mother of God, she was crossing her legs.

"I just don't understand why you're refusing to date mortals."

"Because I want to be honest. With a Vamp, I wouldna have to lie about who or what I am. I want a relationship built on complete honesty."

She lowered her gaze to her hands clenched in her lap. "No . . . secrets, then?"

"Nay. And no judgments. A mortal would have trouble accepting my past, but another Vamp would understand and no' find fault with the things I had to do to survive."

She glanced at him sharply. "You mean using women for food and sex?"

He gritted his teeth. "That's exactly the sort of judgment I'm talking about. I admit I took blood when I needed it, but I have never forced myself on a woman."

"How can you be so sure? Didn't you use mind control?"

"I'm no' a rapist." He turned onto West Thirty-fourth. At least her accusations were doing a good job of squelching his lustful desires. "I willna blame ye for interrogating me since ye were attacked only a few nights ago. I'm sure ye canna help being touchy."

"I'm not touchy. I'm pissed."

"Doona mistake me for a Malcontent. When I enter a lady's mind, I can hear her thoughts, and I never stay where I'm no' welcome."

"You never controlled a woman's thoughts to make her succumb?"

"Nay. In my case, I used mind control to convince women I was older than I looked."

"So you *did* trick them."

"My bloody face was the trick, Toni, and there was no

escaping it. It made people think I was fifteen, when inside I was a fully grown man. I had to use more trickery to make women see me the way I wanted to be. I canna be proud of all that deceit. That's why it is so important now that I be honest. Another Vamp would understand that."

"You could be honest with a mortal."

"I could hardly approach a mortal and say, 'Hello, I'm a vampire. Would you like to go out with me?' I would have to lie to her at first, and I refuse to do that."

"There are plenty of women who would date you because you *are* a vampire."

He pulled to a stop at a red light and faced her. "I doona want to be loved because I'm Undead. No more than ye would want to be rejected for being mortal."

She looked away. "I—I've been too . . . harsh with you."

"Lass, ye have every reason to be suspicious. Ye were almost murdered a few nights ago. But those vampires who attacked you were probably cruel and vicious before they were transformed. Death doesna change a man's heart."

"Then you were a good man," she whispered.

All his desire came flooding back. "I try to be."

Her gaze met his. "What do you want more than anything?"

Right now, he felt like he could gaze into her green eyes for a century or two. They were amazing, the way they flared with anger, twinkled with humor, or softened with compassion. "I want to be loved, honestly and truly loved, for who I am. And I want to love a woman with all my heart for all my life. I want to ache for her mind, for her body, for her companionship."

Her eyes widened. "Oh."

The scent of her hot, rushing blood filled the car, and his nerve endings thrummed in response. He wondered if she had any idea what she was doing to him. Could she feel the waves of desire flowing off him?

Yes, he would swear she did. Her heart was pounding fast. Her breathing was erratic. He leaned closer.

"You—your eyes," she whispered.

He knew they were turning red, for his vision was now tinted pink. He slipped a hand around her neck.

She didn't pull away. Her gaze dropped to his mouth, and he couldn't resist any longer. He kissed her.

Chapter Eight

She stiffened slightly, but he didn't give up. Ian moved his mouth over hers, gently coaxing her to respond. And she did. She relaxed, leaning into him. His heart expanded in his chest, and he pulled her closer.

He nibbled on her bottom lip. Her mouth opened with a soft sigh, inviting him inside. He ran the tip of his tongue across her lips. They were moist and sweet.

A horn blared behind them, and they both jolted in their seats. Toni gasped and pulled away. Ian faced front and realized the light had turned green. He stepped on the accelerator.

Bloody hell, what was he doing? For the last few days, he'd convinced himself that a little flirtation didn't harm anyone. But *kissing?* He couldn't stay in denial anymore. He was breaking the noninvolvement rule, and Toni would be in big trouble if the truth got out.

He glanced at her. Her face was pale, and she was pressing her hand against her mouth.

"Are ye all right?"

"Yes. No." She lowered her hand.

He noticed the slight tremble before she clenched her hands together. "I shouldna have . . . kissed you. I'm sorry."

She closed her eyes briefly. "We won't think about it. Or talk about it. It never happened."

He remained silent, for he knew he couldn't agree. He *would* think about it. He would relive it in his mind, over and over again.

"It doesn't matter anyway," she continued in a breathless voice. "You want a Vamp woman. We're not at all suited for each other. It was a—a mistake."

Mistake, his arse. He'd do it again in a second. He hoped he hadn't frightened her, though. She'd gone through a lot of turmoil lately.

A sudden blast of music erupted, filling the strained silence. Toni gave him a confused look, then glanced around the car. The musical refrain repeated, and Ian began to comprehend the words sung by a female vocalist.

"I think it's coming from yer handbag." He motioned to the bag at her feet.

"Oh, it's my cell phone." She pulled the bag into her lap and fished out the phone. "Carlos changed the ringtone. I guess he likes Pat Benatar."

"Love is a battlefield?"

"His idea of a joke," she muttered as she wrenched the phone open. "Hello? Carlos! How could you do this to my phone?"

Ian tried to listen, but the wail of a nearby police siren made it impossible to hear Carlos's words.

"I don't know where you got that idea." Toni winced as she glanced at Ian. "Our association is purely business."

They were close to Horny Devils, so Ian began looking for a place to park.

"Okay," she continued in a whisper. "I'll talk to you later. Bye." She slipped the phone back into her handbag.

"Something wrong?" Ian asked casually.

"No, everything's fine."

Then why was her heart still racing? "Carlos seemed a bit
. . . different to me."

She shrugged. "He's gay."

Ian recalled the pained expression on Carlos's face when
he'd exited Toni's bedroom. "Did he tell you he's gay?"

"Well, no. We assumed he is, 'cause he acts like it."

"Who is *we*?"

A guarded look came over Toni's face. "Sabrina and I.
She's my roommate. She's visiting relatives at the moment."

There was something wrong; Ian could feel it. Something
other than the forbidden kiss they'd just shared. And he was
more convinced than ever that Carlos was more than he appeared.

He spotted a parking space and pulled over to the curb.
"Toni, before we go in, I have to know—why do ye have an
apartment?"

She unbuckled her seat belt. "It beats living on the street."

"Ye said ye were guarding Vamps because ye wanted free
room and board, but that doesna make sense when ye already have an apartment."

"Yes, I'm paying rent, but the lease is almost up. Believe
me, having a well-paying job with all expenses paid is the
best thing for me right now. It gives me a chance to pay back
my student loans."

"What about yer roommate?"

"She's . . . not broke like me. She gets a nice allowance
every year, and as soon as she graduates, we have a plan for
going into business together."

"So ye see this job as temporary?"

"Yes. A year at the most." She gave him a worried look.
"That's not a problem, is it?"

"Dinna Connor explain what happens when a mortal
guard leaves MacKay Security and Investigation?"

"He said he would erase my memory about vampires."

"He'll erase yer memory of everything. Ye'll lose the year like it never happened."

Her eyes grew wide. "That's . . . too much." She pressed a hand to her chest.

Ian knew he should urge her to quit now. Then she would lose only a few days. But the thought of never seeing her again was painful. "Ye . . . ye should quit and go back to yer normal life."

Her eyes glittered with unshed tears. "My life's not very normal." She blinked and squared her shoulders. "So, are we going in this club or not?"

"We'll go." Relief swept through him. He didn't have to lose her just yet. But relief quickly morphed into apprehension. Something was seriously wrong. A mortal didn't throw away a year so easily. She was up to something. And he would damned well figure it out.

She could lose a year of her life? Toni was numb with shock as she walked alongside Ian. She aimed a quick glance in his direction. Good grief, she'd kissed the man! She'd kissed a vampire. And lived to tell about it.

He hadn't even tasted bloody. Oh, bloody hell. She could lose a year of her life? This was too much to take in all at once. How could she have kissed him? She shoved that thought aside and concentrated on the other thing driving her crazy—losing a whole, freaking year of her life!

Damn that Connor. He'd glossed over that part. He must have figured she'd keep the job forever. But she and Sabrina had plans. Big plans, dammit.

And she'd kissed Ian. A sudden thought made her wince. Had Carlos seen it through his little spy camera? No wonder he'd called afterward. He'd probably wanted to make sure she was all right. After all, she'd just locked lips with a vampire. And what lips. The man sure knew how to kiss. Of course, he'd had several centuries to perfect his technique.

He'd been so sweet and apologetic afterward. Why

couldn't he be mortal? She could fall for him in a second if he were mortal. She glanced at him again. Could she fall for him as a vampire?

He led her into a dark alley. "The entrance is hidden, so mortals willna try to enter."

She spotted a red door in the dim light, with a huge man standing guard. He nodded at Ian, then opened the door.

"Wait a minute." The bouncer raised a beefy hand. His beady eyes focused on Toni, and his nostrils flared. "She can't come in here. She's—"

"She's with me, Hugo." Ian looped an arm around her shoulders and pulled her inside the club.

Loud music assaulted her ears, and flashing lights temporarily blinded her. So this was a vampire nightclub. It looked a lot like a mortal one. She rotated so the camera on her vest could send the images back to Carlos's apartment. He was recording it all there.

She spotted a group of scantily clad ladies pressed close to the stage where a hunky guy gyrated, his sparkly red thong glittering under the lights. Well, Carlos would enjoy seeing that. Other than the male dancer, most everyone else was female. Even the bartender and DJ were women.

She noted a few Vamps sitting at the tables and drinking something red from glasses. Blood, no doubt, but would a picture of them constitute proof of the existence of vampires? It might look like a picture of regular people drinking red wine.

"Can I get ye something to drink?" Ian smiled when she made a face. "They have a few nonbloody drinks."

"A Diet Coke then. I have a final tomorrow." And she was on a mission now, so she needed her wits about her. "I can't stay very long. I should be home by ten."

"I can teleport ye home whenever ye like." He led her toward the tables.

A female suddenly materialized next to the bar with a cell phone by her ear. She hung up, then dashed to the stage.

"What was that?" Toni turned to follow her movements, but she wasn't sure if her camera had caught everything.

"Vamps call if they're teleporting in for the first time," Ian explained. "They use the phone as a sensory beacon to make sure they come to the right place."

"Oh." She wondered if she'd reacted fast enough to catch the Vamp in the act. "Is there a ladies' room?"

"Aye, over there." He touched her shoulder. "Be careful."

"I thought all these Vamps were bottle drinkers."

"They are, but after a few Blisskys and Bleers, they could be drunk and not behave themselves."

"Oh, great." As she strode toward the restrooms, she became aware of the sly looks being cast her way, and the slight flaring of nostrils as each Vamp caught her scent. She felt like a walking appetizer.

She entered the ladies' room and found a beautiful blonde, primping in front of the mirror. No, it wasn't a mirror, but a giant flat-screen TV. Two cameras on the wall were aimed at the row of sinks. Of course. Digital technology was the only way the Vamps could see themselves.

The blonde turned toward her and wrinkled her turned-up nose. "Good heavens, how did you get in here?" she asked with a snooty British accent.

"It was amazing. I pushed on the door, and it opened."

"I wasn't referring to this powder room, you silly gel," the blonde Vamp continued. "I'm one of the owners of this establishment, and we do not welcome your kind."

"Oh, pardon me, Your Highness." Toni refrained from doing a curtsy. "I thought this was a free country."

"What's going on?" A redhead exited a stall. "Hey, Pamela." She looked at Toni and sniffed. "How did she get in here?"

"That's what I'd like to know," Pamela huffed. "I've told Hugo a million times not to let any mortals inside."

"I came with Ian MacPhie." Toni glared at the arrogant Vamps. "I'm his guard, which means I can kick ass."

Pamela laughed. "Ian would never allow a female to guard him. In fact, he would never need a guard at all."

"Did you say Ian MacPhie?" the redhead asked. "Isn't he that gorgeous guy on *Single in the City*?"

"Oh my God!" A brunette burst from another stall. "Ian MacPhie is here?" She glanced at Toni. "Can I meet him?"

"I want to meet him, too." The redhead approached Toni. "Can you set me up with him?"

Damn, she'd gone from feeling like an appetizer to a pimp. A twinge of jealousy jabbed at her, but she steeled herself against it. The kiss had been a mistake. Ian was not her type. She preferred men who were alive, dammit. So she had to accept the fact that he would pursue these Vamp women. One of them would be his starlit, shimmering princess. One of them would be kissing him from now on.

"I know Ian personally," Pamela boasted. "He used to guard me when I was a member of Roman Draganesti's harem."

The brunette turned to Pamela. "Is he really that handsome?"

"And rich?" the redhead added.

"Come with me. I shall introduce you." Pamela aimed a superior smirk at Toni as she sauntered toward the door. "You know I have an interesting theory regarding Ian."

"What is it?" the brunette asked as she trailed behind.

"I believe he's a five-hundred-year-old virgin," Pamela announced.

"Not for long," the redhead muttered.

There was a twitter of laughter as the three women left the room.

"You didn't wash your hands!" Toni called after them. She gritted her teeth. How could Ian prefer them? But at least the room was empty now, and she had complete privacy. She moved out of range of the cameras and dialed Carlos.

She could lose a year of her life. The thought kept haunting her. It wasn't fair, dammit! These Vamps lived for centuries, while her life was way too short. How could they steal a year from her?

"Hello?" Carlos answered.

"Did you get the shot of a Vamp teleporting here?"

"*Menina*, you're at the club?"

"Yes. Aren't you watching?"

"No, I'll watch the video later. Right now I'm on my way to Westchester."

Toni gasped. "You're going to the Proctors' house?"

"Don't worry. They'll never know I'm there. And I finished checking out their financial records. Uncle Joe has a bad habit of going to Atlantic City."

"How do you know?"

"Credit cards leave a trail, girlfriend."

"But how do you know how to—"

"Do you like your new ringtone?" he interrupted.

"No. Your death will be slow and painful."

He laughed. "Now, don't worry about the video. It's recording at my place. You just catch those naughty Vamps doing something vampy, okay?"

"Okay." So he hadn't seen Ian kissing her. "Carlos, when I quit working for them, they're going to erase my memory. I won't remember squat!"

There was a pause. "Bastards," Carlos muttered. "Don't worry. If they erase anything, I'll tell you what happened. You just get the proof we need as quickly as possible. That way, you'll only lose a few days."

She would lose more than a few days. She would lose all memory of Ian. And the kiss. For some weird reason that made her heart squeeze in her chest.

"Are you all right, love?" Carlos asked.

"This really sucks." Toni snapped her phone shut, then strode back into the club.

Chapter Nine

Ian ordered a Bleer and a Diet Coke from the bartender.

"Is Vanda here?" He handed Cora Lee a ten-dollar bill.

"Over there. Sounds like she's all riled up again."

Ian glanced toward the stage. The music had stopped, and the crowd of lady Vamps had gathered around to hear Vanda rail at a dancer.

"This isn't a whorehouse!" she yelled. "You're fired!"

"There goes another dancer." Cora Lee waved her arms in the air. "Woohoo, Vanda! Ian's here!"

The crowd turned in unison to stare at him.

"Is that Ian MacPhie?" one of the ladies asked.

"Sure is," Cora Lee shouted. "Come and git 'im!"

The crowd moved forward. Ian gulped.

Cora Lee giggled, then whispered, "Looks like your wish will come true now. You're sure to get laid tonight."

"Ian!" Pamela called. "I have two ladies who want to meet you." She motioned to the women accompanying her.

"We saw him first!" a lady in the crowd yelled, and they rushed forward.

"Bloody hell." Ian pressed back against the bar.

"Back off!" Vanda unwrapped the whip from her waist and flicked it at the crowd. "You heard me! Line up and wait your turn!"

The ladies scrambled to form a queue. Ian winced at the amount of pushing and cursing. They acted more like wrestlers than ladies. And there were more than fifty of them.

Vanda grinned at Ian. "Isn't this great? That profile I wrote was incredible! Everyone wants to date you."

"I canna date fifty women in one night."

"Sure you can." She wound the whip back around her waist. "It's called speed dating."

"But I already told three women I'd meet them here."

Vanda waved that aside. "We'll let them go first." She turned to Cora Lee. "Don't you have a kitchen timer?"

"Yep." Cora Lee handed over a white plastic timer.

Vanda set it on a table. "We'll give them each five minutes."

"It'll take hours." Ian brought the drinks to the table.

"You got anything better to do?" Vanda eyed the Diet Coke. "What's with the mortal drink?"

"I brought Toni with me. She's the new day guard at the townhouse."

Vanda's eyes widened. "*She?* Connor hired a *woman?*"

Two nights ago, Ian had felt equally as shocked, but now he wanted to defend her. "She's an excellent fighter."

Vanda gave him a dubious look. "I'm picturing a moose woman with a unibrow, who's popping steroids."

Ian stiffened. "Nay! She's—"

"Hey, Ian!" a lady shouted from across the club. "What the hell happened to our date? We talked on the phone last night. Don't you remember?"

"Aye." He tried to recall the sound of her voice. "Ye're Stormy?"

"Tempest." Her eyes flashed with annoyance. "And this is Moonbeam and Cindy." She motioned to the women

beside her. "We talked to you last night. We have seniority!"

"You may come to the front of the line," Vanda ordered. "Ian will begin shortly."

He groaned. What would he say to all these women? "Why are there so many of them?"

"You're the number one profile on *Single in the City*." Vanda beamed proudly. "Everyone's heard of you."

Ian winced. "I wanted to talk to you about that. Connor's upset that ye listed the location and phone number of Roman's townhouse."

"Connor's an old grouch. The women need a way to contact you."

"I understand that, but for security reasons, it's dangerous to have our location known to so many. We doona want some overzealous admirers trying to break in to see me, especially during the day. It's too risky."

"Okay, okay." Vanda fluffed up her spiky purple hair. "I'll take the address off the website."

"And the phone number, too. They can leave a message for me at *Single in the City*."

"All right." Vanda frowned. "But you're playing too hard to get."

"Hey, whassup?" A male Vamp, dressed in an expensive suit, sauntered toward them and winked at the line of waiting women. "Hello, ladies."

"Hi, Gregori," a chorus responded.

Ian was impressed. Gregori knew all these women?

"What's going on?" Gregori kissed Vanda on the cheek. "Are we lining up to do the bunny hop?"

"Ian's doing some speed dating tonight." Vanda lowered her voice to a whisper. "He's looking for his true love."

"Ah." Gregori's eyes twinkled as he regarded Ian. "Shall I warm them up for you?"

Ian scowled. "It's hard enough to be charming once, but fifty times in a row?"

"You can do it, bro. Just be yourself."

Ian's scowl deepened.

Gregori winced. "You might try smiling. You know the ladies love a guy with a sense of humor."

"I'm doomed."

"Chill out, dude. I'll—" Gregori froze. "Good Lord, look at her. She's an angel."

Ian glanced in the direction of Gregori's stunned gaze. *Toni.* "She's mine," he blurted out, then caught himself. "I mean, she's my guard."

"*She's* the guard Connor hired?" Vanda asked.

Gregori snorted. "Yeah, I can see why he hired her."

"Her beauty had nothing to do with it," Ian snapped. "She's an excellent fighter and verra brave and clever."

"Oh." Gregori eyed Ian curiously. "I see."

Ian felt his face heat up. Perhaps he'd come on a wee bit strong. "Actually, I'd appreciate it if ye could keep an eye on her while I'm busy."

"Sure. No problem, bro."

Toni gazed at the long line of girls as she approached. "I thought you only had *three* dates."

"I have a few more now," Ian grumbled as he moved to her side. "I'd like ye to meet some friends of mine. This is Vanda. She manages the Horny Devils."

"And writes fascinating profiles," Toni added with a smile. She held out a hand.

"Nice to meet you." Vanda shook her hand. "I'm working on another project to make Ian even more famous."

Ian swallowed hard. "That's no' really necessary."

"Of course it is. We've got to find your true love." Vanda patted Ian on the cheek. "I'll check on you later." She strode toward her office.

"And this is Gregori." Ian gestured toward him. "He's the vice president of marketing at Romatech."

"I'm delighted to meet you." Gregori took her hand and kissed it. "I've heard about you. My mother, Radinka, told me that she and Shanna will be seeing you tomorrow."

"Oh, that's right." Toni smiled. "They're coming with Howard to help him babysit while I take a final."

Ian frowned at the word *babysit*.

"Well, bro, shouldn't you get to work?" Gregori nodded his head toward the long line of women.

Ian gulped. Work was the right word for it. Flirting with Toni had been fun, but the thought of charming all these women seemed like a bloody chore. "I need a drink first." He sat and swallowed down some Bleer.

Gregori pulled out a chair at the table so Toni could sit. "Where do you go to college?"

"NYU." She sat.

Gregori sat beside her. "That's where I got my MBA."

"I got my bachelor's in business there."

Feeling forgotten and a bit undereducated, Ian gulped down more Bleer. Damn, he should have pulled out the chair for her.

Gregori leaned toward her. "Hey, is old Professor Hudgins still there? Short, bald, wears a bow tie. Looks and talks like Elmer Fudd. 'Today we're wearning about high intewest wates on cwedit cards.'"

Toni laughed, and it sounded like music from heaven. But Ian was aware of an undercurrent of grumbles and curses. The fifty Vamp women were pissed. No doubt they disliked having to wait while he talked to a mortal.

Toni finally stopped laughing and looked at Ian. "Gregori does a great impersonation. He's really funny."

"I bought you a drink." Now that was smooth, he chided himself.

"Thanks." Toni took a sip.

"What the hell are we waiting for?" Tempest yelled from the front of the line.

Ian groaned inwardly.

"The natives are getting restless," Toni observed. She glanced toward the bar and suddenly jumped to her feet when two women teleported in.

"Are ye all right?" Ian asked.

She sat back down. "I guess I'm a little . . . nervous about being here."

"Dance with me," Gregori suggested. "I'll tell the DJ to get back to work." He headed toward the dance floor.

Toni watched him go. "Is Gregori a Vamp?"

"Aye, a verra young one. He was changed after the invention of synthetic blood, so he's completely bottle-fed."

Toni grimaced as loud, pulsating music started. "Oh God, no. Disco?"

"Gregori loves it. Will ye stay with him till ye're ready to go home?"

"I can take care of myself."

. "Toni." Ian leaned forward. "There are fifty Vamp women behind you, all glaring daggers at you. Please stay with Gregori."

She glanced over her shoulder. "Okay, I see your point. I'll go . . . boogie down." She stood and smoothed down her tiny skirt. "Good luck with your dates. Although I have to say you're wasting your time."

With her head held high, she strode past the glaring women, like an angel unafraid of the dark forces around her. But why did she think his dating was a waste of time? Did she think it was impossible for him to find love?

"Hey!" Tempest yelled. "Can we start already?"

"Aye, let's begin." Ian set the timer.

Tempest rushed forward, flung her arms around his neck, and kissed his cheek.

Ian unhooked her arms. "Will ye have a seat, please?"

"Sure." She climbed onto his lap.

"What are ye doing, lass?"

"Sitting." She raked her black-painted fingernails down his chest. "You know why they call me Tempest? I'm as wild as a hurricane."

"I thought we might talk a wee bit first. Ye know, the calm before a storm?"

She ripped the leather strip from his hair and raked her fingers across his scalp. "Why don't you send those other girls home?" She gripped his hair. "I want to get wet and wild with you."

"I doona know you yet." He pried her fingers loose.

"What's to know?" She nibbled on his neck.

"Well, uh, what do ye do for a living?"

She chuckled, low and throaty. "I'm not living, silly, I'm Undead."

"Aye, but we all have bills to pay."

"If I need something, I just *take* it." She nipped at his ear. "Right now, I need you."

"What do ye mean, ye take it?"

"I take stuff from mortals. Money, clothes, whatever."

"Ye steal from them?"

She sat back with an impatient huff. "It's not stealing when they never realize it happened. It's so easy to fuck with their minds. Like, I have a great condo for free 'cause the manager actually thinks I'm paying rent."

Why had he assumed all Vamps were like him? "I'm afraid we're no' well suited."

"What does that mean?"

He picked her up and set her on her feet as he stood. "It was nice meeting you."

"Are you ditching me?" she shrieked. "Nobody ditches me!" She flung the rest of Toni's Diet Coke in his face, then stalked away, cursing under her breath.

Ian wiped his face with a cocktail napkin. One down, forty-nine to go. Maybe Toni was right, and he was wasting his time. He glanced at the dance floor. Gregori was wiggling his hips and pointing a finger up and down. With a laugh, Toni mimicked his move.

Ian sighed and motioned to his second date.

A pretty blonde glided toward him. "Hi, remember me? I'm Moonbeam."

"How do ye do?" He sat and reset the timer.

Moonbeam settled across from him. "Well, I guess I should tell you about myself. I'm an Aquarius."

"That's nice."

"I was born in 1950. My name was Mary. Boring, I know. My parents were like so square. I ran away when I was sixteen, so I could protest the war. I really hate war."

This might be a bad time to mention he was a warrior. Ian noticed Gregori was spinning Toni in circles.

"I went to San Francisco, of course." Moonbeam fiddled with the beads around her neck. "That's where it was happening, you know."

"What was happening?" Ian asked.

"Everything, man. Flower power. Make love, not war. I'm like totally opposed to violence of any kind."

"Then ye would never manipulate or cheat a mortal for yer own gain?"

"God, no. That's like so damaging to your karma."

Ian nodded. This one might have potential. At least she appeared to have good morals.

"So there I was, tripping on acid and enjoying a perfectly good orgy, when this guy comes out of nowhere and bites me on the neck! I mean, I was like totally bummed out when I woke up dead."

Ian blinked. "I see." His gaze wandered back to Toni. Every now and then, when someone teleported in, she would jump to face them. Perhaps teleportation frightened her? If that was the case, he should drive her home. The thought of escaping the club sounded excellent.

The timer rang, and he realized Moonbeam was still talking. He stood. "I'm afraid our time is up."

"Okay. Peace." She hugged him and glided away.

Ian motioned for Cindy to come forward. She launched into a long account of her past two hundred and thirteen boyfriends, while Ian's attention slid back to the dance floor. The music slowed, and Gregori took Toni into his arms. Dammit, he'd told Gregori to watch her, not maul her.

After two more interviews, Vanda sauntered toward him, grinning. "I did it! It's all set up."

His stomach knotted with apprehension as he rose to his feet. "What did ye do?"

"Don't look so worried. It'll be great. Tomorrow night at midnight, Corky Courrant is coming here!"

"The barracuda?" Everyone knew the reporter from *Live with the Undead* was vicious. "Why is she coming here?"

"To interview you!" Vanda announced.

Ian stepped back. "Vanda, no. Hell, no."

"It'll be fun! Trust me."

He shook his head. "No good can come from this. The woman is a monster."

"Don't be such a wuss!" Vanda poked him in the chest. "Corky's show is broadcast all over the world. Every Vamp on earth will see you. And see my club. This is brilliant!"

"What's brilliant?" Gregori walked toward them with Toni.

"Ian's going to be on *Live with the Undead*," Vanda boasted. "They're coming tomorrow to do the interview."

"You're going to be on television?" Toni asked.

"On DVN," Vanda said.

"Digital Vampire Network," Ian explained. "We get it at the townhouse. But I'm no' doing the show."

"Of course you are," Vanda hissed. "I've been working on this for hours. It's all set."

"Be careful with Corky Courrant," Gregori warned.

"Who is she?" Toni asked.

"The star of the show." Gregori splayed his hands in front of his chest. "She has the most humongous"—Ian elbowed him—"commercials," Gregori finished.

"Were ye ready to go home?" Ian asked Toni. "I could drive you."

Vanda grabbed his arm. "You're not going anywhere. All these women are waiting for their chance to date you."

"I can teleport Toni," Gregori offered.

"But she might no' want to teleport," Ian protested.

"I'll be fine." Toni gave him a reassuring smile. "I can't wait to see you on TV."

Ian sighed. Maybe he should go through with it. He didn't want to disappoint Vanda or Toni. And how bad could it be? "Gregori, can I have a word with you in private?"

"Sure." Gregori walked away with him. "What's up?"

"I—uh—thought ye might give me some advice."

"Are your dates not going well?" Gregori whispered.

"I feel like I'm conducting job interviews. I'm no' connecting with them." Not like he did with Toni.

Gregori rested a hand on Ian's shoulder. "Dude, you can do this. You must have charmed ladies out of a pint of blood every night for several centuries."

Ian sighed. "I was never verra sophisticated about it. No one expected me to be. I looked so young, even though I felt old inside. And now I look old on the outside, but inside I feel like a green lad. I doona know what to say."

"You just need to work on your communication skills. First off, practice being a good listener. Women like to talk about their feelings. Even if you think it's totally boring, nod your head and keep listening."

"Okay."

"You should respond with lines like 'How interesting. Tell me more.'"

"How interesting," Ian repeated. "Tell me more."

"That's it. And here's another good one. 'You're absolutely right. How clever of you.' Women like to be complimented on their intelligence."

"Okay." Ian repeated the lines. "Thank you." He walked back to the table with Gregori. Vanda had already rushed off to her office.

"Good night, Ian." Toni smiled shyly.

"Good night, Toni." God, he wanted to touch her. He wanted to kiss her again.

Gregori slapped him on the back. "Later, dude. Let's go, Toni." He led her toward the dance floor.

With a resigned sigh, Ian motioned for the next date to come forward.

"Hi, I'm Amy."

"Please have a seat." Ian looked over at Gregori. He was holding Toni close. That was necessary when teleporting with a mortal, but it didn't make it easier to watch.

"Gosh, when I saw your picture on the Internet, I thought you looked so sexy," Amy began. "But, I swear, you look even better in person!"

"How interesting," Ian murmured. "Tell me more." Damn, Toni was putting her arms around Gregori's neck.

"You want me to talk about how handsome you are?" Amy asked. "Isn't that kinda vain?"

"Ye're absolutely right. How clever of you."

"You jerk! I'm outta here." She stalked away.

He groaned. This night from hell would never end.

Toni and Gregori arrived at the back porch of the town-house, and she used her special key to deactivate the alarm and open the door. He wished her good night, then tele-ported back to the Horny Devils for more dancing. It was odd, but she'd actually enjoyed herself at the vampire night-club.

Unlike Ian. He had looked miserable. She hated to admit it, but a part of her rejoiced over his misery. His theory that only a Vamp would understand him was so wrong. Those bimbo bloodsuckers weren't good enough for him.

She rushed upstairs to her bedroom to get away from the surveillance cameras. She dropped her handbag on the bed and dialed Carlos. "Where are you now?"

"I got back to my apartment about five minutes ago," he replied. "I'm watching the monitor connected to your camera. It went black for a few seconds."

"That was teleportation. Does it give us the proof we need?"

"No, it just looked like a camera malfunction. So is this your luxurious bedroom I'm seeing now?"

"Yes." Toni unclipped the camera from her vest and turned it off.

"Hey!" Carlos objected over the phone. "I want a tour of the house."

"And I want to go to bed." She slipped the camera into a dresser drawer. "I'm not sure if I caught any of the Vamps teleporting, because they just popped up without any advance warning. It was very frustrating." Though not as frustrating as watching those creepy Vamp women throw themselves at Ian.

"I don't know," Carlos replied. "I'll need to review the tape."

"If it didn't work, I have another idea." Toni opened the armoire across from her bed. Inside there was a television that she hadn't bothered to turn on yet. "The Vamps have their own television network called DVN."

"Really? What frequency is it on?"

"I don't know." She turned on the TV. "This looks like a commercial. Something called Vampos. It's an after-dinner mint to get rid of blood breath."

Carlos laughed.

"I'm serious. Now there's a bat flapping its wings. Underneath it says—*DVN, on 24/7 because it's always nighttime somewhere.*"

"Sounds interesting. I'll try to tap into it."

"Now there's a soap opera coming on. *As the Vampire Turns.* If we get a recording of this, won't it prove vampires exist?"

"Not really," Carlos said. "It's not unusual to have vampire shows on mortal television."

"But what about the commercials?"

"We see talking lizards and cavemen in commercials all the time. It doesn't make them real."

"I beg to differ. I have dated a few cavemen." She turned the TV off and wondered how Ian was doing. Was he discovering his shimmering, starlit princess? Was she so fabulous, he'd forgotten about the kiss they'd shared?

"*Merda,*" Carlos muttered. "I don't think the footage from the club is going to help. Every time you spun toward a teleporting Vamp, the picture blurred."

"Damn." How on earth were they going to prove the existence of vampires?

"And I'm afraid we have another problem," Carlos said. "I found the Proctors' house."

"You did? What happened?"

"I talked to the maid, Maria. She's from Colombia, and thankfully my Spanish is good. She said your phone call made the Proctors really nervous."

"Oh dear." Toni tossed her boots in the closet. "Did she say if Sabrina's okay?"

"She was locked in a bedroom upstairs. Maria saw her twice, said she was asleep both times."

"I'm afraid her uncle is drugging her."

"You're right. Maria said he was giving her Haldol. It's a strong antipsychotic. Tends to knock people out."

"This is terrible." Toni paced across the room.

"It gets worse. By the time I got there, the Proctors had packed up Sabrina and taken her somewhere. Maria said they were talking about a mental hospital."

"Oh no!" Toni collapsed on the bed. "Why are they doing this?"

"I'm not really sure, but you can bet it has something to do with the money Bri stands to inherit. I'll find out more tomorrow. I have a date with Maria."

"A date? But aren't you—?"

"I'm working undercover," Carlos said. "The Proctors always give Maria Friday night off 'cause they like to go out. So I'll convince her to let me into Uncle Joe's office.

Shouldn't be too hard. She hates him 'cause he pinches her ass whenever his wife isn't looking."

"Oh, what a great guy."

"I'll call you tomorrow night. Hopefully I can find out which hospital they took Sabrina to."

"I hope so. Thank you, Carlos." Toni hung up. Poor Bri. If she was trapped in a mental hospital, she would need to be rescued somehow. Carlos would help.

Toni took a deep breath. She'd failed her grandmother, and the guilt had gnawed at her ever since. She wouldn't let Sabrina down.

Jedrek Janow lounged in his chair with his feet propped on his desk as he watched DVN. He couldn't believe the amount of information being thrown about. The newscaster on the *Nightly News* had actually reported that the Vamps still had no idea where the evil warlord Casimir was located. Jedrek hoped Casimir was watching. He'd love that part about being an evil warlord.

Then a show came on called *Live with the Undead*, and the buxom hostess announced that Roman Draganesti and his mortal wife were expecting their second child in May.

Jedrek snorted. Why pay spies when he could learn so much for free? Unfortunately, now a stupid soap opera was starting. He turned the television off and set his feet back on the floor. He picked up the photos Yuri had brought the other night and thumbed through them.

A whimpering sound came from the corner of his office. Nadia was still crying.

"Shut up. I can't concentrate with your sniveling."

She sniffed. "I miss my friends."

Of course she did. But the first step in breaking a bitch was isolation. He was making her sit in the corner all night. "Did I say you could talk?"

Tears rolled down her face. "I'm so hungry."

Of course she was. He'd fed earlier that evening, drinking his full from a captured mortal right here in the office while Nadia had been forced to watch. And go hungry. "I've told Yuri to bring me another snack. A blonde. I might let you feed this time."

"Yes, please."

"And when you're done feeding, you will kill the blonde to please me."

Nadia's face paled.

"If you want to eat, you'll have to kill her."

Her shoulders slumped. "Yes, sir."

"That's yes, *Master*."

Chapter Ten

"Oh my gosh," Toni whispered as she peered through the peephole on the front door.

It was nine A.M. on Friday morning, the appointed arrival time for the babysitters, but Toni doubted the two girls with pink-striped hair were Shanna Draganesti and Gregori's mother. They banged on the door once again.

Toni punched the intercom. "May I help you?"

"Where's Ian?" one of the girls demanded. "We tried calling, but all we get is a recording."

"Yeah," the second girl agreed. "He says that he's taken, but we don't believe it. We want to see him!"

Toni groaned. The message Ian had left on the answering machine wasn't working. Some of his admirers were resorting to a more desperate tactic. "Please come back tonight."

"And let the competition get to him first? No way!"

Competition? Toni strode into the living room and peered out the window.

Good grief! There were a dozen more girls pacing up and down the sidewalk. They waved posters in the air. *Pick me, Ian! Ian's so hot!* One girl had a sparkly tiara on her head, and her poster read, *I'm Ian's shimmering princess!*

"Oh my gosh." Toni pulled the cell phone from her pocket and called Howard.

"Oh shoot," he muttered. "They must have gotten the address before Vanda had it removed. We're almost there. We'll park in the back. See you in a few minutes."

"All right." Toni hung up, then gathered her school stuff in the kitchen.

Soon she heard voices on the back porch. She peeked out the window and saw Howard fiddling with his key. Behind him was an older woman with graying hair and a younger, blonde woman, both loaded down with tote bags. A little boy stood close by.

She turned off the alarm and opened the door. "Hi. Thanks for coming."

"No problem." Howard strode into the kitchen and headed straight for the foyer. "I'll see if I can get rid of those girls out front."

"Okay." Toni turned to help the elderly woman put her tote bags on the kitchen table. "You must be Radinka."

"Thank you, yes." Radinka took her hand and regarded her curiously. "Interesting," she murmured.

The pretty blonde deposited her bags on the table. "Hi, I'm Shanna."

"Nice to meet you." Toni extended a hand, but Shanna pulled her into a hug.

"I heard how you were attacked the other night." Shanna patted her on the back. "I'm so glad you're safe now. Are you all right?"

"Yes." Toni was surprised by how sweet and . . . normal Shanna was. Who would ever believe she was the wife of a powerful Undead coven master? And there was an angelic little boy standing close to her.

"This is my son, Constantine." Shanna ruffled his blonde curls.

Toni leaned over. "Hi, Constantine."

He smiled, then buried his face in his mother's coat.

The older woman chuckled. "He won't be so shy once he gets to know you. Gregori told me he met you last night. He was very impressed with your dancing."

Toni laughed. "He's a lot of fun."

"Yes." Radinka's eyes narrowed. "But I do not believe he is the one destined for you, my dear."

Toni blinked. "I—I'm not looking for anyone—"

Shanna touched her arm. "Don't worry. Radinka's always trying to match people up."

Radinka snorted. "There's no trying to it. I can see when two hearts belong together." She pointed to her temple. "I'm psychic, you know."

"Oh. That's nice." Toni didn't know what else to say.

"It doesn't take a psychic to know a bored child will be a problem." Radinka moved one of her tote bags to the floor. "So we brought the little one some toys."

Constantine rummaged through the bag, removed a big picture book, then wiggled onto a kitchen chair. "I want to learn how to read."

"That's wonderful." Toni smiled at him, and he smiled shyly back, his cheeks dimpling.

"Uncle Connor said you were nice. He said you know how to kick a—"

"Whoa, Uncle Connor talks too much." Shanna removed her coat, then turned to her son. "Let's get you out of that jacket."

While Shanna hung up jackets on the hooks by the back door, Radinka unloaded groceries from the remaining bags on the table.

"We weren't sure if you had enough food here." Radinka set a carton of milk in the fridge, then grabbed the kettle from the stove. "I'll make everyone a nice cup of tea."

Constantine eyed the bags of fruit still on the table. "Can I have a banana?"

"Here you go, sweetie." Shanna handed him one, then stashed the bags in the fridge.

Toni was about to offer Constantine some help when she realized he didn't need it. He peeled the banana, then bit off a piece while he studied his book.

He pointed at a word. "Is this *house?*"

She peered over his shoulder. "Yes, it is." What a bright little boy he was. She wondered if he was Shanna's from a previous relationship. Surely Vamp men weren't able to have children. "Thank you for coming today."

"We were happy to." Shanna hooked the empty tote bags on the pegs with their coats. "A delivery man's bringing a tree around noon. We always decorate one for the guards."

"Oh, that's nice." With all the turmoil in her life, Toni had forgotten that Christmas was coming soon.

Radinka set out three cups and saucers on the counter. "We saw those women out front with their posters. I can't believe they're behaving so silly."

"Yeah." Toni sat next to Constantine. "It's crazy."

Shanna shook her head. "Poor Ian. I heard he really had to suffer to get his older looks."

Radinka made tsking noises as she placed a teabag in each cup. "Gregori told me he's doing a television interview to-night with Corky Courrant."

Shanna made a face. "That's a disaster waiting to happen."

"Why?" Toni asked.

Shanna bit her lip, considering. "I should leave Ian a note, begging him not to do it. Is he in the basement?"

"No, he outgrew his coffin. He's on the fifth floor." Toni winced. "In your husband's bedroom."

Shanna laughed. "Well, looks like I'll get some exercise. Be right back." She strode from the kitchen.

Toni was tempted to go with her. She'd seen Ian only once this morning, right before calling in her eight o'clock report. She'd risen at six-thirty A.M. and was having breakfast in the kitchen when Phineas and Dougal had come in for a bedtime snack before retiring to the basement. She'd hoped to see Ian, but he'd gone straight up to the fifth floor without stopping by to see her.

Why had he not wanted to talk to her? She was a bit worried that he'd actually hit it off with one of those fifty Vamps he'd dated last night.

The kettle whistled, and Toni jerked back to the present. She had to stop thinking about Ian so much.

Howard strode into the kitchen. "Those women are psycho! One of them hit me with a poster when I told her Ian wasn't here."

Toni winced. "Sorry. They do seem awfully determined."

Radinka handed Howard a cup of tea. "Such nonsense. Are they still there?"

"I got them to leave, but I'm afraid they'll come back." Howard drank some tea. "I'd better check on the guys. Is Ian still on the fifth floor?"

"Shanna's already on her way up there." Radinka set a cup of tea in front of Toni.

"I'll start in the basement then." Howard gulped down the rest of his tea, then left the room grumbling about crazy women.

"Is this *truck?*" Constantine looked up at Toni, then pointed at another word.

She glanced at his book. "Yes, it is." He had finished his banana. "Would you like something to drink?"

"Can I have some milk?"

"Sure." Toni hunted through the cabinets, but couldn't find any plastic cups. She'd have to give him a glass. She set it in front of him, and he drank without hesitation.

She sat next to him. "How old are you, about four?"

He grinned with a milk mustache. "I'm almost two."

Toni gaped, then shut her mouth quickly since she didn't want to embarrass the little boy. "You're . . . sure?"

"He'll be two in March." Radinka added some milk to her tea. "He's very clever, isn't he?"

More than clever, Toni thought. He was a wonder child.

"Is Toni with us?" Constantine asked.

Radinka tilted her head, considering Toni. "She may not know it yet, but I believe she is."

What did that mean? Toni sipped her tea with a growing sense of confusion.

"Do you want to see what I can do?" Constantine backed away from the table and spun around.

"That's great!" Toni smiled appreciatively.

He gave her a dubious look. "I haven't done it yet."

"Oh, sorry." Toni's mouth dropped open as the young boy slowly rose to the ceiling. "Oh my gosh."

Radinka sat at the table with her cup of tea. "He's very special."

"I'm back." Shanna strode into the kitchen. She picked up her cup of tea and glanced around the room. "Where's Tino?"

A giggle from the ceiling drew her attention, and Shanna snorted. "I should have known." She gave Toni a wry look. "I've been trying to teach him to clean the ceiling fans."

"He—he's floating," Toni said lamely.

Constantine giggled and performed a front somersault.

"Oh, now you're just showing off." Shanna sipped some tea. "You should see him and his daddy play basketball."

"I blocked Daddy's goal by sitting in the hoop," Constantine boasted.

"He—he's really Roman's son?" Toni asked. "How—?"

"Roman's a genius. Don't ask me how, but he inserted his DNA into human sperm." Shanna patted her stomach. "We're expecting another one in May. A little girl."

"Oh. Congratulations." Toni watched Constantine float down to the floor. She couldn't believe it. Shanna and Radinka were sipping tea like it was entirely normal to breed half-human/half-vampire children.

"Did you ask if it was okay before you levitated?" Shanna asked her son.

"Yes, Mommy." He climbed back onto his chair.

"That's good." Shanna sat across from him. "We've been teaching him to be careful about levitating. It's not something we want just anyone to see."

"Like Grandpa." Constantine drank more milk.

"I'm afraid so," Shanna agreed. "My dad is the head of the CIA Stake-Out team. They'd like to eliminate all vampires from the planet."

Toni winced. "That's got to be a little awkward for family reunions."

"Tell me about it. Fortunately, my dad's crazy about his grandson, so he's ignoring the Vamps and concentrating on the Malcontents. But if he found out that Tino's inherited some unusual genes, it could cause a problem."

The little boy slumped over his book. "Would Grandpa not love me anymore?"

"Oh, sweetie." Shanna rushed over to hug her son. "He'll always love you. We all love you so much."

"We sure do." Radinka's eyes glimmered with emotion as she regarded the little boy.

Toni felt a tiny twinge of envy. How lucky this boy was to be so loved. She'd always wanted her mother's love, but it had never happened. Her mom had gone on to marry the man of her dreams and have two more children. Toni had never been welcome there. Her only experience with maternal love had been from her grandmother, and that had ended abruptly when she was thirteen. When she had failed her.

When Toni had first entered the Vamp world a few nights ago, she had expected to find a scary place filled with creepy characters. Instead she'd found a group of Vamps and mortals who were caring and compassionate. It was obvious that they looked out for one another. Shanna had run up five flights of stairs just to leave Ian a note.

Was she with them? That was the question Constantine had asked. With a small shock, Toni realized she could be an accepted member of this extended family—a family that cared for one another and trusted one another. She could be a part of it all. Never rejected again. Never made to feel like she wasn't good enough.

It was so . . . tempting. But alarming, too, for she already had her life planned out with Sabrina. Sabrina was her family, not these people in the Vamp world. As soon as the mess with Sabrina was resolved, Toni could leave the Vamp world forever. Two days ago she'd been eager to leave. Now she was starting to feel . . . wanted. And valued. For the first time, she realized she was getting pulled in two different directions.

"Are you all right, dear?" Radinka asked.

"I—I'd better go." She glanced at the clock over the kitchen sink. "My final starts in an hour."

Constantine placed his small hand on her arm. "You'll be okay, Toni."

Her arm tingled as a surge of warm energy rushed from the little boy's hand. She stiffened, then immediately relaxed as the energy washed over her with a soothing gentleness. Her tension melted away, leaving a sense of well-being and a feeling that she could accomplish anything.

She looked at the little boy, and he smiled back. There was an intelligence in his bright blue eyes that should have been frightening in a child so young, but she felt too relaxed to be concerned. Constantine radiated goodness, so she knew there was no need to be afraid.

He withdrew his hand and focused his attention back on his picture book. Toni gathered her things and said her good-byes. As she walked to the subway station, the little boy's question kept repeating in her mind. *Is Toni with us?* How deep was she getting sucked into this new world? Would it be hard to give it up when she left? Not so hard, if they completely wiped her memory. But how could she give up the memory of Constantine and the others?

How could she give up ever seeing Ian again?

* * *

That evening, Toni was celebrating the end of her college education with a big bowl of triple chocolate ice cream on top of a double chocolate brownie, when Ian walked in.

"Good evening."

He'd caught her with her mouth full. She gulped. "Hi."

He opened his mouth to speak, then apparently changed his mind. He wandered to the refrigerator and took out a bottle of blood. He hesitated, then placed it back in.

"Not hungry?" She scooped more ice cream into her mouth.

"I already ate." He paced across the room, his kilt swishing about his knees.

"Did you see the Christmas tree in the parlor? It's very pretty. Shanna and Constantine decorated it."

"Aye, it's nice." He continued to pace.

He seemed nervous to her. "Are you doing that interview tonight?"

"I think so." He flexed his hands as he paced. "But I have a bad feeling about it."

"Shanna thought you should skip it. Did you see the note she left you?"

"Aye, but Vanda's worked verra hard to set this up. I doona want to disappoint her." He sighed. "She's lined up some more dates for me, too."

Toni stabbed at the brownie. "More Vamp women?"

"Aye." He leaned back against the kitchen counter and crossed his arms across his chest.

And what about the kiss they'd shared in the car? Toni thought about bringing it up, but she'd been the one who'd insisted they never speak of it. She'd called it a mistake. She glanced at Ian. Had he thought it was a mistake?

But what about those moments when their eyes met, and the whole world melted away? Toni could have sworn something was happening between them. Something like a huge magnet drawing them together. Or was she fooling herself? She took her bowl to the sink. She'd lost her appetite.

"Toni, I doona know how to say this, but . . ."

Would he tell her he was attracted to her? "Yes?"

"I canna see myself when I shave. I was wondering if I looked all right. For the interview, ye ken."

"Oh. Okay, let me see." She moved close and examined his cheeks, the line of his jaw, his strong neck, and his dimpled chin. She felt her own face growing warm. "You look fine to me."

Her eyes met his, and her heart did a little flip. Damn, knowing him, he'd heard that. She stepped back.

"I doona have a hairbrush upstairs. I just pulled my hair back."

"I've got one." She rummaged through her handbag on the kitchen table and pulled out a brush. She was about to offer it to him when she realized this was a chance to actually touch his hair. With her heart racing, she motioned to a chair at the table. "Take a seat."

He did.

She stared at the back of his head and his shoulders. Even from the back he was gorgeous. She untied the leather strip around his ponytail and dropped it on the table. She stroked the brush through his thick hair. It shimmered in waves down to his shoulders. His very broad shoulders.

"You have wavy hair." She smoothed a hand over the waves. His hair was as soft as she'd thought it would be.

"When I wore it short, it was curly," he said. "Thank you for helping me. I—I wanted to look good for the interview, but I dinna want to seem vain."

She smiled. "I don't think you're vain." Gorgeous, but not vain. She gathered his hair into a ponytail. She'd never dated a guy with hair this long. It was a lot sexier than she'd realized. She took her time, smoothing the silken strands back from his temples and around his ears.

"Ye have a soft touch," he whispered.

She leaned over to get the leather strip off the table, and her breasts grazed against his head. He glanced up at her, and her breath caught. "Are you all right? Your eyes look kinda bloodshot."

He closed them. "I'm a wee tired."

"Oh." She hadn't thought a Vamp could get tired. She tied the strip around his hair at the base of his neck.

"I dinna know what to wear—breeches or a kilt."

"The kilt is good. It's . . . you. And you want to be yourself. I mean, if a woman doesn't love you for yourself, then she's not the right one for you."

He remained silent.

She stepped back. "Have you met someone you liked?"

"Aye. I have."

Her heart plummeted. "I see. Well, I'm done here."

"Thank you." He rose slowly. "When I told Vanda I was looking for my true love, I told her I wanted a lady Vamp who was honest, loyal, intelligent, and pretty."

Toni's heart sank lower. She didn't match up very well.

"But now I'm starting to realize that there's more to love than meeting a few requirements."

"That's true." She dropped her brush into her bag.

He strode to the kitchen door, then hesitated. "If ye were no' my guard, I could date you."

Her heart swooshed back into place. He wanted to date her?

He frowned. "But if ye were no longer my guard, yer memory would be erased. Ye wouldna know me."

"I know." Her heart squeezed. "It's kinda . . . sad."

"Aye, it is." He turned and left the room.

A little after ten, Carlos called. "I'm on my way home."

Toni was already in her pajamas, lounging in bed. "How was your date?"

"Good. Maria let me into Dr. Proctor's office, and I found a copy of the will. Sabrina can't inherit the bulk of her trust fund until she obtains a college degree. Meanwhile, her aunt Gwen remains the trustee."

"So they're trying to keep her from graduating?" Toni sat up with a gasp. "Carlos! What if they plan to keep her locked up in a mental hospital forever?"

"I'm afraid that's exactly what they're up to," Carlos muttered. "But never fear. I discovered where Dr. Proctor works. Shady Oaks Psychiatric Hospital. I called, but they wouldn't confirm if Sabrina is a patient there."

"We have to find her."

"I know, *menina*. We will. Meet me tomorrow night after you get off work, and we'll go to Shady Oaks together."

"Okay." Toni hung up. She'd find Sabrina. And she'd get her out of that hospital. She wouldn't let her down.

Chapter Eleven

Saturday before dawn, Toni didn't see Ian. He teleported straight to the fifth floor without stopping to say hello. How had the interview gone? Was he avoiding her? He'd mentioned he'd met someone he liked. But he'd also hinted that he wanted to date her. It was so confusing.

Four times during the day, she wandered up the stairs to check on him for her reports. She stood there, staring at him in his death-sleep, searching for answers that weren't detectable on his handsome, blank face.

Right after sunset, Dougal and Phineas marched into the kitchen for their evening breakfast. Toni was having a quick sandwich before leaving to meet Carlos.

"Saturday night." Phineas took a gulp from his bottle of warmed-up blood. "I bet you've got a hot date."

"Something like that." She set her empty plate in the sink. "Why doesn't Ian come down? Isn't he hungry?"

"There's a wee fridge up there with a supply of

blood," Dougal said. "Still, I wish he would come down."

"Yeah. The interview couldn't have been that bad." Phineas drank more from his bottle.

Dougal frowned. "Gregori told me it was verra bad."

Toni's heart stilled. "Why? What happened?"

Dougal shrugged. "Gregori wouldna give details. But they're showing the interview tonight on the telly."

She would have to see it. Hopefully, it would air before it was time to meet Carlos. But poor Ian. Was he hiding in his room out of embarrassment? "You know, this whole dating thing has snowballed completely out of control. The women came back about two hours ago. There are about twenty of them camped out on the front sidewalk."

"Twenty babes? Are they hot?" Phineas rushed from the kitchen.

Toni ran after him and found him turning off the alarm. "Phineas, don't! They're rowdy enough already. Whenever I look out the window, they start screaming."

"Cool." Phineas yanked open the door and was instantly rewarded with squeals. "Ladies." He held up his hands. "Let me introduce myself. I'm Dr. Phang, the love doctor."

"We want Ian!" They pressed forward, knocking over empty beer bottles.

"Careful," Toni warned Phineas.

"Ladies, you have come to the right place. I'm a personal friend of Ian's—"

"Ask him if he wants some of *this*!" One of the girls let out a long squeal while she lifted her T-shirt to flash her boobs like a girl gone wild.

"That's a good start," Phineas said. "Anyone else?"

"Stop it." Toni slammed the door shut and glared at Phineas. "You should be ashamed of yourself."

He grinned.

Dougal's mouth twitched as he reset the alarm. "Come on, Dr. Phang. We need to go to Romatech."

"But the interview is starting in five minutes." Phineas

dashed into the living room and located the remote control. "Don't you guys want to see it?"

"I do." Toni settled on the maroon couch that faced the widescreen TV.

"I'm going to work." Dougal gave Phineas a warning look. "I'll expect ye there in fifteen minutes."

"Okay, okay," Phineas agreed impatiently. "But admit it, bro, you're going to be watching it at Romatech."

Dougal smiled. "Perhaps." He vanished.

Phineas sprawled on the couch next to Toni and turned on the TV. "See that dude? He's Stone Cauffyn. Does the *Nightly News*."

Toni listened to the Vamp newscaster drone on in a boring voice. Suddenly her cell phone went off.

"Love is a battlefield?" Phineas snorted. "Man, that's wack. Love is a many-splendored thing, especially when you're with Dr. Phang."

"I'll keep that in mind." Toni rushed into the foyer to answer the phone. "Carlos?" She glanced at the surveillance camera. "This is not a good time."

"We need to go to Shady Oaks. Get your pretty ass home, girl, so we can go."

"I—" Toni glanced at the television in the next room. "I need to stay here about fifteen more minutes."

"Why? Aren't you off duty when the sun sets?"

"Yes, but . . ." She groaned inwardly. It was happening again. She was getting pulled in two different directions.

"Okay, I'll pick you up on the way. And before you object, I know exactly where you are, *menina*. I Googled Ian the other night and found his profile and address. I'll be there in twenty minutes." Carlos hung up.

"Toni, it's starting," Phineas yelled.

She rushed back to the couch. The TV screen was filled with large words in a flowing script—*Live with the Undead, starring Corky Courrant*.

"Good evening, friends!" A close-up revealed a face with

heavily lined eyes and collagen-enhanced lips. "This is Corky Courrant, reporting from the Horny Devils nightclub in New York City."

The camera pulled back, and Toni recognized the night-club she'd seen the night before. Corky was sitting at a table next to a somber-looking Ian.

"Shit, look at the tits on her," Phineas murmured.

"Tonight we're talking to Ian MacPhie, who has recently posted a very popular profile on the online dating service *Single in the City.*" Corky inclined her head toward Ian. "We're delighted to have you on the show, Ian."

"My pleasure," Ian said.

"This ain't so bad," Phineas observed.

"Looks fine to me," Toni agreed. More than fine. Ian looked gorgeous with his blue eyes and wavy black hair. His green sweater clung to broad shoulders and a firm chest.

"My friends, this is a special night." Corky's smile faded, and she affected a dreamy look. "Every now and then, in the annals of vampire history, there arises a man who stands out among all others. He is the legendary hero who inspires great music and poetry, that perfect man who inhabits the secret fantasies of all vampire women."

Ian shifted in his seat, his face blushing.

"He is the man we all yearn for." Corky glanced at Ian. "And this is *not* his story."

Toni gasped. Ian's face paled.

Corky's eyes gleamed with wicked delight. "No, tonight we have the pathetic story of a lonely, desperate man, so desperate he tries to sell himself online. No, wait, he's so pathetic he has a *friend* sell him online."

"What are you doing?" Vanda marched into view.

"Ah, here is the friend—Vanda Barkowski. Tell me, is it true Ian's too illiterate to write his own profile?"

"He's not—" Vanda began.

"Did you write it or not?" Corky snarled.

"I helped," Vanda admitted, "but he's not illit—"

"I had to wonder what would drive a man to such desperate measures," Corky continued with a smile. "So, before this show, I interviewed two women who are very well acquainted with Ian MacPhie. Here they are . . ."

The screen changed to the blonde bartender.

"You are Cora Lee Primrose, former member of Roman Draganesti's harem?" Corky asked.

"Yes." Cora Lee smiled shyly. "Ian was one of our guards. He was always such a sweet boy."

"Boy?" Corky asked. "He looks thirty in his photo."

"That's because he ate something that made him grow older," Cora Lee explained. "For centuries, he looked like a fifteen-year-old boy."

"That's amazing. What else can you tell us about Ian?"

"Well." Cora Lee chewed on her bottom lip. "He told me why he wanted to look older. He just wants to get laid."

The scene switched back to Corky and Ian, who was frowning.

"That was a joke," he muttered.

Corky scoffed. "The next interview, please . . ."

The scene shifted to another blonde Vamp. Toni recognized her as Pamela, the woman from the restroom.

"I am Lady Pamela Smythe-Worthing, one of the owners of this establishment," she began. "And I have known Ian MacPhie since 1955 when he was assigned to guard those of us who were members of Roman Draganesti's harem."

"I heard he looked like a teenager," Corky said.

"Indeed," Pamela agreed. "He was much too young-looking to be of any interest to us. Personally, I believe Ian MacPhie is a five-hundred-year-old virgin."

"Amazing," Corky said. "So his profile is nothing more than a desperate ploy to finally pop the cherry?"

Pamela smiled. "Precisely."

The scene switched back to Corky and Ian.

Vanda planted her hands on the table and leaned toward Corky. "That's bullshit. Ian's looking for his true love."

"Can you confirm he's not a virgin?" Corky asked calmly. "Have you slept with him?"

"Of course not," Vanda growled.

Corky raised her voice. "Has anyone here slept with Ian MacPhie?"

The camera panned over a hundred faces, all shouting *no*, then returned to a smiling Corky. "I rest my case."

"You told me you would be nice," Vanda yelled.

Corky shrugged. "As a dedicated journalist, it's my duty to always report the truth."

"The *truth?*" Vanda shrieked. "The truth is you're a vicious, lying bitch!" She leaped across the table and seized Corky by the neck.

"Vanda, no!" Ian grabbed her, trying to pull her off Corky, who was getting shaken like a rag doll, although her huge breasts remained remarkably still.

Corky's eyes bugged out as she gasped for air. "Cut!"

A commercial started for custom-made coffins. Toni and Phineas stared at the TV in silence.

"Shit," Phineas finally whispered.

Toni swallowed hard. "That was bad."

"Really bad." Phineas stood as he turned off the TV. "Well, I gotta go to work." He vanished.

Toni dashed up the stairs. Carlos would be here any minute now, but she didn't want to leave without making sure Ian was all right. That was part of her job. Sorta.

She reached the fifth floor, gasping for air, and knocked on the door. No answer. She turned the knob, and it opened. That was a good sign. He hadn't locked her out.

She peered inside. The room was dark except for the light emanating from a television. She opened the door wider and spotted Corky Courrant on the TV.

"My friends, I'm sure you're terribly distressed after watching that vicious woman's attempt to strangle me." Corky sniffed and wiped away an imaginary tear. "But don't cry for me. I'm going to be all right."

The television switched off in the middle of a fake Corky sob, and Toni spotted Ian sitting in the dark.

She slipped inside the room. "Are you okay?"

"I'm fine, Toni. I doona need a babysitter."

"I'm just here as a . . . friend." She approached him.

"Ye watched the interview?" He set the remote on the table beside his chair and picked up a bottle of blood. "Of course ye saw it. The entire vampire world saw it."

"I'm so sorry."

"Save yer pity for Vanda. Corky's suing her."

"That's ridiculous! Corky purposely set out to hurt you. She was cruel and vicious." Toni paced in front of him. "Though I have to admit, Vanda went shrieking across that table like a flying monkey."

Ian's dimples showed, and Toni secretly celebrated that she could still make him smile.

"Vanda is a loyal friend," he said. "I'll pay the damages."

"But it wasn't *your* fault." Toni resumed her pacing. "We could prove Corky was lying. You could get some of the Vamp women you've slept with to come forward and—"

"I have never slept with a Vamp." He took a sip from his bottle.

"Really?" She halted. "So you actually prefer mortal women? Never mind." She began to pace once again. "We'll get one of the mortals you slept with to—" No, that wouldn't work. Mortals wouldn't have been watching DVN.

"Most of them have passed away." Ian took another sip.

"Well, okay. I'll just call that bitch myself and tell her I've slept with you."

A corner of Ian's mouth tilted up. "Ye would lie for me, Toni?"

It wouldn't have to be a lie, the thought sprang to her mind. She winced, wishing she could do a mental rewind. Surely he wasn't doing his vampire telepathy on her. Her cheeks heated up as she slanted a wary glance his way.

He was watching her intently. A flash of red tinted his eyes before he blinked and looked away. He drank some more blood. "Ye should go, Toni."

"All right." She backed toward the door. "Just don't let this get you down, okay?"

He shrugged. "It was a silly notion from the start. Me, trying to be some sort of Romeo when I havena the slightest idea how to be charming or flirtatious."

"That's not true. You've been very charming and flirtatious with me." And one hell of a kisser.

He set the bottle on the table. "I doona know why, but it comes easy with you. But it doesna matter now. I'm pulling out of this dating nonsense."

"What?" She stepped toward him. "You're quitting?"

"A man should be honest with himself, Toni. I'm no' a ladies' man, I'm a warrior. Ye said it yerself the other night, that I was wasting my time."

"But I—" She'd said it out of frustration. And jealousy, she now realized. She'd hated the thought of him preferring a Vamp woman over her.

"Ye know my past transgressions," Ian continued. "Do ye really think a man like me deserves to be loved?"

He didn't feel deserving? Toni's eyes welled with tears. When she'd first met Ian, she'd thought they were totally different, but now she realized they were very much alike.

He'd touched on the last of her morning affirmations, and the one she found the hardest to believe. *I am worthy to be loved.* How could she ever be worthy? She'd always let down those who counted on her. And poor Ian. He didn't feel worthy, either. Her heart ached for him.

"Ye doona need to answer." Ian stood and walked away. "The look on yer face tells me how ye feel."

"But you do!" The words tumbled from her mouth. "You do deserve to be loved."

He turned toward her, a surprised look on his face.

She blinked back her tears. "Don't you dare give up, Ian." She dashed to the door.

"Toni," he whispered her name softly, so softly she wasn't sure she'd heard it.

She paused at the door and glanced back. A flood of longing rushed through her.

He stepped toward her, and she gasped.

His eyes were bright red.

She stumbled from the room and shut the door. Dear God. What was she doing? She was falling for a vampire.

Ian opened the aluminum blinds and peered down from the fifth-floor office. With his superior vision, he was able to count twenty-two women on the sidewalk, all bundled up against the cold and carrying posters. One was wearing a tiara that sparkled in the nearby streetlamp.

A sleek black Jaguar came to a stop in front of the townhouse, and the women wandered over to check it out. Then a slash of light spilled onto the sidewalk from the townhouse. The women squealed and rushed toward the front door. Just as Ian wondered if he would have to fend off a home invasion, the slash of light disappeared.

The driver jumped out of the Jaguar. *Carlos.* He extracted someone from the bunch of excited women and led her back to his car. *Toni.*

With a twinge of annoyance, Ian realized Carlos had rescued her from the mob. The Jaguar sped down the road. What was she up to now? With a greater jab of annoyance, he realized she preferred spending her free time with Carlos.

Or did she just feel safer with a mortal who was supposedly gay? Ian was fairly sure that her rushed exit from the office had meant she was aware of his attraction to her. But she'd also gasped when she'd noticed his eyes. Did his Undead nature frighten her? Probably so. After surviving a vicious vampire attack, why would she welcome the advances of another vampire?

But when he'd kissed her, she hadn't pushed him away. Perhaps there was hope after all. He closed his eyes, picturing her in her tiny skirt. He would stroke her golden thighs, then slide his hand under her skirt to feel the sweet curve of her hip and bottom, and the tender, moist flesh between her legs.

With a sharp breath, he cleared his mind. What a fool he was. Intellectually, he knew a female Vamp presented the most suitable mate for him. Yet here he was, lusting for a mortal. And even worse, the one mortal who was off limits.

She totally intrigued him—physically, emotionally, and intellectually. She was such an interesting mixture of determination and self-doubt, emotional strength and hidden wounds. She reminded him of himself.

And what were her hidden motives for being here? What made an intelligent woman with a bright future guard the Undead and risk losing her memory when she left? He had to know. Last night while she'd slept, he'd teleported into her bedroom and slipped a tracking device into her handbag. He would know exactly where she and Carlos were going.

He wandered back into the bedroom to shower and change clothes. After taking care of the women on the sidewalk, he teleported to the parking lot at Romatech Industries.

Connor showed no reaction when Ian marched into the security office. He simply turned off the television.

Dougal and Phineas gave Ian sympathetic looks before focusing on their shoes. Bloody hell. He hated pity even more than humiliation.

"We'd better make the rounds." Dougal headed out the door. "Come on, Phineas."

Phineas paused halfway out the door. "Man, that Corky bitch was wack. You want me to set her straight?"

"Nay." Ian smiled halfheartedly. "But I appreciate the thought."

"Anytime, bro." Phineas raised a fist and punched the air. "I got your back." He closed the door as he left.

Connor sat behind his desk and quietly studied Ian.

"Have a go." Ian folded his arms across his chest. "I reckon ye're wanting to rant at me."

"I reckon ye've endured enough humiliation for one night."

Ian lifted his chin. "Doona hold back on my account. I have a high threshold for pain."

Connor's face remained blank, though Ian detected an amused glint in his blue eyes. "Ye should have known Corky couldna be trusted."

"I did, and I warned Vanda. She dinna believe me."

Connor lounged back in his chair. "I daresay she believes you now."

"Aye." Ian smiled, recalling Toni's description of her as a screeching, flying monkey.

"The situation is hardly amusing. I hear there are over twenty women camped out in front of the townhouse."

"Doona worry. They're all gone. I took care of it."

Connor gave him a bland look. "And were ye careful with the disposal of the bodies?"

"I dinna kill them!" Ian paused when he saw Connor's mouth twitch. The damned Scotsman was playing with him. "Verra funny."

Connor chuckled as he rose from his chair. He approached Ian and slapped him fondly on the back. "Lad, how did ye manage to make such a mess?"

Ian felt his face redden. "I'm trying to clean it up. I took the names and phone numbers of the women on the street. They were happy to leave after I talked to them a wee bit. The puir lassies were freezing out there."

Connor shook his head. "I canna imagine being that desperate for love."

Ian sighed. Didn't everyone need to be loved? He'd endured twelve days of tortuous pain on Roman's Stay-Awake drug just so he could look older and find true love. "There's another problem. Did ye see how Cora Lee announced to the whole vampire world that I aged? Everyone will wonder how that happened."

"I doubt any Vamps want to age." Connor circled his desk and sat. "But if anyone finds out that the drug enables a vampire to stay awake during the day—"

"The drug could be used as a weapon," Ian finished the sentence. "I'm sure the Malcontents have been dying to know how Roman managed to invade their headquarters during the day to rescue Laszlo. If they figure it out, they'll do anything to get their hands on that drug."

Connor drummed his fingers on the desk. "I'll tell Roman that we need to either hide the drug or destroy it. And we'll increase the security here."

"Roman has the formula in his head," Ian continued. "We'll need to watch out for him."

"Aye." Connor gave Ian a worried look. "When the Malcontents start looking for answers to how ye aged, ye're going to be their first target."

Ian swallowed hard. While he hunted for his true love, the Malcontents could be hunting for him.

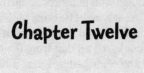

Chapter Twelve

"Is there a point to this?" Toni trudged along in the snow, surveying the ten-foot-high brick wall. Carlos had insisted they inspect the exterior of Shady Oaks before entering the lobby. The visitor parking was in front, the employee parking on the east side, and a guarded service entrance in the back. Now they were on the west side, traversing an area that boasted quite a few shady oaks.

She realized her question had gone unanswered, so she turned to confront Carlos.

He was gone.

"Carlos?" She spun around, and her handbag slipped off her shoulder. "Carlos, where are you?"

"Shhh, not so loud."

She followed the sound of his voice and spotted him high in an oak tree, lying on a thick branch that extended over the brick wall. Good grief, he had to be fifteen feet up. "Carlos, what are you doing?"

She gaped as he jumped from the tree and landed lightly on his feet. "How'd you do that?"

"The real question is why." He strode toward her. "I needed to see over the wall. There's an inner courtyard. All the surrounding buildings open onto it. I think the buildings with numbers on them are the wards where the patients are staying. The other buildings looked like a cafeteria, gymnasium, and indoor pool. It's a fancy place."

"You could tell all that from the tree?"

"Yes, and even better, I saw a handful of patients hanging around the gazebo, smoking. There was one guard with them." He walked toward the front parking lot.

"How is that helpful?" Toni hitched her bag back onto her shoulder and followed him.

"All information is helpful. Now I'll go into the lobby first and check it out. You wait here out of range of the surveillance camera."

"But—" She stopped when the automatic doors swooshed closed behind him. "Great. I'll just wait here in the freezing cold."

The circular drive to the entrance was lined with stone statues and snow-capped boxwood hedges. She could see inside the lobby through the large plate-glass windows. It looked warm and cozy with leather sofas and easy chairs. Carlos was right about Shady Oaks being a fancy place.

He exited, holding a piece of paper in his hand, and met her out of range of the surveillance camera. He stuffed the paper into the pocket of his leather coat.

"What was that?" Toni asked.

"A job application. Now here's the layout. The receptionist is behind the information desk. There are two locked doors on each side of the lobby, leading into the east and west wings. The back wall of the lobby is glass, looking out onto the courtyard. There's a door, but a guard is sitting in front of it."

"So there's no way into the courtyard?" She sighed. "I guess it doesn't matter, since I'm sure the wards are locked up tight."

"The courtyard is accessible. You're forgetting the well-placed shady oak."

She grimaced. "I can't get up that tree."

"You don't have to. I will, and hopefully I can distract the guard and the receptionist in the lobby. That's when you check the patient list I saw on the receptionist's desk. If you find Sabrina's name, make sure you get the ID number. We won't be allowed to even talk to her on the phone without her ID number."

"Okay." Toni stomped the mud and snow off her boots. "I'm not entirely comfortable with this espionage stuff." And how come Carlos was so good at it? "So how are you going to distract them?"

Too late again. Carlos had already taken off. He sprinted around the corner of the complex, headed no doubt for his favorite tree.

"Good grief." Toni marched in place to warm up her feet. She'd give him a few minutes to start whatever he was planning to do. She exhaled, letting the air rush out with a cloud of icy vapor, then strode into the lobby. Showtime. The automatic doors swooshed behind her, and the guard and receptionist both looked at her.

It was long past visiting hours, so she was all alone.

"May I help you?" the receptionist asked, studying her over her black-rimmed reading glasses.

Toni glanced around quickly. She could barely see the courtyard through the window. The gazebo was dimly lit, and the shadows of patients milled about. Their cigarettes flared with little orange lights whenever they took a puff.

The receptionist cleared her throat.

"Ah, I was wondering . . ." Toni edged over to the information desk and spotted the patient list, pinned under the receptionist's elbow. "How does someone get admitted to this hospital? I have a friend with a serious problem."

The receptionist gave her a wry look. "And what exactly is your *friend's* problem?"

Toni realized the woman thought she was talking about herself, so she played along. "Well, I—that is, my *friend* is addicted to . . . sex. Lots of sex. All the time. She can't get enough."

"I see." The receptionist pursed her lips. "Normally your psychologist would refer you here. You are seeing a psychologist, aren't you? I mean, your *friend*."

Toni grinned sheepishly. "Okay, you got me. And yeah, I was seeing a therapist, but his wife caught me giving him a hummer in the backseat of his Hummer, so—"

The receptionist pulled off her glasses. "You had sexual relations with your therapist?"

"Sure. I sleep with all my therapists. And my doctors, my teachers, the plumber, the pigeon guy on the roof." Where the hell was Carlos? "You know, it's a disease."

Screams suddenly erupted from the courtyard, and the guard jumped to his feet to peer through the window.

The receptionist stood. "What's going on?"

"I can't tell," the guard answered. "The patients are running all over the place."

The screams increased in volume and terror. What the hell was Carlos doing? Toni jumped when a patient slammed against the plate-glass window.

"Help!" he shouted. "Let me in!"

The guard punched a keypad to open the door.

"You're not supposed to let them in the lobby," the receptionist warned.

Just then, a loud roar filled the air and shook the glass windows. The screams from the courtyard intensified.

A woman flung herself against the glass. "Help me! It attacked me!"

The guard opened the door, and the two patients scurried inside.

"Look what it did to me!" The female patient showed off her down jacket. The sleeve was ripped open so that the stuffing was falling out. "It's a monster! A black monster with glowing eyes!"

"Doris, take them to the clinic," the guard ordered the receptionist. He removed a Taser from his belt. "Don't worry, folks. I'll take care of this . . . monster." He cast an amused look at Doris. No doubt he suspected the patients at the mental hospital were crazy.

Doris ran over to the patients. "Come. This way." She unlocked the door to the west wing and ushered them inside.

Screams continued in the courtyard, and Toni spotted the shadows of other patients scurrying about, banging on the doors to other buildings. Whatever Carlos was doing, he was scaring the hell out of everyone. Meanwhile, the lobby was empty. She rushed around the desk and thumbed through the patient list. There on the last page was *Vanderwerth, Sabrina. Third ward. VS48732.*

Toni scribbled down the information on a notepad, tore off the page, and stuffed it in her handbag. She dashed out the front door and was halfway to Carlos's car when she slipped on an icy patch and her feet flew out from under her. She landed hard on her hip.

"Ow. Damn." She eased to her feet and hobbled to the car. "Damn." She checked her handbag to make sure the paper was still there.

After a long, nerve-racking minute, she spotted Carlos running toward her. What the heck? He was barefoot, with his boots in one hand and his leather coat in the other. His black shirt was unbuttoned and flapped wildly as he sprinted toward her.

He shifted his jacket to his other arm, then pulled the keys from his pants pocket. With a click on the keypad, the doors unlocked.

He tossed his shoes and jacket on the backseat. "Did you get the info?"

"Yes." She opened her door. "What happened to you?"

"Hurry." He slid into the driver's seat. "I overheard the guard calling the police."

She climbed in with her hip complaining, then buckled up. "What did you do? I heard so much screaming."

"I created a diversion." He backed the car out, then zoomed toward the exit.

She eyed his bare chest and partially buttoned pants. "Oh my God. Don't tell me you streaked."

"Something like that." He pulled out onto the street. Police sirens wailed in the distance. "We'll come back tomorrow after things have calmed down. Visiting hours are five P.M. on Sunday. Can you make it?"

"I think so." Toni squinted as two police cars raced past them with flashing lights. She glanced over her shoulder and saw them pulling into the hospital parking lot. What had caused the guard to call the police? She recalled the woman with the slashed jacket. And the woman's frantic words—a black monster with glowing eyes.

A twinge of unease knotted her stomach. What on earth did Carlos do?

Ian stashed the six vials of the Stay-Awake drug in the safe room in the basement of Romatech—a room completely encased in silver so that a vampire could teleport neither in nor out. The silver room was equipped with its own air supply and enough food, water, and bottled blood to keep a mortal or Vamp alive for three months.

Meanwhile, Connor and Roman were making sure the recipe for the Stay-Awake drug was erased from all computer files. Now there were only two sources for the formula—a CD in the silver room and Roman's brain. Connor wanted to send Roman and his family into hiding, but Roman didn't think the situation was dire enough yet.

Since Ian still had a few vacation days left, Connor didn't expect him to stick around, so he teleported back to the townhouse. In the fifth-floor office, he connected the computer to the tracking device in Toni's handbag. He zoomed in on her location. Shady Oaks Psychiatric Hospital? Why would Carlos take her there? The light started blinking. They were on the move.

His cell phone rang, and he retrieved it from his sporran. "Hello?"

"Ian, this is Vanda," she whispered. "I need you to come to the club, but not to the entrance or the main room. Teleport straight to my voice."

"What's wrong?"

"Just come here *now!*" she hissed.

"All right." He focused on her voice. A few seconds later, he arrived in a dark room next to Vanda.

He glanced around. Scattered on the floor around low tables were overstuffed, tasseled pillows in red, purple, and gold silk. The walls were covered with sheer drapes of red and gold. On the tabletops, candles flickered inside golden mosaic glass, casting sparkly lights around the room. Music and more light filtered through the open cutwork of carved wooden screens that lined one side of the room.

"What is this place?" he whispered.

"The VIP room," Vanda replied. "Since we were harem ladies, we thought it would be cool to make it look like a harem. The screen folds open, so the VIP customers can look over the railing at the action below. But if they want privacy, we close the screen."

Ian peered through a hole in the screen. Sure enough, the Horny Devils nightclub was below. In front of the stage, lady Vamps bounced merrily in time with the music while the male dancer on stage spun around in a black, flowing vampire cape. Beneath the cape he was naked, except for a black bow tie and red, sparkly bikini underwear.

Ian winced. Dracula would roll over in his grave.

"By the way, all the girls down there have been asking about you," Vanda said. "They want to meet you."

"Why? So they can laugh at me?"

Vanda snorted. "Actually, they all want the honor of being the one to take your virginity."

"Bloody hell," he muttered. "Did ye tell them they're about five hundred years too late?"

"I tried to, but they prefer Corky's version. I suspect they think being your first will make them famous and give them some airtime on Corky's show."

"Och. So it's fame and no' me that attracts them. Was there an important reason ye called me here?"

"I'm afraid so." Vanda peered through the screen. "Look at the bar."

His gaze shifted to Cora Lee, whose blonde head was close to a stocky male Vamp. Ian's stomach twisted as recognition clicked in place. "Dammit to hell."

Vanda cast him a worried look. "Then you know who he is?"

"Aye. Jedrek Janow." Ian had last seen the murderous Malcontent in the Ukraine the night he'd gone there with Jean-Luc and others to help rescue Angus and Emma. Jedrek had been there with Casimir, but when the Malcontents started to lose the battle, both Jedrek and Casimir teleported away, leaving their Russian comrades behind to be vanquished.

Shanna's father and his CIA Stake-Out team maintained a constant surveillance of the Russian-American vampires, and they kept Connor informed since he'd managed to plant the listening devices in their headquarters. Unfortunately, the bugs had been destroyed a few nights ago. Jedrek was being thorough.

"He usually hangs out in Eastern Europe," Ian explained, "but he's recently been put in charge of the Russian-American coven in Brooklyn."

"But he's Polish," Vanda protested.

"Half Polish, half Russian, and Casimir's right-hand man." Ian regarded Vanda curiously. "How do ye know him?"

A hint of pain flickered across her face. "Let's just say he got along really well with the Nazis. He's a vicious killer, and he enjoys it."

"A Malcontent poster boy." Ian peered through the screen. "He's drinking Bleer to fool Cora Lee into thinking he's a regular Vamp."

"Unfortunately, it's not that hard to fool Cora Lee."

Ian strained his ears, but he couldn't hear Jedrek's low voice over the din of loud music and squealing women. "I need to know what he's saying."

Vanda frowned, considering. "If I go down there, he'll recognize me and—oh, I know. There's an intercom on my desk that connects to the bar. I use it when I need to talk to Cora Lee. This way."

She strode to a door partially hidden behind a sheer red curtain. Ian followed her down a flight of stairs and into her office.

"Is this it?" He reached for the intercom on her desk.

"Wait. It's a two-way connection," she warned him. "We'll have to be perfectly quiet."

He nodded and pushed the button with his finger.

"So you know Ian?" Cora Lee asked.

"Sure," Jedrek replied with a fake Brooklyn accent. "We go way back. I can't get over the way he looks now."

"I know! I didn't even recognize him at first," Cora Lee confessed. "I can't believe he got older like that."

"And you say it happened in Texas?" Jedrek asked.

"That's what Ian told me."

"Sweetheart, could you get me another Bleer? This stuff is freakin' fantastic. Roman is a genius."

"He sure is. You know him, too?"

"Who doesn't? The guy's famous," Jedrek commented casually. "But you know what? He looks a bit older, too."

"Yep, all of a sudden he turned gray at the temples."

"But he didn't go to Texas, did he?" Jedrek asked.

"Nope, he was here when it happened. Land sakes, I can't imagine why anyone would want to look older."

"They would if there was a really important, secret purpose behind it," Jedrek said.

Vanda gasped, and Ian shook his head to remind her to stay quiet. No doubt she had grasped the full danger of the situation. If the Malcontents acquired the means to stay awake during the day, they would slaughter Vamps who were helpless in their death-sleep.

The phone on Vanda's desk rang, and Ian quickly lifted his finger off the intercom button to break the connection. Vanda grimaced and answered the phone.

Ian dashed back up the stairs to the VIP harem room and peered through the screen. Cora Lee must have heard the ring, for she'd answered her phone. With a confused look, she hung up. Meanwhile, Jedrek was scanning the surroundings, his eyes narrowed. No doubt he suspected something.

Ian considered teleporting down to challenge him, but before he could weigh the pros and cons, Jedrek vanished.

"What's happening?" Vanda rushed into the room.

"He's gone."

"That damned phone," Vanda muttered. "It was the dancer I fired Thursday night. He heard Corky was planning to sue me, so he decided to have a go at me, too. The bastard."

"I'll get the name of Angus's solicitor," Ian offered. "He's the best in the Vamp world. And doona fash over Corky. I'll pay to settle with her. I canna have ye suffering on my account."

"But I'm the one who attacked her." Vanda dragged a hand through her spiky hair. "And now we have this mess with Jedrek Janow. He's not going to stop until he knows what caused you to age. And if he gets his hands on that drug—"

"I know. They'll kill us in our sleep."

Vanda pressed a hand to her brow. "This is all my fault. I made you too famous, and now you're in danger. Jedrek will hunt you down. He'll—he'll—"

"It will be all right."

"But I completely screwed up," she cried. "You're like one of my little brothers to me. And I lost all of them. I can't stand to lose you, too, not when it's all my fault."

"Shhh." He pulled her into an embrace and patted her on the back. "I doona blame you, Vanda. Yer heart was in the right place. But I would appreciate it if ye could tell Cora

Lee and Lady Pamela to keep their bloody mouths shut."

"I will, I will." Vanda stepped back and sniffed. "And I'll keep trying to find you the perfect mate. I'll make a list of the girls who want to meet you, and I'll interview them myself to weed out the ones who just want to be famous."

Ian figured that was all of them, but he didn't want to belittle Vanda's offer. "That would be great. Thanks."

She squeezed her eyes shut. "I want you to be happy, Ian. And *safe*." When she opened her eyes, anger flashed in them. "So help me, if that Jedrek bastard hurts—"

"Vanda, promise me ye'll do nothing about Jedrek Janow. Leave him to me and Connor."

She heaved a sigh. "Okay, but please be careful. He'll want answers, and you're the one who has them."

"I know." Ian realized Jedrek could be hunting for him right now. And the first place he'd search would be Roman's townhouse. "I need to use your computer."

He dashed down the stairs to Vanda's office and accessed the tracking device in Toni's handbag. She was back at the townhouse. All alone.

Ian's stomach clenched. *Toni*, he thought, just before he teleported away.

Chapter Thirteen

A hot shower helped take the chill out of Toni's bones and relieve the ache in her bruised hip. She leaned over to wrap a towel around her wet hair, and as she straightened, she accidentally brushed her hip against the counter.

"Ow!" She eyed the bruise. It had swollen to a lovely shade of purple that coordinated well with the red scars on her torso and breasts.

"Toni!"

She jumped at the sound of Ian's voice coming from her bedroom. Her hip knocked against the counter. "Ow! Dammit!" She grabbed on to the towel bar to keep from falling.

"Toni, are ye all right?" Ian pounded on the door. "Is someone hurting you? Should I teleport in?"

"No!" What was he doing out there? "I . . . I have the entire offensive line from the New York Giants in here. Oh yeah, I'm feeling good! Second down and eight to go."

There was a pause. "Ye're jesting, right?"

She snorted. "Brilliant, Sherlock."

"Come out now. We need to talk."

Not that again. "I don't have any clothes. Go away."

"I'll close my eyes."

Now it was her turn to pause. "I don't believe you."

"Brilliant, Sherlock."

Damn him. She wrapped a towel around herself. "Go away."

"No. I've come to rescue you."

"From what? Mildew?"

"I'll step into the hall so ye can get dressed. Please hurry."

She heard footsteps and a door click shut. She peeked out. The bedroom was empty.

She eased toward the dresser. "Why are you pestering me? I'm off duty now." She dropped her towel and quickly pulled on some panties.

"This canna wait," Ian spoke from the hallway. "We're in danger from a Malcontent assassin named Jedrek Janow. He's the new master of the Russian-American coven in Brooklyn, the bastards who attacked you before. Jedrek wants information about the drug I took in order to age, so he'll be searching for me."

Any irritation Toni had felt sifted away, only to be replaced by a twinge of fear. She reached behind her back to hook her bra. "How serious is this?"

"Verra serious. If he comes to the townhouse, he willna come alone. He'll bring other Malcontents with him, and everyone here, including you, will be attacked."

A chill prickled her skin with gooseflesh. "They know about this townhouse? I thought it was a secret." Damn, she had thought she was safe from them.

"Roman's home is a secret, but this place has always been known in the Vamp world. Every spring, Roman hosts a conference at Romatech, and coven masters come from around the world to attend. They always stay here, and Angus's company provides security. Are ye decent now?"

She could be attacked again? God, no. Memories of that night threatened to wash over her. No, not again.

A form appeared before her, and she gasped.

Ian's eyes widened. "Toni."

Her hands fluttered around her panties and bra. Damn! Her undies didn't cover up much. And her scars! She glanced at his face and saw his expression go from shock to horror.

"Go away!" She turned her back to him. Dammit, what was worse? Being caught almost naked or seeing a guy's horrified reaction to it?

"Toni, ye're covered with bite marks."

"I know. I was there when it happened." She rushed to the closet and yanked a pair of jeans off a hanger.

"And yer hip. It's bruised something terrible."

"Stop looking at me!" She pulled on the jeans. "I fell in a parking lot."

"At the Shady Oaks Psychiatric Hospital?"

She gasped, and the jeans slid down to her knees. "How—" She noticed his gaze drifting south, and she jerked the jeans back up. "How did you know?"

"I'm a verra good investigator."

Damn him. She zipped up her jeans. "You've been spying on me?"

He strode toward her. "Is that yer suitcase there?"

She jumped aside to keep some distance between them. "What are you doing?"

He opened the suitcase on her dresser and started filling it with her clothes. "Finish getting dressed now."

She didn't care for his authoritarian tone. Or that he'd been spying on her. She jerked a T-shirt off a hanger and pulled it on. "Fine. I'll get dressed. Then you won't have to look so horrified at the sight of my body."

He paused with a handful of her panties in his fist. "I was angry when I saw how those bastards punctured you with holes. I wasna horrified. Yer body is beautiful."

How could she stay angry when he said that?

He dropped the panties in her suitcase. "Please hurry. We need to go."

"Where are we going?" She ran into the bathroom, grabbed her hairbrush, toothbrush, cosmetic bag, and contacts, then tossed them into the suitcase.

"I'll take you to Romatech. Security is much tighter there. Then the lads and I can return here to fight the bastards if they come."

She liked the idea of being safe, and she really hated the idea of seeing the Malcontents again, but something about Ian's plan annoyed her. She didn't like being a weak damsel in distress. She sat on the bed to pull on her socks. "I'm not going to hide and leave all the fighting to you guys. I was hired to fight."

Ian smiled as he grabbed clothes from her closet and dumped them in her suitcase. "Ye're a brave lass, and I commend ye for it, but this is no' yer fight."

Normally she would agree. Why risk her life over a vampire dispute? But the night the Malcontents attacked her, it became personal. As much as she hated seeing them again, she had to do it. She jerked on her boots. "This *is* my fight. I won't cower in fear. I'll do what I was hired to do."

Ian zipped her suitcase shut. "Sweetheart, ye were hired as a day guard. That means ye're supposed to fight daytime enemies, namely mortals. Ye're off duty at night for a reason. Ye canna survive against a vampire foe."

"I pinned Phineas down the other night."

"A lucky break."

"Look, *sweetheart*." She marched toward him. "I'm good. I'm damned good. Do you need a demonstration?"

"Perhaps ye do." He vanished, and a second later he was behind her, pulling her against his chest.

She reacted quickly, ramming her elbows into his chest. It was like hitting a brick wall.

His hands moved to her neck and face, and his voice was

soft against her ear. "The next sound ye would hear is the snapping of yer neck."

Rage swept through her. Dammit to hell, was there no winning against them? The memory of her attack flooded back and sucked her under, drowning her in horror. She shook her head, trying to dislodge the memories, but they filled her mind, playing back every excruciating detail. A shudder almost doubled her over.

"Toni, it will be all right," Ian whispered.

"No!" She fought back the tears, but the more she struggled, the more her emotions swelled. She broke free from Ian and staggered back. "I—*I hate your kind!*"

His face paled. She pressed a hand to her mouth, startled by the intensity of her outburst.

His mouth thinned, and pain glinted in his eyes. "At least ye're being honest now."

She splayed her hands across her scarred rib cage. "They chewed on me like I was food. Like I wasn't human. I was just a piece of *meat*." Tears rolled down her face, and she wiped her cheeks. "I couldn't fight them. They took over my mind, and it was like my soul was squashed."

He pulled her into his arms. She stiffened, but he held her tight. "Lass, I would never harm you. Ye can trust me."

She took a slow, shuddering breath, and let it out. "I know." She burrowed her face in his thick sweater and let his scent fill her nostrils. He smelled clean, but earthy. Sweet, but manly.

He rubbed a hand up and down her back. "I hope I do see those bastards tonight. I'd love to skewer them for what they did to you."

She rested her cheek against his shoulder. He still didn't quite understand. She appreciated his desire to protect her, but she didn't really want a protector against evil vampires. What she wanted was a way to protect herself. And given their superior abilities, she didn't think such a way existed. And that's what bothered her the most—the inequality and injustice of it all.

"I wish I could whip your ass," she whispered.

Ian chuckled. "That's my girl."

She nestled her cheek deeper into his thick sweater. He was surprisingly warm and wonderfully solid. When he released her and stepped back, she wanted to throw herself back into his arms.

"We need to go, lass." He dragged her suitcase off the dresser.

She pulled on her coat and grabbed her handbag. "Are you driving?"

"Teleporting. It's faster." He grasped the handle of her suitcase with one hand and extended the other toward her. "Ye'll need to hold on to me."

"Oh." Not a problem. She slid her arms around his neck.

"Closer." His arm tightened around her waist.

She pressed against his solid chest. "Like this?"

He closed his eyes briefly. "Aye."

Her breath caught when his eyes opened. "What's the deal with your eyes? They keep turning red."

"It's a normal reaction for a vampire."

"I don't think so." She studied the red, glowing irises. "None of the other Vamps do that."

"Good. I wouldna want to fight any of my friends."

"What are you talking about?"

He gave her a wry smile. "Toni, when my eyes turn red, it's because I'm wanting you verra badly."

She swallowed hard. "But it's been happening for days."

"Aye, since I first met you. But doona let it worry you. I know ye hate our kind."

"I don't hate you, Ian. I don't hate any of the good Vamps. Maybe I did at first, but now . . ."

He watched her carefully. "How do ye feel now?"

A flood of emotions brought tears to her eyes. "I—I have a lot on my mind. Not just you, but my friend Sabrina. I'm so very worried . . . and confused." She shouldn't feel so damned attracted to a vampire.

"Tell me what's going on. I might be able to help you."

She studied his handsome face and saw genuine concern and compassion. She wanted to trust him. Dear God, she wanted to stay in his arms forever. "I'll think about it."

"Good. Hang on, sweetheart." He pulled her tight, and everything went black.

As soon as Ian was assured that Toni was safely ensconced in the silver room at Romatech, he teleported back to the townhouse with Dougal and Phineas.

When they materialized on the back porch, they heard the high-pitched buzz of the alarm inside the townhouse. They instantly drew their swords. There were only two explanations for the alarm—either a mortal had broken into the townhouse and didn't hear the alarm, or a vampire had teleported inside and didn't know the proper combination required to turn the alarm off.

Dougal quietly unlocked the back door and let it swing open. They waited, swords ready, for someone to poke his head out the door and look. If it was a Malcontent, his head wouldn't stay attached for long.

No one fell for the bait. Ian moved to enter, but Phineas pulled him back.

"It's you they want, bro. Stay between us." Phineas entered first.

The kitchen was a mess. Cabinets and drawers hung open, and the contents were scattered on the countertops.

"They must be looking for the drug." Dougal started to punch in the combination to turn off the alarm.

"Nay." Ian stopped him. "If we turn it off, we'll be announcing our arrival."

Dougal grimaced. "Ye're right, but the noise is bloody annoying."

"Yeah, sounds like a cat on crack," Phineas muttered. He positioned himself by the swinging door. "Ready?"

Ian nodded, and the three Vamps zoomed into the foyer. A

quick glance assured them that the intruders were not on the first floor. Books were tumbled onto the floor in the library, and the parlor had been ransacked.

They zipped downstairs to the cellar. Phineas's bed had been slashed, and the coffins ripped apart.

"Shit." Phineas studied the broken picture frame of his family. "We're too late."

"We should check Roman's office," Ian suggested. "I'm sure they've realized that he invented the drug."

"We go together," Dougal said. "Aim for the fifth-floor landing."

The trio teleported to the landing outside Roman's office and bedroom. The two doors were open, and inside, voices were speaking in Russian.

Ian eased toward the office door and spied Jedrek Janow at Roman's desk, fiddling with the computer. The Malcontent cursed and pounded a fist on the keyboard. Then he started rifling through the desk drawers.

Dougal peeked into Roman's bedroom, then raised two fingers to indicate two men. Ian lifted one finger. It was three against three. He gave Dougal and Phineas a questioning look, and they both nodded.

Ian charged into the office, headed straight for Jedrek. The assassin glanced up and reached for the sword he'd left on the desk. Ian was already swinging his sword down for a killing blow when Jedrek teleported away.

Ian's sword ripped through an empty office chair. "Bloody hell." He spun to see if Jedrek had materialized behind him.

He hadn't. The Russian coven master reappeared in the bedroom next to his two followers.

Ian moved toward them while Dougal and Phineas flanked him.

"Just the man I was looking for," Jedrek sneered. "Stasio, Yuri, take the man in the middle."

The two Malcontents lunged toward Ian, but Dougal and Phineas jumped in front, and each engaged in battle. Ian cursed inwardly at being treated like a helpless pup. He headed for Jedrek, but the coward vanished once again.

Ian whirled just as Jedrek's hand gripped his arm from behind. A dizzying sensation stole over him, and he realized Jedrek was attempting to teleport away with him. He slashed his sword down onto Jedrek's arm, and the man yelped in pain just before disappearing completely.

"You coward!" Ian shouted at the now empty space.

A cry of pain drew Ian's attention back to the sword fights. Phineas had sliced his opponent's torso. The Russian stumbled back, and Phineas stabbed him in the chest. The Russian turned gray, then crumbled into a pile of dust on the floor.

The second Russian shouted in anger, then teleported away, leaving Dougal cursing in his wake.

"I did it!" Phineas lifted his sword in the air. "Did you see that? I was a killing machine!"

Dougal slapped him on the back. "Yer first kill. Congratulations."

Phineas raised his hand to give them both a high five. "Oh yeah, Dr. Phang strikes again!"

Ian smiled wearily. After a few centuries of killing Malcontents, he no longer felt the thrill. He strode back to the desk and turned off the alarm. "Jedrek was injured. I doona think he'll try anything else tonight. Let's go back to Romatech."

Roman and his family would be safe for the time being. And so would Toni.

As soon as Jedrek Janow materialized in his Brooklyn office, he felt the pain of his slashed arm. He dropped his sword on the floor and clasped a hand over the wound. Blood seeped through his fingers and dripped onto the expensive Turkish rug. "Damn."

"Sir, you're bleeding," the guard at his door said.

"Brilliant observation, moron," Jedrek growled. "Get Nadia in here now."

"Yes, Master." The guard zoomed away.

Jedrek pulled his ripped and bloody sweater off and tossed it in the litter bin.

The guard returned with Nadia in tow. She hovered by the doorway, refusing to look at him.

He knew she was angry. She hadn't enjoyed killing the blonde. "Bring bandages. You will bind my wound."

She lifted her chin defiantly. "Your wound will heal during your death-sleep."

"That's five hours from now, bitch. Bring the bandages now."

She trudged off. Still too much spirit, but he would break her soon.

"You." He glared at the guard. The guy's name was Stanislav, but Jedrek didn't like to call people by their names. It made them think that somehow you liked them. "Give me your shirt."

"Yes, Master." Stanislav unbuttoned his white shirt.

Meanwhile, a form wavered, then solidified by the desk. It was Yuri. He sheathed his sword and avoided looking at Jedrek.

"Where's Stasio?" Jedrek demanded.

"He—he's dead," Yuri whispered.

"Then he should have fought better." Jedrek grabbed the shirt Stanislav offered and wrapped it around the cut on his forearm. The white cotton turned red with blood. "Who killed him? Was it one of those damned Scotsmen?"

"No," Yuri replied. "It was the black vampire."

"Black?" Stanislav asked. "I wonder . . ."

"Out with it," Jedrek growled.

"There was a black guy in our coven for a while," Stanislav explained. "Phineas McKinney. Alek transformed him because he was a drug dealer, and Katya needed his help to make Nightshade."

Unfortunately, the now-deceased Katya had used up all the Nightshade in her failed attempt to deliver Angus MacKay to Casimir. Jedrek had hoped to find some of the drug here in the office, but no such luck. "Where is this Phineas? If I'd had some Nightshade tonight, I could have paralyzed Ian MacPhie and brought him back."

"I haven't seen Phineas in over a year." Stanislav tilted his head, concentrating. "Last time I saw him, he was here in the office. Said he was looking for Katya, but she and Galina had already gone to the Ukraine."

Jedrek narrowed his eyes. He'd debugged this office when Katya was master, then again when he'd become coven master. Someone in the coven had been playing both sides. "Look through the photos on my desk. There's a picture of a black Vamp who works for MacKay."

Stanislav shuffled through the photos, then stopped. "This is him. Phineas McKinney."

Jedrek gritted his teeth. "And when Phineas was here in the office, did you tell him where Katya was?"

Stanislav opened his mouth to answer, then snapped it shut when realization struck. He gulped audibly.

"What did I say about incompetence?" Jedrek growled.

Yuri drew his sword and awaited the order.

Stanislav stepped back, his face pale. "I thought he was on our side. He helped us make the Nightshade."

Jedrek inhaled deeply. Fear radiated from Stanislav like the sweetest of perfumes. "You will have one chance to redeem yourself. You will kill Phineas McKinney."

"Of course." Stanislav nodded enthusiastically. "It'll be my pleasure."

Yuri sheathed his sword with a disappointed look.

"First you will find me a snack," Jedrek told Stanislav. "This wound has left me famished."

"Yes, Master. Right away." Stanislav left just as Nadia arrived, her hands filled with bandages and tape. She approached him with a wary look.

"You took too long." Jedrek perched on the edge of his desk and lifted his wounded arm. "Wrap it up tight."

"Yes, Master." She began rolling the gauze around his forearm.

He noted the bruises on her arms where he'd dug his fingers into her earlier. "I enjoy hurting you."

Her hands shook as she bandaged his arm. Good, she was showing the proper amount of fear. He loved instilling fear in others. It gave him power over them. People bowed in fear before gods.

"What about the drug?" Yuri asked. "And Ian MacPhie?"

"I need to heal first." Jedrek flexed his hand. "Tomorrow we will strike again. We'll get our answers. And Vamps will die."

Chapter Fourteen

A dinging sound nudged Toni from her sleep. Where was she? Oh right, the silver room at Romatech Industries.

A flash of light drew her attention, and she stiffened when she realized she wasn't alone in the dark room. Then she recognized the red and green plaid kilt. The broad shoulders and black ponytail that curled on the end.

The red exit light above the door cast a dim, red glow across the room. Ian removed a bottle of blood from the microwave. That must have been the source of the dinging sound. She glanced at the bedside clock. Time to get up for work. She sat up, and the rustle of sheets caused Ian to turn toward her.

"Och, I dinna mean to wake you."

"It's okay. It's time for me to get up."

"Ye can sleep late if ye like."

She immediately collapsed onto the bed. "Oh God, yes."

He chuckled. "Everyone is staying here for their death-sleep. There are a few bedrooms here in the cellar, all with surveillance cameras. Howard's in the MacKay office, watching over us."

Toni glanced up at the camera in the corner. The red light indicated it was turned on.

"There's a second office for day security," Ian continued. "They watch over the mortal employees and guard the building. I hear it's verra busy upstairs during the day. Lots of mortals making synthetic blood, bottling it, and shipping it to hospitals and blood banks."

"You're not worried one of the mortal employees will stumble onto a Vamp in his death-sleep?"

"The mortals are no' allowed in the basement. Ye need a special key card to make the elevator come here or access the stairway. I left one on the table for you here."

"Did I miss anything while I was sleeping?"

He shrugged on shoulder. "The townhouse was invaded."

"What?" She sat up. "The Malcontents were there?"

"Aye. Phineas killed one. He was verra proud of himself. Jedrek tried to teleport away with me, but I slashed his arm to get free."

"Good grief," Toni whispered. This was awful. "Are you okay?"

"Aye." Ian finished his bottle and rinsed it out in the kitchen sink. "We expect they'll try something tonight, so ye should get more rest while ye can."

"Okay. I'll just go to the bathroom first." She padded to the bathroom. Once she was done, she shut the door behind her and let her eyes adjust to the red-tinted darkness. Ian was no longer in the kitchen.

She moved toward the bed and halted. There he was, on the far side, lying on top of the covers, wearing his kilt, a white T-shirt, and his knee socks.

"What are you doing?" She glanced around the room.

There was only one bed. Maybe if she pushed the easy chairs together, she could manage—

"I willna molest you, lass. Verra soon, I'll no' be able to move." He clasped his hands together over his stomach and studied the ceiling. "Though I hope ye willna have yer way with me while I'm unable to defend myself."

She snorted. "Right. Because there's something so irresistible about a corpse."

His mouth curled into a half smile as he looked at her. "If it bothers you to sleep next to me, I can lie on the floor. Once I'm dead, I'll hardly know the difference."

"I've dated a few guys with the same level of sensitivity," she muttered while she debated whether to climb back into bed.

He yawned and closed his eyes. "I'll be gone soon."

She sat on the edge of the bed. "Does it hurt?"

"To know there's a beautiful woman lying next to me, and I'll no' be able to touch her?" His eyes opened and glimmered with humor. "It's a living torture. But no' for long."

She scoffed. "I meant does it hurt every morning when you die?"

He lay there, his gaze roaming over her slowly, lingering here and there as if he were memorizing every tiny detail. Her skin tingled, responding to his gaze. Just when she thought he wouldn't answer, he spoke softly.

"It's like slipping into a black hole, so black and deep there is no light, no feelings, no thoughts." He blinked slowly, the twinkle in his eyes fading. "I wish I could dream."

"What would a vampire dream about? Big vats of blood? A shiny, new coffin with leather upholstery?"

"Nay. I would have a lovely dream." A hint of a smile played on his lips as his eyes drifted shut. "About you." His face went lax.

Me? Toni's heart raced. He would dream of her? She leaned close to study him. "Are you dead yet?"

He didn't answer. He just lay there, the most gorgeous man she'd ever known. Her gaze settled on the dimple in his chin. She'd wanted to touch it the other day. She'd reached for it, but had lost her nerve.

She would have the nerve now. But not the opportunity. She glanced up at the surveillance camera. It wouldn't do for Howard to see her touching Ian's face.

She slipped under the covers and lay on her back beside him. God help her, she wanted to snuggle up to a dead body. This was wrong on so many levels.

She rolled over, putting her back to him. So wrong. And yet, it was starting to feel so right.

Thank God there was a different receptionist working at Shady Oaks Sunday evening. Toni had worried about Doris being there and recognizing her from her sex addict routine. She tried to look a little different by wearing her glasses instead of contacts and pulling a knit cap down low to cover her blonde hair.

Carlos had picked her up at Romatech. The sun had still been up, and all the Vamps still dead. Howard had assured her everything was under control, so she was free to go. Still, she felt that uneasy sensation of being pulled in two different directions. Ian had thought the Malcontents would attack again. She hated not being there to help.

"We're here to see Sabrina Vanderwerth," she told the receptionist.

"You'll need to sign in and fill out this form."

While Carlos signed them in, Toni quickly filled out the form, including Sabrina's name and ID number.

The receptionist checked the form against her records, the same records Toni had snuck a peek at the night before. "I'll need your IDs." She examined their driver's licenses, then filled out name tags for them.

"I'll hold your licenses here until you return and sign out."

She handed them the clip-on name tags. "Wear these at all times. You cannot bring any personal items or food or drinks into the wards. Do you understand?"

"Yes." Toni was directed toward the guard, who went through her handbag, then patted her and Carlos down.

He unlocked the door. "Follow the sidewalk across the courtyard, then turn right to Ward Three."

As they crossed the courtyard, Toni looked around. Inside each building, another guard was posted. She shivered. The place was like a prison.

Carlos opened the door to Ward Three and followed her into a small foyer. The guard checked their name tags and took their request form, which he placed in a sliding metal box. It slid into a nurses' station, all enclosed in glass.

"Put your coats and personal items in these bins." The guard motioned to some plastic bins on a table.

While they filled the bins, a brawny male nurse entered the nursing station and examined their request form. "Come to the door," he spoke through an intercom.

There was a buzzing sound, then the metal door opened.

The male nurse motioned for them to enter. Toni noted his name tag said Bradley. And the hall smelled of disinfectant and despair.

"Are there visitors for me?" a young man asked as he shuffled toward them in corduroy house shoes. His Spider-Man pajamas were crumpled, and the red color had faded to pink.

"They're not here for you, Teddy," Bradley growled. "Go back to the men's room."

"Okay." Teddy ran a hand through his dark hair that had a streak dyed white down the middle, making him resemble a skunk. He shuffled back down the hall.

"This way." Bradley led them to the right. "Sabrina will be in the women's rec room. We keep the men and women separated except at mealtime. It's better that way since we get the occasional sex addict."

Toni winced.

"Here you are." Bradley motioned to an open area, then strode back down the hallway.

A female nurse sat behind a counter, watching everyone. In the middle of the plain white room, there were two tables, surrounded by orange plastic chairs. More plastic chairs lined the three walls. A television, mounted high in a corner, played an animated movie with the volume turned down low. The air was stuffy and warm. Stifling.

Two middle-aged women sat along the wall, across from the television, staring dumbly at it. One's hand kept twitching, and the other one's mouth drooped open. Their eyes looked dead. Toni's heart squeezed in her chest.

In the corner, a young female patient sat beside a male visitor, her husband perhaps? They were both quiet, as if they no longer knew what to say to each other.

Toni's heart was already breaking when she spotted Sabrina. She was wearing flannel pajama bottoms and a blue T-shirt. Her hair, usually a bouncy and shiny blonde, was dull and frizzy. She sat at a table, swinging her feet back and forth as she studied a magazine. Her sneakers flopped loosely on her feet. The shoelaces had been removed.

As Toni moved closer, she realized it wasn't a magazine Sabrina was looking at, but a coloring book. She flipped through the pages, then stopped at a page that hadn't been colored yet. She removed a broken pink crayon from a plastic bin and started to color.

This was the ace student at NYU who had made the dean's list for the past six semesters? Toni squeezed her eyes shut. *I will not cry in front of her. I'll be strong.*

"I could kill her uncle," Carlos whispered.

Toni took a deep breath and pasted a smile on her face. "Hi, Sabrina!"

Bri turned toward them, her face blank, then she blinked. "Toni! Carlos!" She stood. "You came to see me."

"Of course we did." Toni gave her a hug. "We've been worried about you."

"You're looking good, *menina*." Carlos hugged her, then sat across from her at the table.

Toni sat next to her. "How have you been?"

"I'm okay." Bri held up her arm to show them the blue plastic ID band around her wrist. "I got promoted to blue today. I'm so glad not to be yellow anymore."

"What's wrong with yellow?" Toni asked.

"It's for suicidal patients." Bri selected a green crayon from the bin. "Not that I was suicidal."

Toni swallowed hard. "That's good," she whispered.

"They just put everyone on suicide watch when they first get here," Bri explained.

"I wonder why," Carlos muttered as he glanced around the bleak room.

"I was so lonely," Bri continued. "I had to eat all my meals alone, and I had to sit here by myself when the others went to the gym."

"Hi, Sabrina."

They turned to see Teddy shuffling into the room.

He cricked his head to the side. "You have visitors?"

"Teddy!" Bradley marched toward him. "How many times do I have to tell you to stay in the men's rec room?"

"Okay." Teddy wandered back down the hall.

"Crazy moron," Bradley muttered as he followed.

"I'm not crazy," Teddy protested.

Sabrina went back to coloring as if everything was normal. "I met Teddy at lunch today. I think he's lonesome. No one ever comes to visit him." She smiled at Toni. "I'm glad you came."

I will not cry. Toni smiled back. "I'm glad, too."

"Teddy's not crazy," Bri whispered. "He's just very sad. He was in a car accident with his girlfriend, and she died. He was driving, so he feels guilty."

Toni nodded. "It's terrible to feel like you've failed someone you love." And God help her, she was going to fail Sabrina if she didn't get her out of this place. "We want to get you back home."

"I'm trying to get better. I'm having delusions."

"You're not delusional," Toni insisted.

"I have to admit it if I'm going to get better. That's what my therapist says. Anyway, lots of people here are delusional." Bri smiled. "Even some of the guards. Last night, they said there was a giant black cat running around the courtyard."

Toni glanced at Carlos, but his face remained blank.

Bri took a purple crayon from the bin. "I have to color Jasmine's hair purple. They took all the black crayons away 'cause they were too depressing."

Toni stifled an urge to scream. How could anyone stay at this place and not get depressed? "Bri, I did what you asked. I went to Central Park to see if any vampires would come and attack me."

Bri shook her head while she colored. "Vampires aren't real."

"You're right," Carlos said quickly, then gave Toni a pointed look when she started to interrupt. "You should tell your uncle that you made a mistake. You were simply traumatized by the attack. But you're all better now, and he should let you out of here."

Toni knew that strategy wouldn't work. Bri would need her uncle's okay in order to be released, and he would never give it.

Bri dropped the purple crayon back into the bin. "Uncle Joe wants me to stay here until they get the right combination of meds for me. It might take a few weeks."

Or forever, Toni thought wryly. As long as Uncle Joe was in charge of Bri's future, she would have none.

Toni had wanted to help Bri by proving the existence of vampires, but so far, she'd failed to come up with any proof. And now she doubted Uncle Joe would acknowledge any proof. It simply wasn't in his best interest to ever let Bri out of this hospital.

A sense of panic grew in Toni as the minutes ticked by. Carlos asked mundane questions like what they'd eaten for supper. Toni was finding it hard to even breathe.

"Would you like to have this picture?" Bri asked as she finished coloring.

"Yes." Toni forced a smile.

Nurse Bradley strode toward them. "Visiting hours are over," he announced.

"Tomorrow we're making Christmas stockings and putting up a tree." Bri handed the picture to Toni. "Can you come back?"

"Of course. I mean, I'll try." Toni was afraid Uncle Joe would deny her access once he saw her name on the visitor sign-in sheet.

"Let's go." Bradley motioned impatiently.

The couple in the corner separated. The husband headed down the hall. The woman sank into her chair and silently began to cry.

"This way, please." Bradley glared at them.

Toni hugged her friend, then quickly walked away before Bri could see the tears in her eyes. She followed Carlos back into the foyer and winced when the heavy metal door shut with a final click.

They slowly put on their coats and gathered their belongings, so the visiting husband would leave before them. A few minutes after he exited, they started across the courtyard.

The cold air slapped Toni's face, bringing her a sense of urgency. "We have to get her out," she whispered.

"I know," Carlos replied. "I've been trying to come up with a plan all evening."

"Her uncle will never release her." Toni's voice rose in panic. "We'll have to—"

"Shhh," Carlos warned her. He motioned to the oak tree

and its massive branch that extended over the wall. "I could try to get her up that tree, but there's still the problem of getting her out of the ward. The damned place is locked up tighter than a nun in a chastity belt."

"We have to do something."

"I can't see a way out of here."

She grabbed Carlos's arm. "Don't say that! There's got to be a way." They just needed to get past the guards and the locked doors. "Oh my gosh, I know how to do it."

"How?" Carlos asked.

"We teleport her out."

"We can't do that."

"But we know someone who can."

"You're going to ask that vampire, Ian?" Carlos asked. "Are you sure he can be trusted?"

"I think so. I hope so." He'd offered to help her. And the more Toni thought about it, the more she knew it was the only way.

Toni insisted Carlos drive her straight back to Romatech. It was dark by the time they arrived. The guard at the entrance gate recognized her and waved them through.

Carlos stopped the car by the front door. "I know you want to talk to Ian alone, but leave me in the loop. This will require some planning."

"Okay." She pulled her knit cap off and fluffed up her hair. She wanted to look decent for her talk with Ian.

"Once Bri is out, we'll need a safe place to keep her. We can't just take her back to her apartment."

"Why not?" Toni snapped her eyeglasses into their case, then dropped them in her handbag. Her eyesight was a little fuzzy from a distance, but it would be fine for a close-up conversation. She pulled the visor down to check herself in the mirror.

"Toni, her uncle might suspect we're behind her disappearance and charge us with kidnapping."

That made her pause. She flipped the visor back up. "But Bri would come willingly with us."

"Are you sure? After all she's been through, do you expect her to trust the next vampire who comes along?"

"Well, I did." Toni winced. "But I had strong motivation. I was trying to help Bri." Tears threatened her once again. "We have to get her out of there."

"I agree. I don't like what those meds are doing to her. She's lost all her fight. She's not herself anymore."

"I know." Toni dragged in a shaky breath. She was barely retaining control over her emotions.

Carlos patted her arm. "It'll be all right, *menina*." He glanced in the rearview mirror. "What the hell is that?"

Toni glanced over her shoulder. The parking lot was well lit, and she spotted a short man, bundled up against the cold, trudging toward the front door of Romatech. He had a large black garbage bag slung over one shoulder. "He's carrying something kinda bulky."

"He?" Carlos glanced back, then shifted his gaze back to the mirror. "He doesn't show up in the mirror. All I see is a bag floating along in the air."

"Really?" Toni snapped down the visor to look in the mirror. Sure enough, the garbage bag was moving on its own. "That looks so weird. He must be a Vamp."

They sat in the car and watched the short man go through the front door.

"I wonder what he's got in the bag," Toni murmured.

Carlos snorted. "A dead body?"

Toni swatted him. "These Vamps aren't like that."

"You've known them for a week, Toni. How can you be sure what they're capable of?"

"They saved me when I was in trouble. Let's just hope they can save Sabrina." She opened the car door to get out. "I'll call you tomorrow."

Carlos waved, then drove back to the entrance gate.

Toni entered the large foyer with its gleaming marble

floors and huge potted plants that concealed surveillance cameras and metal detectors. She turned down the hallway on the left, headed for the MacKay security office.

The short Vamp with the stuffed garbage bag was half-way down the hall. He stopped at a door and punched in a number on the keypad.

The door across the hall opened, and Shanna hurried out. She stopped. "Laszlo! How good to see you."

"Mrs. Draganesti." The short man bowed slightly. "How do you do?"

"I'm fine." She moved closer to him. "What did you bring?"

He opened his bag, and she peered inside.

"Laszlo, these are wonderful! Thank you!"

He blushed. "I'd better get them inside." He scurried inside the door with his mysterious bag.

What the hell was going on? "What's up?" Toni motioned toward the locked door.

"Toni!" Shanna gave her a hug. "Have you seen my office yet?" She pointed at the dental office across the hall.

"No." Toni suspected Shanna was trying to change the subject.

"You need to make an appointment," Shanna continued. "All the MacKay employees get two free checkups every year. Well, actually, not free. Angus pays for it. Have you met Angus?"

Definitely trying to change the subject. "No, I haven't."

"Hi, Mommy! Hi, Toni!" Constantine called out.

Toni spotted him hovering about four feet off the floor in the room next to Shanna's office. This had to be his nursery. The doorway was partially closed off by the bottom half of a door. The top half was open, and Constantine had levitated so he could see them in the hallway.

"Hi, Constantine." Toni peered into his playroom. It was full of toys, books, stuffed animals, a twin bed, and some comfy chairs. "Wow, you have a lot of stuff."

"You can say that again," Radinka muttered as she returned some books to a bookcase. "You two had better hurry up, or you'll be late for Mass."

"Okay." Shanna leaned over the door to hug her son. "I'll see you afterward, sweetie." She started down the hall, then stopped when Toni didn't join her. "Aren't you coming?"

"I'm sorry, but I need to talk to Ian." Toni gestured toward the security office.

"Howard's the only one there right now." Shanna moved closer. "All the Vamp guys are at the chapel, making sure it's safe. They're worried the Malcontents will try something tonight."

"Like what?"

Shanna sighed. "They blew up our chapel last summer. Luckily, no one was there at the time."

Toni winced. "That's terrible."

"Yeah." Shanna glanced toward the nursery and lowered her voice. "That's why I'm leaving Tino in the nursery with Radinka. Just in case. Come on. You need to meet Father Andrew. He's wonderful."

Toni followed her down the hall and into the main foyer. "I don't know if I should go. I wasn't raised Catholic."

Shanna grinned. "Neither was I. But these old Vamps are so medieval, it's all they know. Did you know my husband was a monk?"

"I didn't know that." Toni followed Shanna into the right wing. She wondered how old Ian was exactly, but didn't want to draw attention to her interest in him. "Are all the guys medieval?"

"No. Gregori's young. Roman transformed him in 1993, when some Malcontents attacked him outside in the parking lot. Poor guy was just picking up his mom from work."

"How sad." Toni grimaced. But it did explain how he managed to have a mortal mother who was still alive. "What about Connor and . . . Ian?"

"They were transformed after some battle in Scotland in

the 1500s, changed the same night, so they've always been close. Roman changed Connor, and Angus changed Ian."

"They wanted to be changed?" Toni asked.

"Oh yeah. They were both mortally wounded. It was either be changed or die." Shanna entered a room on the right. "This is our fellowship hall, where everyone visits after church. I just want to make sure everything's ready."

The room had two long tables, both draped in long, white tablecloths. It was obvious that one was meant for Vamps, and the other one for mortals. The mortal table boasted a cheese/deli tray, a veggie and dip tray, a bowl of punch, and a plate of chocolate chip cookies.

The other table had two large bins filled with ice and bottles of blood. The microwave was in the center of the table, flanked by rows of glasses.

"Ladies, the service is starting," a male voice spoke from the hallway.

There was no mistaking that deep, lilting voice. Toni's heart fluttered in her chest. When she turned to face him, her heart did a bigger flip.

"We'll talk later." Shanna patted Toni on the arm, then hurried from the room.

Toni approached Ian, and her heart speeded up under his intense scrutiny. "I need to talk to you."

He raised his eyebrows. "Are ye ready to finally confess yer secrets?"

Her face heated. All the other Vamps had trusted her from the beginning. Only Ian had suspected her of a hidden agenda. "How do you know I have secrets?"

He leaned close and whispered, "Yer heart is racing. Yer cheeks are on fire." He smiled slowly. "And now yer eyes are flashing an angry, but lovely, shade of green."

"You're like a human lie detector." She glared at him. "It's very aggravating to lose the option of lying."

He chuckled as he curled a hand around her elbow. "They say confession is good for the soul."

The sound of singing drifted from the chapel. Deep, male voices. The Vamps were singing a hymn.

"Why does a Vamp worry about the state of his soul?" she whispered. "You could live forever."

"None of us live forever."

"So you're praying for salvation?" She guessed that made sense. Who would need redemption more than a vampire?

"I pray for many things, Toni." His hand slid down her arm, then lingered by her fingers. "I pray ye'll trust me with the entire truth."

And she would pray that he understood.

Chapter Fifteen

Ian found comfort in the old, familiar chants and prayers. Over the centuries, the world powers could change, technology advance, mortal friends pass away, but Mass remained much the same. And the scent of Christmas remained the same. He breathed deeply, enjoying the scent of fir tree garlands and lit Advent candles.

Tonight there was another scent, one that kept luring him away from holy thoughts. Type AB positive. His favorite flavor. It emanated from Toni, who sat beside him in the back row. She'd removed her jacket and folded it on her lap. Her hands clenched together so tightly her knuckles gleamed white. What had happened to make her desperate enough to reveal her secrets to him?

When he'd first wakened and realized she was gone, he'd checked her tracking device on a computer. She'd gone back to that psychiatric hospital. By the looks of her clenched hands and pale face, something at the hospital had upset her. Was it somehow connected to her taking the job as their guard?

Father Andrew began his homily, and Ian tried to

focus on the priest instead of the heavenly body next to him.

"As you know, I never reveal anything I hear during confession," Father Andrew began. "But I would like to speak tonight about a common thread I've heard many times, and each time I hear it, it grieves me greatly. Many of you believe you don't deserve happiness or love. You feel you are not worthy."

Ian heard Toni breathe in sharply.

"Whereas a mortal has one short lifetime to experience regret," the priest continued, "a Vamp can live much longer and rack up a greater amount of regret and guilt. Some of you believe you've taken the grand prize in unworthiness, that there is no hope for your soul. You fear God can never forgive you. And because of your self-condemnation, you're unable to forgive yourself."

Toni pressed a hand to her mouth. Ian saw her eyes were squeezed shut. What was wrong? He hoped she wasn't going to cry. He couldn't bear to see a woman cry.

"You know your past failures, your mistakes," Father Andrew said. "But know this, too—you are still children of the Heavenly Father, and your Father loves you."

A small noise came from Toni that sounded like a stifled whimper.

"Do not believe you are unworthy of love, for God loves you. And do not let your past sins torment you. If God can forgive you, why can you not forgive yourself?"

Toni jumped up and ran out the back door.

Ian stared at the closed door. Dammit to hell. Why would she be so upset? He'd seen her personnel file. She was only twenty-four years old. Her worst offense was a bloomin' traffic ticket. She was an angel compared to the bloody Vamps in this room, himself included.

Father Andrew droned on and on and showed no sign of stopping anytime soon. And Toni was off somewhere, crying.

He slipped out the door and followed the sound of her sniffles. She was sitting in the refreshment room, doubled over with her face in her hands.

"Toni, are ye all right?" Stupid question, he chided himself. The lass was crying.

She sat up and wiped her face. "I'm okay."

"What's wrong? Did the priest upset you?"

"I'm sure he means well." She stood and wandered toward the table of mortal food. "I'm sure he's right about forgiveness, but . . ."

Ian stepped closer to her. "But what?"

"I—I've never been able to forgive myself."

"Lass, what could ye have possibly done? Ye're so young and . . . innocent."

She turned toward him, and he winced at the sight of her tear-stained cheeks. "I—I let my grandmother die."

He hadn't expected that. "It must have been an accident."

"I didn't mean for it to happen." Tears streamed down her face.

He couldn't take it, so he pulled her into his arms and rubbed her back. "What happened?"

"I was in middle school, and by then, my grandmother's health wasn't very good. I learned to do the chores. And I was used to getting myself up in the morning, and fixing my lunch, and catching the bus. I always hugged Grandma before I left."

Ian could see that Toni had learned to be strong and independent at a young age.

"One night, Grandma was having trouble sleeping. I could hear her up a lot. But that morning, when I came in to say good-bye, she was sleeping well. I didn't want to wake her, so I went on to school. But when I came home that afternoon, she was still there." Toni stepped back and grabbed a napkin off the table to wipe her face, but the tears kept coming. "She died while I was gone."

"Sweetheart, she died naturally. It wasna yer fault."

"But I knew she'd been sick the night before. I keep thinking about what I should have done differently. If I had called 911 that morning, she might have lived. Even my mother said I'd done a lousy job of taking care of her. She wouldn't let me live with them after Grandma died. She sent me to a boarding school."

Ian winced. "Lass, I doona mean to offend, but yer mother is a bloomin' arse."

Toni blinked.

Apparently his observation had taken her by surprise. "Ye can believe me. I'm a bit of an expert when it comes to mums. I was fifteen when I was transformed. I thought I could go back home, but my mum wouldna accept me."

Toni's red-rimmed eyes widened. "Why not?"

"Och, how did she put it? I was a monstrous creature from hell. She feared if I got a wee peckish, I might slaughter my younger brothers and sisters."

"That's ridiculous! Anyone who knows you would know you could never hurt someone you love."

Her declaration filled his heart. And the way her eyes flashed with angry indignation, he thought he'd never seen a woman more beautiful. "I appreciate yer faith in me." He stepped closer. "Are ye all right now?"

She blew her nose in the napkin. "I think so. I'm really sorry about this. I've been an emotional wreck lately, and you keep seeing me at my worst."

"Nay, I think ye're at yer best."

She gave him a dubious look. "With my watery eyes and red nose?"

He wanted to kiss her watery eyes and red nose.

"Actually, I was referring to yer compassionate heart."

She snorted. "I'm not feeling very compassionate. I was just thinking that *your* mom was a bloomin' arse."

He chuckled. "At least we both survived."

"You know, when I first met you, I thought we were totally

different. Alive, dead." She motioned to herself, then him.
"Modern, old-fashioned. Intelligent, not so intelligent."

"Excuse me?"

She grinned. "I'm kidding. But I was wrong. We actually
have a lot in common."

"Ye mean our heartless mothers?"

"More than that. We share the same worries and fears.
That we're not worthy. That we'll fail someone we love." Her
face grew sad again.

He touched her face and smoothed his thumb over her
damp cheek. "Ye have more deep, dark secrets to tell me?"

"I'm afraid so."

"Och, ye're so deep."

"And dark." She smiled. "Thank you. I feel a lot better
now."

"Will ye tell me yer full name?"

She winced. "That's too dark."

"Lass, it canna be that bad." He touched her other cheek,
so her face was cradled in his hands. He could hear her heart
racing. He moved closer.

She didn't back away.

He dragged his thumb along her jaw. Her mouth opened
slightly, and she licked her lips. Ah, he wanted to feel that.
He slid his thumb over her bottom lip, gliding over the moisture. She drew in a sharp breath.

"Your eyes are red again," she whispered.

"I know." He moved closer till his chest was grazing hers.

Her gaze drifted down to his mouth. The napkin fell from
her hand and fluttered to the floor. Slowly she raised a hand,
then touched the dent in his chin.

It was simple movement, but he interpreted it as permission. She'd pushed the yes button, and that was all that mattered. To hell with the rules, to hell with reason.

He held her face and kissed her lightly once, twice. She
leaned toward him, and his passion broke loose with a wild,
devouring kiss. He pulled her close, one hand at the back of

her neck, the other at her waist. He pulled her so close, her feet came off the ground. She wrapped her arms around his neck and kissed him back.

A hunger he'd kept restrained for nights was unleashed. He couldn't taste her enough. Her lips, her tongue. He explored her mouth and nibbled her lips. She was sweet; she was trembling; she was clutching him tight. And he wanted more. It felt like he'd wanted her for centuries.

He trailed kisses down her neck, then tickled her with his tongue on a path to her ear. She shivered.

"Toni," he whispered, then drew her earlobe into his mouth.

She moaned and ran her fingers into his hair. "Ian."

He smoothed his hands down her back, then cupped her bottom and gently squeezed. He was returning to her mouth for more kissing when he heard someone clearing his throat.

He froze. Froze with his hands planted firmly on Toni's rump. This was bad. He glanced over his shoulder. Connor stood in the doorway. He'd averted his face, but his jaw was shifting as he ground his teeth.

Ian released Toni and stepped back. She glanced at him, then at Connor, her eyes wide.

Ian cleared his throat. "This was my fault. I take full responsibility for it."

"No," Toni whispered and shook her head.

"I'll have a word with you in private, Ian." Connor turned and strode down the hall.

He tried to give Toni a reassuring smile. "I'll be right back."

She didn't look very reassured. He hurried into the hallway to catch up with Connor.

Halfway to the foyer, Connor opened a door to a conference room. "This will do."

Ian glanced back. People were leaving the chapel and wandering into the refreshment room. He hoped Toni would be all right.

"Close the door behind you," Connor said quietly as he marched to the end of a long conference table.

Ian shut the door. "I will ask ye no' to reprimand Toni. I instigated the . . . incident, and I take full responsibility for it."

"How noble. I wouldna expect less from you." Connor stopped at the head of the table and rested a hand on the back of a chair. "But I wasna born yesterday. 'Twas quite obvious that she was no' being forced."

A thrill shot through Ian, and he stifled a grin. It was true—she had been willing. More than willing. She'd kissed him back. She'd moaned with pleasure. She wanted him. And he wanted to shout with joy.

"She willfully broke the rules." Connor rubbed his brow. "I have no choice but to fire her."

"No!" Ian walked toward him. "She was crying when I found her. She was verra upset, and I took advantage."

"Ian." Connor regarded him sternly. "What has come over you lately? Ye've been back less than a week, and ye have a mob of females hounding you. Hundreds of phone calls and e-mails. Women camped out on the sidewalk. I heard ye dated fifty ladies in one night, and then there was that interview."

"Things have gotten a little out of control, but—"

"More than a little!" Connor's eyes flashed with anger. "Is it no' enough to have hundreds of women throwing themselves at you? Why would ye seduce the one woman ye canna have? Is it because she is forbidden?"

"Nay. I guarded Roman's harem for fifty years. I never misbehaved with any of them. Toni is . . . different. Special."

"Unemployed," Connor added wryly.

"Ye canna fire her. We need her."

"Dammit, Ian." Connor pounded a fist on the back of the chair. "How can ye expect me to ignore the rules?"

Ian took a deep breath. He had to come up with something fast, or Connor could be erasing her memory tonight. "What if the Malcontents already know she's working for us? If we fire her and erase her memory, she would be totally defenseless against an attack."

Connor frowned. "Ye make a good point, but 'tis based on an assumption."

"We canna gamble with her life. She's been doing an excellent job for us, and she can still do it. I willna interfere with her duties."

Connor paced away, deep in thought. "I hired her for a probationary period of two weeks. I could let her complete those two weeks before making a final decision." He glanced at Ian. "Can ye keep yer hands off her for another week?"

He wasn't sure he could for thirty minutes. "I can try."

"*Try?* Have ye no' heard of restraint, man?"

Ian gritted his teeth. The more he told himself he couldn't have Toni, the more he wanted her.

Connor sighed. "I'll delay my decision for another week." He headed for the door. "Meanwhile, if ye care for the lass, ye'll bloody well leave her alone."

"I do care for her, but . . . do ye no' understand how I feel? Have ye never felt the fierceness of . . . longing?"

A sad look came over Connor's face. "Aye, it is fierce. It rages like a wildfire, but leaves you with naught but ashes." He left the room.

What had happened to Connor to make him such a pessimist? Ian knew that a relationship between a mortal and Vamp rarely worked. Eventually they broke up or the mortal agreed to change over. Shanna had agreed to become a Vamp sometime in the future. Did he really want to involve Toni in a relationship where he'd have to suck her dry till she was dead, so he could change her?

Connor was right. If he really cared for her, which he did, he'd leave her be. He'd let her find love with her own kind. And he would keep looking for love among the Vamps.

* * *

"What's wrong?" Shanna asked.

Toni sighed. She knew she looked like a mess. How on earth had Ian found her attractive? She filled a plate with cheese cubes, carrot sticks, and broccoli, and what the heck, a few chocolate chip cookies. "I'm doing my Rudolph-the-red-nosed-reindeer impersonation."

Shanna handed her a cup of punch. "Are you unhappy with your job here?"

"No." She bit into a cookie.

The fellowship hall was filling up fast with churchgoers. Toni hated for everyone to see her swollen, red eyes, but she didn't want to run off just yet. She still needed to talk to Ian. "I have a close friend who's in the hospital. I just came from visiting her, and I was all smiles while I was there, but now . . ."

"Now the stress has caught up with you," Shanna observed. "I'm so sorry. If you need some time off, I'm sure we can arrange it."

"You're very kind." Unfortunately, she might have lots of time off very soon. Connor was probably going to fire her. Fired for kissing a vampire. Who would have known her life could be so risqué? But she'd known it was against the rules.

Would she do it again? In a heartbeat.

It had been the most phenomenal kiss of her life. Not one of those fumbling ones like she'd had in the past where she'd spent the entire kiss wondering if she was doing it properly, or wishing like hell that the guy knew how to do it properly. There'd been no wondering or wishing at all. She'd simply been swept away into a glorious daze of pure sensation. It was the kind of kiss she'd always dreamed of.

And Ian was the romantic hero she'd always dreamed of. Strong, but sweetly vulnerable. An endearing mixture of pride and uncertainty. Bold enough to kiss her and damn the consequences. Exciting, noble, clever, sexy—perfect in every way. Except one. He was a vampire.

"Shanna, can I ask you a personal question?"

"Sure."

"I was wondering how you . . . well, is it difficult being in a relationship with a vampire?"

"Ah." Shanna sipped some punch. "I suppose it depends on the vampire. I lucked out with Roman." She looked around the room, and Toni could tell the instant she spotted her husband. Her eyes softened.

Roman must have felt her gaze or heard her say his name, for he turned away from his conversation with Father Andrew and smiled at her.

"He's the love of my life," Shanna whispered. "And Constantine, too. I'm totally amazed by them."

"But how do you handle the different hours?"

"Tino and I keep late hours. We stay up to one or so in the morning, so we can spend time with Roman. Then we sleep late in the morning. I take dental appointments from three in the afternoon till about nine at night, so I can see both mortals and Vamps. It's a bit of a challenge, fitting in family and a career, but it's that way for all women, so I don't think my situation is all that strange."

"I see what you mean." Toni popped a piece of ranch-dipped broccoli in her mouth.

"So which hunky Vamp guy are you interested in?"

She nearly choked. Her eyes watered, and she gulped down some punch. "I didn't say I was."

Shanna grinned. "Never mind. I think I know who."

"It was a hypothetical question," Toni insisted. "I was just wondering how a Vamp and mortal could make it work, and obviously, you and Roman are doing it well, so I asked. That's all."

"Uh-huh." Shanna gave her a knowing look. "Well, hypothetically speaking, I think he's a great guy, and you'd be crazy to pass him by."

Toni wondered if she was referring to Ian, but didn't dare ask. "I don't mean to be a downer, but I just don't see how it can last, not when the mortal continues to age, and the Vamp doesn't."

Shanna nodded. "It was a tough decision, and not one I took lightly." She rubbed a hand over the bump where her second child was growing. "I've decided to change over eventually, but I wanted to wait till the children are a bit older."

Toni gaped. "You're going to become one of them?"

Shanna's eyes twinkled in merriment. "Ooh, scary! They're not monsters, you know. I realize it might take a while for you to see that. It took me a while. Well, only about a week." She laughed. "I fell for Roman so fast."

Toni could relate to that. There was something so special about Ian. He'd intrigued her from the start. And she could recognize herself in him. If he had to come up with four morning affirmations, she figured his would be identical to hers.

"I feel so fortunate to be a part of their world," Shanna continued. "I have the best husband and most wonderful little boy—"

"He's gone!" A shout came from the hallway, along with the sound of running. Radinka halted at the doorway, gasping for air. "Tino! He's gone!"

Roman strode toward her. "He's not in the nursery?"

"Oh my God." Shanna spilled punch as she set down her cup. She rushed toward Radinka. "What happened?"

"I don't know. I only turned my back on him for a second. I don't—"

"Dougal, Phineas, go check—" Roman started to give an order, but the two guards had already zoomed out the door.

"I'll take the east wing. Ye take the west," Dougal shouted at Phineas.

"Tell Connor!" Roman yelled after them. "And Howard!"

All the other Vamps and Father Andrew rushed from the room to help with the search.

"Oh my God." Shanna clutched Roman's arm. "What if he was kidnapped? What if the Malcontents—"

He squeezed her shoulder. "We won't panic yet. He might have just levitated and climbed over the door."

"I've told him a million times not to do that," Shanna said.

"From now on, I'm stationing a guard at the nursery," Roman said quietly. "I'll check the parking lot."

Shanna paled. "Don't go alone. This could be a trap."

Roman zoomed down the hall, shouting for Connor. Shanna and Radinka strode down the hall, calling out Constantine's name.

A wave of panic froze Toni. Would the Malcontents kidnap a child? If they teleported away with Tino, how would Roman ever find him? She wished she could do something to help, but she didn't know what. For the first time, she actually wished she was a Vamp so she could move faster and fight better.

She stepped forward and trod on something. It was the napkin she'd dropped before kissing Ian. She leaned over to pick it up and spotted something odd. The tablecloth had moved.

As the shouts for Constantine grew dimmer in the distance, Toni heard a small, whimpering sound. She circled to the back of the table and dropped to her knees. She lifted the bottom edge of the tablecloth.

Constantine gasped. He was hugging his knees to his chest, and his pink cheeks were wet with tears.

"Tino," she whispered. "How did you get here?"

"I don't know," he wailed and covered his face. "Mommy's going to be mad at me."

"Honey, no." Toni pulled him out from under the table and held him in her arms. "They're just scared. We need to tell them you're all right."

"No!" Tino clutched her shoulders. "Mommy told me not to leave the nursery. She'll be mad at me."

"She only sounds upset 'cause she's so scared. Believe me, she'll be thrilled to know you're all right."

He sniffled. "They won't be mad?"

"No, honey. They love you so much." Toni stood, still holding the little boy, then strode into the hallway. "He's here! Tino's fine!"

The Vamps must have heard her first, for Dougal and Phineas zoomed toward her. Connor, Ian, and Roman zipped toward them a few seconds later.

"Daddy!" Tino reached for Roman, who grabbed him and held him tight.

The other Vamps returned with Howard Barr and Father Andrew trailing behind. There were shouts of delight and slaps on the back.

"You found him?" Roman asked Toni. "I can't thank you enough."

"Way to go, Toni!" Phineas gave her a high five.

"Well done." Connor nodded at her.

She felt her face heat up. Was he going to fire her now? She glanced at Ian. Passion flared in his eyes, then he turned away.

"Constantine!" Shanna ran toward them, followed by a gasping Radinka.

Roman zoomed to them quickly, and Shanna flung herself at her husband, sandwiching their little boy between them.

"Thank God." Shanna hugged him tight.

"I was so scared." Radinka's eyes filled with tears. "I could never forgive myself if anything happened to you." She touched the boy's cheek.

They all walked back to where the crowd was gathered.

"Who found him?" Shanna asked. "Where was he?"

"Toni," several Vamps answered at once as they smiled at her.

Her heart expanded with a warm feeling. For the first time in her life, she felt like she belonged to a whole family.

"Oh, thank you." Shanna hugged her.

"He was afraid you'd be mad at him," Toni whispered. "I found him hiding under the table." She motioned with her head toward the fellowship hall.

"Oh my goodness." Shanna turned toward her son. "How did you get in there without anyone seeing you?"

"I don't know. Can I have a cookie?"

"Tino," Roman spoke quietly. "You've been told not to leave the nursery alone."

"I didn't mean to." Constantine wiped his nose. "I was just thinking about you and Mommy and how much I wanted to be with you. Then it was so dark, and I couldn't see anything. Then I was there behind the table, and I fell down 'cause I was dizzy. And then I heard everybody shouting, and I thought you were mad at me."

"Oh my God." Shanna pressed a hand to her mouth.

"Everything went black?" Roman asked his son. "You were in the nursery, then suddenly you were here?"

When Constantine nodded, everyone exchanged shocked looks.

"Tino, you teleported." Roman looked at everyone and grinned. "My son can teleport!"

The Vamps cheered. Toni's mouth fell open.

Shanna gasped for air, her face very pale. "Oh God, this is terrible."

"Are you mad at me, Mommy?" Constantine asked.

"No, no." She hugged him, then gave her husband a pointed look. "Can you teach him to control this?"

"Yes," Roman assured her. "It'll be all right."

"Come." Radinka escorted Shanna into the fellowship hall. "I think you'd better sit down."

Shanna winced. "A toddler who can vanish at will?"

Everyone filed into the fellowship hall, and Roman set his son next to Shanna. He returned a few seconds later with plates of food for both of them. Constantine happily munched on cookies.

Radinka looked around. "Where's Gregori?"

"I haven't seen him," Toni replied.

Radinka huffed. "That rascal. He told me he would come

to church." She marched to the mortal table to fill a plate with food.

Toni edged toward Ian. "Am I still employed?"

He glanced toward Connor, who was busy congratulating Roman. "Aye, for now. The final decision will be made in a week."

Toni exhaled with relief. A week would be enough time for them to rescue Sabrina. Then it would be okay if she lost her job. But she still dreaded having her memory wiped. Carlos could fill her in on the facts, but he couldn't tell her how she had felt while she'd lived with the Vamps. She would forget how wonderful it had felt to be a part of their family. And she would forget all about Ian.

"If I lose this job, I can live with that. But I don't want to lose my memory."

Ian frowned at his shoes. "I'll do what I can for you. But it would be better for us not to be alone."

Toni swallowed hard. He was backing off. Was he doing it to save her job? Or had the kiss not meant that much to him? She could have sworn there'd been a ton of passion. "I still need to talk to you."

He glanced at Connor. "This is not a good time. I—I promised Vanda I would go to the club tonight."

She gritted her teeth. "Still looking for the perfect lady Vamp to share eternity with?"

He swore under his breath. "I have never lied to you, Toni. I said from the beginning that I wanted a Vamp."

"Right. 'Cause they're so superior."

"Better suited," he corrected her.

"Fine. But I still need your help with something really important. When you find some time in your busy dating schedule, let me know." She marched from the room before she succumbed to an urge to slap his handsome face.

Chapter Sixteen

Jedrek Janow hid behind a large maple tree, on the grounds at Romatech. He'd instructed Yuri to park a mile away from the entrance gate. Then they'd teleported onto the grounds and zipped through the woods to the main building.

"The parking lot looks completely covered with surveillance cameras," Yuri whispered. He crouched next to Nadia behind a snow-capped bush. "And the guards sweep through these woods every fifteen minutes. We can't stay long."

"We don't need to." Jedrek eyed the number of cars in the parking lot. There were more Vamps here than he'd expected. "Are they workaholics or holding an orgy?"

"They have a mortal priest who performs Mass for them on Sunday night," Yuri said.

"And you forgot to mention that to me?" Jedrek ground out between clenched teeth.

"We thought they stopped," Yuri protested. "They did stop for a while. We blew up their chapel last August."

So the sweet little bottle-sucking morons had started going to church again. They made him want to puke. "I hope they're praying for salvation. They'll need it." He glanced at Yuri's long duffel bag. "Get the RPG ready."

"Yes, Master." Yuri unzipped the bag and carefully removed the shoulder-launched rocket weapon. He loaded a grenade.

"I heard the Vamps have a party after Mass," Nadia whispered. "They give out free Chocolood."

"And how would you know that?" Jedrek asked softly.

She eyed him warily. "I never went. It was some of the other girls in the coven. They were curious."

"Stupid cows," Jedrek grumbled. "Tell me, Nadia, have you ever watched a vampire burn to death?"

She shook her head.

"Answer me."

"No, Master. I have not."

"You're in for a special treat. You will show your gratitude to me later tonight."

She hugged her knees to her chest. "Yes, Master."

He smiled. She was bending to his will now.

Yuri lifted the rocket-propelled grenade to his shoulder. "Ready."

"Good. We'll wait for them to return to their cars, then blow a few of them up," Jedrek said. "And when the survivors are running about like frightened little mice, we'll locate MacPhie or Draganesti and get the information we need." His attention snapped back to Romatech when the front door burst open.

A lone figure ran out.

"Jackpot," Jedrek whispered. It was Roman Draganesti. He was running around the parking lot, looking frantically for something. "The fool is unarmed. Take him."

Yuri set the RPG down and pulled a long silver chain

from his duffel bag. He wrapped the ends around his heavily gloved hands.

Just then, two sword-wielding Highlanders zoomed out the front door, headed straight for Draganesti.

Yuri hesitated.

"Is there a problem?" Jedrek asked dryly. He recognized the Scotsmen as Connor Buchanan and Ian MacPhie.

"That's Buchanan," Yuri said. "He's the one who killed Sashenka."

"Then you should be eager to avenge him."

Yuri slowly drew his sword. "I'll be outnumbered."

Jedrek rolled his eyes. He was surrounded by cowards. He unsheathed his own sword. "Keep Buchanan busy. I'll grab MacPhie and teleport away with him."

Just then, Draganesti halted and cocked his head toward Romatech. He raced back inside, followed by the two Scotsmen. The door banged shut.

"You fool," Jedrek hissed at Yuri. "Your cowardice ruined our chance."

Yuri hung his head.

Nadia shivered. "It's cold. Can we go home now?"

"I still don't know what caused Ian MacPhie to age," Jedrek grumbled.

"Why do we need to know?" Nadia asked. "Nobody wants to age."

Jedrek wrapped a hand around her neck and squeezed. "You dare to question me?"

"I was wrong. Forgive me, Master."

Jedrek released her. His real concern was how Draganesti had managed to invade their Brooklyn headquarters during the day. He just had a sneaking suspicion that MacPhie's sudden aging was somehow connected. He wanted answers. Tonight.

After a few minutes, a lone car pulled into the parking lot. A young man emerged from the black Lexus. Jedrek recognized him from the photos he'd studied. This was Gregori Holstein, vice president at Romatech and good friend to Roman Draganesti.

"He'll know their secrets." Jedrek turned to Nadia. "Talk to him. Distract him, so Yuri can take him."

"Yes, Master." She edged toward the parking lot.

Gregori removed a stuffed black garbage bag from the trunk of his car. He was singing to himself, repeating two words. *Staying alive, staying alive.* How fitting.

"Teleport him here," Jedrek ordered. "I want some time with him."

"Yes, Master." Yuri crept toward the parking lot, keeping low.

"Excuse me." Nadia approached Gregori.

He turned toward her. "Miss, what are you doing here?"

"Is this where they have the party with free food?"

"Yes." Gregori looked at her closely. "Are you all right, miss?"

"I'm so . . . very hungry." Nadia stumbled to the side.

Gregori dropped his garbage sack and caught her. Yuri zoomed up behind him to grab him, and a second later, they both materialized next to Jedrek.

"What the—" Gregori grimaced as Jedrek looped the silver chain around his bare neck. Gregori's skin sizzled where the silver burned it.

"The silver will keep you from teleporting away." Jedrek passed the ends of the chain to Yuri. "I have a few questions."

"Go to hell," Gregori growled.

"He sent out a telepathic message," Nadia warned him as she joined them in the woods.

"I heard it." Jedrek grabbed Gregori's head and plunged into a swift and ruthless psychic assault. It was a trick he'd learned over the centuries. He'd accidentally destroyed a few brains before he'd perfected his technique.

Gregori stiffened, trying to resist the invasion, but he was a young vampire, easy prey for Jedrek. He swept through Gregori's memories like flipping through a scrapbook, until he found the one he wanted.

A short Vamp in a white lab coat was talking to Draganesti. "The results are clear, sir. For every day you take the Stay-Awake drug, you will age a year. I recommend you stop using it immediately."

"That's why he turned gray?" Gregori asked.

"Silver," a blonde woman corrected him. "Roman, I agree with Laszlo. I don't want you to take the drug anymore."

"But you need help during the day with the baby," Roman protested.

"Master," Yuri hissed. "They're coming!"

Jedrek noted the guards pouring into the parking lot. He released Gregori, and the Vamp slumped forward, held up by the silver chain around his neck. "Shove him back to the parking lot."

Yuri yanked the chain free and pushed Gregori toward the parking lot. The injured Vamp stumbled toward the parked cars just as the guards zoomed toward him.

Jedrek grabbed the RPG and rested it on his shoulder. He selected the car closest to Gregori and the Vamp guards. He smiled as he pulled the trigger.

Toni was sitting in the security office with Howard Barr, silently ruminating over Ian's pigheaded behavior, when Howard jumped to his feet.

"Shit!" He punched the alarm, then ran to the stash of weapons. He stuffed a pistol in his belt.

"What?" Toni scanned the monitors, but couldn't see well without her contacts.

"Someone kidnapped Gregori from the parking lot!" Howard charged out the door with swords and pistols.

"Oh my gosh." Toni threw on her jacket and stuffed a

Taser and some wooden stakes in her pockets. Her heart raced. It was time to face her demons. She sprinted down the hall.

The Vamps, naturally faster, had already grabbed weapons from Howard and zoomed outside. Shanna was in the foyer, trying to hold a wriggling Constantine and comfort Radinka at the same time.

"I don't care what they said, I have to go out there!" Radinka rushed to the front door.

Toni beat her there. "Stay behind me." She flung open the door and dashed outside.

Boom! An explosion ripped through a car. Pieces of metal and glass shot outward while flames and smoke burst upward into the night sky.

Toni halted in shock. Behind her, Radinka screamed. Constantine started crying.

Toni walked forward slowly. An odd, echoing noise buzzed in her ears, making the screams and shouts seem far away, and though she knew she should move faster, her body wasn't cooperating. A car was on fire, but with all the parked cars nearby, more explosions could happen any second. Heat from the fire lapped at her face. Smoke cleared, and she saw bodies lying on the pavement.

Something snapped inside her, and suddenly she could run. "Ian!" She charged forward, her boots crunching on shattered glass. Where was he?

"Gregori!" Radinka ran to her son and collapsed beside him. He lifted a bloody hand to her face.

Toni gasped, then coughed as smoke invaded her lungs. Her eyes stung as she desperately searched for a red and green plaid kilt. "Ian!"

He rose to his knees on the glass-strewn pavement, then slowly stood. Blood trickled down his legs.

"Ian!" She ran to him and cried out when he straightened. His face was torn and bleeding.

She clutched his shoulders. "Oh, Ian. Your beautiful face." Tiny shards of glass were embedded in his skin.

"Careful, ye'll cut yerself," he whispered. "Go back. It's no' safe here."

"I don't care." She plucked a shard of glass from his sweater.

"I'm sorry I was rude to you," he said. "I really doona want to date anyone else."

"That's good." Tears filled her eyes. "I'm afraid I'm becoming very . . . selfish where you're concerned."

His smile looked a bit gruesome with all the blood on his face. "Can ye help the wounded get back inside?"

She looked around and saw that most of the Vamps had risen to their feet and were grabbing their weapons.

Wincing, Ian leaned over to retrieve his sword. "I need to check the grounds. They could still be here."

"You're not in any shape to fight."

"They're only flesh wounds." He flexed his bloody hand around the hilt of his sword. "Dougal, Phineas, come with me!"

The three bloodied warriors dashed toward the woods.

Connor lifted Gregori in his arms and strode back to Romatech, Radinka jogging alongside them. Roman helped Howard Barr to his feet.

"I can walk." Howard limped toward the front door with a slash in one leg.

Shanna ran to Roman, still holding Constantine in her arms. Other than a few scrapes, Roman looked fine.

"Hurry back inside," Roman warned them. "There could be more explosions."

In the distance, sirens wailed.

Toni wondered how they would explain this to the police. She glanced around the parking lot. It wouldn't do to have swords or wooden stakes lying about. She spotted a black garbage bag on the ground next to a black Lexus.

She peeked inside. Video games? Had Gregori brought these to work? They were all brand-new and unopened.

"I'll take that." Dougal grabbed the bag and zoomed to the front door.

"But—" Toni jumped when Ian suddenly appeared beside her. "What's the deal with the sack of toys?"

"A secret Santa thing." Ian ushered her toward the front door. "The woods are clear, but we could tell where they'd been hiding."

"Yeah, man." Phineas dashed up to them. "The freakin' cowards teleported away."

Toni winced at the blood on Phineas's face. "You two need some medical attention."

"Roman and Laszlo can patch us up," Ian said.

They entered the foyer and found everyone headed to a waiting room. Toni glanced down the hall and spotted Dougal with the garbage sack of video games. He was opening the locked door across from the nursery.

"Come." Ian ushered her into the waiting room.

Father Andrew was praying with Radinka. Others were sitting silently as if the full force of shock had finally overcome them.

Connor was pacing back and forth, with Constantine following him, mimicking Connor's gait. When the little boy spotted Toni, he ran up to her with his arms raised. She picked him up and gave him a hug.

"Roman and Shanna are in the operating room with Gregori," Connor explained. "He was hit the worst."

"Will he be all right?" Toni realized Constantine had closed his eyes and was falling asleep on her shoulder.

"He has some major cuts and burns," Connor said, "but if he makes it till sunrise, he'll be able to heal during his death-sleep."

The operating room door opened, and Roman and Shanna stepped out.

"Gregori will be fine," Roman announced, and everyone sighed with relief.

Radinka rushed forward. "Can I see him?"

Roman nodded. "He's conscious. Laszlo's giving him a blood transfusion."

After Radinka went into the operating room, Roman moved toward Connor and Ian and lowered his voice. "Some bad news. Gregori said a Malcontent did a Vulcan mind meld on him, whatever that is, and the Malcontents now know about the Stay-Awake drug."

"Then they'll know ye're the inventor," Connor said. "I want to take you and yer family into hiding tonight."

Roman frowned. "Very well. But I want to tend the wounded first and deal with the police."

"Howard can deal with the police. We're leaving as soon as possible," Connor ordered. He turned to Ian. "Ye'll be in charge here."

"But what about the Christmas Ball?" Shanna asked.

Connor shrugged. "'Tis no' important."

"Of course it is," Shanna protested. "Everyone's coming. We have to do it, Roman."

"I'm more concerned about your safety—"

"We'll be safe," Shanna interrupted. "Angus and Emma are coming. And Jean-Luc, Zoltan, Giacomo—they'll all be here. You can't get any safer than that."

Roman exchanged a glance with Connor. "She makes a good point. We'll have a small army here."

"And I refuse to let the Malcontents destroy our Christmas," Shanna argued. "If we cancel, it'll look like we're scared of them."

Connor hesitated. "They could still try to infiltrate the party. And they would target Roman for capture because he knows how to make that damned drug."

"It's a costume ball," Shanna said. "They would have trouble recognizing him." Her face lit up. "I know! We have a hundred Santa Claus costumes. All the men can wear the same costume. It'll totally confuse them."

Roman grinned. "I like it."

A hundred Santa Claus costumes? Toni wondered. Why would a bunch of Vamps have Santa costumes? Was it somehow related to what Ian had called the secret Santa thing?

Connor nodded slowly. "'Tis crazy enough it might just work. But we're still leaving tonight. We'll come back for the ball on Tuesday."

"Agreed." Roman was halfway back to the operating room when Dougal opened the waiting room door.

"Roman, the police are here."

"Howard will handle it," Connor said. "Where is he?"

"Laszlo was bandaging his leg." Roman peered inside the operating room. "Howard, are you done? The police are here."

"I'm on it." Howard limped across the waiting room to join Dougal in the hallway.

Roman's gaze wandered over the Vamps in the waiting room. "Phineas, you're next." He strode into the operating room with Phineas following him.

"Come on, Connor. I'll look at your cuts." Shanna ushered the Scotsman to the operating room.

"Ye're a dentist, no' a doctor," Connor grumbled.

"If I can pull teeth, I can pull the glass out of your face." She shoved him inside and glanced back. "You're next, Ian."

Toni winced. "That's going to be fun."

Radinka left the operating room, smiling. "Gregori's going to be just fine. Here, let me take the little one and put him to bed." She took the sleeping Constantine in her arms and left the room.

"Ye should get some sleep, too," Ian told Toni. "Ye've had a rough day."

"It wasn't all bad." Her gaze wandered to his mouth. Be-

tween the terrible hospital visit and the awful explosion in
the parking lot, there had been a glorious kiss.

Hopefully, Ian would know what she was referring to,
since she didn't dare mention it in a room full of Vamps
with super-powered hearing.

He stepped closer. "Ye doona regret it? Ye called the first
one a mistake."

"I was confused. I'm still confused." She shook her head.
"I don't know what to make of all this. And I still need to
talk to you. It's really important."

"Ye're ready to spill yer secrets?"

"After they take care of your cuts."

"I'm fine." He glanced around the room. "No' here. Come
on."

He led her from the room.

Chapter Seventeen

Ian strode down the hallway. "Ladies' or gents'?"

"Excuse me?" Toni asked.

"Which restroom do ye prefer? I want to wash up a bit."

"Oh. Ladies', I guess. If you don't mind."

He smiled. "As long as it's empty." He pushed open the door to the ladies' restroom. "Hello?"

Toni followed him inside and looked under the stalls.

"Romatech is fairly empty on Sunday night. Just a few people who come to Mass." He turned on a water faucet and washed his hands in the sink.

She stood behind him. "You're not in the mirror. I can see myself like you're not even there. It's so creepy."

"Thank you." He cupped water in his hands and splashed it on his face. Blood swirled around the sink. "Now tell me yer secrets." He yanked paper towels from the dispenser and pressed them to his face.

"Careful," she warned him. "You don't want to push any glass further in."

"Obviously I canna see what I'm doing." He tossed the towels in the trash.

"Here, let me." She dampened some paper towels and folded them into a pad. Then she gingerly patted his brow.

"Yer secrets?"

"All right." She plucked a shard of glass from his hair and tossed it in the trash. "After my grandmother died when I was thirteen, I was shipped off to a boarding school in Charleston. I was miserable until I met Sabrina."

"Yer roommate?"

"Yes. She came to school after both her parents died in a small plane crash. She'd been an only child, so she was really alone. At first I just thought it was cool that there was someone there who was more miserable than me. But then I got to know her, and we became best friends. More like sisters, really."

"Aye." Ian could relate. Connor and Angus had always been like older brothers to him.

Toni threw the bloodied paper towels in the trash and made a fresh pad. She dabbed at his cheeks. "Sabrina and I came up with a master plan for our future, and we've been working on it for years. You know how some celebrities adopt kids from foreign countries?"

"Aye."

"We plan to do that on a bigger scale. We'll run an orphanage that's a real loving environment, like the family we always wanted. And we'll rescue kids from around the world. I've been studying business and sociology so I can run the orphanage, and Sabrina's getting a master's in education so she can run the school. And Carlos already has some orphans for us."

This was not what Ian had expected. It was a huge undertaking. "Ye'll need a great deal of money."

Toni carefully wiped his chin. "Sabrina's parents left her a huge inheritance. Eighty-five million."

Ian's eyebrows rose.

"She can only inherit the full amount once she graduates from college. Her parents didn't want her to be a useless trust fund baby."

Ian nodded slowly, although his mind was racing. If Toni had such big plans, why was she here, working as a guard? And she certainly didn't intend to stay. It would be terribly selfish of him to try to keep her here when she had such a noble plan for her future.

"Everything was going according to plan till last Sunday," Toni continued. "Sabrina was attacked in Central Park. She ended up in the hospital with cracked ribs, contusions, and . . . bite marks."

Ian inhaled sharply. "Malcontents."

"Yes. She was hysterical when the police questioned her. She claimed she'd been attacked by vampires."

"Those fools. They should have erased her memory."

Toni's eyes widened. "You think it's all right, what they did?"

"No, of course not. But any vampire, good or bad, knows there is nothing more important than keeping our existence a secret."

Toni winced as she threw away the dirty paper towels. She pulled more towels from the dispenser. "Let's clean up your knees."

She started to kneel, but Ian levitated till his knees were even with the sink. "It'll be easier this way."

"Oh." She glanced up at him. "This is weird."

"Thank you. Back to yer story . . ."

"Right." She gently tugged his bloody knee socks down. "Sabrina's trust is handled by her aunt and uncle. Her uncle's a psychiatrist, and he diagnosed her as psychotic and delusional. He put her in a mental ward."

"She's the one at Shady Oaks Psychiatric Hospital?"

"Yes." Toni's eyes flashed with anger. "Her uncle wants her money, so he'll make sure she's never released. Carlos and I went to see her tonight, and it was awful."

Ian lowered himself to the floor. "Ye went there before Mass?" No wonder her emotions had been so raw.

Toni nodded. "I can't fail her like I did Grandma. I've got to get her out of there."

He squeezed her hand. "And ye thought ye would need my help? Is that why ye took the job as my guard?"

"I do need your help, but that's not exactly how things happened. After Sabrina was attacked, she asked me to find the vampires who attacked her, to prove she wasn't delusional."

Ian stiffened. "Ye purposely went to the park to be attacked?"

"I didn't think anything would happen, 'cause I didn't believe vampires were real. But—"

"Ye were viciously attacked," he finished her sentence. "Ye could have died if Connor hadna come along."

"Believe me, I know how bad it was. Connor offered to erase my memory, but I couldn't do that, not when I'd just found out that Sabrina was right. So I took the job, hoping I could get the proof she needed."

A chill came over Ian. "Ye intended to prove our existence?" He let go of her hand. "Ye took an oath that ye would never expose us."

Toni winced. "I know."

"Do ye no' understand the full importance of our secret? If our existence becomes public knowledge, there would be millions of mortals wanting us destroyed. There would be slayers roaming the streets with their bloody stakes. There'd be scientists wanting to experiment on us or dissect us. And if they ever found out about the healing properties of our blood, we'd be hunted like animals and drained dry. Exposure means extinction."

She paled. "I never meant to hurt anyone. I thought I could give the proof to a psychiatrist or lawyer who would keep it confidential. Sorta like your Father Andrew."

"That's a terrible risk to take. Ye canna guarantee some-

one would keep quiet, especially if he considered us a serious threat to mankind."

"The Malcontents *are* a serious threat."

"Ye canna expose them without exposing us! And we're
the only ones capable of defeating them. I canna believe
ye would take such a risk with our lives." He paced away
from her.

"I didn't understand at first how nice the Vamps are. Once
I got to know you all, I knew I couldn't hurt you."

"That's bloody generous of you." Ian frowned at her. "Ye
should have told me this from the start."

"I didn't know if I could trust you. It took me a few days
to get to know you."

Ian didn't know what to think. He just felt a nagging sense
of betrayal. "I—I have to think about this." He headed for
the door.

She followed him. "Ian, you must know I could never hurt
you."

He felt too confused to even know how to answer. "Go to
bed, Toni. I'll see you tomorrow."

"Ian, I'm sorry."

He couldn't bear to see her stricken face, so he marched
back to the waiting room. Shanna was ready to see him. He
sat on an operating table, thinking things over while Shanna
plucked glass from his face and knees.

He couldn't believe Toni had planned to spill their secret.
Maybe she didn't understand how important it was. But
surely, Connor had explained it to her.

To her credit, she had noble intentions. She was trying to
save her friend Sabrina. Ian would feel that way about his
friends. But she'd intended to expose the Vamps. That made
his gut wrench.

When Shanna was done, he wandered down the hall. Toni
had signed a contract, swearing to protect them. How could
she have planned to betray them?

But she hadn't. Should he blame her for her intentions

before she'd gotten to know them? After the Malcontents had attacked her, she might have easily thought all vampires were evil and should be exposed.

But she'd practiced deception. He'd sworn to himself that nothing was more important in a potential mate than honesty and loyalty. Was that why this frustrated him so much? He was seeing Toni as a potential mate. God knew he wanted her. He ached with desire for her. He thought about her all the time. But could he trust her?

After an hour of getting nowhere, he decided he needed advice. He teleported to Vanda's office at the Horny Devils. After she recovered from the shock of his scarred face, he gave her the details of Toni's story.

Vanda sat behind her desk, frowning. "That little bitch."

Ian stiffened. "She doesna deserve that. She's trying to save her friend who's in danger."

Vanda's eyebrows rose. "Are you defending her now? I thought you were angry with her."

"I'm no' angry." He paced across the office. "I'm confused."

"Why? This problem's so easy to solve."

He stopped. "Ye think so?"

"Sure. Fire her ass and erase her memory. Then she's no longer a threat, and she's out of your life for good."

Out of his life? A surge of panic swept through him. How could he bear to lose her? "But . . . what about her friend?"

"Who gives a shit? She doesn't owe you any money."

"She's trapped in a mental ward—"

"Yeah, yeah, by the evil uncle. Boo hoo. That's one person. One mortal. And Toni was ready to expose us all to danger because of it."

"Only because she cares so deeply," Ian protested.

"She's not the only one," Vanda muttered.

Ian scowled at her. "Fine, I admit it. I care about her. I wouldna be this upset if I dinna care."

"A week ago, you swore to me that all you wanted was a

Vamp. I have a list right here of twenty Vamp women, all vetted by me and eager to meet you. You could start seeing them tonight."

A week ago, that would have sounded wonderful. But now Toni was in his life and everything was changed. "I doona want to date anyone else. Take my profile off the dating site."

"Ian, she was planning to betray us."

"But she never did. She never did anything to harm any of us." He was finally able to appreciate her predicament. She wanted to save Sabrina because she loved her. And she hadn't exposed him because she cared about him. He'd seen that clearly on her face when she'd frantically searched for him in the parking lot. She truly cared about him. But at the same time, she couldn't bear to fail her friend. Her heart was getting split in two.

All he had to do was help her rescue her friend. Then she would no longer be pulled in two directions. She would be free to come entirely to him.

And that's what he wanted more than anything. He wanted Toni to be free to love him. She was the one he wanted.

Toni woke slowly. She'd had trouble sleeping all night, for it felt like a heavy weight was pressing against her chest. *Ian*. She'd lost Ian. She rolled onto her back and realized she was not alone.

"Ian?" She sat up. He was there beside her.

Relief swept through her. He couldn't be angry with her if he'd climbed into bed with her, right? Last night she'd feared their relationship was over. He'd looked so upset.

He looked perfectly peaceful now. He was lying on his back, his hands folded over his stomach.

She checked the clock on the bedside table. Eight-forty-five? She'd set the alarm for six-thirty. He must have turned it off before climbing into bed with her.

She turned back to him. For the first time since she'd known him, he wasn't wearing a kilt. He had on flannel pajama bottoms, although still a red and green plaid, which made her smile. He'd showered off all the blood and grime.

She leaned closer to examine the cuts on his face. They looked much better already. She lifted one of his hands. The gashes had closed and the scars were fading. By sunset he would be back to his usual gorgeous self.

She realized suddenly she was holding hands with a dead man. And she didn't flinch or let go. Why wasn't she freaked out? She glanced at his face. He was still the same brave warrior who had charged to Gregori's rescue, the same selfless hero who had insisted she go to safety while he stood there bleeding, the same sweet man who had kissed her passionately and then taken all the blame for it.

She climbed out of bed and went to the bathroom. There she found a note taped to the mirror.

   Toni,

   *I want to help you rescue your friend. Please forgive
   me for being an arse.*

                                                    Ian

With a laugh, she pressed the note against her chest. Ian understood. She could trust him. And Sabrina would be saved. She ran back into the bedroom. "Thank you, Ian. Thank you."

He just lay there.

She sat on the bed, smiling at him. "You're not an arse. You're a wonderful man."

And she was falling in love with him.

A thrill shot through her. How could she not love him? He was the dearest, sweetest, sexiest man she'd ever met.

She studied his face as love continued to swell inside

her. This wasn't at all like her two past relationships. She'd thrown herself into those affairs with a desperation born from her mother's rejection. She'd needed to feel loved.

This was different. She hadn't meant to fall for Ian. For the first time, it wasn't about her and her need to be loved. It was all about Ian and the love she felt for him. It had become painfully clear to her when the explosions had gone off and she'd feared him dead.

She touched the dimple on his chin. She couldn't run away from him. She'd be running from her own heart.

She showered and dressed and left Ian locked safely in the silver room. When she stepped out of the elevator onto the ground floor, she was immediately surprised by all the people. Real people. They were bustling up and down the hall. Most of them were wearing white lab coats. They all had Romatech name tags clipped on their pockets.

On the way to the MacKay security office, she called Carlos on her cell phone. "Guess what? Ian agreed to help us rescue Sabrina."

"That's great!" Carlos lowered his voice. "So tell me, *menina*, what did you do to convince him?"

She snorted. "I talked to him."

"Come now, you must have been . . . friendly."

"Carlos, we need to rescue Bri as soon as possible. Do you think we can do it tonight?"

"Yes." His voice grew more serious. "I'll draw up some plans and come see you this afternoon."

"Good." Toni hung up and strode into the security office. Howard was sitting behind the desk, his bandaged leg propped on a chair.

"Sorry I overslept." She sat beside him.

"No problem." He waved at the monitors. "Nothing much going on. Day security is getting the mess cleaned up in the parking lot."

Toni gazed at the monitors that showed the parking lot.

A wrecker was hauling the burned car away. "What did the police say about last night?"

Howard munched on a doughnut. "They're used to Romatech getting bombed. I told the officer in charge that we've been targeted by a group of psycho fanatics who are opposed to the synthetic manufacture of blood. Which is pretty much the truth, actually."

Yeah, you couldn't get any more psycho than the Malcontents. Toni scanned the other monitors. One showed a bedroom with several twin beds. Phineas and Dougal were stretched out in their death-sleep. The silver room was displayed on another monitor. Oh great. Had Howard seen her touching Ian's face? "Doesn't day security think it's strange that we're in here, watching dead people sleep?"

"They have their own office. They keep out of our business." Howard pushed a pastry box in her direction. "Want a doughnut?"

"Sure." She selected a plain one. "So what happened while I was sleeping?"

"Connor took Roman and his family and Radinka into hiding about three in the morning. No one knows where. It's better that way when jerks like Jedrek can pick through your brain."

"Jedrek's the guy who attacked Gregori?"

"Yep." Howard finished his doughnut and licked his fingers.

And Jedrek had been the one who'd tried to capture Ian. Toni sighed. She doubted they'd seen the last of him.

Howard slid a paper across the desk. "This is the list of stuff to do for the Christmas Ball. Shanna and Radinka were kinda upset that they wouldn't be here to help, but I told them not to worry."

Toni gulped down the last of her doughnut. The list was a mile long. "And all this has to be done before tomorrow night?"

"Don't worry. It's covered. I gave a copy to Todd Spencer, the VP of production during the day. He knows what to do. Shanna gives a Christmas party every year, and then there's the Vamp conference and Gala Ball every spring."

"Todd must be a mortal. Does he know about Vamps?"

Howard shifted in his chair. "Todd knows a lot of things. He's already got some workers setting up chairs and tables."

"Number one is decorate the big Christmas tree," Toni read aloud from the list. "I don't recall seeing a tree."

"It'll be delivered around noon." Howard drank from his coffee cup.

Toni glanced down the list. Item number ten was confirm the band. A phone number was listed. "I'll go ahead and call this band."

Howard chuckled. "Wait till tonight. The High Voltage Vamps couldn't light a lightbulb right now."

"It's a vampire band?"

"Yeah, they play all the big Vamp parties and weddings." Howard stood and limped toward the door. "Come on. I'll show you the ballroom."

Just to the right of the main foyer, there were a number of meeting rooms with partitions that could be folded back like giant accordions. Toni was surprised by how large the ballroom was. The back wall was mostly windows that over-looked a garden. In front of the windows, Todd Spencer was overseeing a group of workmen who were erecting a stage. Howard introduced her.

"Glad to meet you," Todd yelled over the noise as he shook her hand. "It's about time MacKay hired a woman."

Toni looked around the huge room, bustling with workers. "How many people work here during the day?"

"Over two hundred now, divided into four departments," Todd explained. "Research, production, packaging, and shipping."

"Can I do anything to help?" Toni asked.

"You can help decorate, if you like." Todd showed her the plastic bins filled with ornaments and greenery.

Howard limped back to the security office to watch the monitors, and Toni spent a few hours spreading tablecloths and draping garland. She grabbed a quick lunch in the Romatech cafeteria and called Shady Oaks.

"I'd like to talk to Sabrina Vanderwerth in Ward Three." She recited the ID number.

"I'm afraid we can't allow that," the receptionist answered. "Her doctor has left strict instructions that she's not to receive any visitors or outside calls."

Toni winced. Uncle Joe had discovered their visit. "Can't we get a second opinion on that? Surely it helps the patient to know there are people who care about them."

"The decision is final." The receptionist hung up.

"Damn." She went back to the ballroom and discovered the fifteen-foot Christmas tree had arrived. She helped decorate for a few hours, then wandered down to the MacKay office. "How's it going?"

Howard motioned toward the monitors. "They're still dead, but they should be up in about twenty minutes."

The phone on the desk buzzed, and Howard picked it up. "Yes?" He listened, then covered the receiver with his big, beefy hand. "It's the guard at the entrance gate. Someone's come to see you. Drives a black Jaguar."

"That must be Carlos." Toni headed toward the door.

"Carlos who?" Howard asked her.

"Carlos Panterra."

"She confirmed his name," Howard told the guard on the phone. "Let him in."

Toni hurried to the front door and stepped outside just as Carlos was parking his car. It was chilly with the sun going down, so she rubbed her arms as she walked to his parking place.

He climbed from his car, looking like a spy all dressed in

black. He motioned toward the blackened area surrounded with orange cones. "What happened there?"

"Some vampires came by last night. Blew up a car and caused some injuries. Nothing major."

Carlos glanced at the burned area, frowning. "Are you saying your vampires don't play well with other vampires?"

"Mine are the good guys who drink from bottles. The bad ones are called Malcontents. They're the ones who attacked me and Sabrina. They hate the guys I work for."

Carlos gave her a worried look. "Toni, you've stepped into a war."

She shivered. "I know."

"You're cold. Let's get inside." He opened his trunk and removed a laptop and a long roll of white paper. "I brought the plans, so we can go over everything. We're doing it to-night, right?"

"Yes." At least she hoped Ian would agree to do it tonight.

Carlos motioned toward a duffel bag. "I packed some clothes and shoes for Sabrina. And some rope and duct tape, just in case."

"Good." She wondered once again if Carlos was more than an anthropology student.

He shut the trunk and walked with her to the front door. "Are you safe here?"

"I think so. The Vamps feel secure enough that they're having their big Christmas Ball tomorrow night."

"Partying in the face of danger? I think I like your Vamps." Carlos grinned as he opened the door. He entered, and his smile immediately faded. He sniffed, and a wary look crossed his face. "Careful." He held out an arm to block her entrance.

"What's wrong?"

"Danger," he whispered.

Chapter Eighteen

"Carlos." Toni peeked around his broad shoulders. "There's nothing wrong."

"Who is that?" he whispered, motioning with his head toward the large man at the far end of the foyer.

"That's my supervisor, Howard," Toni whispered back.

Howard suddenly stiffened and turned to face them. His nostrils flared as his gaze riveted on Carlos. He limped forward. "You are Carlos?"

"Yes." Carlos watched Howard carefully.

"I'm Howard Barr. Can we have a word in private, please?" He motioned toward the security office.

Carlos nodded and strode down the hall with him.

What the hell? Toni inched forward so she could see the two men disappear into the security office. Was Howard gay? Though she could have sworn their reaction to each other had been one of suspicion, not attraction.

She wandered down the hall toward the security office. Sheesh, she didn't dare barge in on them. Her attention was momentarily snagged by the mysterious locked room across from the nursery. She tried the doorknob, but no luck.

She waited awhile, then the security office door opened. Carlos exited with a perplexed look on his face.

"Are you okay?" she asked.

"Yes." He strode toward her, carrying his laptop and roll of paper. "Something very strange just happened."

Toni winced. "You don't have to tell me."

"Howard just offered me a job."

"*What?* You would work as a day guard like me?"

Carlos nodded. "I happen to have some . . . skills that are highly valued at MacKay Security and Investigation."

"Like martial arts?"

"That, too." Carlos ran a hand through his long black hair. "I warned Howard that I've always been a wanderer, but he said they had clients all over the world who needed guarding, and I could transfer from one place to another."

"Did he tell you about the Vamps?" Toni whispered.

"No, he called them clients. I'm going to consider it. The pay is excellent, and I have a lot of expenses."

"That's true." Toni knew Carlos was supporting a few orphans in Brazil. It was one of the things that had first attracted her and Sabrina to him. He was also paying for his education and research trips to South America and Malaysia. "Howard's a nice boss. He used to be a defensive lineman for the NFL, but he's as sweet as a teddy bear."

Carlos gave her a sharp look. "Yeah, I noticed. So where can we discuss the plans for Sabrina?"

Toni led him down the hall till she spotted a room labeled *Conference*. She peeked inside and flipped on the light. "This will do."

Carlos strode into the room and went straight to work, setting up his laptop, then spreading out the roll of white paper. "I drew the layout for Shady Oaks, so Ian will know exactly where to teleport." He tapped his finger on a rectangle labeled Ward Three.

Toni leaned over to study the map. "This is very good." Carlos would make an excellent employee for MacKay Security and Investigation.

"*Menina*, I know I've been teasing you about Ian, but I'm wondering if it's wise to get involved with him. Don't get me wrong, he's a nice guy, but he is a vampire."

"He wouldn't bite me." Toni blushed as memories of last night's glorious kiss filled her mind. "At least, not for food."

Carlos frowned. "After we rescue Sabrina, you should quit your job here and forget these vampires exist."

"That would be rather rude, don't you think? To just use Ian for his super abilities, then tell him adiós. And how can you tell me to quit when you're planning to work here?"

"You have special plans with Sabrina. I don't. And the truth of the matter is Ian is not your kind."

She planted her hands on her hips. "I'm surprised at you, Carlos. I would expect you, of all people, to be more understanding and tolerant."

"I am tolerant of anything two humans want to do with each other, but he's not exactly human."

"He's more human than anyone I know. And I love him."

"You've known him exactly a week."

"And a hell of a lot has happened in that time." Toni pressed a hand to her chest. "I'm becoming a different person now. I feel like I'm finally growing into a whole person—one who's capable, strong, and worthy. I'm not a wounded child anymore. And I like what's happening to me. I'm not going to give it up."

"All right, then." Carlos touched her shoulder. "I'm very happy for you."

She gave him a hug, then wandered to the window to peek out the blinds. "The sun has set. I'll go get Ian."

"Okay. And change clothes. Dress all in black." Carlos moved to his laptop. "Give me your cell phone."

"Why?" She removed it from the pocket of her khaki pants.

"Because you need a new ringtone." He took her phone. "Love is no longer a battlefield for you."

"Put on something nice," she warned him, then left to find Ian.

He was in the silver room, still in his pajamas, finishing his breakfast.

She grinned at him. "I got your note. Thank you for helping us." She rummaged through her suitcase and found some black cargo pants. "Carlos wants us to dress in black."

Ian's eyebrows rose. "Are we doing it tonight?"

"Yes. Is that all right?"

"Aye." Ian set his empty bottle in the sink. "I should stay here most of the night in case Jedrek tries something, but it shouldna take long to teleport yer friend out."

She located a black T-shirt, but unfortunately it had bright white letters on the front. *Am I Crazy or What?* She showed it to Ian. "The perfect shirt for breaking into a mental institution."

He chuckled. "Ye do want to be properly dressed for every occasion." His face grew more serious. "I'm sorry for the way I reacted last night."

"There's no need to apologize. I was wrong to ever consider telling your secret."

His eyes gleamed. "Ye've gone to amazing lengths to help yer friend. Ye've survived a brutal attack, ye've taken a job with the Undead, and ye're about to do some serious breaking and entering. That kind of loyalty is verra rare."

Her eyes grew misty as her heart swelled with love. "You tell me the loveliest things." He made her realize how worthy she truly was.

He glanced at the surveillance camera, then motioned with his head to the bathroom. "Ye need to change clothes?"

"Right." Toni gathered up her black clothes and dashed into the bathroom. She gasped when Ian followed her in and shut the door. "What—?"

He pulled her into his arms and planted his mouth on hers.

Her clothes tumbled to the floor as she melted into his kiss.

He suckled her bottom lip, then nibbled kisses down her neck. "Did ye need help getting out of yer clothes?"

"You rascal." She slid her fingers into his soft hair.

He tugged her navy polo shirt up and slipped his hands underneath. "I want you." He surveyed the tiny bathroom with his red, glowing eyes. "This is . . . a challenge."

"Ian." She placed her hands on his cheeks. "We don't have time right now. And I don't really want a quickie in the bathroom."

His mouth curled up. "No' verra romantic, huh?"

She grinned. "I think you're very romantic, but Carlos is waiting upstairs, and we have a job to do."

"I understand." He kissed her quickly on the mouth, then exited the room.

She changed clothes, then found him in the kitchen pulling a black sweater over his head. He had on black leather pants and looked deliciously naughty. She almost called him back into the bathroom for a quickie.

"Let's go." She grabbed her coat and took the elevator with Ian to the first floor. "We were getting the ballroom ready today for the big party."

He nodded. "Phineas said he would teach me how to dance more modern, so I could dance with you. I only know how to do the minuet and waltz and a few country dances."

She grinned at him as they exited the elevator. "You want to dance with me?"

"Aye. Phineas said I needed to know how to do pop blocking and jam-on-it."

She laughed. "You're going to hip-hop in a kilt?"

"Actually I'll be wearing a Santa costume, along with ninety-nine other men."

"How come there are so many Santa costumes?" She motioned to the locked door across from the dental office. "What's the deal with the secret Santa thing?"

"If I told you, it wouldna be a secret."

She swatted his arm. "I told you *my* secrets."

"No' all of them. I still doona know yer full name."

"I see no reason to divulge that at this time."

"It canna be that bad. My name is Ian David MacPhie."

"That's a good name. It's easy to confess." She opened the door to the conference room. "Here we are. Carlos has everything planned."

"I'm used to making my own plans." He marched inside, frowning. "Good evening, Carlos."

"Hi, Ian. Nice pants. Love the leather. Here's your phone, Toni."

She slipped her cell phone into a pants pocket.

Ian examined the map of Shady Oaks.

"This is Ward Three." Carlos pointed at it. "That's where they're holding Sabrina. There's a guard just inside the front door, but I spotted a back door here. Do you think you can teleport in undetected?"

Ian gave him a bland look. "I've teleported into Langley undetected."

Carlos arched a brow. "Then I'll take that as a yes."

Toni stifled a grin. She hoped these two guys wouldn't get into a pissing match.

Ian nodded. "I can do it."

"I'll wait for you in the car. I can park here or here." Carlos indicated the front parking lot and the back service entrance.

"Use the parking lot," Ian said. "It'll be less conspicuous."

"Agreed."

Ian slanted a look at him. "Ye've done work like this before."

Carlos rolled up the map. "My research has led me into some strange places and situations."

"What kind of research?"

"Unusual, primitive cultures, mostly in South America

and Southeast Asia." He moved to his laptop. "This is the route I'll use to drive us to the hotel. It's an inconspicuous place in Queens. I paid cash in advance."

Ian studied it a moment. "Looks good. I need to check on things here, so ye drive there with Toni. Then she can call me, and I'll teleport there to meet you."

"Agreed." Carlos shut his laptop. "Let's do it."

At Shady Oaks, Carlos parked his Jaguar in a dark corner. Toni called Ian, and he materialized beside her in the parking lot.

"I'm coming with you," she told him.

"Nay. I canna teleport two people at the same time."

Stubborn man. "Then you can make two trips."

Carlos exited the driver's seat. "What's wrong?"

"Toni wants to put herself in danger," Ian muttered.

"You have to take me with you," Toni insisted. "How else will you know which one is Sabrina?"

"I expect she can tell me her name."

Toni gave him an exasperated look. "She could be asleep. Or if she's awake, she could scream and raise the alarm. If I'm there, I can keep her calm."

"I think Toni's right," Carlos said.

Toni shot him a grateful smile.

Ian's jaw shifted. "All right."

"You'll find it easier to approach from the west," Carlos suggested.

"I can manage," Ian growled. "Come on, Toni."

She strode alongside him as they moved through the parking lot, angling to the west side of the hospital. "Carlos just wants to help. He really cares about Sabrina."

"And you."

She wondered if he was jealous. "We're just good friends."

"I doona mean to be a grouch," Ian muttered. "I'm just used to doing this kind of work on my own."

"Why?"

He remained silent as they walked along the west wall. Finally he spoke, "I never wanted to work with the other guys, 'cause they would invariably treat me like a child."

"Oh. I'm sorry. It must have been terribly frustrating to look like a fifteen-year-old for so long."

"Almost five hundred years." He glanced at her. "I'm glad ye never knew me that way. Ye've always seen me as a man, as the man I felt like inside all those years."

"You're a wonderful man, Ian."

He took her hand. "Och, yer puir fingers are frozen." He sandwiched her hand between his.

"That's the oak tree Carlos climbed." She pointed with her free hand. "The courtyard is just over the wall."

He released her hand. "I'll take a look."

She blinked when he started to rise to the top of the wall.

"All right. Come." He extended his left hand toward her.

"I can't—" She stopped when his body dropped a few feet. He grabbed her hand and pulled her into his arms. Then he levitated back to the top of the wall.

She flung her arms around his neck.

His teeth flashed white in the dark. "Ye doona need to choke me, sweetheart. I willna drop you."

"Sorry." She tried to relax. "I'm not used to floating six feet off the ground."

"That is Ward Three, aye?" He pointed.

She squinted to see across the dimly lit courtyard. "Yes." No doubt he could see much better than she.

"Ye see the shadowy area to the right of the building? It's close to the back entrance. We'll teleport there first."

"Okay." She steeled her nerves. The black, dizzying sensation sucked her in, then she stumbled as her feet landed on hard ground.

"Steady." He led her toward the back door. It was locked, of course, but through the glass window they could see a plain hallway, lined with doors on each side. The doors were open, and light spilled from several onto the shiny linoleum floor.

A female nurse padded down the hall in white athletic shoes. "Eight o'clock! Lights out!"

The lights clicked off, leaving the hallway dimly illuminated with a few emergency lights. The nurse walked away, presumably toward the nurses' station by the main entrance.

"Those must be the bedrooms," Ian whispered. He pulled her to his side. "Let's go."

Darkness swirled around her once more, then she found herself with Ian in the hallway. The air was hot and stuffy. She took the left side of the hall, while he took the right. They moved silently across the floor, checking the name tags next to each door.

Four doors down, she spotted the name *Vanderwerth, Sabrina*. She motioned to Ian, and they both slipped inside the dark room. She could barely make out the twin-sized bed on a raised platform. There were no dressers, just open shelves like bookcases. No place to hide anything. No lamps, no mirrors. A body was huddled under the plain blanket. Sabrina's blonde hair gleamed dully on the pillow.

Toni hunched down beside her. "Bri, can you hear me?" She touched her shoulder.

Bri moaned. "Leave me alone, you creep."

"Sabrina, it's me, Toni."

"Toni?" She rolled onto her back. "You can't be Toni."

"I *am* Toni. I've come to get you out of here."

Sabrina rubbed her eyes. "I'm just dreaming. I'm so delusional."

"No, you're not." Toni grabbed her hand and squeezed. "It's really me. Now come on. We're leaving."

Bri struggled to sit up. "I'm kinda sleepy. Can't you come back in the morning?"

"No, we're leaving now." Toni realized her friend was too doped up to think clearly. She located her slippers beside the bed and shoved them on her feet.

"This is taking too long," Ian whispered. "I'll just grab her and go."

Bri squinted at Ian's dark shadow. "Who are you?"

"He's a friend," Toni explained. "Ian. He's going to help you escape."

Bri giggled. "Escape? You can't escape from here."

"No' so loud, please," Ian whispered. He leaned out the door to check the hallway. "Hurry. I hear someone coming."

"He talks so cute," Bri whispered.

"He's Scottish." Toni pulled Bri to her feet and led her to the doorway. "Ian will take you first, then come back for me."

Bri glanced at the back door. "We can't get out that way. It's locked."

"Ian can get you out." Toni removed her jacket and put it on Bri. "It's cold outside."

"Sabrina, do you have visitors?" A male patient shuffled toward them. His Batman pajamas were faded to a dull gray, but the gold bat on his chest still gleamed.

"Hi, Teddy," Bri answered.

Ian groaned.

"I'm going to escape," Bri announced, then giggled.

Ian stepped close to Toni and whispered, "Keep him quiet. When I come back for you, I'll erase his memory."

"Okay." Toni buttoned up her jacket on Bri. "Don't be afraid. You can trust Ian."

Sabrina startled when Ian wrapped an arm around her shoulders. "What are you—"

She vanished, along with Ian.

Teddy gasped. "Oh my God!"

"Not so loud," Toni whispered. "I can explain."

"He's a superhero!" Teddy exclaimed. "He rescued her with his superpowers!"

"Teddy, are you out of bed again?" a male voice boomed in the distance.

"Aw shoot, it's Bradley," Teddy muttered. "I wouldn't have to roam around if he wasn't so—"

Toni grabbed Teddy by the shoulders. "Don't tell him Sabrina escaped. Do you understand?"

He blinked. "Okay."

Toni ran into Sabrina's room, climbed into bed, and covered herself up to her ears.

"Teddy, what are you doing out of bed?" Bradley's voice sounded closer.

"I—I saw a superhero! He was just here, and then poof! He vanished."

"You are crazier than hell," Bradley muttered. "Get back to your room."

"I'm not crazy," Teddy mumbled. His shuffling footsteps grew dim.

Toni exhaled with relief. Sabrina's escape was still a secret. She froze when she heard a sound. Was Ian back so soon? Her skin prickled as all her senses went on alert. Something was wrong. Footsteps approached her bed. She squeezed her eyes shut.

"Sabrina," Bradley whispered and stroked her hair.

Bile rose in Toni's throat. Oh God, she wanted to leap out of bed and slam a fist down his throat. But she didn't dare. She couldn't let him know that Bri had escaped. She needed to buy some time to give them a chance to get away.

She swallowed hard. Was this why Bri had called her a creep earlier? Bradley must have touched her before while she was groggy on medication.

"Sabrina," Bradley whispered again.

There was a dull thud, and a body fell on top of her.

Toni scrambled out of bed and away from Bradley's body. He was sprawled across the bed, unconscious.

Teddy stood there, holding a thick book. "I don't like him. He's a bad man."

"Thank you, Teddy."

He smiled sheepishly. "I haven't been taking my meds. I knew I needed to watch that creep."

Ian zoomed into the room, and his gaze fell on the unconscious nurse. "What happened?"

"It's a long story," Toni said. "But Teddy saved me from being molested."

Ian stepped toward Bradley. "This man was taking advantage of the women here?"

"He's been trying to," Teddy said. "That's why I roam the hall at night."

"Bastard." Ian placed a hand on Bradley's head. "There. He'll sleep till morning. Let him explain his presence here in Sabrina's bed."

"Cool," Teddy whispered. "You have some kick-ass superpowers, man. What's your name?"

"Ian."

Teddy frowned. "Dude, you gotta get a better name than that. And you need a cape."

Ian chuckled. "Like a vampire cape? I have one of those somewhere."

"That would be awesome, man."

Ian approached Teddy. "I have to erase yer memory now."

Teddy stepped back. "No! This is the coolest thing that's happened to me in ages. I want to remember it."

"Ian." Toni gave him a pleading look. She understood how Teddy felt. She didn't want to lose her memory, either.

"Toni, he knows we helped Sabrina escape."

"Take me with you," Teddy begged.

"Nay." Ian shook his head.

"Seriously, dude. If you take me with you, then I can't tell anyone what you did. Not that I would, but they might try to hypnotize me or something. I'm not really crazy, you know. I was just depressed, 'cause I didn't have anything to look forward to, but with you guys, I could be really happy."

Ian hesitated. "Once ye know our secrets, there is no going back."

"Cool."

Ian frowned. "You must understand the danger of being with us. We are at war with some evil creatures."

Teddy shook his fist. "Awesome!"

Ian gave Toni a questioning glance.

She shrugged. "Teddy, do you know what you're doing?"

"I'm not stupid," he grumbled. "I was head of the math department at St. Bartholomew's Academy."

"Ye're a teacher?" Ian asked.

"Yes." Teddy eyed them warily. "Does that mean I'm not cool enough to hang out with superheroes?"

"Actually, I think ye're exactly what we need." Ian motioned for him to follow. "Come."

"Cool." Teddy followed him into the hall. "Are we beaming up to the mother ship?"

Toni peeked out the door and saw them teleport away. *Beam me up, Scotty.* She wondered why Ian was interested in Teddy's teaching background. And while Teddy certainly had good credentials, he seemed a little shaky on reality. She didn't want to find fault with him, though, not when he'd saved her from the perverted nurse.

Bradley had fallen across the bed sideways. She tugged at his body to align him better with the bed.

She noted Bri's belongings on the open shelves. Two sets of clothes and another set of pajamas. She slipped on Bri's jacket, then spotted some underwear on the shelf.

She glanced at Bradley, and inspiration struck. She grabbed a pair of Bri's panties, then stuffed them into Bradley's hand. Then she took one of Bri's bras and fastened it around his head like a cap. Let him try to explain that in the morning.

Ian zipped into the room. "I think Teddy's a bit disappointed to be sitting in a car instead of a spaceship." He eyed the nurse. "That's interesting."

"I like it." Toni gathered up the rest of Bri's belongings. "Shall we go?"

Ian smiled. "There's never a dull moment with you, Toni." He teleported her to the parking lot.

Toni opened the Jaguar's passenger door and peered inside.

Teddy was squashed into the tiny backseat with Sabrina. She leaned against him, her eyes droopy with medication.

"Bri, Carlos is going to take you to a hotel where you can rest," Toni told her.

Bri blinked at her. "I thought I was in bed. How did I get here?"

"You'll be fine," Toni insisted. "You just need some rest. I'll come see you tomorrow."

"No." Bri struggled to sit up. "Don't leave me." Her face crumpled. "I think I'm going crazy. I don't know how I got here."

Toni winced. "All right. I'll come with you. Just a minute."

"We have to hurry, *menina*," Carlos warned her.

Ian touched her shoulder. "It's all right. Go with yer friend. Ye can call me later, and I'll teleport over to bring you home."

She threw her arms around him and kissed him. "How can I ever thank you?"

His mouth twitched. "I'll think of something. I'll see you later." He stepped back and vanished.

Toni climbed into the Jaguar. "Let's go."

"Were you kissing that man, Toni?" Sabrina asked.

"Sure she was," Teddy replied. "The superheroes always get the girl."

Jedrek sat at his desk, studying the photo of Roman Draganesti and his family. How could a man be so smart and stupid at the same time? His Stay-Awake drug was fantastic. But the idiot had used the drug so he could babysit? If the moron had any sense at all, he would give the drug to his Highlander thugs, and they would spend the daytime killing their enemies who rested helplessly in their death-sleep.

It could happen. Jedrek had ordered twice as many daytime guards. But as tough as the Russian mafia guys were, he didn't like depending on them for safety.

What he needed was that damned drug. Then he could

spend a few days killing Vamps. He thumbed through the stack of photos, relishing the thought of staking them all. MacKay and his wife. Buchanan. MacPhie.

"Master?" Yuri entered the office, followed by Stanislav. "You wanted to see us?"

"We need to plan our next move," Jedrek announced.

"They're having their Christmas Ball tomorrow night at Romatech," Stanislav suggested.

Jedrek shook his head. "Too predictable." His hand paused on the photo of the black Vamp. "Remember this one?"

"Yes," Stanislav answered. "Phineas, the traitor."

Jedrek arched a brow. "You haven't killed him yet?"

Stanislav gulped. "I will, Master."

"See that you do." Jedrek resumed flipping though the photos. He stopped on the mortal girl with blonde hair. He'd seen her last night after the bombs had gone off. She'd run across the parking lot, screaming MacPhie's name. The ground had been littered with wounded men, but she'd gone straight to MacPhie.

"What do we do next?" Yuri asked.

Jedrek stroked his finger over the photo of the blonde mortal. "I know exactly what to do."

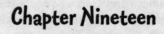

Chapter Nineteen

Tuesday night, Toni walked into a ballroom full of Santas. The dancing had already started, and several Santas whirled around the dance floor, waltzing with their partners. The women's costumes were a bit more varied. A few were dressed like Mrs. Claus with long, full skirts, white aprons, and white frilly bonnets on top of silver wigs. Other women wore outfits reminiscent of the costumes worn by the Rockettes in their Christmas show.

Toni did a double take. The two Rockettes by the reindeer ice sculpture looked male.

She headed toward the table with real food. As far as she knew, only mortals who knew about Vamps had been invited to the ball. The other mortal employees at Romatech had gone to a party for them earlier in the afternoon.

She scanned the room, searching for Ian, but all the Santas looked alike. They even wore padding inside their red velvet coats to give them fake bellies. Under their red hats, they sported bushy white wigs and beards. The only departure from the norm were a few Santas sporting swords—in case the Malcontents showed up uninvited. Even Toni had a few wooden stakes in her belt.

She noticed one Santa who was different. He was about a foot shorter than the others, and he fidgeted with the black buttons on his jacket. That had to be Laszlo, the scientist who had helped in the operating room and delivered a bag of stuff to the mystery room.

At the mortal table, there was a Mrs. Claus and a little girl who were having a snack of cheese and fruit.

The woman smiled at Toni and extended a hand. "Hi. I'm Heather Echarpe, and this is my daughter, Bethany."

"I'm Toni." She shook hands, then smiled at the little girl. "What a beautiful dress."

"My new daddy made it for me." Bethany's face lit up, and she pointed across the room. "Look, Mama. It's Constantine. Can I go see him?"

"Sure, sweetie." Heather gazed fondly at Tino, who was dressed like a miniature Santa without the beard.

Bethany dragged Constantine onto the dance floor while the waltzing adults managed to avoid running over them. Tino and Bethany reached the middle of the dance floor, where they started jumping and giggling.

Toni popped a grape in her mouth. "So you must be the one who married the famous fashion designer."

"Yes." Heather smiled. "Jean-Luc is here somewhere. Lost in a sea of Santas."

"Yeah, I can't tell who's who."

Heather bit into a strawberry. "It's for the best, I suppose. It would totally confuse any Malcontent who crashed the party." She stepped closer to Toni. "I hope you don't mind, but Shanna told me about you."

"Oh?"

Heather smiled. "Don't worry, it was all good stuff. I just wanted to say that Ian's a great guy, and I hope it works out for you."

"We—we're not going out or anything. I'm a guard, so it's against the rules for us to get involved."

"Since when does love follow the rules?" Heather lowered her voice. "Ian was in Texas when he took the drug to grow older. He was in so much pain, it nearly killed me to watch. I begged him to stop, but you know what he said?"

"What?"

Heather's eyes grew moist. "He said all the pain was worth it if he could find true love."

Toni's heart squeezed in her chest. "I'm going to look for him. Excuse me." She started across the ballroom.

The band switched to a modern song, and she noted a disco Santa on the dance floor. Gregori, she thought with a smile. He was back to his normal self.

She'd arrived a bit late to the ball because she'd spent too much time in the silver room, fussing with her hair and makeup. She wanted to look good for Ian.

She'd had a late night, making sure Sabrina was all right before Ian had teleported her back to Romatech. She'd been so tired, she'd gone straight to bed. Today she'd called the hotel twice. Carlos had told her that Bri was sleeping most of the time, and Teddy was watching television. She hoped to see Bri tomorrow, but for now, she was eager to see Ian.

All day long, her heart had been light with joy. She couldn't wait to see him. It was just a shame she hadn't been able to dress a bit sexier. Shanna had insisted she wear this specific costume.

She wandered toward a group of Santas who were talking to one another. They noticed her and smiled.

She quickly checked their eyes. No Ian. "Excuse me." She backed away.

"*Bellissima*, don't run away." A Vamp Santa with sparkling brown eyes took her hand. "Allow me to introduce myself. I am Giacomo di Venezia. Please call me Jack, like my other English-speaking friends do."

"I'm Toni Davis."

He kissed her hand. "*Bellissima*, you are the guard Connor hired? He didn't tell me you were a goddess." He turned to the other men. "She is a vision of beauty, no?"

"Ye're embarrassing her, Jack," a second Santa said with a Scottish accent. He extended a hand. "Welcome to MacKay Security and Investigation. I'm Robby MacKay."

Toni shook his hand. "You're related to Angus?"

"Aye, but he's much, much older than me," Robby said with a grin.

"How do you do?" The third Vamp in the group held out his hand. His eyes were almond-shaped, and his accent was thicker. "I am Zoltan Czakvar from Budapest."

"Oh." She shook his hand. "I'm Attila the Hun."

The men laughed.

"Will you dance with me, Attila?" Zoltan asked.

"Perhaps later. I'm . . . looking for someone right now."

"Ah." Jack nodded his head. "*Amore*. I'm afraid her heart is already taken, Zoltan."

Zoltan bowed. "Then we will hope he is worthy of you."

"Okay." Toni smiled as she left the three guys. There was something definitely appealing about Vamp men.

She wandered by another group of men, but none of them looked familiar. Then she saw someone who was easy to recognize. He was the only black Santa in the room. He was drinking blood from a wineglass, along with another Santa.

"Phineas." She lifted a hand.

"Hey, sweetness." He gave her a high five and a knuckle pound. "What's up?"

She recognized the second Santa as Dougal. "Hey, Dougal. Have you seen Ian anywhere? I can't find him."

"The last time I saw him," Dougal said, "he was at the refreshment table, having a Bleer."

Phineas eyed Toni's costume. "Girl, what are you supposed to be? You look like the Jolly Green Giant's little ho."

Toni gritted her teeth. "I'm an elf."

Dougal laughed. "She makes a good elf."

"Thanks," Toni muttered.

Phineas snorted. "So do you live in a tree and bake cookies? Whatcha got for me in your oven?" He winked.

She swatted his arm. "I'll sic the Jolly Green Giant on you."

She marched off, feeling even more ridiculous in her costume. She had a red feather in her silly green hat, and jingle bells on her green slippers that made noise with every step. If anyone else made fun of her costume, she might have to stake him into oblivion.

She circled the dance floor. The music had changed to a slow, modern dance. She spotted Heather dancing with a Santa, probably her husband, Jean-Luc. And Shanna was dancing with another Santa, probably Roman. As she neared the Vamp refreshment table, she saw the two questionable Rockette ladies talking with another Santa.

One of them pressed a hand against the Santa's chest. Her fingernails were painted a bright red. "Oh my God, look at you! You're all grown up!"

Toni winced. The Rockette's voice was definitely male.

"Our sweet little boy," the second male Rockette said. "All grown up and so handsome." He waved a hand in front of his face. "I'm think I'm going to cry."

"Don't you dare, Tootsie," the first Rockette warned. "If you start crying, I'll completely lose it, and I just hate runny mascara. Don't you, Ian?"

"I wouldna know," he growled. He spotted Toni, and relief flooded his face. "Toni, I've been looking for you."

"Oh my!" The Rockette named Tootsie looked Toni over. "Has our little Ian found a sweetheart?"

Ian pulled her to his side. "Toni, let me introduce you to Tootsie and Scarlett. They teleported here from New Orleans."

Toni smiled politely. "How do you do?"

Scarlett pressed a hand to his chest. "Oh my God, isn't she just the prettiest thing?"

Tootsie's red-painted lips trembled. "They're so precious together. I—I can't help it. I'm going to cry!"

Scarlett huffed. "Well, don't get *me* started."

Ian backed away, dragging Toni with him. "Excuse us, but I promised Toni I would dance with her."

Scarlett sighed. "That's so sweet."

"And romantic." Tootsie dabbed at his eyes with a lacy handkerchief.

Ian led Toni farther away.

She glanced back, and the two male Rockettes were still watching them with tears in their eyes. "They seem very fond of you."

"They're verra friendly." Ian put his hands around her waist. "Thank you for rescuing me."

She rested her hands on his shoulders and matched his steps as he swayed to and fro. "Where did you meet them?"

"In New Orleans, a few years back. I was doing an investigation for a Vamp with amnesia."

"Really? Did you find out who he was?"

Ian nodded. "He was a cowboy with a secret baby."

Toni laughed.

"I'm serious." Ian grinned, and it made his white beard twitch. "And what are ye supposed to be?"

"An elf, and don't you dare make fun of me."

"Are ye kidding? Yer red tights are driving me crazy."

She bumped against his fake belly that stuck out above his belt. "Is that padding in there, or are you happy to see me?"

His beard twitched again. "And what are these?" He fingered the wooden stakes in her belt. "Are ye intending to use them on me?"

"Maybe. If Santa doesn't give me what I want for Christmas."

"And what do ye want?"

She almost said, *You*, but she hesitated. "It's a secret."

"Another secret?" His blue eyes twinkled. "Are ye ever going to tell me yer full name?"

She shrugged. "Maybe never."

"But I need to know. I'm making a list. And checking it twice."

She laughed.

"Tell me, Toni." He pulled her closer. "Have ye been naughty or nice?"

A warm feeling swept through her. She wanted this man so much. She curled her hands around the back of his neck. He tightened his hold on her.

She glanced at his eyes, and suddenly felt the warmth ratchet up a few degrees. "It might be fun to get a little naughty."

A red tint flared in his eyes. "We could go somewhere private. No one would notice one less Santa in the room."

Toni licked her lips. The thought of ripping his beard off to kiss him was very exciting. "Your eyes are turning red."

"Your heart is beating faster." He leaned close, his white beard tickling her cheek. "I'd like to peel those red tights down yer legs."

"I might let you," she teased. "If you give me what I need."

His eyes glowed a deeper red. "Sweetheart, I have what you need."

She grinned. "What I need is a few answers. I have some questions for you."

"My favorite color is green. Like yer eyes."

"Not that question." She smoothed her hands down his chest. "I could make it worth your while. If you answer, I'll . . . take something off."

His eyebrows rose. "Now that *is* naughty."

"Of course you have to agree to the same terms. If I answer one of your questions, *you* have to take something off."

"Agreed." He glanced around the room. "We'll leave separately. Meet me in the hall in three minutes." He strode away, leaving her alone on the dance floor.

She wandered back to the refreshment table for mortals with her mortal heart pounding in her ears. Good grief, what had she just agreed to? She wanted some answers, but stripping for them was likely to get out of hand.

Good. She smiled to herself. She wanted him. He wanted her. There was no denying that red glow in his eyes.

She took a few deep breaths to calm herself, then drank some punch. Out of the corner of her eye, she noticed a Santa leaving the ballroom. She drained her cup, then strolled toward the exit. She wandered down the hall in the direction of the chapel. Where was he?

A door to the right cracked open and an arm in a red velvet sleeve reached out and grabbed her. She gasped, then laughed as a Santa hauled her into a dark room. He shut the door and pinned her against it.

"You'd better be Ian."

"Aye." He nuzzled her neck.

"Take off that beard. I want to kiss you."

He chuckled. "Ye're a demanding lass." He locked the door, then led her into the room.

It was a conference room, she noted, with a long table surrounded by a dozen chairs. Ian had left the lights off, so the only light came from the red exit sign over the door and the lights from the parking lot outside the large plate-glass window.

"It's snowing outside." She wandered alongside the table. "Should we close the blinds?"

"It's one-way glass." He sat in a chair midway down the table. "So what's yer full name, Toni?"

"That again? Does it really matter?"

"I'm only curious because ye'll no' tell me."

"Okay, okay." She perched on the table next to him and propped one foot up on the arm of his chair. "But it'll be worth two articles of clothing."

He wrapped a hand around her ankle. "All right."

She leaned back, bracing her weight on her hands. "I only know what my grandmother told me, so my knowledge of the events is a bit sketchy. It appears my mother had a desire to marry a racecar driver when she was seventeen. She went to the Daytona 500 to find a driver and jumped a guy in a jumpsuit in a garage. She was a bit pissed to discover afterward that he was just a mechanic and even more pissed when she discovered herself pregnant."

Ian shook his head. "Yer mum continues to confound me."

"I guess she needed a reminder never to make such a stupid mistake again, 'cause she named me after the racetrack where I was conceived."

"Yer name is Daytona Five Hundred?"

"No." She glared at him. "Just Daytona. Isn't that humiliating enough? Please don't tell anyone."

His white beard twitched. "Daytona Davis. I like it."

"Daytona Lynn, actually. It's a Southern thing. Now strip, Santa. Two items."

He removed his red Santa cap with the attached wig. "That's one." He took off the beard. "And that's two." He tossed them on the table. "Yer turn."

"What's the secret Santa thing? And what are you all hiding behind the locked door across from the nursery?"

He circled his fingers around her ankle again. "That's two questions."

"But they're related, aren't they?"

"Och, now that's three."

She nudged him with her foot, and the bell on her slipper jingled. "Just answer the question."

He smiled. "Roman started the Secret Santa Pact in 1950 when he became coven master. We have a few Vamps around the country who work the night shift, sorting mail for the post office. Each year, they gather the letters addressed to Santa, and we collect toys. Then on Christmas Eve, some Vamps dress up like Santa to deliver the goods, including places like halfway houses and women's shelters."

Toni sat silent for a while, absorbing this latest news. What more proof did she need that these Vamps were kind and noble? "That is so awesome."

"Thank you." He pulled both her feet into his lap and removed one of her green slippers. "We enjoy it quite a bit." He took off the second slipper. They jingled when he tossed them on the table.

"You mean you're one of the Santas?"

"Aye. I've been doing it since I came here to work in 1955." He slid one of her fuzzy red socks off. "There are a hundred of us now." He pulled off her other sock.

"What are you doing?"

"I answered yer questions." He threw the socks on the table. "Two questions."

"But you removed four articles of clothing."

"Nay. Socks and shoes come in pairs." He wrapped his hands around one of her feet and began massaging it.

How could she argue when it felt so good? "Okay. Ask your next question."

He sat there, quietly rubbing her foot while he considered. "Do ye want children?"

That surprised her. "Yes."

He removed his belt and sword and slid them down the table to the pile of clothes.

"That's it?" she asked. "One lousy belt?"

"'Twas an easy question for you."

"Do *you* want children?" She knew the answer wouldn't be easy for him. He could never have children if he married a Vamp.

"If I ever have children, I would consider myself greatly blessed."

"That's a bit evasive. But still nice." She uncinched her brown leather belt, and her wooden stakes clattered onto the table.

He stood and shoved the stakes across the table, so that they tumbled onto the floor.

"A bit sensitive about those, aren't you?"

"Aye." He plucked the feathered cap off her head and tossed it onto the pile of clothing.

"What are you doing?"

"Ye asked a question, and I answered it. In fact, I just answered another one." He tugged at the lacings on her green elfin tunic.

"Stop that." She swatted his hand away. "Those questions didn't count. That was normal conversation. Now ask an official question, please."

"Verra well." He sat back down in his chair and studied her. "What do ye want most in life?"

"That's a big one. You'll have to remove five articles of clothing for that answer."

"Four."

"All right, four. But I get to choose which ones."

He smiled. "Agreed."

What did she want the most? "Every morning, I start my day with four affirmations. I guess you could say they're what I want most in life. Or what I want to believe the most. The first one is I deserve to be happy."

"Aye, ye do."

She slid off the table. "I'm taking your boots." She yanked them off and smiled at his argyle socks. So Scottish.

"Yer second affirmation?" he asked.

"I will accomplish my goals."

He nodded. "Ye have worthy goals."

She unbuttoned his red velvet jacket. "Take it off, Santa."

He tossed the jacket on the table, along with the small pillow that had masqueraded as a belly. "Go on."

"Number three is I will achieve something meaningful with my life."

"That is important. That's why I fight the Malcontents." He stood when she tugged on his white T-shirt. He pulled it over his head and tossed it aside.

She eyed his bare chest. The patch of black, curly hair, the strong pecs, the six-pack abs. His red velvet pants were tied at his hips by a white drawstring. She took the end of the white cord in her fingers and gently pulled.

"And the fourth affirmation?"

She glanced up at his face. "It's always been the hardest one for me to believe." And the hardest to confess. Her eyes stung with tears. "I am worthy to be loved."

"Lass." He smoothed back her hair. "I have never met anyone more worthy of love than you."

"Ian." She touched his face. "That's what I think about you."

He pulled her into his arms and kissed her. She kissed him back with all the passion that had grown inside her for days. He slanted his mouth over hers and invaded her with his tongue. Her knees grew weak. There was such hunger in his kiss. It made her feel desperate. Feverish.

She raked her hands down his smooth, bare back. "I want you."

"Ye have me." He wadded her green elfin tunic in his fists and pulled it up and over her head. Her long-sleeved red T-shirt soon followed. Before she could lower her arms, he had her bra unclasped.

"You're very quick."

"Aye." He flung her bra aside. "Like you, I intend to accomplish my goals." He cupped one of her breasts.

Her nipples hardened under the gaze of his red, glowing eyes. She squeezed her thighs together. "What is your goal?"

"To make ye moan." He rubbed his thumb over a tight nipple, and she did moan. "To make ye shudder and scream." He leaned over to take her nipple into his mouth. He suckled, teased her with his tongue, then gently tugged.

She shuddered and leaned back in his arms.

"I want to feast on you." He gave his attention to her other breast.

Through a haze of sensual pleasure, she recalled that word *feast*. He was tormenting her nipple with his tongue. Were his fangs next? "You want to bite me?"

He lifted his head and gave her a look of admonishment. "I'm no' doing this for food."

"But you said *feast*."

His mouth quirked. "I was referring to oral sex. Do ye have any objection to letting me kiss and suck on you?"

She gulped. "No, that would be fine."

He slid his fingers underneath the waistband of her red tights and slowly tugged them down. "And ye'll no' be shy about getting all juicy when ye come on my face?"

"No," she squeaked.

He smiled as his hands curved over her bare rump, dragging her tights down further. "Naughty lass, ye're no' wearing undies."

"I learned that from you." She smoothed her hands over his biceps, then over his shoulders and onto his chest. "You're the most beautiful man."

He snorted. With her tights rolled halfway down her thighs, he grabbed her at the waist and set her on the table. Then he grasped her tights and finished dragging them down her legs.

"I've been wanting to touch yer legs for days." He lifted them and rested her ankles on his shoulders. "So long and golden, kissed by the sun." He slid his hands down to her thighs and turned his head to kiss her calf.

Toni squirmed on her bare rump, becoming more and more aware of the slow, throbbing need between her legs. He moved forward, coming closer to her core, kissing the inside of her knee, her thigh. The red glow of his eyes in the dark sent a thrill through her. God, she wanted him.

"Please." She fell back onto the table. She hooked her feet around the back of his neck to pull him closer.

He stroked his fingers across her belly, and she trembled. "By all the saints, I can smell yer scent. It's so sweet. I canna resist tasting you."

His words struck a primeval need inside her, making her even more wet. And ready. She opened her thighs to him.

His eyes burned red. He dragged his fingers into her curls, then leaned forward. "I want to see yer face when I touch you for the first time."

She focused on his red eyes, then gasped when his fingers slid between her legs. She shuddered as he stroked her gently, easing his way between her sensitive folds. She saw a flash of white teeth as he smiled.

"Ye're so verra wet." He inserted a finger inside her. "And verra warm."

"Yes." She pushed against him.

"Och, puir lass." He waggled his finger inside her. "Ye're in sore need of attention." With his other hand, he tweaked her clitoris.

She squeaked. He pressed against her, and she pushed back.

She dug her fingernails into the table. "Please, hurry."

He removed his finger. "We'll take it slow next time." He sat in a chair and rolled it up to the table. Meanwhile, he cupped her bottom and pulled her up to his face.

"This, sweetheart, is what I mean by a feast." He pounced on her, dragging his tongue over her engorged skin, probing, tasting, licking.

Toni squirmed, and he held her steady. She panted, closing her eyes as all sensation centered on her hot skin and his glorious mouth. He tickled her clitoris, then sucked on it gently. She cried out. Her legs tensed. His tongue flitted.

She screamed. A heart-stopping, delicious shudder crashed over her, then swelled up to crash over her again and again.

"Och, Toni." He stood and pulled at the drawstring on his red velvet pants. "I'm dying for you."

He stopped suddenly, tilting his head and frowning.

"What is it?" She struggled to sit up. Her body was a melted heap of frazzled nerve endings.

"Bloody hell," he muttered. "The alarm has gone off."

Chapter Twenty

Ian cursed again as he threw on his Santa coat. With vampire speed, he buttoned it up and yanked on his boots.

What bloody awful timing. He would have been tempted to let Connor or Angus deal with this, but the alarm had been triggered by an emergency psychic call for help from Phineas. Ian had taught the young Vamp how to fence. He had to be there for Phineas, no matter how much he wanted Toni. And God, he wanted her.

She was leaning over to pull on her red tights. Her long blonde hair fell forward, partially hiding her flushed face. She straightened, flipping her hair back as she wiggled the tights over her hips. By all the saints, he'd never realized that putting clothes on could be so sexy.

"Bloody hell," he whispered.

"Is it bad?" She snatched her bra off the floor.

"Aye. It's downright painful. I'm rock hard and about to explode." He belted on his sword.

She paused with her bra half on. "I was referring to the attack."

He glanced at the window overlooking the parking lot. It was still snowing, so visibility was bad. "I can hear them outside. Phineas must have been making the rounds."

He put on his beard, wig, and hat. "Stay here. I'll be back as soon as possible."

"But I should help. It's my job." She pulled on her red T-shirt.

"Stay here," he repeated. "There are plenty of Vamps to take care of the matter."

"You don't think I'm strong enough to fight a Malcontent, do you?"

"Honestly, I'd rather no' find out." He teleported to the parking lot and saw the tracks in the snow where other Vamps had crossed the pavement to the woods. He heard the clash of swords in the distance. Drawing his own sword, he zoomed toward the noise.

As he entered the woods, the snowfall became lighter as snowflakes were caught by the canopy overhead. He spotted a dozen red Santa suits in a clearing. They were standing still, so each had a slight dusting of snow on his hat and shoulders. Most of the Santas had formed a loop around a pair engaged in a duel. Phineas and a Malcontent, dressed in black. They circled each other slowly.

Two more Santas had a second Malcontent pinned against a tree with their swords poised to strike his heart.

Ian joined the circle of Santas. "What happened?" he whispered to the man on his right.

"Phineas was making his rounds in the woods here," the Santa answered, and Ian recognized Robby MacKay's voice. "Two Malcontents jumped him, and he called for help. We sounded the alarm and came running."

Swords rang out as the Malcontent lunged at Phineas. He parried the attack and forced the Malcontent to retreat.

"We captured that one." Robby nodded toward the second Malcontent pinned against the tree. "The other one challenged Phineas to a duel, and he accepted."

Ian watched the duel carefully, gauging each one's skill. They appeared evenly matched, though he detected more desperation from the Russian.

"Let's go, Stanislav!" the captured Malcontent yelled. "Let's get the hell out of here!"

"The second I see your body start to teleport, I'll stab you through the heart," one of his captors warned. Ian recognized his French accent. Jean-Luc Echarpe.

"The devil take it," the second captor grumbled. It was Angus. "Let's just skewer the bastard and get it over with."

"I'm unarmed!" the captive shouted.

"Ye were armed two minutes ago before ye threw yer sword down," Angus argued. "Look, Yuri. Aye, no need to look surprised. I know who ye are. 'Tis a simple matter of being time-efficient. If we doona kill ye now, ye'll just come back, and we'll have to do it later. So I say we slaughter you now. 'Twill save us all a lot of time."

Jean-Luc chuckled. "You expect him to agree with you?"

"If you're as good and noble as you claim to be," Yuri said, "then you'll never kill an unarmed man."

"Och, I hate it when they say that," Angus growled.

Jean-Luc pressed the point of his sword against Yuri's throat. "Don't be a coward, Yuri. Pick up your weapon, and we'll settle this like men."

"Now ye've scared him," Angus said. "I think he's wet his pants."

"I did not!" Yuri protested. "Stanislav, I'll leave without you."

Stanislav was busy with Phineas. Both men eased slowly to their right, their legs bent, their swords ready.

"Stan the man, you're going down," Phineas spoke softly. "Why are you doing this? I always thought you were pretty decent. You were the only Russian I could stand to talk to."

"You double-crossed me, you bastard." Stanislav slipped in the snow and quickly righted himself. "You tricked me into telling you where Katya was."

"She was a bitch, Stan. Haven't you realized yet that you're on the wrong side? You're one of the bad guys."

"Traitor!" Stanislav lunged forward, swinging his sword wildly.

Phineas blocked each move, and Stanislav fell back, breathing heavily.

Phineas circled him. "You're not going to live through this, Stan."

"Let's go!" Yuri yelled.

"I can't!" Stanislav wiped sweat from his brow. "Jedrek will kill me if I don't kill Phineas."

"You're up shit creek." Phineas advanced, and with an expert thrust, he sent Stan's sword flying from his hand.

Stanislav backed away.

Phineas grazed the tip of his sword on Stanislav's chest. "The way I see it, you have three options. You can be killed by me, killed by Jedrek, or you can join our side."

"Now wait a minute." Angus strode toward them. "I seriously doubt we could ever trust this bastard."

Stanislav vanished. Ian turned just in time to see Yuri teleport away, too.

"Merde," Jean-Luc muttered.

Angus sighed. "Ah well." He patted Phineas on the back. "Ye did well, lad."

Phineas sheathed his sword. "I should've killed him when I had the chance. I just . . ."

"Dinna want to?" Angus asked. "That's what makes you one of us, lad. We kill when we have to, but we doona relish it."

"But he'll just come back," Phineas said.

Angus rested an arm around his shoulder. "There are always bad vampires in want of killing. I've lived over five hundred years, and that has never changed. One thing that time has taught me is there's no need to be in a hurry to kill."

"Aye, that's true." Connor spoke from the circle. "Ye kill one, and two more show up the next night."

"It's freezing out here," Roman observed. "Let's get back to the party."

The Santas walked back to the parking lot. Ian sheathed his sword.

Robby leaned toward him and whispered, "Ye'd better wash her scent off before Connor or Angus get a whiff of you." He strode off to join the other Santas.

Ian winced. He waited till all the Santas had entered Romatech, then he zoomed down to the silver room. With vampire speed, he showered and redressed.

He sprinted to the stairs. When he heard a dinging sound behind him, he glanced back. The elevator doors opened, and Toni stepped out.

"Toni." He strode toward her. So much for her doing as he asked and staying in the conference room.

She spun around. "Ian. What are you doing down here? I thought you'd be with Phineas."

"I was, but . . . what are you doing down here?"

She lowered her voice. "I was in the foyer, finding out what happened outside, when Emma MacKay whispered to me that I should retire for the evening. She's one of the big bosses, so I didn't want to argue, but I got the impression that she knew what we'd been doing . . ."

"Vamps have a verra good sense of smell. I received a similar warning."

She stepped closer. "They can smell that we . . . you know?"

"I know verra well. Unfortunately, a few others have noticed, too."

"Good grief," she muttered. "Can't we get a little privacy around here?"

Ian grinned. "Are ye so eager to jump in bed with me?"

"Quiet." She glanced around the hallway. "I don't want to get you in trouble. And I don't want to get fired. I sure don't want to lose my memory, not after . . . you know."

"Are ye referring to how ye gushed all over my face?"

She winced. "We shouldn't talk about that." She glanced around the hallway again.

"We're all alone, sweetheart."

She scanned the ceiling. "But there are surveillance cameras around here somewhere."

"Aye. That's why I havena taken you into my arms." He folded his arms over his chest. "I just took a cold shower, and it dinna help."

"Oh, Ian." She sighed. "I don't know where we can go. All the bedrooms down here have cameras."

"I'll figure out something. It'll be easier once Connor takes Roman back into hiding. And Jean-Luc is having a house party in Texas, so a lot of the guests are teleporting there later tonight."

"That's good." Toni yawned.

"Ye're tired. Go on to bed, sweetheart." As he watched her enter the silver room, he knew he could never give her up. He wasn't sure how he could fit into her plan to run an orphanage and school. But he knew he loved her enough that he couldn't bear for her to sacrifice any of her dreams. Somehow they would make it work.

Connor wouldn't dare erase her memory if she was engaged to him. That was a big step, but it didn't cause any warning signals to flare up inside him. It simply felt right. And exciting.

The next morning, Toni called Carlos to see how Sabrina was faring.

"She's fully awake now," Carlos reported. "And full of questions. She wants to know why she can't go home. And how you managed to get her out of the hospital. I asked Teddy to stay quiet till you got a chance to talk to her, but he keeps dropping hints about superheroes."

"Tell her I'll explain everything this evening when I get off work," Toni said. "Or I'll try to."

"There's another problem," Carlos continued. "The local stations have posted Bri's photo on their television newscasts. They say she's been kidnapped. I don't dare take her anywhere she can be noticed."

Toni winced. They couldn't stay hidden in a hotel forever.

"I thought we could meet you at that vampire nightclub," Carlos suggested.

"The Horny Devils? Why?"

"It's a great place to hide. No mortal would ever look for her there. And I doubt any Vamp would call the police to report her. It's also a really good place to convince Bri that vampires are real."

"I don't know." Toni frowned. "It might scare the hell out of her."

"The male Vamps there are strippers. They'll seem harmless." Carlos lowered his voice. "Bri still thinks she's delusional. We have to give her proof that she's right, or she'll end up back in a mental hospital."

"Okay, okay. I'll ask Ian to take me there tonight. We'll meet you at five-thirty." She hung up.

Early that afternoon UPS delivered a small blue box for her from Tiffany's. With her heart racing, Toni pulled out a gold heart-shaped pendant on a gold chain. It came with a note—*All my love, Ian.*

He loved her. She could hardly concentrate on anything for the rest of the day. She didn't want Howard to know she'd received a gift from Ian, so she slipped the heart underneath her polo shirt and let it nestle between her breasts.

When the sun went down, she hurried to the silver room to change clothes. "Thank you, thank you!" She grinned at Ian as she ran into the bathroom to change.

"We need to go to the Horny Devils," she called out to him. He was in the kitchen drinking his breakfast. "We're supposed to meet Carlos, Bri, and Teddy there."

"They're going to the Horny Devils?" he asked. "Why?"

"So we can convince Bri that she's not delusional." She pulled on a pair of jeans and a green sweater, then opened the door. "Can you teleport me there?"

"Aye." He pulled his cell phone from his sporran. "Let me warn Vanda. And I'll need to tell Howard that we'll be gone for a little while."

Five minutes later, Toni arrived with Ian in the alley outside the Horny Devils.

Carlos was already there with Bri and Teddy. He motioned to the bouncer. "That guy wouldn't let us in."

Bri gave Ian a suspicious look. "Why are we here? I just want to go home."

"We can't go to the apartment, Bri," Toni said. "Your uncle would look for you there. We need to hide you here for a while."

Bri cast a nervous glance at the huge bouncer. "What is this place?"

"I bet it's their secret Batcave!" Teddy exclaimed.

"It's more like a nightclub," Toni explained. "Vanda is expecting us, right?"

"Aye," Ian answered. "She agreed to let you hide in the VIP room. She even had some mortal food delivered."

"Mortal?" Bri whispered.

"I knew it!" Teddy leaned close to her. "He's from another planet. That's why he has superpowers here."

"I'm no' a superhero," Ian grumbled.

"Of course you are!" Teddy insisted. "You have superpowers, man. And I'm gonna be your sidekick."

"Ian, we have to tell them the truth," Toni said.

He frowned. "Are ye sure they can handle it?"

"Sabrina deserves to know that she was right all along." Carlos looked at Sabrina. "*Menina*, you were never delusional."

Bri shook her head. "No, I was wrong. Vampires aren't real."

Ian glanced at Carlos. "Ye know the truth then?" He gave

Toni a disappointed look. "Ye were no' supposed to tell anyone."

"Carlos needed to know what was going on," Toni said. "And besides, he knows how to keep a secret."

Ian regarded Carlos curiously. "Aye, he certainly does."

Carlos exchanged a quick look with Ian before turning back to Sabrina. "*Menina*, remember how you were attacked by some vicious vampires?"

She shook her head. "I was mistaken."

"You asked me to go to Central Park and find them," Toni said. "Those same vampires jumped me."

Bri gasped. "No!"

"Yes. I was attacked. And I might have died if a guy with a sword didn't come along and save me."

"Did he have superpowers?" Teddy asked.

"Yes," Toni replied. "He stabbed one of the attackers, and he turned to dust. The other two vanished. Then the guy with the sword teleported me to Romatech."

"Is that another planet?" Teddy asked.

Ian groaned.

Toni smiled. "It's Romatech Industries. They manufacture synthetic blood. Connor, the guy who saved me, told me he was a good vampire."

"Whoa," Teddy said. "A good vampire?"

Bri shook her head. "There's no such thing."

"Yes, there is," Toni insisted. "Just like mortals can be good or bad, vampires can be good or bad." She motioned to Ian. "He's a good vampire."

Bri backed away, a look of horror on her face. "He's one of them? He bites people?"

"Nay." Ian frowned at her. "I drink bottled blood from Romatech."

"And you have superpowers," Teddy added. "That is so cool. I guess you're fighting the bad vampires?"

"We call them Malcontents," Ian explained. "They call themselves the True Ones."

"Toni." Bri sidled up close to her and whispered, "Why are you hanging out with . . . *him*?"

"Ian's one of the good guys," Toni whispered back. "I've been working for them since I was attacked."

"Why? Are they controlling you?"

"No. I wanted to find a way to prove you were right. You were never delusional, Bri. Your uncle's been holding you prisoner and keeping you drugged so he can control your money."

"But he—he's my uncle . . ."

It was sad to watch. Toni could see Bri figuring it all out step by step as the emotions flitted across her face. Disbelief, then shock, then horror, then anger.

Her face flushed. "I was never sick."

"No, sweetie." Toni gave her shoulders a squeeze.

She gave Ian a wary look. "And vampires are real." She closed her eyes and shuddered.

"Let's go inside," Ian suggested. "Hugo, these people are with me."

Hugo grunted and opened the door.

Ian strode inside with Carlos and Teddy. Bri hung back, clinging to Toni.

"It's okay," Toni insisted. "This is a nightclub for Vamps." When Bri's face paled, she continued, "They all drink from bottles. It's perfectly safe."

Bri let Toni pull her inside. Bright flashing lights and loud music greeted them. Bri stayed close to Toni, and her gaze flitted nervously about. Toni noted the usual bunch of scantily clad girls bouncing to the music, close to the stage.

"Those girls are hot," Teddy said. "Are they all—?"

"Undead, yes." Carlos looked curiously about.

The girls squealed when a dancer strutted onto the stage, dressed like a pirate. He tossed his tricorne hat into the crowd, and the ladies scrambled to claim it as a souvenir. More clothes flew through the air till the dancer was down to his bikini underwear. He turned his back to the crowd to show off the skull and crossbones printed on the back of his underwear. He rotated his hips suggestively.

"Oh my," Sabrina whispered.

"He's very talented," Toni agreed.

"Ladies, are ye coming?" Ian stood by Vanda's office, watching them with a wry look on his face. Carlos and Teddy were waiting with him.

"We're coming." Toni tugged on Bri's arm.

She glanced back at the dancer. "I'm starting to feel much better now."

Toni laughed. "It's good to have you back." She joined Ian at Vanda's office, and he arched an eyebrow at her. Her face grew warm. "I was just looking."

His mouth twitched, and he knocked on Vanda's office door.

She greeted them. "Come on in. I've got everything ready."

As Toni entered, she smiled. "Thank you for your help."

"No problem." Vanda regarded her sternly.

Toni had a feeling she didn't approve. As Ian introduced everyone, Vanda's gaze flitted over Bri and Teddy, then came to rest on Carlos. Her eyes narrowed suspiciously.

Carlos smiled slightly. "I like your cat suit."

"Thanks." Vanda adjusted the whip she used as a belt. She opened a door that revealed a narrow staircase. "This is the back entrance. I figured you don't want anyone to see you going up there."

"That is correct." Ian led them up the stairs.

Toni stepped through some hanging strands of beads and brushed back a gauzy curtain. "Good grief."

"Wow," Bri whispered. "It's beautiful. It looks like Princess Jasmine's boudoir."

"Glad you like it." Vanda swept into the harem-styled room. "As you can see, there's food and drink on the table and plenty of big cushions for resting." She pointed at two doors across the room. "That's the restroom and the main stairs."

"It's perfect." Toni wandered over to the carved wooden screen. She could see the club below. "Thank you, Vanda."

She adjusted her belt with an annoyed look. "Ian's a good friend. I'd do anything for him."

"So would I." Toni glanced at Ian. He was at the refreshment table, pouring himself a glass of Bleer.

Vanda stepped closer. "Would you give him up?"

Toni stiffened. "Why would I do that?"

"Because he wants a true mate," Vanda insisted. "Someone who can spend eternity with him. You can't do that."

"I don't know how things will work out," Toni said. "But I do know I'm in love with him." She heard a gasp behind her.

"You're in love with a vampire?" Sabrina screeched.

Toni winced as everyone stared at her with shock or dismay on their faces. Everyone except Ian. He was watching her intently, his eyes sparkling with emotion.

She lifted her chin. "Yes, I'm in love with Ian."

He walked toward her, a smile slowly forming on his lips.

Vanda scowled at him. "You said all you wanted was a vampire."

"I changed my mind." Ian was grinning now, and the sharp points of his fangs showed.

Sabrina pressed a hand to her chest. "Toni, how could you?"

"How could I not?" She pulled the heart pendant out from behind her green sweater. The gold chain and heart glimmered in the soft overhead lights. "Thank you for sending me your heart."

Ian halted and his grin faded. "I dinna send that."

Toni blinked. "But it came this afternoon with a note that said, *All my love.*"

Ian zipped toward her, and with a quick wrench of his wrist, he broke the chain around her neck.

"Ian—" Toni gasped when he dropped the pendant on a low table and smashed it with his fist.

He picked up a small metal piece.

"That's a tracking device," Carlos said.

Ian dropped the device on the floor and crushed it with his heel. "I'll summon Phineas and Dougal here, and we'll teleport everyone to Romatech." He stepped away, closing his eyes briefly.

Toni realized he was sending out a psychic message.

Sabrina clutched her arm. "Who—who would want to follow us? Is it my uncle or the police?"

"Worse," Carlos muttered.

Teddy's eyes lit up. "The evil forces! They're upon us!"

Shots exploded below in the club, and screams filled the air.

Chapter Twenty-one

Ian dashed to the wooden screen to see what was happening below. He spotted Jedrek Janow with a pistol in his hand and a sheathed sword hanging from his belt. Jedrek shot twice in the air and laughed when the women scurried about, screaming. Thankfully, most of the women had enough sense to teleport away.

"Toni, call Dougal and Phineas, so they can use yer voice to teleport straight to this room. And tell them to bring extra weapons." When Ian had sent out a psychic message, he'd merely summoned them to the Horny Devils. But now he didn't want them to accidentally teleport into the turmoil below. And he didn't want to send another psychic message that Jedrek could overhear.

Toni whipped her cell phone from her pants pocket.

Sabrina started crying, and Teddy tried to comfort her. Vanda and Carlos were peering through the wooden screen.

"They're taking hostages," Carlos said quietly.

Ian looked at the scene below. About ten of the

lady Vamps had frozen in fear and failed to teleport to safety. Stanislav and Yuri were using silver ropes to lasso them like frightened heifers, while Jedrek stood on stage, smiling as the silver burned their skin and made them scream. The women were herded together, and a Malcontent woman looped more silver rope around them to keep them confined and unable to teleport away.

Phineas and Dougal materialized next to Toni, carrying five swords and some wooden stakes.

Ian passed a sword to Carlos. "Do ye know how to wield it?"

"I can learn." Carlos gripped the hilt. "Why don't you use guns?"

"We can recover from most bullet wounds, but a sword through the heart is permanent." Ian offered the last spare sword to Vanda.

"No thanks." She untied the whip from her waist. "I'm more comfortable with this."

"Can I have a sword?" Teddy approached him.

"Teddy, no!" Sabrina pulled him back. "We shouldn't get involved."

"I want to be a hero, too," Teddy insisted.

Ian passed him the sword. "Ye'll guard the women."

"He can protect Bri." Toni grabbed some wooden stakes. "I'm not staying here."

"Ye are—" Ian was interrupted by Jedrek's booming voice.

"Ian MacPhie! I know you're here. Bring me the Stay-Awake drug or I'll start killing." Jedrek's voice was muffled by screams from the hostages.

Ian motioned for Phineas and Dougal to join him at the screen. "We'll teleport at the same time. I'll take Jedrek."

Phineas peered through the screen. "I'll take Stan."

"Then I'll take Yuri," Dougal said.

"And I'll take the woman," Toni added.

Ian stiffened. "Nay. Ye're staying here."

"*I* will take the woman." Vanda glared at Toni. "I can teleport. You can't."

Toni glared back. "I can handle the silver ropes to untie the hostages. You can't."

"Ye're no' going—" Ian was interrupted by Jedrek.

"Don't think you can attack me, MacPhie!" he shouted from the stage. "We have a hostage here, and she'll die if anyone comes close to me. Nadia, you will kill the blonde to please me."

"Yes, Master." With gloved hands, Nadia tied a blonde hostage to the dancer pole on the stage.

"Oh no," Vanda whispered. "It's Cora Lee."

The bartender struggled against the silver ropes that bound her and sizzled against her bare skin. "Let me go!"

Jedrek pointed his handgun at her. "Silver bullets, my dear. They really hurt." When Cora Lee whimpered, he smiled. "Your fear makes you even more attractive."

"Vanda," Toni whispered. "Do you have any wire cutters around here?"

"Maybe. There's a tool kit in my office."

"Toni." Ian regarded her sternly. "Ye are no' going down there." When she opened her mouth to argue, Ian continued, "This is no' a friendly request. I'm yer boss. Ye'll do as I say."

Her eyes flashed with anger.

Ian turned to Carlos. "Ye both stay here."

"You can't order me around," Carlos growled.

Ian ignored him and motioned to the other Vamps. "We teleport on three." He counted, and they vanished.

Ian materialized beside Jedrek and with the first swipe of his sword, he sent the gun flying from Jedrek's hand.

Jedrek jumped back, spotted the blood seeping from his cut hand, and yelled, "Kill the blonde, Nadia!"

Ian glanced over to see Cora Lee, still tied to the pole,

squirming and crying. Nadia was too busy avoiding Vanda's snapping whip to follow her master's orders.

Ian charged at Jedrek, but he vanished.

"Damn!" Ian spun around to see where the coward had teleported.

Dougal and Phineas had engaged their opponents, and the clash of swords mingled with frantic screams from hostages. Jedrek reappeared, standing on the bar. He drew his sword, and blood dripped from his hand.

Good, let his grip grow slippery. Ian jumped from the stage and stalked toward him. *Let him grow weak from the loss of blood.*

Jedrek kept his eyes on Ian as he reached down and nabbed some paper napkins off the bar. He pressed the napkins against his bleeding hand.

"Amazing how much those little cuts can bleed," Ian observed.

With a sneer, Jedrek tossed the bloodied napkins to the floor.

From the corner of his eye, Ian noticed Toni slipping from Vanda's office. Dammit, no! She had wooden stakes stuffed in her waistband and wire cutters in her hand. Staying low, she dashed to the back of the hostages.

He couldn't let Jedrek see her. Jedrek had sent her the heart pendant. He knew Ian cared for her, and that made her a prime target. By all the saints, she should have known that. She should have minded him and remained hidden.

Ian zipped quickly to the bar and leaped on top, forcing Jedrek to face him and turn his back to Toni. Ian lunged, slashing his sword with full force. Jedrek teetered on the edge of the bar, losing his balance, then vanished.

"Damn!" Ian spun around. How could he fight the cowardly bastard if he kept teleporting?

From his position on the bar, Ian could see most of the room. Already the group of hostages had dwindled from ten to six. Another vanished, making it five. Toni was obviously freeing them as quickly as she could. But her own success would be her downfall, for with no hostages left, there would be no one for her to hide behind.

Jedrek reappeared on the stage. "This one will die, Mac-Phie!" He lunged toward Cora Lee.

"No!" Vanda snapped her whip at him. It tangled around his sword arm.

"You bitch!" He grabbed the whip and yanked Vanda toward him. She released her whip to keep from being pulled onto his sword. "I should have killed you in Poland. You would always hide in the caves like a rat."

Vanda scrambled back.

"It will please me, Nadia, for you to kill the blonde," Jedrek ordered.

"Yes, Master." Nadia advanced on Cora Lee.

"And I will kill *you*, Vanda." Jedrek lifted his sword.

Ian teleported to the stage and intercepted Jedrek.

"Help me!" Cora Lee screamed as Nadia came closer.

With an angry shriek, Vanda leaped on Nadia's back. The two women tumbled onto the stage, scrambling for the dropped sword. Ian wanted to help, but he was fending off Jedrek's attack.

Behind Jedrek, he spotted Toni sneaking onto the stage. Oh, hell no. He fought furiously, attempting to keep Jedrek fully engaged. Toni ran past them and clipped the silver ropes holding Cora Lee to the pole. Cora Lee scrambled off the stage, crying. Meanwhile, Nadia reclaimed her sword, and she stalked toward a weaponless Vanda.

Toni grabbed the silver rope that had bound Cora Lee and charged, swinging the ropes at the back of Nadia's head. Nadia cried out in pain. The air smelled of burnt hair.

Ian leaped back as Jedrek's sword narrowly missed slashing his stomach. He needed to pay better attention. He lunged at Jedrek, but the bastard vanished once more.

"Bloody hell!" Ian wheeled around, searching for his opponent.

Jedrek appeared next to Toni.

"No!" Ian zoomed toward them, but Jedrek vanished, taking Toni with him. "No!" Fear seized his throat in an icy grip.

Relief swept over him when he saw Jedrek reappear on the bar with Toni. At least the bastard hadn't taken her to some secret place to torture and kill her. Ian jumped from the stage and ran toward them.

His relief was short-lived. Jedrek yanked Toni against his chest and pressed his sword to her neck. Ian froze.

"Comrades, to me!" Jedrek shouted, and the three other Russians teleported to the bar. "You see, MacPhie, we only need one hostage when we have the right one." With a hissing sound, his fangs sprang out.

He nuzzled his mouth against Toni's cheek. His fangs scraped her skin, leaving a pink mark. She squeezed her eyes shut. "I can smell her fear, MacPhie. No wonder you like her so much. She tastes delicious."

Ian swallowed hard as bile rose in his throat. He had to save Toni, but God help him, he didn't know how. The second he attacked, Jedrek would slice her throat.

"You know what I want, MacPhie. Bring me the drug."

Should he play along to buy some time? Despair roiled in Ian's gut, threatening to smother his ability to think. He couldn't bear to lose her. He couldn't bear to fail her. He dropped his sword, and it clattered on the cement floor.

Jedrek smiled. "You have five minutes."

A loud crash sounded overhead. Everyone looked up as splintered pieces of wood rained down. And through the cracked opening of the wooden shutters, a giant black panther leaped into the air. It roared, and the sound echoed in the stunned silence of the nightclub.

With Jedrek distracted, Ian retrieved his sword and moved

toward him. Unfortunately, Jedrek realized the panther was headed straight for him. He pivoted, dragging Toni with him so she'd take the full force of the animal's attack. He extended his sword, obviously hoping to skewer the panther as it landed.

With Jedrek's back turned to him, Ian zoomed forward and stabbed the Malcontent's right shoulder. Jedrek cried out and dropped his sword. His hold on Toni loosened enough that she was able to duck just as the panther slammed into them. Its massive paws caught Jedrek on the shoulders and knocked him and Toni off the bar. Ian jumped to the right as the panther flew past him, hit the ground, and rolled onto its feet. Toni had landed on top of Jedrek. She dove to the left just as the panther pounced. Jedrek shrieked as razor-sharp claws ripped through his shirt and scored his chest with bloody stripes.

Toni screamed and scooted away on her rump. The panther looked at her, then turned toward the bar, its amber eyes narrowing on the three Malcontents. They teleported away. Jedrek, too. The cat, realizing its prey had escaped, roared in anger.

Dougal and Phineas approached slowly, their swords pointed at the beast.

"Shall we kill it?" Dougal asked.

"Nay!" Ian shouted. "Leave him be."

The panther swung toward him, snarling, then focused its familiar amber eyes on Toni. As its head turned, Ian noted the gleam of two gold studs in its pointed ears. Of course. He should have known. But he would have never guessed a panther.

The giant cat stalked toward Toni.

"No." She scrambled back and tried to get to her feet, but her legs were shaking.

Ian flung himself in front of her. "Carlos, no."

The panther growled low in its throat.

"Carlos?" Toni whispered.

Ian heard a dull thud and glanced back. Toni was sprawled on the floor in a dead faint. "Och, lass." He squatted beside her and brushed her hair from her face.

"That's Carlos?" Phineas lowered his sword and whistled under his breath. "Hello, kitty."

The panther padded toward Toni on its huge paws. Ian was relieved to see its claws were in, but those teeth were awfully sharp. One nip and Toni would be a were-panther for life. Was that what Carlos wanted?

The cat lowered its head to sniff her.

"By all the saints, doona bite her," Ian whispered.

The panther whipped its thick tail around so hard and fast, it knocked Ian onto his knees. Then it trotted toward Vanda's office. Toni had left the door slightly ajar, and the cat squeezed through.

"I thought he smelled like a shape shifter," Dougal said. "But I assumed he would be a black wolf."

"Me, too." Ian supposed Carlos was headed back to the harem room to change and dress. When Sabrina screamed, he knew the panther had arrived.

"God, I hate shape shifters." Vanda had found her whip and was looping it around her waist.

"You know of them?" Ian asked.

Vanda shrugged. "Long story. Just get that cat out of here, okay?"

"He saved Toni's life," Phineas reminded her.

"She wouldn't have needed saving if she'd followed orders," Vanda snapped. "You should fire her ass, Ian."

"No!" Cora Lee strode toward Vanda. "Toni cut me free. She freed all the hostages. And she kept that terrible Nadia from killing you, Vanda. Land sakes, I've never seen a mortal be so brave."

"Okay, okay, she's brave." Vanda tightened her whip. "But she still can't follow orders."

Yes, she'd disobeyed a direct order. Ian tamped down on the anger simmering inside him. She'd disobeyed him and come bloody close to dying. And he'd been helpless to save her. If it hadn't been for Carlos . . . his anger spiked. Dammit. That was the real cause of his anger. Carlos had saved her. He had not.

He heard her moan softly. He patted her cheek, and her eyelids flickered. "Toni, wake up."

She blinked at him with a dazed look. "What happened?"

"Ye fainted."

She struggled to sit up. "That's crazy. I never faint." She looked around. "The Malcontents?"

"They teleported away," Ian explained. "I doubt we'll see them again tonight. Jedrek's in bad shape."

Toni looked around again. "Carlos? He's a—?"

"Were-panther." Ian helped her to her feet. "It's rather unusual."

"Well, duh." She glanced up at the shattered wooden screen. "I didn't think such creatures existed."

"I've never known one who shifted to a cat." Ian noticed Hugo stumbling into the nightclub. His hands were tied behind his back with silver rope, and blood oozed from a bullet wound in his thigh.

"Oh my God!" Vanda rushed to him.

"We'll take him back to Romatech," Ian offered. "Laszlo can remove the bullet."

"I'll take him." Dougal grabbed Hugo's arm, and they both vanished.

With a sigh, Vanda ran a hand through her short, spiky hair. "Everyone's gone, so I'm closing for the night. I just hope the customers will come back, that we're not ruined."

"Land sakes, don't you worry about that," Cora Lee said. "This place will be notorious. We'll be packing them in."

"I hope so." Vanda set an overturned chair upright. "Let's get the place cleaned up."

Cora Lee surveyed the room, frowning. "Lady Pamela sure picked the right night to take off."

Ian grabbed Toni and teleported to the VIP room. Phineas arrived shortly after them. Sabrina gasped at their sudden appearance and retreated across the room.

Carlos was back in his human form and gave them a nervous glance as he buttoned his shirt.

Toni approached him slowly. "You saved my life."

"I wanted to tell you about my . . . condition, but—" He glanced at Sabrina, who was regarding him with horror. "I didn't want to lose your friendship."

"Carlos." Toni wrapped her arms around him. "You will always be my friend."

He hugged her back. "Thank you, *menina*. You know I would do anything for you."

She gave him a wry look. "I thought I saw a puddy tat."

He grinned. "You did, you did."

They both laughed. Ian felt a mixture of emotion—a twinge of jealousy and a surge of pride. Toni was so generous and accepting. She'd risked her life to save Vamps she didn't even know, and she remained loyal to her friends no matter what.

"It's not funny," Sabrina muttered from across the room. "I saw him change. It was awful."

"It was awesome, man." Teddy blushed. "Though it was kinda freaky when he started stripping."

"That was nothing," Sabrina argued. "What about the black fur sprouting out and the claws and the sound of bones breaking and shifting?" She shuddered.

"Yeah, that was cool." Teddy's face brightened with excitement. "Do you have a name, dude? Like Panther-Man?"

"No." Carlos sat on a low table to put on his socks and shoes.

"Oh, come on." Teddy sat beside him. "You superheroes are totally ignorant about how to behave. How do you expect to get famous without cool names?"

"We doona want fame." Ian stood in front of Teddy. "Listen to me. Ye canna speak of us. Ever. If the outside world learned of our existence, they would kill us."

"That's true." Carlos slipped on his shoes. "My kind was discovered by a land developer in the Amazon. He sent out hunters to destroy us all. They're tracking down my people and killing them."

Toni pressed a hand to her chest. "Carlos, I'm so sorry. That's terrible."

"I managed to save some of the children. Their parents were slaughtered."

"Those are the orphans you're supporting?" Toni asked.

Carlos nodded. "Five of them. Our numbers are dwindling fast. I've been searching Malaysia because there are panthers in the jungle, and odd stories are told in the villages. I've been hoping to locate more of my kind."

"I'll tell Angus," Ian said. "He'll be happy to fund yer research. His company has always been supportive of werefolk."

Carlos's amber eyes gleamed. "That would be wonderful, thank you."

"What other kinds of shifters are there?" Teddy asked.

"Most of the ones I've met are wolves." Ian went to the refreshment table to pour himself a Bleer. "Of course, Howard isn't."

"What?" Toni looked confused. "Howard's a shape shifter?"

Carlos helped himself to a sandwich off the refreshment table. "You said it yourself, Toni. He's a teddy bear."

Ian snorted. "No' nearly as cuddly as a teddy bear once he's shifted, believe me."

Toni's mouth dropped open. "My supervisor is a *bear*?"

"Aye. Howard Barr." Ian drained his glass.

"That is so incredibly awesome," Teddy whispered.

"No, it isn't!" Sabrina screamed. "I can't take it. Panthers and vampires and bears—"

"Oh my!" Phineas quipped.

"You're all monsters!" Sabrina edged toward the main staircase. "I'm getting out of here!"

"Bri, wait!" Toni ran toward her. "You can't go. You have no money. No ID."

"And the police are looking for you," Carlos added.

"Like that's *my* fault?" Sabrina glared at them. "You took me from my room."

"We rescued you," Toni said, frowning.

"You made me a penniless fugitive." Sabrina lifted her chin. "Now I'm going to my apartment to get the key to my safety deposit box. I have a passport in there and lots of cash, so I don't have to hang around with *monsters*!"

Carlos walked toward her. "You can't go to your apartment, Bri. The police will look for you there. And it's a good ten hours before the banks open."

"I am not spending the night with *vampires*!"

"Calm down, *menina*." Carlos raised his hands. "I'll take you somewhere safe for the night. Another hotel."

"I'm not going anywhere with *you*." Tears streamed down Sabrina's face. "You're an animal."

Carlos halted, and he scowled at her. "That's why I never told you my secret. Vanderkitty told me you couldn't handle the truth."

Sabrina gasped. "You—you talk to my cat?"

Ian was fast losing patience. There was no way he was letting Sabrina leave with the knowledge she now possessed.

Sabrina glared at Carlos. "You said you had orphans for our orphanage, but they're animals like you."

Carlos's face flushed with rage. "They're children in need of a home and education. And compassion."

Sabrina wiped tears from her face. "I can't possibly put them with normal children. They might bite them or . . . eat them."

"Enough!" Ian moved toward Toni as he sent a psychic

message to Phineas to take Sabrina. "Miss Vanderwerth, yer fear is an unfortunate result of yer ignorance."

She gasped. "How dare you!"

Ian wrapped an arm around Toni. "Ye and yer friend are coming to Romatech. No arguing. No *disobeying*." That earned him a dirty look from her. He glanced at Carlos. "Ye can come if ye like."

"I'll come tomorrow," Carlos said. "And I'll bring Teddy."

Sabrina squealed when Phineas grabbed her. Ian vanished, taking Toni with him.

Chapter Twenty-two

"They're holding us prisoner!" Sabrina trudged about the silver room.

"They're keeping us safe." Toni opened a can of chicken noodle soup and poured it into a saucepan. "This room is lined with silver so no vampires can teleport in."

She didn't dare tell her friend that she knew how to unlock the door. The last thing they needed was Bri running around White Plains, claiming she'd seen vampires and were-panthers. She'd end up back in Shady Oaks before the night was over.

Bri collapsed into an easy chair. "This is crazy."

Toni stirred the soup as it heated on the stove. "You'll find it easier to accept everything once all the drugs are out of your system."

"Why would I want to accept *vampires*? And Carlos—I can't believe him. I feel so betrayed."

"Your uncle was the one who betrayed you." Toni tamped down on the anger she'd been squelching for hours. First Ian had tried to order her around. Vanda had treated her like a lowly worm. Carlos had somehow *forgotten* to tell her he was a shape shifter, even after she'd told him about vampires. And Sabrina was acting like they'd ruined her life instead of rescuing her.

Toni gritted her teeth. "I'm sure Carlos can't help being born a shape shifter, no more than I could help being born an illegitimate embarrassment."

Sabrina yawned. "That's it, isn't it? You accept all these . . . weirdos because they're outcasts, and you've always felt like an outcast, too."

Toni started to argue, but paused. Sabrina could be right. She'd always felt a natural empathy toward anyone who felt unworthy or didn't fit in. Ian's fear that he didn't deserve true love because of his jaded past—that had touched her deeply. It had made her determined to prove him wrong. And her eagerness tonight to jump into danger to rescue Vamps—was she still trying to prove she was worthy?

"I can't believe you're working for the Undead," Bri grumbled. "I mean, you get attacked by vampires, and then you go to work for them? That's crazy."

"There's a world of difference between the Malcontents who attacked us and the Vamps I've been working for." Toni poured soup into two bowls and brought them to the table.

"They both look violent to me." Sabrina sat at the table and yawned. "I'm so tired."

"You've been on some strong meds." Toni set two spoons on the table.

Bri rubbed her eyes. "I can't believe I saw one of my best friends turn into a panther."

"We'll try to get you back to a normal life as soon as possible. You'll need your IDs. Do you know where your handbag is? Shady Oaks or your uncle's house?"

Bri ate some soup while she considered. "I don't remember much. I think it's still at Uncle Joe's house."

"We'll get it back."

Bri frowned. "When you say *we*, you mean you and that vampire?"

"Yes. Ian."

"He was bossing you around."

"He was anxious to keep me safe." Toni had realized too late how vulnerable she would be. She'd always fought well in practice sessions, but the good Vamps fought with honor. The Malcontents resorted to vanishing and taking hostages. "It's hard to compete with a vampire."

"Exactly." Bri set down her spoon. "You can't compete with them, Toni. You don't belong in their world. Whatever possessed you to join up with them?"

"I did it for you. I wanted to find proof that they existed, so I could prove you weren't delusional."

Bri's eyes filled with tears. "I'm sorry. Here I am, giving you a hard time, when you've been such a good friend. You've always been there for me."

Tears burned Toni's eyes. "Careful, or we'll both start blubbering."

Bri sniffed. "It scares me for you to be with those creatures. I don't want to lose you."

"You haven't lost me."

Bri frowned. "You said you were in love with him."

Toni set down her spoon. "I am."

"How long have you known him? A week?"

"A little bit longer." Toni took her bowl to the sink.

"But not very long. Can a relationship forged that quickly last an entire lifetime?"

Toni rinsed out her bowl, then cleaned the saucepan. Bri's comments stung, but she knew her friend was truly concerned about her. "I'm not sure how things will work out." Or if they even could. "But I do know I love him."

"He's very good-looking, I'll grant you that, but Toni, he's *dead*."

"Only half the time."

"You want half a life?" Sabrina yawned again.

"Go on to bed. You're exhausted." Toni took her bowl to the sink.

"We've been working on our plan for ten years."

"I know." Toni rinsed out her bowl.

"You can't live in both worlds, Toni."

She turned and saw Bri climbing into bed. The same bed where she'd seen Ian in his death-sleep, where she'd touched the dimple in his chin. "I really do love him."

"It was a chapter in your life, but it's over," Bri whispered. "Just like the hell I've been through the past week. It's time for us to move on."

Toni turned down the lights so Bri could sleep. Then she collapsed in the easy chair. A dull ache was spreading in her chest. It grew more and more as reality sank in.

For the last ten years, she'd clung to their mission of the orphanage. It had kept her going when the workload from school had seemed too hard. It had given her a noble purpose and identity when she'd felt unimportant and unworthy. She hadn't expected Ian to come into her life, or love to bloom in her heart and make her feel whole.

A few times during the last week, she'd felt pulled between two worlds—her new world with the Vamps and her old world with Bri. When Ian had offered to help her rescue Bri, she'd felt elated, as if the two worlds were finally connecting and she could have both.

The ache in her chest intensified, squeezing her heart. What if the two worlds could never coexist? What if she was forced to choose? How could she fail Sabrina after all they'd been through? How could she ever give up Ian?

It was midmorning when Toni awoke in the large bed. She glanced at Sabrina sleeping peacefully beside her and wondered where Ian was spending his daily death-sleep. Probably next door with the other guys.

She showered and skipped her morning affirmations. They seemed like a cruel joke now. Yes, she was worthy to be loved, but that didn't guarantee it would work out. She dressed in her uniform and slipped her cell phone into a pants pocket. Time to go see the bear. Her supervisor.

She took the elevator to the first floor, then strode down the hall. What kind of bear was he, anyway? A friendly little brown Boo Boo Bear or a huge grizzly? An image flitted through her mind of Howard turning bright yellow and fluffy with a sunburst on his tummy. She snorted. Well, why not? If vampires could be real, so could Care Bears.

She passed some mortal employees going about their daily work. As far as they knew, they were making synthetic blood for hospitals. They were, actually. They had no idea that the night shift consisted of Vamps who were making Chocolood, Blood Lite, Bubbly Blood, Blissky, and Bleer.

Night and day. Two different worlds. Could she possibly live in both?

She passed by Constantine's closed nursery. She missed the little guy. As she walked past Shanna's dental office, she noted the sign on the door. *On vacation, will return soon.* Shanna, who managed to exist in both worlds, still had major problems keeping herself and her family safe.

Toni entered the MacKay security office. "Hi, Howard." *Don't think of him as a bear.* "Sorry, I'm late."

"No problem. You haven't missed anything." Howard sat behind the desk, looking like his usual cheerful self. "Not much going on today."

Not a grizzly, Toni thought. Far too friendly and easygoing. Maybe a pink Cheer Bear. She sat beside him just as he pushed the doughnut box her way.

"Thanks." Toni hesitated with her hand halfway in the box. There were plain doughnuts and bear claws. She quickly grabbed a plain one and scanned the monitors. She could see Sabrina still sleeping in the silver room. Phineas and Dougal were on the twin beds in the guardroom, while Ian lay dead as a doornail on the floor. Poor guy. Though he would hardly notice a hard floor.

"So I heard it got rough at the Horny Devils last night." Howard grabbed a bear claw from the box.

"Yeah, pretty grisly." She winced and crammed the doughnut in her mouth to keep from talking.

"Like a virgin," a female voice sang.

Toni sat up and looked around.

Howard chuckled. "Your pants are singing."

Toni jumped up and pulled the phone from her pocket. She opened it, cutting off Madonna's claim that she'd been touched for the very first time. Carlos's idea of a joke, no doubt. He could laugh all the way to hell. "Hello?"

"*Menina*, how are you?"

"Carlos." Toni walked across the office. "I swear I will have you declawed."

He laughed. "I see you like your new ringtone. How is Sabrina?"

"She's still asleep." Toni glanced at the monitor.

"Are you able to talk freely?"

"Sure. I'm in the security office with Howard Bear—uh, Barr." She winced.

Howard chuckled and grabbed another bear claw.

"*Menina*, the police were just here in the apartment building, looking for you and Bri. They knocked on all the neighbors' doors to ask about you."

Toni swallowed hard. "So they think I'm involved in her disappearance?"

"They suspect you. They questioned me, too, and asked to see my apartment."

"Good grief, what about Teddy?"

"Don't worry. I sent him out this morning with some money and instructions to buy new clothes and a new hairstyle. We're supposed to meet in Washington Square at three."

"He's fine, then?" Toni had worried that Teddy wasn't quite ready for the real world.

"He's very happy. The police are looking for him, too.

They had photos of him and Bri. I gather the hospital takes pictures of all the patients when they're admitted. I acted very shocked and concerned, of course, about Bri's disappearance."

"Good." Toni could just imagine Carlos putting on a convincing show for the police.

"They think Teddy and Sabrina might have developed a romantic relationship and escaped together."

"Did they say anything about the nurse, Bradley?" Toni asked.

"No, I suspect the hospital wants to keep that little problem a secret."

Toni checked the monitor again. Bri was still asleep. "I asked her about her purse. She thinks it's still at her uncle's house."

"Hmm." Carlos paused. "I could drive over there and see if the maid would give it to me."

"But we would still have the problem of her uncle Joe wanting her back in the psych ward."

"And problems with the police," Carlos added. "I'll bring Teddy this afternoon, and we'll discuss strategy."

"Okay, sounds good."

"I—I hope Bri can get over her fear of me," Carlos said sadly.

"I hope so, too." Toni hung up. She also hoped Bri could get over her fear of five orphaned were-panther children. Those poor kids needed help. They needed acceptance and love, so they wouldn't grow up feeling like monsters who deserved to be butchered like their parents.

"A guard's coming." Howard stood and lumbered toward the door.

Toni noted the daytime Romatech security guard on a monitor. He was holding a small gold box.

Howard opened the door. "Yes?"

"This was delivered to the front gate. For Toni Davis."

"Thanks." Howard closed the door and offered the small gift box to Toni.

She eyed it warily. "Do they expect me to fall for that again?"

Howard smiled. "This is legit. I saw Ian order it online last night."

"Really?" She grabbed the box and unraveled the golden ribbon. Inside the box, on a bed of cotton, lay a beautiful, gold filigree heart. She grinned. With the filigree design, it was obvious there was nothing hidden within the heart. It was pure.

Wedged in the top of the box was a note.

My dearest Daytona,

You've brought sunshine back into my life.

                                                    Ian

She pressed the note to her chest as her heart constricted with emotion. In that moment, she knew no matter what happened, she would not make a mistake as long as she followed her heart.

When Ian awoke Thursday evening, he warned Dougal and Phineas to be extra vigilant. Jedrek would be completely healed after his death-sleep and no doubt plotting to avenge his embarrassing defeat at the Horny Devils.

While Phineas and Dougal made a sweep of Romatech and the grounds, Ian called Angus to give him an update and request extra guards. Angus was still at Jean-Luc's home in Texas. Since Jack and Zoltan were planning to return to Europe soon, they agreed to stay in New York for a few nights before teleporting east. They would arrive before dawn.

A quick check of the monitors in the security office showed

him Toni's location. She was in the Romatech cafeteria with Sabrina, Carlos, and Teddy. He studied the monitor screen closely. Toni was wearing the heart necklace he'd ordered. That was a good sign. She was laughing with Carlos and Teddy. Sabrina was eating quietly, casting an occasional wary look at Carlos.

According to Howard, Carlos, and Teddy had arrived an hour ago and filled out employment applications for MacKay Security and Investigation. Carlos would make an excellent guard when he wasn't busy tracking down more of his own kind. As for Teddy, Ian had different plans for him. He stopped in Shanna's office to pick up her folder, then he proceeded to the cafeteria.

Toni's pretty green eyes lit up when he approached. Her hand moved to the golden heart on her chest. "Thank you."

"Ye're welcome." He kissed her cheek, then greeted the others.

Sabrina watched him curiously. "He's wearing a kilt," she whispered to Toni.

"He's a medieval Scotsman," Toni whispered back.

"Oh." Sabrina's eyes widened.

"We have some nachos left." Carlos motioned to a plate on the table. "But I don't suppose you're interested."

"I already ate." Ian sat at the end of the table.

"Anyone we know?" Carlos's amber eyes twinkled. "Ouch." He glared at Toni.

Ian smiled for he'd heard the kick underneath the table. "I mostly drink AB positive. It's my favorite flavor." When Toni's cheeks turned a pretty pink, he inhaled deeply. "Smells like heaven on you."

Her blush deepened. "You can taste a difference between different blood types? And you can tell which type people have?"

"Aye." When Sabrina grimaced and turned away, Ian realized he'd better change the subject. He tapped the folder he'd brought from Shanna's office. "This is something that

Roman and Shanna have been working on since Constantine started levitating at the age of three months."

He glanced at Sabrina and Teddy. "I should explain. Roman Draganesti is the owner of Romatech and inventor of synthetic blood."

"I already told them who's who," Toni said.

"And Howard told Teddy and me about the war against the Malcontents," Carlos added.

"Good." Ian opened the folder. "Roman and Shanna have a second child on the way. Heather and Jean-Luc plan to have children, too."

"You're talking about half-vampire children?" Sabrina asked, her nose wrinkled.

"Aye, it's the only way we can be fathers," Ian glanced at Toni, wondering how she would feel about giving birth to such a child.

Her gaze met his, and her eyes widened. Did she know what he was thinking? Did she know how deeply he was falling in love with her?

Carlos cleared his throat.

Ian broke eye contact and removed a few large photos from the folder. He slid them down the table. "This is a property in upstate New York that Roman recently purchased. There's a mansion, numerous other buildings, a pool, tennis courts, and three hundred acres."

"Wow." Teddy grabbed a picture. "It's huge."

Toni studied a picture of the main house. "It's beautiful." She passed the photo on to Sabrina.

"Impressive." Carlos looked at an aerial shot of the extensive grounds. "Roman must be extremely wealthy."

"Aye, but this is no' meant to be a show of wealth. Roman's keeping it a secret. He and Shanna realized some time ago that the children would need a safe place to be educated and learn their special skills."

Teddy looked up from the photo he was examining. "You plan to turn this mansion into a school?"

"Aye." Ian handed them the rest of the photos. "You understand the need for secrecy about this? The children attending this school will be unique."

"What about were-children?" Carlos asked. "Would they be welcomed there?"

"Yes." Ian nodded. "Any child with abnormal abilities. Or children who simply know too much. Heather's daughter falls into that category."

"This is so cool!" Teddy thumbed through different photos. "A school for future superheroes! Would they live on campus?"

"They could." Ian shrugged. "Some of the Vamp children could be teleported there if they wanted to live at home."

"This is great." Toni passed another photo to Sabrina. "I can't wait to introduce you to Constantine. He's so smart and sweet. And he can already levitate and teleport."

Sabrina remained quiet, frowning at the photos.

"Look at this." Carlos pointed at a picture of a lake. "There's an island here. It would be the perfect place for my kids to practice their panther skills without putting any other kids in danger."

Toni leaned forward to look. "That's an excellent idea."

"The main problem Roman and Shanna face," Ian continued, "is finding teachers and administrators who can be trusted."

"Count me in," Teddy said.

"Me, too," Carlos said. "I'd love to bring my orphans there."

Ian gave Toni a questioning look. "What do you think?"

"I think it was very wise of Roman and Shanna to plan ahead like this. I don't think Tino could be happy in a normal school." She turned to Sabrina. "This would be an interesting place to run, don't you think?"

Sabrina slowly stacked the photos. "It's a beautiful place. And an interesting idea." She gave Toni a worried look. "But this was not our plan. We wanted to help children who were homeless, starving, and suffering. This Constantine has a billionaire dad to take care of him. What about the children who have nobody? We can't turn our backs on them just because these mutant children are more interesting."

Toni's cheeks turned pink. "Don't call them mutants, please."

Sabrina's eyes narrowed. "You're not planning on having any, are you?"

An awkward silence fell upon them. Ian watched Toni carefully, but she avoided his eyes. Her blush reddened. Was she embarrassed to be involved with him?

Sabrina pushed the stack of photos away. "This is admirable, but it's not our plan. Toni and I have been working on our own plan for ten years."

Toni closed her eyes with a pained expression. A twinge of panic crept into Ian's gut. What if she decided to completely leave the Vamp world behind? What if she left him?

He grabbed the stack of photos. "There's three hundred acres here. We can build more buildings. We doona need to turn children away."

Toni finally looked at him. "We could fit a regular orphanage in there?"

Ian took her hand. "We would have to okay everything with Roman. But I do want ye to keep both worlds. Ye shouldna have to choose one or the other."

Her eyes glimmered with moisture. "That would be good."

"Look at this field behind the mansion." Carlos showed a photo to Sabrina. "It would make a perfect soccer field."

She snorted. "I can see where your priorities are."

"Come on, Sabrina." Teddy leaned forward. "This is the coolest opportunity ever."

She sighed. "I'll think about it. I still need some time to adjust to . . . everything." She glanced warily at Carlos and Ian. "And I still have a year of school left. That is, if I can go back to school without my uncle trying to lock me up."

"We were just talking about that before you arrived." Toni

selected a chip from the tray and bit into it. "We need to get Bri's purse from her uncle's house and somehow convince him to leave her and her money alone."

Carlos grabbed a salt shaker and sprinkled more salt on the chips. "The police came by today, looking for Bri, Teddy, and Toni. We need to get this mess straightened out before one of us gets arrested."

Ian considered as he stacked the photos back into the folder. "Where does this uncle live?"

"Westchester." Carlos munched on a chip. "I've been there before. I think I could get the maid to bring me Bri's things."

"I should go," Sabrina said.

Ian shook his head. "Nay, ye'll be safer here with Teddy." He stood. "Carlos, drive Toni to the uncle's house. Then call me, and I'll teleport there to meet you. I have to go somewhere else first."

"Where?" Toni asked. "What are you planning?"

"I left my cape in Scotland. But Roman has a vampire cape and tuxedo at the townhouse. I need to get into costume first."

Toni's eyes widened. "Costume?"

Teddy grinned. "Cool! I always said you needed a cape."

Sabrina frowned. "What are you going to do my uncle?"

"Doona fash. I'll no' be violent." Ian smiled. "But I doona believe yer uncle will enjoy his encounter with Count Dracula."

Chapter Twenty-three

"You look very handsome." Toni adjusted Ian's black tie. He'd just materialized in the alley behind the Proctors' house in Westchester.

"I'm supposed to look scary," he muttered.

More like sexy. Toni ran her fingers over his elegant black tuxedo. His black satin cape was lined in red, and his black hair curled inside the stand-up collar. "If I was making a vampire movie, I'd hire you in a second."

Carlos cleared his throat. "If you two are finished admiring each other, we'll get on with this." He approached the back kitchen door and knocked lightly.

The maid peered out the window and smiled when Carlos waved. She opened the door and spoke to him softly in Spanish. He motioned to Toni and Ian, and the maid nodded.

"Maria's letting me sneak up the back stairs,"

Carlos told them. "I'll collect Bri's stuff and meet you downstairs. She says the doctor's in the library at the front of the house."

"I'll go around." Ian disappeared into the shadows.

Carlos slipped up the back stairs, while Maria escorted Toni to the library.

Dr. Joe Proctor was pacing behind his desk, talking on his cell phone. "Look, Jenkins, you're supposed to be the best PI in the business. Don't tell me you can't find one lousy girl." He paused, rubbing a hand over his balding head. "Yeah, I realize she must be getting help. It's—" He spotted Toni at the library entrance. "I'll call you back."

He dropped his phone on the desk as he approached Toni. "Who are you?"

"I'm Toni Davis, Sabrina's roommate."

He hesitated, then broke into a big grin. "Toni, how wonderful to meet you. You must be terribly worried about Sabrina. Let me assure you, I am sparing no expense to find her. You wouldn't happen to know anything about her disappearance, would you?"

"You'll never find her."

His smile morphed into a snarl. "You helped her escape, didn't you?" He strode back to his desk and grabbed his phone. "I'm handing you over to the police. Of course, you could avoid being arrested if you just tell me where Sabrina is."

"Go ahead. Call the police. I'd like to report some crimes. Let's see, there's medical malpractice for claiming Bri was delusional when she wasn't."

He lifted his chin. "Any psychiatrist would agree with my diagnosis."

"Then there's the embezzlement of her trust fund and holding her prisoner so you could steal more of her money."

He snapped his phone shut. "You can't prove any of that."

Toni strolled toward him. "Once the police investigate

your financial records, it'll be very clear. You imprisoned Sabrina. You poisoned her mind. You tried to steal her entire life from her."

"No, no." He waved a hand in the air. "I wouldn't have kept her locked up forever. I just needed a little money to pay off a few gambling debts."

"And then there would have been more gambling debts."

Proctor's eyes narrowed. "Those guys would have killed me. I didn't have any choice."

"Those guys are the least of your problems. Have you wondered how Bri escaped?"

He watched her warily. "Of course I wondered."

"You locked her away because she said vampires are real. But only a vampire could have helped her escape."

"You're as crazy as she is." Proctor's eyes lit up. "I'll lock you both up."

Toni smiled. "You can try. But first let me introduce you to someone." She lifted a hand to cue Ian, who was waiting outside by the window.

His body materialized in the middle of the room.

Proctor gasped and stepped back. "What? This—this is some kind of trick."

Ian raised his arms, spreading his cape wide. "You doona believe in the existence of the Undead?"

Toni bit her lip to keep from laughing. Ian's fake Transylvanian accent still had a touch of Scottish in it.

"Im-impossible," Proctor breathed.

Ian zoomed toward the desk at vampire speed. Proctor stumbled back and knocked against the bookcase.

"Ye will believe." Ian levitated into the air.

Toni winced as his head almost bumped the ceiling. At least Proctor looked truly terrified as he cowered behind his desk. She just thought Ian looked incredibly cute.

He dropped onto the desk, and with a flash, his eyes glowed a brighter blue and his fangs sprang out. Toni flinched. That wasn't very cute.

Proctor huddled on the floor, lifting his arms in a defensive posture. "Don't hurt me. Please."

With a hiss, Ian flipped his cape back over his broad shoulders. Toni wobbled as her knees grew weak. Good grief, he was in full monster mode, and all she could think of was *Bite me*. How strange that the Malcontent attack had left her terrified and disgusted, while the thought of Ian biting her made her skin tingle with anticipation.

Her face heated up, and she flushed all over, feeling the rush of blood through her veins. Rushing faster and faster as if it needed to escape, as if it were calling to him.

Ian turned to look at her, and a surge of lust nearly knocked her off her feet. She gasped as the blue glow of his eyes turned red hot. Oh God, he knew she was turned on.

She stepped back, lifting a hand to her throat. Her heart beat wildly. Her thighs squeezed together with sudden, hot need. Good grief, no wonder women had offered him blood over the centuries.

Ian turned back to the trembling doctor, huddled on the floor. He reached out his right arm, and Proctor flinched as if an invisible force had struck him.

"Ye are under my control." Ian's eyes glowed an intense blue, and Toni realized he was using mind control. "Ye are lowly, and I am yer master."

"You are lowly, and I am your master," Proctor whispered, his eyes wide and glazed.

Ian grimaced. "Nay. *I* am the master."

"You are the master," Proctor said.

Toni stifled a grin. Ian wasn't very good at being an evil monster. No wonder she adored him.

"Listen and obey," Ian ordered. "Ye'll never steal from Sabrina again. Ye'll never interfere in her life. Ye'll be an honorable uncle to her. Do ye understand?"

"Yes, Master."

Ian turned to Toni. "Anything else?"

"Call off the police," she whispered.

Ian extended his arm again. "Ye'll cease yer search for Sabrina and Teddy. Ye'll tell the police it was all a mistake. Ye'll fill out the proper release forms. Ye'll never gamble again. And ye'll pay off yer debts, using yer own resources."

Proctor nodded. "Yes, Master."

Ian jumped down from the desk to stand beside the doctor. "Ye'll tell no one about this night. I know how to find you, Joseph Proctor."

"Yes, Master."

"Are you done?" Carlos asked at the entrance, his arms full of Bri's belongings.

The maid looked curiously at Ian.

"One more thing." Ian turned to Proctor. "Ye will treat yer maid with respect." He laid his hand on Proctor's head, and the doctor slumped into a deep sleep.

"Thank you, *señor*." Maria crossed herself, then led them to the back door. "Is Sabrina okay?"

"Yes," Toni told her. "Thank you for your help."

"Gracias." Carlos kissed the maid's cheek.

Maria giggled as she shut the door.

"You were wonderful!" Toni hugged Ian. "Thank you."

He smiled and kissed her brow.

"Get a room," Carlos muttered as he strode to his car. He dumped Bri's stuff in the trunk.

Ian held Toni's hand as they walked back to Carlos's car. "Zoltan and Jack will be arriving before dawn. There's no' enough room for everyone at Romatech, so we'll go back to the townhouse for our death-sleep."

"Are you sure it'll be safe there?" Toni asked.

"It'll be safe during the day," Ian answered. "The Malcontents will be as dead as we are. And Howard will spend the day there. Carlos, too."

"All right." Toni stopped next to Carlos's Jaguar. "Coming with us, Dracula?"

"I'll see you later, sweetheart." He vanished.

* * *

But she didn't see him later. After Carlos drove her back to Romatech, and they told Sabrina and Teddy the good news, Bri immediately wanted to go home and see Vanderkitty. Then, with everyone at Toni's and Bri's apartment, they ordered in Chinese food and celebrated.

Howard had asked Carlos to start his security job right away, so Carlos packed some clothes to take to the town-house. Toni packed some more of hers. She was nervous about leaving Bri alone, so Teddy offered to stay overnight at the apartment.

It was ten P.M. by the time Carlos and Toni arrived at Roman Draganesti's townhouse on the Upper East Side, and it took thirty more minutes for Carlos to inspect and admire each room. He chose the bedroom next to Toni's for his own.

"This is perfect for me, *menina*." He ran his hand appreciatively over the bed's wood and wrought-iron footboard. "I love this Spanish decor."

"I believe the room belonged to a medieval Spanish lady named Maria Consuela," Toni said.

"What happened to her?" Carlos hefted his suitcase onto the red velvet bedspread.

Toni tried to remember what Dougal had told her about the former harem when she'd moved in more than a week ago. She'd been so insulted by the idea of a harem that she'd tuned out half of what he'd said. "My room belonged to some medieval chick called Princess Joanna. She and Maria Consuela weren't too thrilled about being co-owners of the Horny Devils, so they sold their shares to Vanda and moved back to Europe. London, I think."

Carlos unzipped his suitcase and began removing clothes. "I have to thank you, girlfriend. This is the best possible job for me. Howard said they'll work around my remaining classes so I can finish my master's."

"That's great." Toni eyed the pile of bikini underwear Carlos had piled up. One was spotted like a leopard, and another was striped like a tiger.

"And they'll work around my research trips, too. I would never find another employer that understanding."

"Well, the Vamps know how much they need mortals they can trust." Not that Carlos was entirely mortal. Carlos *Panterra*. Toni mentally slapped herself on the brow. She should have known. She winced when he set another item on the bed. Good grief. Those were the biggest nail clippers she'd ever seen.

"It's just so wonderful, *menina*. I've always had to keep my secret . . . well, secret, you know. But with this job, I am free to be myself. In fact, being a shape shifter actually adds to my value. And I've found a home for my orphans."

Toni smiled. "I'm very happy for them. And you."

Carlos skirted the bed and hugged her. "Thank you so much."

"Thank you, Carlos. You've always been a great friend." She resisted the urge to pet him behind the ears. The guy was practically purring. "I'll let you settle in. We have to be up before sunrise, you know." She moved toward the door.

He grabbed a stack of clothes and headed for the dark, ornately carved wooden dresser. "What are you going to do, *menina*? Will you stay with Ian or go back to Sabrina?"

That was the question of the day. Toni fingered the heart pendant on her chest. "I'm hoping that it won't be an either/or situation. That Sabrina will come around in time."

Carlos nodded. "Sometimes you must dare to believe."

Toni went to her bedroom, repeating those words to herself. *Dare to believe*. She loved Bri, and she loved Ian. She had to believe it would all work out.

She overslept in the morning, and didn't wake until she heard Carlos banging on her door.

"I'll be right down," she called out. Damn, damn, damn. She hated these early mornings. She rushed through her shower and threw on her uniform. She was hurrying down the stairs, pulling her damp ponytail through a scrunchie, when she spotted Zoltan Czakvar and Giacomo di Venezia, aka Jack, coming up the stairs.

"*Bellissima*, you are as lovely as ever." Jack bowed.

Boy was he full of it. Toni appreciated the compliment, but she knew her male uniform was baggy and ugly, and she was wearing very little makeup. "You guys retiring for the night—I mean, day?"

"Yes. We'll be in guest rooms on the fourth floor," Zoltan said. Between his yawn and his Hungarian accent, he was hard to understand.

"*Bellissima*, will you check on me personally?" Jack's brown eyes twinkled.

"If you like. Sure."

"*Molto bene. Ciao, bellissima.*" Jack started up another flight of stairs.

Zoltan trudged behind him. "You're planning to sleep in the nude, aren't you?"

Jack chuckled.

Toni rolled her eyes, then ran down the stairs. Hopefully, Ian was still awake. In the foyer, she met Dougal and Phineas heading down to the basement.

Phineas yawned. "Good night, sweetness."

"Good night. Or morning." These guys were confusing her. "Have you seen Ian?"

"Already gone to bed." Dougal shut the cellar door behind him.

Too late. Dammit. It was hard having a boyfriend on the graveyard shift. She trudged into the kitchen.

"Good morning." Howard sat smiling at the kitchen table, munching on a bear claw.

Doughnuts, again? If she kept eating those, she'd be as big as a bear. She noticed Carlos was spooning something from a bowl into his mouth. It looked a bit healthier. "What are you eating? Meow Mix?"

Howard snorted with laughter, while Carlos gave her a bland look.

Toni smiled sweetly. "I hear they have a new anti-hairball formula."

"It's cereal." Carlos showed her the box.

"Hmm, Special K for kitties? Can I have some?" She fetched a bowl.

"If you'll stop being catty," Carlos grumbled.

"Sorry." She patted him on the head. She knew she was being ornery. She was just so disappointed about not seeing Ian. It would be a long, long time till sundown.

After breakfast, she offered to go check on him. "Is he on the fifth floor?"

"Yes." Howard finished his cup of tea. With extra honey, no doubt. "What do you say, Carlos? Are you up to a martial arts session? I want to see how well you can fight."

"You're on." Carlos and Howard headed down the basement stairs, while Toni started the long climb to the fifth floor.

She was breathing a bit heavily by the time she reached the fifth-floor office. The room was dark, the aluminum shutters closed. An empty blood bottle sat in the sink at the wet bar. Ian must have had a snack before going to bed.

She opened the double doors leading into the bedroom. Light spilled from the partially closed bathroom.

"You left the light on. Shame on you." She approached the left side of the bed.

Ian was lying there in his white T-shirt and plaid flannel pajama bottoms. He'd folded back the tan suede comforter to lie on the cool cotton sheets. His black hair was loose from its leather thong and made a dramatic contrast to the white pillowcase.

He was in the usual position he assumed for his death-sleep. Flat on his back, big feet pointed to the ceiling, hands clasped neatly over his flat stomach. He'd probably learned this position from centuries of sleeping in a coffin.

Toni did a double take to the area below his clasped hands. There was a definite bulge in his pajama bottoms. She leaned over for a closer look. Good grief, he'd fallen into his death-sleep with a hard-on. Was it possible for a stiff to be that stiff?

She straightened with a deep breath. "Naughty boy," she whispered and glanced at his handsome face. A shadow of dark whiskers lined his strong jaw. His black eyelashes were so thick. She would hate him if she didn't love him so much. She reached out to touch the cute dimple in his chin.

His eyes suddenly opened. She jumped. A hand locked around her wrist in a tight grip. She gasped.

"Surprise." He seized her by the arms and rolled her onto the bed.

Chapter Twenty-four

He'd certainly surprised her. She lay on the bed, her bonnie mouth dropped open. He rolled onto his side to face her and propped himself up on an elbow.

"You—you're not dead," she whispered.

He smiled. "No' at the moment."

"How? You took that drug? The Stay-Awake drug?"

"Aye. I know where it's hidden."

She sat up. "But Ian, it makes you grow older."

"One year for each day." He shrugged one shoulder. "So I'll look twenty-eight instead of twenty-seven."

Her mouth fell open again. "You were willing to age a year?"

"To spend a day with you, aye."

"That's so sweet." She stretched out, facing him. "But are you sure you should be sweet? I mean, you're awake, and the bad guys are asleep."

His smile widened. She was as much a warrior as he was. "So ye want to slaughter them while they're unable to defend themselves?"

She winced. "I realize it's not a very honorable thing to do, but they would do it to you in a second."

"Aye, they would, so we'll have to make sure they never get that drug." He reached out to brush a tendril of damp hair off her cheek. "Actually, I would be tempted to kill them all and be done with this mess, but they have about twenty Russian mafia guys guarding them with high-powered assault rifles."

"Oh." She made a face. "That would be nasty."

"Aye, verra nasty. Ever since Roman visited them during the day, they've been extra vigilant." He trailed a finger along the line of her jaw. "And then there's the problem of me burning to a crisp if I go out in the sun."

"I guess we'll have to stay inside."

"Aye." He skimmed his finger over her ear.

"I guess we could think of something to pass the time." Her eyes twinkled as she glanced at his pajama bottoms. "It looks like you've been thinking ahead of me."

He smiled wryly. "A man should never be unprepared."

It was true that while he lay in bed, waiting for her to arrive, he'd grown aroused just thinking about making love to her. He knew his eyes were turning red now. A red tint shaded the room, making Toni's skin look pink and ripe with blood. It would be a challenge to keep control. He'd purposely filled up with synthetic blood to make it easier.

The way she'd looked at him when he'd unleashed all his Vamp power in Dr. Proctor's library—that had stretched his control to the max. He'd heard her heart racing. He'd smelled the scent of her arousal. He'd wanted to leap on her and sink his fangs into her neck.

His gums tingled, and he collapsed on his back, squeezing his eyes shut. *Control.* He didn't dare make love to her if he couldn't control himself.

"Are you all right?" she whispered.

"I doona want to influence you in any way. If ye stay in

my bed, it should be yer decision. But know that I will make love to you."

"Well, I was sorta counting on that." Her voice sounded muffled, then something soft fell on his face.

He brushed it aside and opened his eyes. There was a navy polo shirt in his hand. *Her* shirt. She sat beside him, sliding her bra straps off her shoulders. The heart pendant he'd given her was nestled between her breasts.

"Are ye certain?"

"Do I look uncertain?" She flung her bra on the floor.

He pounced, pushing her onto her back. "I love a decisive woman."

She smiled. "I love an aggressive man."

He splayed a hand around her rib cage. "I know ye havena known me for verra long."

"But I've waited for you for years."

"For centuries. I think my heart recognized you the verra first night we met. It just took a few more nights for my brain to catch up."

She touched his face. "I was the same way."

He skimmed his hand up to cover her breast. "I want ye to know that I'll be faithful. I love ye dearly. That will never change."

"Oh, Ian." She wrapped her arms around his neck. "I love you, too."

He leaned down to kiss her lips. They were soft and moist, and they opened sweetly. He swirled his tongue inside, exploring and tasting. She quivered beneath him, so fragile in her mortality but so strong with passion. She was everything he wasn't. Everything he craved. Life and light. Pure and good.

Her tongue skimmed along his teeth, then swirled bravely around the sharp point of one of his fangs. He groaned. Did she know how badly she was flirting with danger? She pressed her tongue against the point.

With a sharp breath, he broke the kiss. Her skin, her neck,

her breasts—they all looked pink and delicious through his red-tinted eyes.

"By all the saints, I want you." He trailed kisses down her throat to her breasts. Her pounding heart echoed in his ears, pounding faster and accelerating the flames of his passion. He scooped a hand behind her back and lifted her rib cage in the air. Her back arched, pressing her breasts against his mouth. With a moan, she flung her arms to the side, as if surrendering her body to his needs.

And he needed her. Every inch of her. He nibbled and suckled on her plump nipples till the tips grew hard in his mouth. He sucked on one and pinched the other one lightly. When he tugged on both, she gasped.

"Oh, please." She grasped his T-shirt and pulled.

He yanked his T-shirt over his head and threw it. Then he unbuckled the belt around her hips and attacked the waistband and zipper of her khaki trousers. "Bloody hell, I never thought I'd be removing a pair of men's pants."

She laughed and tried to help him by lifting her hips in the air. He groaned at the sight. He tugged her pants down to her ankles, but was halted by her athletic shoes. With a quick flick of his wrists, they went flying into the air. Her socks and trousers followed.

"I love yer legs." He grasped an ankle and lifted her bare leg so he could plant kisses along her calf.

"Take off your pants."

"Now?" He tickled the underside of her knee.

Her leg jerked. "Yes. Now."

He lowered her ankle onto his shoulder, then rose to his knees to pull his pajama bottoms down. His erection sprang out.

She propped herself up on her elbows to get a better look at him. "Wow."

"I hope ye doona expect me to dance like that guy at the Horny Devils." He tossed his pajamas on the floor.

"What guy?" she murmured, her eyes glued to his crotch.

The more she stared, the more swollen he became. At this rate, he wasn't going to last another minute. He needed to distract her quickly. "Now, where were we?" He kissed her ankle.

"No." She slid her leg off his shoulder and leaned forward. "I want to touch you." She circled her hand around his erection.

"Och, lass. I canna endure this for long."

"Aw, come on." She squeezed gently. "You're a tough guy."

"Aye." He hissed in a breath as she teased the tip with her thumb. He'd already leaked a drop, and she spread the moisture around. "I am tough." He gritted his teeth. "I'm a seasoned warrior."

"A real he-man." She shoved him back onto the bed.

His head was halfway off the end of the bed. He gasped when her mouth enveloped him. He crushed the comforter in his fists. He could handle this. He wasn't a green boy. "I—I grew a few inches over the summer."

She made a sound of appreciation deep in her throat. Her fingers tickled his balls, then squeezed. Her tongue was swirling around him. The room swirled around him. He couldn't believe it. This was different from all the sex he'd had over the centuries. Maybe it was because his equipment was slightly different—bigger and more mature. Or maybe it was because Toni was . . . Toni. She was making love to him. He never wanted it to stop.

But it was going to stop, and bloody well soon.

"Nay! Toni!"

She looked up at him just as he lost control. With a groan, he spurted on her chest. He retained enough control to turn away from her. Mortified, he ejaculated all over Roman's suede comforter. And the damned stuff kept coming.

"Och, lass. I'm so sorry. I'm no' used to this longer . . . I dinna control it properly." He lowered his head, too ashamed to look at her.

The sound of giggling broke the silence. He looked warily at her. She was rolling from side to side, laughing so hard there were tears in her eyes.

His face heated up. "Och, it is truly every man's desire to be laughed at in bed."

"Ian, you're so cute. Och, mercy! Me cock is too big. It's out of control!" She mimicked his Scottish accent and laughed some more. "You poor baby. It's so sad to be over-endowed. I think I may have to cry."

He glowered at her. "Ye're certainly enjoying this."

"Of course." She sat up, wiping her eyes. "I am so thrilled that I could make you lose control."

"Really?"

"Oh yes! It's like an amazing power trip." She flexed her biceps. "Mere mortal drives hunky, immortal vampire past the brink of his control. I feel like Superwoman!"

"Ye liked it?"

"Oh God, yes." She pressed a hand to her chest, then laughed some more when her fingers landed in cum. She grabbed the edge of the sheet and wiped her hand and chest.

Ian was amazed. He could embarrass himself with Toni, and she still loved him. He was the luckiest man on earth.

"And I have to say that I really appreciate those extra inches." Her gaze dropped to his crotch. "You are magnificent."

"Thank you." He was feeling much better now. "I could easily be persuaded to lose control again, since it makes ye feel so good."

Her mouth twitched. "That's real noble of you."

"I aim to please. In fact, now that I'm no longer in danger of exploding, I can devote more time to pleasing you."

Her eyebrows rose. "That sounds good."

"Aye." He trailed his fingers up her bare leg. "It will be my mission to drive you past the brink of control."

"I love a man with a mission."

He arched a brow. "Off with yer undies, lass."

With a giggle, she lay back. "Aye, aye, medieval warrior." She hooked her thumbs in the waistband of her panties and slowly wiggled out of them. "You may have your lusty way with me."

"That I will." He admired the way she moved her hips.

When her undies reached mid-thigh, she couldn't reach any farther with her hands. "Could you be so kind as to offer me some assistance?"

"My pleasure, dear lady." He hooked a finger in her undies and dragged them down her legs.

"Why thank you kindly, sir." Her Southern accent grew more pronounced, and she gave him a sultry look.

He chuckled. He should have known making love to Toni would be like nothing he'd experienced before. She filled his heart with joy. "You are most welcome, fair lady."

He tossed her panties in the air. When they defied gravity, he looked up and spotted them hanging from the light fixture.

Toni reclaimed his attention when she planted one foot to the right and then, with a seductive sway of her hips, she planted the other to the left. She opened her legs. "I do hope you'll enjoy the view."

"Aye, I do." He could see the moisture glistening on her tender folds. He inhaled deeply, savoring the scent of her arousal. "Och, lass, ye are the most beautiful of all fair maidens."

"Hmm. You are too kind." She wiggled her hips provocatively. "I shall endeavor to accommodate your manly size." She grinned at him.

"I'm going to suck on you till yer eyeballs pop out."

Her eyes widened. "Okay."

He grasped her ankles and placed them around his neck. "Hold on, sweetheart. This could get wild."

She giggled.

He seized her hips and buried his face in her scent. She

gasped when he started to lick and trembled when he sucked. He inserted two fingers and stroked her gently. With panting breaths, she moved her hips in rhythm with his fingers.

She was so wet now. So hot. So beautiful. And he was growing hard again. He enjoyed one last look at her wet, engorged flesh, then moved in for the final assault. He flicked his tongue, increasing his speed as only a vampire could do. Her legs clenched. Her hips rose. Almost there.

With a squeal, she jolted. Her inner muscles spasmed around his fingers. Her whole body shuddered.

He kissed her trembling thighs and lowered her feet to the bed. He kissed her belly, her breasts. He held himself poised over her, and the tip of his erection grazed her slick opening.

"Ian." She skimmed her hands up his back to his shoulders.

"I want to see the love in yer eyes when I enter you," he whispered.

"You have it." She looked at him. "I love you."

He slid inside her. A mixture of sensations surged through him. Joy, love, erotic pleasure, and a primordial, male triumph as he took possession. He intended to make love slowly, but she was so beautiful, so sexy, so loving, that they were soon hurtling together toward a climax. They couldn't get close enough. Her legs locked around his waist, and they ground their bodies together.

His orgasm hit hard. He pumped into her with a speed and ferocity that only a vampire could do. She screamed and came with a shuddering rush. She clung to him as her body continued to spasm.

"Oh my." She panted, trying to catch her breath.

He rested his brow against hers as their breathing slowly returned to normal.

"I hope I dinna hurt you," he whispered.

"No. It was . . . wonderful. Spectacular. Mind-blowing."

"Aye." He collapsed beside her and pulled her close.

Her eyes flickered shut. "You wore me out."

"Aye." He shut his eyes and nuzzled his chin against her hair. A man could easily want an eternity of this.

Toni woke up, slowly becoming aware that she was naked and cold. She sat up. In the dim light that spilled from the cracked bathroom door, she spotted Ian beside her. Her gaze drifted down his naked body and back to his face. Gorgeous man. So sexy. And so sweet to age another year just to be with her. Had the drug worn off? He certainly looked dead to the world.

She glanced at the bedside clock. Good grief. It was almost noon. Carlos and Howard had to be wondering what had happened to her. She pulled the sheet up to cover Ian to his chest. Then she went to the bathroom and took a hot shower.

She padded back into the bedroom with one towel wrapped around her head and another around her body. She found her polo shirt on the floor on one side of the bed and her bra on the other. She glanced up at the wrought-iron chandelier above the bed. Her underwear was dangling from one of the spiky branches. She doubted she could reach it, even if she stood on the bed. What a shame she couldn't levitate like the Vamps.

Maybe she could find something that would knock her panties down. She looked inside the closet and smiled at the kilt hanging there. She stroked the softness of Ian's sweater and leaned close to smell his scent. She spotted the black leather pants he'd worn the night they rescued Bri. Behind that was the tuxedo he'd worn to play Dracula. And then there was the vampire cape.

She skimmed her fingers down the sleek, black satin. The stand-up collar was so cool. She glanced back at Ian, still dead to the world.

Well, why the heck not? She dropped her towels to the floor and grabbed the cape. She twirled around, flourishing the cape like a matador. Then she swirled it onto her shoulders and tied the strings at her neck. She clasped the edges with her fingers so she could lift her arms and spread the cape wide. Whoosh, she ran across the room, letting the cape billow behind her. Then she executed a few lunges in a Paso Doble style. Happy with that, she bent her right elbow, letting the cape cover the bottom half of her face. Like Snidely Whiplash, she stalked across the room.

She jumped onto the foot of the bed and lifted her arms wide. With an ominous glare at Ian, she said in a spooky, low voice, "I am your master."

"Like a virgin," a female voice answered.

Toni jerked around. That had to be her cell phone. Her pants were somewhere on the floor.

Madonna claimed she was being touched for the very first time.

"Oh, hush." Toni jumped down from the bed and strode about the room, searching for her pants. "You're about as virginal as I am."

"That's debatable," a male voice said.

With a squeak, she spun around. "Ian?"

"Toni?" His eyes widened as he took in her costume, or lack of costume.

She whipped the edges of the cape together to conceal her nude body. "I thought you were dead. Again."

His mouth twitched. "I wouldna miss this for anything."

Her face heated up.

"Like a virgin," Madonna taunted her.

She snatched the phone from her pants pocket. "Hello?"

"*Menina*, what happened to you?" Carlos asked. "You went upstairs to check on Ian and never came back."

"I—I'm fine. Ian's fine." She glanced at the bed. Ian was grinning at her.

"Did you fall asleep?" Carlos asked. "I know you were tired this morning."

"I . . . slept a little. Sorry."

"It's okay. Nothing's happening. I just thought you might be hungry. Howard's making some paninis in the kitchen. You want one?"

"I—uh . . ." She watched Ian stroll past her into the office. The view from the back was great. He removed a bottle of blood from the small fridge at the wet bar and popped it into the microwave.

"Toni, what's going on?" Carlos demanded. "Do you need some help up there?"

"No! I—I'm fine, really."

"He's awake, isn't he?" Carlos demanded. "Either that, or you have developed some tastes that are way too kinky."

"Okay, he's awake," she confessed.

"Howard told me about the Stay-Awake drug," Carlos said. "I guess you two are putting it to good use?"

"Oh yeah."

Carlos chuckled. *"Ciao, menina."* He hung up.

"They know what we're doing?" Ian removed his bottle from the microwave and poured the blood into a glass.

"Yes." She dropped her phone and wandered into the office. "Are we going to be in big trouble?"

"No one has a way to contact Connor right now, so I wouldna worry about it." Ian sipped from his glass as he watched her approach. "That cape looks better on you than it does me."

"I don't think it's the cape you're looking at." She swept the cape open for a second to flash her body.

Ian smiled and took another sip. "Something amazing happened."

"Oh yeah, the sex was great." She perched on a bar stool.

He chuckled. "That, too. But Toni, I actually fell asleep." He leaned toward her, resting his elbows on the bar. "It was so strange. I havena slept in centuries."

"Wow."

He drank more blood. "I'd forgotten what it was like. Death-sleep is so . . . blank. It's nothing but death and total oblivion. But this was sweet and . . ."

"Restful?"

His eyes glimmered with moisture. "I had a dream. I dreamed of you."

"Oh . . . my." She noticed the tears in his eyes were reddish in color.

He touched her face. "I would have never thought it possible."

She took his hand. "What did you dream?"

His mouth quirked. "Ye did a striptease dance for me in a vampire cape."

"Really?" When he laughed, she made a face at him. "Very funny. What was the dream?"

His eyes softened. "I'll tell you someday."

"Hmm." She scooted off the bar stool. She walked away from him, then flipped one side of the cape back to reveal a rounded hip. "I have ways of making you talk."

She gasped when he zoomed up to her at vampire speed. "I have ways of making you scream." He untied the strings at her neck and pushed the cape off her shoulders.

The satin material pooled on the floor, the red side up. Ian lifted her in his arms, then laid her down on the scarlet satin.

"Well, why not?" She gave him a wry look. "We've stained everything else in this place."

With a laugh, he zoomed back to the bar and grabbed his glass. An inch of blood still remained in the bottom. "Ye've given me an idea."

"You're going to stain the carpet?"

"Nay." He knelt beside her and drizzled the blood over her breasts and down her torso.

"Eeuw. I hope you plan to clean that up." She forgot to be indignant when his tongue lapped the blood off her breasts.

He followed the trail of blood down her torso, then licked the last remaining drops from her belly button.

She squirmed on the red satin, enjoying the decadent feel of it against her backside. Ian returned to her breasts to suckle. She felt his teeth nibbling ever so gently and recalled the look of his fangs when he'd gone into full Dracula mode. His eyes had glowed blue, intense with Vamp power, then they'd turned red as he'd looked hungrily at her. The old bite marks on her breasts and torso itched, but not with fear or repulsion.

She felt desire. And need. "Ian."

He glanced up at her, and the red glow in his eyes tugged deep within her. Her bite marks burned.

She raked her hands into his long black hair and gripped his head tight. "Bite me."

He blinked. "Nay. Doona say that. I willna use you for food. I'm no' hungry."

"I am. I have a deep . . . hunger inside me."

"Toni, ye're reacting to my Vamp power. I'll try to tone it down."

"No, let it loose."

He studied her curiously. "Do ye know what ye're asking? Ye were attacked. Ye have terrible memories."

"I want to turn that terror into something beautiful. Can you do that?"

"I can keep it from hurting. But it is all an illusion. Mind control. And I know how ye feel about that."

"I'm not afraid of *your* mind. I love you."

He hesitated, frowning.

"Do it. Do it all. I want to experience everything with you."

He closed his eyes. "Ye're so verra tempting. I can smell yer blood, hot and delicious. I can hear it rushing through you, calling to me."

"Take me."

His eyes opened, and she gasped at the startling blue. A

wave of icy cold air struck her forehead, then swept down her body, prickling her skin with gooseflesh.

I am with you. His voice reverberated in her mind, and her entire body tingled as if he were blowing his breath over her. He nuzzled her neck. *We will share mind, body, and blood.* He licked her neck, and she gasped as the same sensation happened between her legs.

It had to be an illusion. But one hell of an illusion. All the tingling on her neck was echoed below. Her need grew more desperate, and the tingles grew into throbbing pulses, demanding satisfaction.

She wrapped her legs around him. "Take me now."

His fangs extended with a small hissing sound that made her ache for him. She shuddered as his erection pressed against her and his teeth softly scraped her neck. Soon, soon it would happen.

He plunged into her core with so much force, she barely noticed the prick on her neck. And then he was loving her, taking her body and blood. *I am inside you in every way. Ye are mine, and I am yers.*

With each suck at her neck, a shudder of pleasure skittered through her. Then he pulled away from her neck. *I doona want to take too much.* He licked the bite wounds, and the shudders continued, intensified with each bodily thrust into her core.

His pace picked up. *I can feel ye coming. We're coming together.*

And they did. Toni cried out just as she heard his roar of pleasure thunder through her mind. She'd never felt anything like it. Their bodies shuddered together like a choreographed dance. Their minds pulsated in shared pleasure. Amazing, she thought, or did he think that? She could no longer tell who was who. They were one.

"Ian," she whispered as their breathing returned to normal. Even their breaths were in sync.

Do ye feel how much I love you? His voice filled her mind.

A warmth flooded her and brought tears to her eyes. Then a chill swept through her, and he was gone. Gone from her mind, but lying next to her with love in his eyes.

And she knew, then and there, that nothing would stop her from spending her life with Ian. No friendships or villains could stop her from loving him.

Even death couldn't come between them.

Chapter Twenty-five

That evening, just after sundown, Toni was sitting in the parlor with Ian, Carlos, Howard, and all the Vamp guys, watching the Digital Vampire Network. Stone Cauffyn of the *Nightly News* droned on and on. Phineas and Jack made everyone laugh with their impersonations of the boring newscaster.

Stone turned his head. "What is the meaning of this?"

The camera swerved, and Toni gasped. Jedrek Janow was approaching the newscaster's desk with a pistol in his hand. "Take him," he ordered, and a Russian Malcontent rushed past him to loop silver rope around Stone Cauffyn.

"What are you doing?" Stone asked. "This is highly irregular."

"On me!" Jedrek demanded, and the camera shifted to him. "You, cameraman, will do as I say if you want to live."

The camera didn't budge.

Jedrek nodded. "Good, now show our audience what we have behind door number one." He motioned to his right.

The camera panned to the door. Yuri and Stanislav entered the recording studio, each dragging a hostage.

Toni gasped. "They have Corky Courrant."

"And another woman," Ian muttered.

"I say we let him kill Corky," Phineas said.

"Shh." Ian turned up the volume as Jedrek spoke.

"As you can see, we have taken over DVN. Your regularly scheduled programming has been canceled for a far more interesting show. Ian MacPhie, you have twenty minutes to bring me the Stay-Awake drug, or I start executing people on live television."

Toni remained stunned and speechless, while the men all started to talk at the same time. How many men did Jedrek have? Who knew the layout at DVN?

The Vamp men suddenly leaped to their feet.

"Sorry!" a voice called from the foyer. Gregori entered the parlor. "Didn't mean to trigger the alarm."

Dougal rushed into the foyer to turn off the alarm.

Gregori glanced at the TV. "I saw what was happening. I thought I should warn you in case you didn't know."

"Do ye know the layout at DVN?" Ian asked.

"Sure. I've done a bunch of commercials there. Got some paper?" Gregori asked.

Toni ran to the desk. She collected some paper and pens, then dropped them on the large, square coffee table.

Gregori sat on one of the couches and began drawing.

"Phineas, Dougal, go below," Ian ordered. "Bring up some weapons. Howard, do ye know where DVN is?"

"It's in Brooklyn." Howard stood. "You want me to drive there?"

Ian ran a hand through his hair while he considered. "We doona want to teleport into a trap, so I think we should attack from the outside."

"Agreed," Zoltan said.

Their attention was snagged by a scream emanating from the television.

"You're burning my skin, you bastard!" Corky Courrant screeched as Yuri looped silver rope around her wrists.

The other woman whimpered as she was tied up.

Stone Cauffyn looked curiously at his ropes. "I say, what do you expect to gain from this?"

Jedrek sneered. "The world. With the Stay-Awake drug, I can rule the vampire world."

Stone gave him a bland look. "No such drug exists."

"Of course it does. Ian MacPhie took it. That's how he aged." Jedrek moved behind Corky and slid his hand around her neck. "I have you to thank, Ms. Courrant. You're the one who brought him to my attention."

Corky's eyes widened as his hand tightened. "If I helped you, then why don't you let me go?"

Jedrek tilted her head back to force her to look at him. "I enjoy watching blondes die. Isn't that so, Nadia?"

The camera swerved to a small brunette standing next to Stone. "It pleases the master when I kill a blonde," she whispered.

"You can't kill me!" Corky screamed. "I have fans." She glanced at the captured woman beside her. "Kill Tiffany. She's blonde. And she slept with my boyfriend."

"No!" Tiffany squealed. "I'm too young to die. And too pretty."

"Pretty?" Corky snorted. "Men just tell you that so you'll sleep with them."

"That's not true. I've been told I'm pretty by hundreds of men."

"And how many of those men did you sleep with?" Corky snarled.

Tiffany's eyes widened.

"Enough!" Jedrek rolled his eyes. "Gag them, Yuri, before I kill them now."

Yuri plastered a strip of duct tape over Tiffany's mouth.

Corky struggled with her ropes. "You can't kill me! I'm entertaining. Kill Stone! He's as boring as hell."

"Why, I say—" Stone stammered. "That seems uncalled for. I happen to find myself somewhat interesting."

Jedrek held Corky's head still while Yuri stuck duct tape across her mouth. Then he turned to inspect Stone, who stared blankly back at him. "What do you do?"

Stone blinked. "I read the news."

Jedrek strolled toward him. "And?"

"I have . . . nice hair."

Jedrek rolled his eyes. "This man is boring. I can't even sense any fear from him. Let him go."

Stone looked mildly surprised. "I must say, that is rather good news."

Nadia untied the silver ropes binding him and led him to the door. Corky tried to trip him as he passed by.

Jedrek paced in front of the two blonde hostages. "Now the question is which one of you shall I kill first? Or perhaps Ian MacPhie will come to save you."

Corky and Tiffany strained against their ropes.

Jedrek smiled. "That's it. Show me your fear. Let it ooze from your pores so I can revel in the smell." His gaze lowered to Corky's overly abundant breasts. "We'll need an extra long stake for this one."

Yuri chuckled. "Yes, Master."

Corky's scream was muffled and desperate.

Jedrek inhaled deeply. "Ah, the smell of fear." He turned to the camera. "Are you afraid, MacPhie? Are you going to let these women die so the entire Vamp world will remember you as a coward?"

"Go to hell," Ian muttered.

"I'm done," Gregori announced. He'd drawn a detailed schematic of DVN at vampire speed.

Phineas and Dougal whooshed into the room, their arms piled high with weapons. They set them down on the floor.

"Howard and Carlos, arm yourselves and get going," Ian ordered.

As the two mortal men grabbed swords, stakes, and daggers, Toni looked at Ian. Did he have other plans for her, or was he trying to completely leave her out? "Ian?"

His eyes met hers. "Can ye stay here?"

She shook her head. "For better or for worse. I'm with you."

A pained look crossed his face. "All right. Go with Howard."

She quickly gathered some weapons.

"Find a dark, secluded place nearby," Ian said. "Then call us, and we'll teleport. We'll have a plan by then."

"Okay." Howard motioned to Carlos and Toni. "Let's go."

On the way to DVN, Howard drove like a madman. "Don't get into a battle with a vampire, Toni. They're too fast and strong. They'll use mind control to freeze you."

"I understand." She couldn't compete with them. The vampires would always be superior. Even Howard and Carlos had abilities that she would never possess.

Howard drove onto the Brooklyn Bridge. "Carlos, if they try to take over your mind, shift. They can't control us when we're in animal form."

"I'll be ready for them," Carlos said.

Toni turned to look at Carlos in the backseat. "Be careful," she whispered.

"You, too, *menina*." Carlos winked.

Toni nervously fingered the wooden stakes in her lap. "I wonder how many men Jedrek has."

"Well, he had two men and a woman in the studio with him," Howard said. "And at last count, the Russian coven was down to about a dozen."

"So there could be ten more scattered about the building," Carlos concluded.

Toni mentally counted their number. Three mortals and six Vamps. Ian, Phineas, Dougal, Zoltan, Jack, and Gregori.

Howard parked in a dark alley next to the DVN parking

lot. They immediately called the townhouse, and within seconds, the six Vamps were there, fully armed. Moonlight gleamed off their swords and daggers. Ian explained the plan. All the men nodded, but Toni shook her head.

"No, Ian. It's too dangerous for you."

"I'm the one he wants. This is the best way."

"Shhh." Phineas held up a hand. "Someone's coming."

The men spread out in the alley, and soon Toni heard a yelp.

"I say, there's no need for violence."

Toni blinked. It was Stone Cauffyn.

"What are ye doing here?" Ian demanded as Phineas dragged the newscaster forward.

"Are you the good guys?" Stone asked. "I was hoping you'd come. I want to help." He patted his perfect hair. "I want a piece of the action because I'm *not boring*!"

"Shhh." Ian hushed him. "Can ye wield a sword?"

"No, but I'm real good with a hairbrush. Oh, and I know where there's a secret entrance. Will that help?"

"Yes. Ye'll take the mortals in through the secret entrance," Ian ordered. "Gregori, go with them. The rest of you, ye know what to do. Let's go." He strode toward the end of the alley.

Toni ran to join him. "Ian, please don't do this. There has to be a better way."

"I've weighed the options, Toni. If we attack, Jedrek will kill the hostages. This way, he'll think he's won, and he'll be easier to defeat." He gave her a worried look. "If I begged you to stay here in the alley, would ye do it?"

"You know I can't. I have to be there for you."

Ian sighed. "Doona try to take on a Malcontent."

"Yeah, yeah, the vampires are superior. I've heard it before. I'm not good enough."

Ian stopped and took her hand. "No one is more valuable to me than you. Doona blame me for being terrified for yer safety."

"I feel the same way about you."

"I'll be fine. Trust me." He kissed her brow, then skirted the alley wall to enter the DVN parking lot.

Toni said a silent prayer for him. Hot tears stung her eyes, but she blinked them away. No time for that now.

Phineas, Dougal, Zoltan, and Jack moved stealthily into the parking lot, keeping themselves hidden, while Ian strode straight to the entrance door.

"Let's go." Howard motioned for her, Carlos, Gregori, and Stone to follow him. They crept along the back of the DVN parking lot, staying in the shadow. They stopped behind two large cars to watch.

Ian approached the entrance, where two Malcontent guards pointed their rifles at him. He raised his hands. "I'm Ian MacPhie. I've brought the drug for Jedrek."

One guard held his rifle on Ian while the other patted him down. "No weapons."

"What about his purse?" The Malcontent pointed his rifle at the leather pouch in front of Ian's kilt.

"It's a sporran." Ian opened it and showed them the vial of greenish liquid. "I'm to deliver this personally."

Toni's breath caught. Did he really have some of the drug with him?

The guard checked Ian's sporran. "There's nothing else inside. Let's go." He opened the door and motioned for Ian to enter.

The guards scanned the parking lot, and not seeing anything, they both went into the building to escort Ian to Jedrek.

About five minutes later, Toni saw a blur of movement as Phineas and Dougal zipped at vampire speed toward the now unguarded entrance. They slipped inside. Two more figures crept from the shadows. Zoltan and Jack stood on each side of the door, pressed against the wall.

Gregori cursed under his breath. "Their alarm just went off. There must be a Malcontent in the security office, and he spotted our guys."

"We knew that could happen," Howard whispered.

"At least the recording studios are soundproof," Gregori said. "Jedrek can't hear it."

Toni recalled the plan that Ian had explained in the alley. Phineas and Dougal were supposed to take over the security office as quickly as possible.

The two guards who had escorted Ian returned. They ran out the front door with swords drawn, but they didn't get far. Zoltan and Jack jumped them, and in a flash, both guards were nothing but piles of dust on the pavement.

Zoltan and Jack sheathed their daggers and drew their swords. Then they rushed inside. Their mission was to zoom through the building, killing any Malcontents they came across. From what Toni could tell, they looked quite capable of the job.

"All right, Stone, let's go." Howard gave the newscaster a push.

They ran to the side of the building. Stone moved a heavy potted plant to reveal a trapdoor in the pavement next to the building. He pulled on a metal ring to lift the door and revealed a staircase leading into the basement.

Howard pulled a small LED flashlight from his utility belt and flipped it on. "Let's go."

"This is all storage," Stone whispered, once they were downstairs. "No one comes down here except Tiffany and the boss when they want to—"

"We gotcha," Gregori muttered. "Take us to the stairwell that's closest to the control room."

"This way." Stone led them across the vast storeroom and up a narrow flight of stairs.

"Me first." Gregori drew his sword.

"Of course." Stone let him pass.

Gregori cracked open the door and peeked outside. "It's clear." He led them down an empty corridor. The sound of clashing blades could be heard in the distance. As Toni passed beneath a security camera, she could only hope they were being watched by Phineas or Dougal and not the Malcontents.

"This is it." Gregori stopped by a door with a sign that read *Control Room*. Clashing blades could be heard inside. Gregori flung open the door. Toni followed him just in time to see Zoltan slash his sword across a Malcontent's neck, then skewer him through the heart. The dead vampire turned to dust.

Zoltan swiveled to face them and bowed. "The room is yours." He zoomed out the door.

"Wow." Toni watched Zoltan disappear around a corner.

"I'm glad that guy's on our side," Carlos muttered.

Gregori cursed. "Look at this." He motioned to the wall that was covered with twelve monitors.

Toni gasped. All twelve monitors showed the same scene, the studio where the *Nightly News* was aired. Ian had been stripped to his kilt, and Nadia was casually looping silver rope around his bare chest. Red welts appeared on Ian's skin, and the sizzling sound made Toni's stomach lurch.

"We have to get him out of there." Toni pulled her dagger from her belt.

"We will, soon," Gregori assured her. "Ian wanted to make sure we had the rest of the building completely under our control and as many Malcontents as possible killed before we make our final move on Jedrek."

Howard stood guard at the door, while they all watched the monitors, unable to help Ian.

"Ye have the drug," Ian spoke through gritted teeth. "Let the hostages go."

Jedrek lifted the vial of greenish liquid. "How can I be sure this is really the Stay-Awake drug? You might have filled it with poison. Is it poison, MacPhie?"

Ian glared at him.

"Is it poison?" Jedrek shouted.

Nadia looped some silver rope around Ian's neck and pulled it tight. His neck sizzled.

Toni swallowed hard at the bile rising in her throat.

Ian glowered at Jedrek. "It's no' poison. Try it and see."

Jedrek nodded slowly. "You want me to drink it." He strode to Corky and ripped the duct tape off her mouth.

She screeched. "That hurts, you bastard."

"This might hurt worse. Hold her!" Jedrek ordered, and Yuri held Corky's head still.

Corky glued her lips together, but Jedrek pinched her nose till she opened her mouth to gasp for air. Jedrek poured some of the greenish liquid down her throat.

Back in the control room, the door opened slowly and Phineas peered inside. "Don't shoot," he told Howard.

"Do you have the security office?" Howard asked.

"Yeah. I left Dougal there. Zoltan and Jack are doing one final sweep. We're almost ready to move on Jedrek."

"Thank God." Toni motioned to the monitors. "Have you seen what they're doing to Ian?"

"Yeah." Phineas grimaced. "There's a monitor in the security office that shows us what's on air. More importantly, the whole vampire world is seeing what they're doing to Ian. And he has a bunch of admirers out there."

"So?" Toni didn't want to hear about all the Vamp women who still wanted to date Ian.

"So, they're all showing up outside," Phineas said. "We can see the parking lot on a monitor, and there's got to be fifty angry Vamp women out there. They're all screaming that Ian MacPhie must be released."

"Good grief," Toni breathed.

"It's getting wild out there," Phineas continued. "Those women have whips and baseball bats."

"I have an idea." Gregori went to the wall of shelves and grabbed a camera. He turned it on and looked at the monitors. "How do I get this to show up there?"

"Here." Stone went to the control panel and flipped some switches. A bottom monitor showed them in the control room as seen through Gregori's camera.

"And how do we get this on air?" Gregori asked.

Stone showed them which switches to use. He handed Carlos the earphones and took a small one for himself.

"I'll let you know when we're ready." Gregori headed out the door. "Let's go, Stone."

Phineas and Howard stood guard while Carlos studied the control panel. Toni watched the monitors, wondering how Ian was faring. She couldn't see him at the moment because the cameraman was still focused on Corky. The Vamp world was waiting to see if Corky was going to die from poison.

"How do you feel?" Jedrek asked her.

"I—I'm fine."

"You don't feel anything at all?"

Corky glared at him. "I feel great, actually. Full of energy like I could kick your ass all the way to China."

"Gag her." Jedrek said, and Yuri stuck the tape across Corky's mouth.

Jedrek paced across the room and stopped in front of Ian. "Full of energy? That sounds about right." He lifted the vial to his mouth and drank the entire contents.

He sneered in Ian's face. "You realize what will happen, MacPhie? The sun will rise, and you'll fall into your death-sleep while I remain awake. You'll be the first one I'll kill."

Ian remained silent.

"Master?" Yuri asked hesitantly. "What if he's taken the drug, too?"

Jedrek turned sharply to look at Ian, who simply stared back. "It won't matter. We'll just keep him tied up. He won't be able to defend himself."

"Master!" another male voice called, and the camera swerved to the door where Stanislav was entering. "Master, the Vamps have invaded the building."

Jedrek gritted his teeth. "Do I have to tell you what to do? Just kill them."

Stanislav paled. "They were too fast. I—I can't find any of our men."

"What?" Jedrek shouted.

"Look!" Toni pointed at the bottom monitor. Gregori and Stone were in the parking lot. "They're ready."

Carlos flipped the switches and spoke into the headphone. "You're on."

Stone's face filled almost all the monitors now, while Jedrek was relegated to one monitor on the bottom row.

"This is Stone Cauffyn, reporting live from the parking lot of DVN," the newscaster shouted. "As you can see, this is definitely *not boring!* Over fifty Vamp women and a few men have gathered here in support of Ian MacPhie, who is being held prisoner inside. In fact, more Vamps are teleporting here as I speak."

Gregori panned the camera along the angry mob. They shook their fists and baseball bats in the air. "Set Ian free! Set Ian free!"

"I have their ringleader here," Stone continued, and Gregori aimed the camera back on him. "Vanda Barkowski, do you have anything to say?"

Vanda lifted a fist, holding her whip. "You're going down, Jedrek! Nobody hurts our Ian MacPhie. We love Ian!"

The crowd took up her shout. "We love Ian! We love Ian!"

"Oh please," Toni muttered inside the control room.

"Look at this." Carlos turned up the volume on the monitor showing the studio where Jedrek was waving his hands in the air.

"What the hell is going on?" Jedrek glared at the monitor in the studio. "What is Vanda Barkowski doing on national television? How did she steal my place?"

"The Vamps must have taken over the control room," Stanislav said.

Jedrek whirled around to glower at the Malcontent. "They cut me off? This is *my* show!" He pulled his pistol from his belt, zoomed to Ian, and pressed the barrel of the gun against Ian's forehead. "Put me back on *now!*"

Toni gasped. "Carlos, quickly."

"I got it." He put Jedrek back on air.

Jedrek glanced at the monitor and saw himself. "That's more like it. Stanislav, Yuri, go take back the control room now!"

"Yes, Master!" They ran from the recording studio.

Toni gulped and tightened her grip on her dagger. "They're coming."

Carlos jumped to his feet and drew his dagger. Howard took up a position by the door with his dagger in hand.

Phineas raised his sword. "I'll take one. The three of you take the other."

The door burst open. Stanislav zoomed toward Phineas, and their swords clashed.

Yuri halted when he spotted Carlos and Toni. "Mortals," he sneered. He pointed his sword at them. "This will be too easy."

With a bearlike growl, Howard leaped on Yuri's back and plunged a dagger into his side. Yuri screamed and threw Howard off his back with so much force that Howard flew across the room and crashed into the wall of shelves. Contents from the shelves spilled down on Howard. He didn't move.

Yuri sucked in a hissing breath as he looked at his bleeding wound. "You'll pay for this." He lifted his sword and charged.

Carlos dunked, and Toni leaped to the side. She heard Phineas cry out and glanced his way. Oh no! Stanislav had managed to stab Phineas in the shoulder.

A blur shot past her, and she whirled, lifting her dagger.

"No!" Carlos shouted.

Yuri caught her from behind. He pressed the edge of his sword against her neck. "Drop your weapon." The sword pinched her skin. "Drop it!"

She let her dagger tumble to the floor.

"Stand back!" Yuri shouted.

With a stricken look, Carlos stepped back. The clash of swords echoed in her ears as Phineas continued to fight Stanislav. A low growl emanated from Carlos as he ripped his shirt off. She realized he was going to shift.

Yuri cursed, then Toni gasped as everything went black.

Chapter Twenty-six

Toni materialized right into a shootout. Yuri jerked them both down to the floor as bullets sprayed overhead. She looked quickly about. Corky and Tiffany had dropped to the floor and were squirming out of the way.

Jedrek was shooting at Jack and Zoltan. They must have just charged into the studio. Jack jumped behind Stone Cauffyn's desk while Zoltan rushed in the opposite direction, taking shelter behind an unmanned camera. The cameraman was huddled on the floor behind his camera.

Jedrek's pistol made some empty clicking noises. With a curse, he threw it aside and drew his sword. Zoltan rushed forward to engage him, while Jack dashed toward Ian to press a dagger into his hands.

"Stop!" Nadia ran at Jack, her sword raised.

Jack lunged at Nadia, forcing her to retreat.

"No!" Yuri lurched forward to help Nadia.

With a quick slash, Jack nearly sliced off Yuri's arm. Blood splattered. With a screech, Yuri fell to the floor. Jack turned him to dust, then went after Nadia.

Toni swallowed hard. She couldn't let this violence freak her out. Yuri's sword was lying on the floor, and she needed to grab it. She stumbled to her feet, but an icy cold assault knocked her flat on the floor. The familiar icy wave swept through her, freezing her body.

You cannot move. Jedrek's command rang in her head.

He zoomed toward her. "You will drop your swords!" He pointed his sword at Toni's heart.

She stared at the sharp point, poised to kill her. Her body couldn't budge. She couldn't even turn her head. Out of the corner of her eye, she saw Ian's stricken face.

Swords clattered on the floor. Jack and Zoltan had surrendered.

Oh God, what if Jedrek killed them? What if he killed Ian? And all because she was unable to function on their level. An old, familiar shame swept through her. Always unworthy. Never quite good enough.

"Tie them up," Jedrek ordered.

Nadia looped silver rope around Jack's wrists.

Jedrek strolled over to them. "What shall I do with you two? Shall I kill you now? Giacomo, the famous son of Casanova." He stopped in front of Zoltan. "And the mighty Coven Master of Eastern Europe. I should tie you both to a lamppost and let the sunrise burn you to death."

Toni noticed from the corner of her eye that Ian had cut the silver ropes looped around his chest and wrists. He stuffed some rope into his sporran. Nadia was too busy tying the new prisoners, and Jedrek was too busy taunting to notice.

She had to help Ian. His poor chest and hands were covered with red welts. God help her, she couldn't lie here helpless while he tried to save everyone. And how could he save anyone if Jedrek kept control of the situation by threatening to kill her? She had to fight this. Somehow, she had to break through Jedrek's mind control.

Toni concentrated hard on Ian. On how much she loved

him. On how strongly she wanted to help him. Her fingers twitched. She glanced at Jedrek and Nadia. Their backs were turned to her as they tormented Jack and Zoltan. Her hand jerked awkwardly to the wooden stake in her belt. Slowly she closed her fist around it.

She turned her head and saw Ian watching her. He nodded slightly.

He was counting on her. She focused hard. Her love for Ian had to be stronger than Jedrek's power.

"Jedrek, have ye figured out yet that ye've been tricked?" Ian asked, and Jedrek whirled to face him. "Do ye really think I would give you the Stay-Awake drug? That vial was naught but an energy drink."

Jedrek's face turned red with rage. "I'll kill you now!" He ran at Ian, raising his sword in the air.

Ian lunged to the floor to grab Jack's sword, then jumped to his feet to deflect Jedrek's first swing.

With Jedrek's mind fully engaged, Toni was better able to defy his mind control. She eased to her feet.

Ian's sword flashed so quickly, it was clear Jedrek was out-matched. With a flick of his wrist, Ian sent Jedrek's sword flying through the air.

Jedrek backed up.

With his free hand, Ian pulled a length of silver rope from his sporran. "Nay, this time ye willna teleport away." He dropped his sword and leaped forward, looping the silver cord around Jedrek. He pulled the Malcontent against his chest.

Jedrek struggled and kicked, but Ian held him tight. "Now, Toni!"

As she ran forward, she noted the shocked look on Jedrek's face. A mere mortal was about to kill him.

He attacked her with a wave of psychic power. *You are under my control. Drop that stake now!*

Her hand shook. Icy power streamed through her, threatening to freeze her in place. She forced her feet to move forward. One step. Two.

Jedrek's eyes widened. "No! You will fear me! You will feel the power of fear!"

"I'll show you fear, you bastard!" She stabbed the stake through his heart.

His cry faded as his body disintegrated.

Her mind was free. She dropped the stake, and it fell onto a pile of dust.

Ian tossed the silver rope aside. "Toni." He pulled her into his arms. "Ye were amazing."

She leaned on him, closing her eyes in relief. Jedrek was dead.

"To please the master, I will kill the blonde," a voice whispered behind her.

"No!" Ian yanked Toni to the side.

She jolted when a dagger plunged into her side. Stunned, she saw Ian grab at Nadia, but the female Malcontent teleported away. She looked down at the dagger in her side. How strange. Then a burning pain ripped through her and dragged her into oblivion.

Panic gripped Ian. He swept Toni up in his arms, and the dagger clattered to the floor. It must not have been in very deep. A good sign. But she was losing so much blood.

He shot a pleading look at the camera. "Roman, Connor, if ye hear me, come to Romatech. Please."

The door burst open, and Phineas, Dougal, Howard, and Carlos rushed in. Ian knew they could take care of the hostages, so he teleported straight to Romatech.

"Laszlo!" He zoomed to the operating room.

"I'm here!" Laszlo opened the door for him. "I saw what happened on the television. Put her on the table." He rushed to the sink to wash his hands.

Ian laid Toni on the operating table. Forms wavered in front of him. Roman materialized, holding Shanna, while Connor appeared with Constantine in his arms.

"Oh, thank God," Ian breathed. "She—she's losing so much

blood." Already the sheet beneath her was stained red.

Roman and Shanna ran to the sinks to wash their hands. Connor disappeared, then returned with Radinka.

Laszlo snapped on a pair of surgical gloves. "You realize she may have to go to a hospital?"

"Yes, of course." Ian didn't know how to help. He pulled off Toni's shoes and socks.

Laszlo grabbed a pair of scissors and began cutting away her polo shirt. Ian unbuckled her belt and pulled it out from underneath her.

"Ian, stand back." Roman snapped on gloves.

"I canna lose her." Ian flinched when Connor grabbed his arm to pull him back.

"Get out of their way, lad. Let them do their job."

"Is Toni hurt bad?" Constantine asked, his bottom lip trembling.

"She'll be fine," Connor said.

"How is she?" Radinka asked.

"She'll be fine," Connor repeated as he handed Tino to her.

Radinka forced a smile. "Of course she'll be fine." She hurried from the room with the little boy. "Let's wait outside."

Ian watched helplessly as Toni lay on the table bleeding. "By all the saints, I canna lose her."

"She'll be fine, lad," Connor murmured.

Ian turned to him. "I love her, and I willna let ye fire her. I doona care what the rules say."

"Calm down, lad. No one wants to fire her. We saw what she did on the telly. She overcame vampire mind control and staked a vicious Malcontent assassin. It was truly an amazing feat for a mortal."

"She *is* amazing." Ian looked at Roman. "Ye have to heal her!"

"We'll do our best," Roman said calmly. "The wound is shallow. No major organs were affected." He gazed at the monitor that Shanna had hooked up to show Toni's vital signs. "Her blood pressure's very low, but that's to be expected." He tossed a bloody pad into a metal pan.

Laszlo passed him another pad. "We could give her a transfusion. She's AB positive."

"Do whatever ye have to do!" Ian demanded. "I'm no' going to lose her!"

"Calm down." Shanna walked toward him, carrying a tray of gauze pads and a bottle of something nasty, no doubt. "You've been burned. Let's get you cleaned up."

Ian waved a dismissive hand. "I doona care. I'll heal during my death-sleep."

"Ian," Shanna spoke sharply. "Those wounds need to heal cleanly."

He groaned. "Fine." He endured the stinging medicine she applied to his burns. It served him right for failing to protect Toni. He'd been so relieved to hold her in his arms, he hadn't seen Nadia sneak up on them.

"It's all my fault." He watched Toni on the operating table. She looked so pale. "I dinna get her out of the way fast enough."

"We saw it on TV," Shanna said. "It was terrifying. Everything was happening so fast."

"Aye," Connor agreed. "Ye did well, lad. The Malcontents lost about ten men, and we dinna lose a single one."

But he'd failed to keep Toni safe. Ian gazed sadly at her. "Can ye fix her?"

"We're trying," Roman said. "But we're not surgeons."

Laszlo nodded. "We've never had to repair internal injuries. Vamps always heal naturally from within."

"Because of our vampire blood." Roman looked at Laszlo. "I've always been curious about how well our blood can heal. What if we give her a transfusion of vampire blood instead of regular synthetic blood?"

Laszlo fiddled with a button on his lab coat. "We could

give her a sedative to keep her unconscious. That might simulate death-sleep enough that the vampire blood would start to heal her internally."

"Are you planning on turning her?" Shanna asked. "We should have her permission."

"This won't transform her," Roman said. "She would have to be drained completely and in a vampire coma. And then she would have to drink from a vampire and ingest the blood in order to change. This would keep her mortal, but we could see if the vampire blood heals her."

Laszlo nodded. "It would be very interesting to see if it works."

Shanna gave the two men a dubious look. "You want to experiment on her. Wouldn't it be safer to take her to a hospital?"

"She would have to undergo surgery in a hospital," Roman argued. "If our theory works, she'll heal naturally and quickly."

"Indeed." Laszlo twisted a button. "We'll be able to tell fairly quickly if it's working or not. If it doesn't, then we can take her to a hospital."

"Then let's get on with it." Ian strode toward the operating table. "I'll give her my blood."

"We'll need to make sure your blood is compatible." Laszlo swabbed Ian's arm with antiseptic.

"It should be. I drink AB positive all the time."

"So I see." Roman glanced at the bite marks on Toni's neck and frowned at Ian.

"I—I dinna force myself on her."

"How recent?" Laszlo cleaned Toni's arm and inserted a needle.

"About nine hours ago." When Ian received some confused looks, he explained. "I took the Stay-Awake drug, so we could have some time alone."

Connor muttered a curse under his breath.

Roman exchanged an amused look with his wife. "Well, since your blood came from Toni, it should be a perfect match."

Lazlo rolled a second gurney up to the operating table. "Get on."

Ian lay on top, and soon his blood was being pumped directly into Toni. Roman and Lazlo kept a close watch on Toni's wound, while Shanna watched her vital signs.

"The bleeding stopped," Roman whispered.

Lazlo fiddled with a button. "That's a good sign."

"Blood pressure's still too low," Shanna murmured.

"Sir, I believe that tissue is closing," Lazlo exclaimed.

"Yes, it's working," Roman announced. "Let's sew her up."

Thirty minutes later, Toni's wound was continuing to heal but her vital signs were still problematic. The transfusion had left Ian weak and hungry, so he rested on the gurney while he drank several pints of synthetic blood. AB positive, just in case Toni needed some more.

A loud cheer erupted from the waiting room. Connor's announcement about Toni's recovery had been well received.

Shanna shook her head. "We shouldn't celebrate just yet. She's running a fever."

Ian said a silent prayer for Toni as he slipped off the gurney. Connor had brought him a navy polo shirt from the security office. He put it on and peeked out the door to see who was in the waiting room.

His mouth fell open. Everyone was there. Jean-Luc and Heather from Texas. Angus, Emma, and Robby. Zoltan and Jack were there. Their burned wrists had been bandaged by Lazlo. Dougal was there, unharmed.

Phineas's shoulder was bandaged.

Ian walked up to him. "Ye were injured?"

"It's nothing." Phineas waved a dismissive hand. "Stan managed to poke me a little, that's all."

"Did ye finish him off?"

"I wish." Phineas made a face. "When Carlos shifted into

a panther, Stan freaked out and ran. Ran straight into the parking lot, and the women out there nearly tore him to shreds before he managed to teleport away."

"So he's still alive."

"Yeah." Phineas shrugged and winced. "I'll have to watch my back from now on."

"Doona fash," Dougal said. "We'll watch yer back."

Ian spotted Carlos sitting between Sabrina and Teddy. Carlos must have called them about Toni.

Teddy grinned as he approached. "Hey, man, I heard you guys defeated the evil forces."

"Toni killed Jedrek," Ian said. "She was amazing."

Sabrina snorted. "She could have gotten herself killed. I told her to stay away from you . . . Vamps. It's not safe to be around you."

"The mortal world is dangerous, too," Carlos told her.

"But Toni has no business trying to fight evil vampires," Sabrina insisted. She glared at Ian. "I swear, if something happens to her, I'll sue your ass. I'll—"

She paused when Constantine climbed up on the chair next to her. "My gosh, little boy, how did you get in here? What are you doing with these . . . people?"

"These are my friends," Constantine said. "I'm worried about Toni."

"Toni's going to be all right," Ian told the little boy. He just hoped it was the truth.

Constantine gave Ian one of his bright, angelic smiles. "Good. I like Toni."

"Who are you?" Sabrina whispered.

"I'm Constantine. My mommy is like you, and my daddy is a vampire."

Sabrina's eyes widened with horror. "Oh my God." She flinched when Tino touched her arm.

Constantine gazed at her with his wide blue eyes. "It's going to be all right."

Sabrina's horrified expression slowly melted away. She

glanced down at Constantine's hand. "What did you do?"

"You were hurting," Tino said. "Do you feel better now?"

"Yes." Sabrina's eyes widened with wonder. "I do."

This gave Ian an idea. "Tino, would ye like to see Toni?"

Constantine jumped in his seat. "Yes! I like Toni."

Ian picked the boy up in his arms. "She's still hurting. Do ye think ye can make her feel better?"

"I'll try."

In just the short amount of time it took to carry Constantine into the operating room, Ian noticed that the pain from his burns had lessened.

"Hi, Mommy! Hi, Daddy!" Constantine grinned at his parents.

"Goodness." Shanna took him from Ian. "I thought you'd be asleep by now."

"I want to see Toni," Tino announced.

Shanna hesitated. "She's not feeling well, sweetie."

Constantine stuck out his bottom lip. "I want to help her. I like Toni."

"All right, sweetie." Shanna set him on the gurney next to Toni.

He reached out to touch her, then withdrew his hand. "She's hurt bad." He stretched out beside her and wrapped his little fingers around her hand.

"Look at this." Roman motioned at the vital signs monitor.

"Her fever's going down," Shanna whispered.

Constantine yawned as he gazed at Toni. "She's going to be like me." His eyelids shut, and he drifted off to sleep.

"Thank you, Tino." Ian smoothed a hand over the little boy's blonde curls.

Toni was going to be all right.

Toni woke slowly as if she were climbing out of a deep, dark hole.

"Look. She's coming to."

"Oh, thank God."

She heard Carlos's voice, followed by Sabrina's. Her eyes flickered open. Their faces hovered over her, their features fuzzy and unclear. She spotted another person at the foot of the bed. Ian? She blinked, trying to focus. What was wrong with her eyes?

"Hi, Toni," the third person said.

"Oh." She swallowed her disappointment. "Hi, Teddy."

"How do you feel, *menina*?" Carlos asked.

"I'm fine, I think." She lifted a hand to rub her eyes. "My eyes are burning."

"I was afraid of that," Sabrina said. "They didn't realize you wear contacts." She fumbled in her handbag and pulled out a compact mirror.

Toni sat up.

"Careful." Carlos grabbed the bed's control device. "Let me adjust the bed for you." With a humming noise, the back of the bed rose up to support her back.

"I'm in a hospital?" Toni asked.

"No, this is the operating room at Romatech," Carlos explained. "Ian brought you here."

Toni tried to focus on the compact mirror. She removed one contact and passed it to Sabrina. "Where's Ian? What time is it?" She removed the other contact.

"It's just after five." Sabrina tossed the contacts in the trash.

"In the morning?" Toni blinked.

"Evening," Teddy said. "You slept all day."

Toni looked at him. Then at Carlos and Sabrina. Then around the room. "Oh my gosh."

"What's wrong?" Sabrina rushed back to her side.

"My eyesight. It—it's perfect. Without contacts." She handed the compact back to Sabrina and looked around the room once more. Her sight was more than perfect. She could read the fine print on a poster across the room above the sink. It described the proper procedure for washing hands.

She caught Carlos and Sabrina exchanging a worried look.

Something was wrong. She lifted the sheet and blanket to look at her side. The last time she'd looked, there'd been a dagger stuck in her. She touched the area gingerly, expecting to feel some pain. Nothing.

Underneath the sheet, she pulled up her hospital gown. She peeked at her side. There was a faint scar, barely noticeable. She touched the scar. No pain or tenderness. And all the bite marks that had dotted her torso were gone.

Alarm crept into her. She must have slept for weeks to be this healed. "How long was I out? Was I in a coma?"

"*Menina*." Carlos touched her arm. "You were wounded last night."

"Last . . . but that doesn't make sense." She grabbed his hand. "Tell me what happened."

He winced. "Toni, lighten up. You're about to crush my bones."

She released his hand. Her sense of alarm grew into full-fledged panic. "I hurt you?"

Carlos flexed his fingers. "You seem a lot stronger."

"Oh my God." Sabrina stepped back, her eyes widening.

"Will someone please tell me what happened?" Toni grasped the railing beside her so she could lower it and get out of bed. She gave it a little push, and it broke completely off.

Sabrina gasped.

"She's Superwoman!" Teddy announced, grinning.

"What?" Toni dropped the bed railing, and it clattered on the floor. "Oh no." Great eyesight, super strength. Was she still alive? She touched her teeth to see if she'd acquired any pointed fangs.

"Relax, *menina*." Carlos patted her arm. "You're not a Vamp."

She exhaled with relief. "Oh, thank goodness. Not that I have anything against them. I'm really fond of them, and I love Ian. But I'd really hate to die and miss it. I mean, I'm glad I'm still alive. I really like to eat." Good grief, she was babbling like an idiot. "I'm just so confused. How did I heal so fast?"

Just then, Ian walked into the room, carrying two vases of flowers. He grinned at Toni. "Ye're awake. How do ye feel?"

"I have perfect eyesight." She looked him over. He was looking great in his jeans and blue sweater that matched his eyes.

"That's good." He set the vases on the counter.

"I didn't have perfect eyesight before," Toni said.

"What did you do to her?" Sabrina demanded. "She—she's ripping the furniture apart with her bare hands!"

"She's Superwoman," Teddy added.

Ian looked at the broken railing on the floor.

"It was an accident," Toni said. "I didn't mean to. I just pushed a little and . . ."

Ian nodded. "We thought something like this might happen. Ye could have heightened senses and abilities."

Toni swallowed hard. "What kind of abilities?"

"Ye'll be verra strong and fast." Ian walked toward her. "Constantine was the one who made us realize it when he said ye would be like him—mortal but with special powers. I hope ye doona mind."

"Mind?" Teddy said. "This is so awesome! Toni will be like the bionic woman, but without the metal parts."

Toni sat there, stunned. She glanced at Sabrina, and her friend was staring at her with a shocked expression. "How—what did you do to me?"

"We gave you a blood transfusion." Ian perched on the end of the bed. "My blood."

"You filled her up with vampire blood?" Carlos asked.

"Awesome," Teddy whispered.

"Are you trying to turn her into a vampire?" Sabrina asked.

"Nay." Ian rested a hand on Toni's foot. "We were only trying to heal her. Ye see, vampires heal naturally during our death-sleep because of our blood. We thought my blood might be able to heal Toni. And it did. Sorta." He shrugged one shoulder. "Constantine helped, too."

Sabrina approached the bed. "That sweet little boy helped heal Toni? He—he helped me, too."

"You met Constantine?" Toni asked.

Sabrina nodded. "You were right. He's a very special child." She turned to Ian at the foot of the bed. "Then Toni is still mortal?"

"Aye. She's entirely normal except for having a few extra abilities. We're no' exactly certain what kind of powers she'll have."

Toni leaned back against the bed. Would she be able to levitate or teleport? "I—I'm really a Superwoman?"

Ian smiled. "I'm just grateful I dinna lose you. I've never been more frightened in my life."

"Oh, Ian." She reached a hand toward him, and he slid down the bed to take her hand and kiss it. "How are you? You had so many nasty burns."

"All healed." He leaned closer to kiss her brow.

"You must be hungry." Carlos motioned for Teddy and Sabrina to come with him. "We'll get you some food."

"We'll be back." Sabrina gave her a worried glance as she left the room.

Ian looked her over carefully. "How do ye feel, sweetheart?"

"I feel great." She flung her arms around his neck and hugged him. "I'm so glad it's all over. And I love those flowers. I can smell them from here."

"Aye, ye have stronger senses. The white lilies are from me, and the red roses are from Vanda."

"Vanda?"

Ian grinned. "They've been showing yer assassination of Jedrek Janow on DVN. Ye're a hero. And Vanda's verra happy that he's dead. I gather she had some bad history with him. Anyway, she wanted me to tell you that she was wrong about you. She says we're perfect for each other, and ye should jump my bones at every opportunity."

"She said that?"

Ian's mouth twitched. "Well, I added that last part."

Toni snorted. "I'm glad Vanda decided I'm good enough. I should be now that I have some super Vamp abilities. It always irked me that you guys were superior."

"Toni, doona say that. I have never considered you less than worthy. Ye've always been brave and fearless. Ye rescued yer friend from her greedy uncle. And look at what ye did last night. Ye defied Jedrek's mind control. He was desperately trying to stop you from staking him, and ye just kept coming. It was amazing. I doona know how ye did it."

"You don't know how?" She touched his face. "It was simple. My love for you was more powerful than his hatred."

Ian took her hand and kissed it. "I love you, Toni. I admire you and respect you. Just the way ye are. Ye doona need vampire blood running in yer veins to be worthy. Ye were always a superwoman."

Tears filled her eyes. *I am worthy to be loved.*

Ian squeezed her hand gently. "I have to tell you that yer new abilities may no' be permanent. Our bodies replenish themselves over time. Of course, if ye want to retain some Vamp power, I'll be happy to share my blood with you."

"I'll share mine with you, too." She grinned. "As long as our love is permanent, that's all that matters."

He pulled her into his arms. "Ye will always have my love."

Epilogue

Christmas Eve

Dressed in his Santa suit, Ian set down his bulky red bag on the threadbare carpet. He'd teleported with Toni, who was wearing her elf costume beneath a red woolen coat. The wood frame house in rural Virginia was small—small enough that they had to very quiet. He could hear the parents snoring in a nearby bedroom, their four children crowded in a second bedroom.

Sabrina had given them the information about this family. The father had been injured in a farm accident, and they were barely scraping by. Only four little presents, wrapped in newspaper, sat under the Christmas tree.

Ian opened his sack, and Toni helped him remove several boxes of warm winter clothes. A plastic bag contained a frozen turkey. Then came the toys—a video game set, some books, and a pretty doll for the little girl.

With his bag empty, Ian grabbed hold of Toni to

teleport. She pointed up to the roof. With a wry look, he did as she asked.

They landed on the roof, ankle-deep in snow.

He held her steady. "Why did ye want to come up here?"

"It's more like Santa Claus. Where do we go now?"

"Back to Romatech. My bag is empty." He touched her red nose. "Are ye sure ye want to keep traveling with me? Ye look half frozen."

"I am, but this is just too cool. When I think about these people waking up in the morning to find all that stuff—I love it!" She flung her arms around his neck.

"Careful." He widened his stance. "These roofs can be verra slippery."

She cuddled up to him, then glanced down. "Either you have something in your pocket, or you're getting excited."

"Both." He reached in the pocket of his red velvet pants and felt the small black box. Should he give it to her now? Back at Romatech, they would be surrounded by noisy people, rushing to get all the presents out tonight.

He looked around. Stars twinkled in a clear sky. Moonlight gleamed off white, snow-covered pastures. The air smelled of cedar and fresh snow. "This is a lovely spot, aye?"

"Yes. Very peaceful." She rested her head on his shoulder. "I have a present for you at the townhouse. But before I give it to you, I was hoping you'd tell me about that dream you had of me."

He kissed her brow. "I dreamed ye were round with child. Our child."

"Really?" She leaned back to look at him. "Why didn't you tell me?"

"I dinna want to push you into something ye might no' want." Although he hoped she did want children. He took the black box from his pocket. "I have a present for you, if ye'll accept it. I hope ye like it." He opened the box to show her the ring.

"Oh my." She took the box. "It's so . . . beautiful."

Ian went down on one knee. "Daytona Lynn Davis, will ye—" Snow shifted beneath him, then suddenly a block of snow went sliding down the roof, taking him with it.

"Ian!" she cried.

He went flying off the edge of the roof and fell on his back on a thick bank of snow. "Oof."

He saw Toni skidding down the roof like a surfer. She jumped off the edge and landed neatly beside him.

She laughed. "Being a Superwoman has its perks. Are you okay?"

"I was trying to propose." He started to sit up.

"Yes!" She flung herself on top of him, pushing him back onto the snow. "Yes, I'll marry you."

He grinned. "We dinna lose the ring, I hope?"

"Nope. Right here." She showed him the box.

He pulled off her mitten so he could slide on her ring. "I dinna know what else to get you for Christmas."

She hugged him there in the snow. "All I want for Christmas is my vampire."

**Warm up the winter nights
with a sizzling hot read!
With four upcoming
Romance Superleaders
from bestsellers
Elizabeth Boyle, Laura Lee Guhrke,
Kerrelyn Sparks, and Kathryn Caskie,
you won't even feel the cold . . .**

Coming September 2008

Tempted By the Night

An exciting new paranormal romance by *New York Times* bestselling author

ELIZABETH BOYLE

Lady Hermione Marlowe has loved the rakish Earl of Rockhurst from afar forever, defending his scandalous ways at every turn. One of her greatest desires is follow after him, completely unseen, so as to reveal his true noble nature . . . and then, much to her shock, Hermione finds herself fading from sight as the sun sets, until she is completely invisible! Freed of the confines of Society, she recklessly follows the earl into the temptations of the night and shockingly discovers that his disreputable veneer is merely a cover for his real duty: safeguarding London as the Paratus, the Protector of the Realm.

✳

Thomasin appeared in the same state of shock. "Oh. My. Goodness," she managed to gasp, her eyes wide with amazement as she gazed somewhere over Hermione's shoulder. "You are never going to believe this, Minny."

India blinked and tried again to speak, her mouth wavering open and shut as if she couldn't quite find the words to describe the sight before her.

"What is it?" Hermione asked, glancing over her shoulder and only seeing the narrow, tall figure of Lord Battersby behind her. Certainly his arrival wouldn't have India looking like she'd swallowed her aunt's parrot.

"Oh, let me tell her," Thomasin was saying, rising up on her toes.

"No, let me," India said as she finally found her voice. "I saw *him* first."

Him. Hermione shivered. There was only one *him* in the *ton* as far as she as concerned.

Rockhurst.

Oh, but her friends had to be jesting, for the earl would never make an appearance at Almack's. She glanced at both their faces, fully expecting to find some telltale sign of mirth, some twitch of the lips that would give way to a full-blown giggle.

But there were none. Just the same, wide-eyed gaping expression that she now noticed several other guests wore.

Turning around slowly, Hermione's jaw dropped as well.

Nothing in all her years out could have prepared her for the sight of the Earl of Rockhurst arriving at Almack's.

"Jiminy!" she gasped, her hand going immediately to her quaking stomach. Oh, heavens, she shouldn't have had that extra helping of pudding at supper, for now she feared the worst.

And here she thought she'd be safe at Almack's.

"I didn't believe you," she whispered to India.

"I still don't believe it myself," India shot back. "Whatever is he doing here?"

"I don't know, and I don't care," Thomasin replied, "but I'm just glad Mother insisted we come tonight, if only for the crowing rights we will have tomorrow over everyone who isn't here."

"Oh, this is hardly the gown to catch his eye," Hermione groaned. "It is entirely the wrong shade of capucine," she declared, running her hands over the perfectly fashionable, perfectly pretty gown she'd chosen.

Thomasin laughed. "Minny, stop fussing. The three of us could be stark naked and posed like a trio of wood nymphs, and he wouldn't notice us."

"True enough," India agreed. "You have to see that you are too respectable to garner his fancy."

"He fancied Charlotte," Hermione shot back, trying to ignore the little bit of jealousy that niggled in her heart as she said it.

"Oh, I suppose he did for about an hour," India conceded, "but you have to admit, Charlotte was a bit odd the last few weeks. Not herself at all."

Hermione nodded in agreement. There had been something different about Charlotte. Ever since . . . ever since her Great-Aunt Ursula had died and she'd inherited . . . Hermione glanced down at her gloved hand. Inherited the very ring she'd found yesterday . . .

Beneath her glove, she swore the ring warmed, even quivered on her finger, like a trembling bell that foretold of something ominous just out of reach.

"Did you hear of his latest escapade?" Lady Thomasin was whispering. There was no one around them to hear, but some things just couldn't be spoken in anything less than the awed tone of a conspiratorial hush.

India nodded. "About his wager with Lord Kramer—"

"Oh, hardly that," Thomasin scoffed. "Everyone has heard about that. No, I am speaking of his renewed interest in Mrs. Fornett. Apparently she was seen with him at Tattersall's when everyone knows she is under Lord Saunderton's protection." The girl paused, then heaved a sigh. "Of course there will be a duel. There always is in these cases." Lady Thomasin's cousin had once fought a duel, and so she considered herself quite the expert on the subject.

"Pish posh," Hermione declared. "He isn't interested in her."

"I heard Mother telling Lady Gidding, that she'd heard it from Lady Owston, who'd had it directly from Lord Filton that he was at Tatt's with Mrs. Fornett." Thomasin rocked back on her heels, her brows arched and her mouth set as if that was the final word on the subject.

"That may be so, but I heard Lord Delamere tell my brother that he'd seen Rockhurst going into a truly dreadful house in Seven Dials. The sort of place no gentleman would even frequent. With truly awful women inside."

Hermione wrinkled her nose. "And what was Lord Delamere doing outside this sinful den?"

"I daresay driving past it to get to the nearest gaming hell. He's gone quite dice mad and nearly run through his inheritance. Of so my brother likes to say."

"And probably squiffed, I'd wager," Hermione declared, forgetting her admonishment to Viola about using such phrases. "I don't believe any of it. Whatever is the matter with Society these days when all they can get on with is making up gossip about a man who doesn't deserve it?"

"Not deserve it?" Lady Thomasin gaped. "The Earl of Rockhurst is a terrible bounder. Everyone knows it."

"Well, I think differently." Hermione crossed her arms over her chest and stood firm, even as her stomach continued to twist and turn.

"Why you continue to defend him, I know not," India said, glancing over where the earl stood with his cousin, Miss Mary Kendell. "He's wicked and unrepentant."

"I disagree." Hermione straightened and took a measured glance at the man. "I don't believe a word of any of it. The Earl of Rockhurst is a man of honor."

Lady Thomasin snorted. "Oh, next you'll be telling us he spends his nights, spooning broth to sickly orphans and bestowing food baskets to poor war widows."

India laughed. "Oh, no, I think he's like the mad earl in that book your mother told us not to read." She shivered and leaned in closer to whisper. "You know the one . . . about the dreadful man who kidnapped all sorts of ladies and kept them in his attic? I'd wager if you were to venture into the earl's attics, you'd find an entire harem!"

"Oh, of all the utter nonsense! How can you say such dreadful things about a man's reputation?" Hermione argued. "The earl is a decent man, I just know it. And I'll not let the Lord Delameres and the Lord Filtons of the world tell me differently."

"Well, the only way to prove such a thing would be to follow him around all night—for apparently only seeing the truth with your own eyes will end this infatuation of yours, Hermione."

She crossed her arms over her chest and set her shoulders. "I just might."

"Yes, and you'd be ruined in the process," Thomasin pointed out. "And don't think he'll marry you to save your reputation, when he cares nothing of his own."

India snapped her fingers, her eyes alight with inspiration. "Too bad you aren't cursed like the poor heroine in that book we borrowed from my cousin. Remember it? *Zoe's Dilemma* . . . No, that's not it. *Zoe's Awful* . . . Oh, I don't remember the rest of the title."

"I do," Lady Thomasin jumped in. "*Zoe or the Moral Loss of a Soul Cursed.*"

India sighed. "Yes, yes, that was it."

Hermione gazed up at the ceiling. Only Thomasin and India would recall such a tale at a time like this. She glanced over at the earl, and then down at her gown. Oh, she should never have settled on this dress. It was too pumpkin and not enough capucine. How would he ever discover her now?

Thomasin continued, "You remember the story, Minny. At sunset, Zoe faded from sight so no one could see her. What I would give to have a night thusly."

"Whatever for?" India asked. "You already know the earl is a bounder."

Their friend got a devilish twinkle in her eye. "If I were unseen for a night, I'd make sure that Miss Lavinia Burke had the worst evening of her life. Why, the next day, every gossip in London would be discussing what a bad case of wind she had, not to mention how clumsy she's become, for I fear I'd be standing on her train every time she took a step."

Hermione chuckled, while India burst out laughing.

"I do think you've considered this before," Hermione said.

Thomasin grinned. "I might have." Then she laughed as well. "If you were so cursed, Hermione, you could follow Rockhurst from sunset to sunrise, and then you'd see everyone is right about him."

India made a more relevant point. "Then you could end this disastrous *tendré* you have for him and discover a more eligible *parti* before the Season ends."

And your chances of a good marriage with them, her statement implied, but being the bosom bow that India was, she wouldn't say such a thing.

Still, Hermione wasn't about to concede so easily. "More likely you would both have to take back every terrible thing you've ever said about him."

"Or listen to your sorry laments over how wretchedly you've been deceived," Thomasin shot back.

Hermione turned toward the earl. Truly no man could be so terribly wicked or so awful.

Oh, if only . . .

Coming October 2008

Secret Desires of a Gentleman

The final book in the *Girl-Bachelor Chronicles*
by *USA Today* bestselling author

LAURA LEE GUHRKE

Phillip Hawthorne, Marquess of Kayne, has his life mapped out before him. He is a responsible member of the peerage, and rumor has it he may become the next prime minister. And then he runs into Maria Martingale. Twelve years ago, Maria was the cook's daughter, and she fancied herself in love with Lawrence Hawthorne, the marquess's younger brother, but Phillip quickly put an end to that romance. Now Phillip, still as cold and ruthless as he had been all those years ago, is concerned Maria will ruin things for Lawrence and his impending marriage, so he does the only thing he can think of to distract her—seduction.

Maria started down the street, still looking over her shoulder at the shop. "Perfect," she breathed with reverent appreciation. "It's absolutely perfect."

The collision brought her out of her daydreams with painful force. She was knocked off her feet, her handbag went flying, and she stumbled backward, stepping on the hem of her skirt as she tried desperately to right herself. She would have fallen to the pavement, but a pair of strong hands caught her by the arms, and she was hauled upright, pulled hard against what was definitely a man's chest. "Steady on, my girl," a deep voice murmured, a voice that somehow seemed familiar. "Are you all right?"

She inhaled deeply, trying to catch her breath, and as she did, she caught the luscious scents of bay rum and fresh linen. She nodded, her cheek brushing the unmistakable silk of a fine necktie. "I think so, yes," she answered.

Her palms flattened against the soft, rich wool of a gentleman's coat and she pushed back, straightening away from him as she lifted her chin to look into his face. The moment she did, recognition hit her with more force than the collision had done.

Phillip Hawthorne. The Marquess of Kayne.

There was no mistaking those eyes, vivid cobalt blue framed by thick black lashes. Irish eyes, she'd always thought, though if any Irish blood tainted the purity of his oh-so-aristocratic British lineage, he'd never have acknowledged it. Phillip had always been such a dry stick, as unlike his brother, Lawrence, as chalk was from cheese.

Memories came over her like a flood, washing away twelve years in the space of a heartbeat. Suddenly, she was no longer standing on a sidewalk in Mayfair, but in the library at Kayne Hall, and Phillip was standing across the desk from her, holding out a bank draft and looking at her as if she were nothing.

She glanced down, half-expecting to see a slip of pale pink paper in his hand—the bribe to make her leave and never come back, the payment for her promise to keep away from his brother for the rest of her life. The marquess had only been nineteen then, but he'd already managed to put a price on love. It was worth five hundred pounds.

That should be enough, since my brother assures me there is no possibility of a child.

His voice, so cold, echoed back to her from ten years ago, and shaken, she tried to gather her wits. She'd always expected she'd run into Phillip again one day, but she had not expected it to happen so literally, and she felt rather at sixes and sevens. Lawrence she'd never thought to see again, for she'd read in some scandal sheet years ago that he'd gone off to America.

His older brother was a different matter. Phillip was a marquess, he came to London for the season every year, sat in the House of Lords, and mingled with the finest society. Given all the balls and parties where she'd served hors d'oeuvres to aristocrats while working for Andre, Maria had resigned herself long ago to the inevitable night she would look up while offering a plate of canapés or a tray of champagne glasses and find his cool, haughty gaze on her, but it had never happened. Ten years of beating the odds only to cannon into him on a street corner. Of all the rotten luck.

Her gaze slid downward. Phillip had always been tall, but standing before her was not the lanky youth she remembered. This man's shoulders were wider, his chest broader, his entire physique exuding such masculine strength and vitality that Maria felt quite aggrieved. If there was any fairness in the world at all, Phillip Hawthorne would have gone to fat and gotten the gout by now. Instead, the Marquess of Kayne was even stronger and more powerful at thirty-one than he'd been at nineteen. How nauseating.

Still, she thought as she returned her gaze to his face, twelve years had left their mark. There were tiny lines at the corners of his eyes and two faint parallel creases across his forehead. The determination and discipline in the line of his jaw was even more pronounced than it had been a dozen years ago, and his mouth, a grave, unsmiling curve that had always been surprisingly beautiful, was harsher now. His entire countenance, in fact, was harder than she remembered it, as if all those notions of duty and responsibility he'd been stuffed with as a boy weighed heavy on him as a man. Maria found some satisfaction in that.

Even more satisfying was the fact that she had changed, too. She was no longer the desperate, forsaken seventeen-year-old girl who'd thought being bought off for five hundred pounds was her only choice. These days, she wasn't without means and she wasn't without friends. Never again would she be intimidated by the likes of Phillip Hawthorne.

"What are you doing here?" she demanded, then grimaced at her lack of eloquence. Over the years, she'd invented an entire repertoire of cutting, clever things to say to him should they ever meet again, and that blunt, stupid query was the best she could do? Maria wanted to kick herself.

"An odd question," he murmured in the well-bred accent she remembered so clearly. "I live here."

"Here?" A knot of dread began forming in the pit of her stomach as his words sank in. "But this is an empty shop."

"Not the shop." He let go of her arms and gestured to the front door of the first town house on Half Moon Street, an elegant red door out of which he must have just come from when they'd collided. "I live there."

She stared at the door in disbelief. *You can't live here,* she wanted to shout. *Not you, not Phillip Hawthorne, not in this house right beside the lovely, perfect shop where I'm going to live.*

She looked at him again. "But that's impossible. Your London house is in Park Lane."

He stiffened, dark brows drawing together in a puzzled frown. "My home in Park Lane is presently being remodeled, though I don't see what business it is of yours."

Before she could reply, he glanced at the ground and spoke again. "You've spilled your things."

"I didn't spill them," she corrected, bristling a bit. "You did."

To her disappointment, he didn't argue the point. "My apologies," he murmured, and knelt on the pavement. "Allow me to retrieve them for you."

She watched him, still irritated and rather bemused, as he righted her handbag and began to pick up her scattered belongings. She watched his bent head as he gathered her tortoiseshell comb, her gloves, her cotton handkerchief, and her money purse, then began placing them in her handbag with careful precision. So like Phillip, she thought. God forbid one should just toss it all inside and get on with things.

After all her things had been returned to her bag, he closed the brass clasp and reached for his hat, a fine gray felt homburg, which had also gone flying during the collision. He donned his hat and stood up, holding her bag out to her.

She took it from his outstretched hand. "Thank you, Phillip," she murmured. "How—" She broke off, not knowing if she should inquire after his brother, but then she decided it was only right to ask. "How is Lawrence?"

Something flashed in his eyes, but when he spoke, his voice was politely indifferent. "Forgive me, miss," he said with a cool, impersonal smile, "but your use of Christian names indicates a familiarity with me of which I am unaware."

Miss? She blinked, stunned. "Unaware?" she echoed and started to laugh, not from humor, but from disbelief. "But Phillip, you've known me since I was five years—"

"I don't believe so," he cut her off, his voice still polite and pleasant, his gaze hard and implacable. "We do not know each other, miss. We do not know each other at all. I hope that's clear?"

Her eyes narrowed. He knew precisely who she was and he was pretending not to, the arrogant, toplofty snob. How dare he snub her? She wanted to reply, but before she could think of something sufficiently cutting to say, he spoke again. "Good day, miss," he said, then bowed and stepped around her to go on his way.

She turned, watching his back as he walked away. Outrage seethed within her, but when she spoke, her voice was sweet as honey. "It was delightful to see you again, *Phillip*," she called after him. "Give Lawrence my best regards, will you?"

His steps did not falter as he walked away.

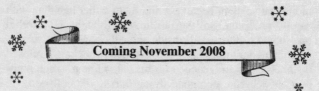

Coming November 2008

All I Want for Christmas Is a Vampire

The latest in the *Love at Stake* series
by *New York Times* bestselling author

KERRELYN SPARKS

*Vampire Ian MacPhie is on a mission—he's on the lookout
for true love. He claims that all he wants is another vampire. . . . until Toni Duncan comes along. Toni's best friend
is locked up in a psycho ward, deemed insane when she con-
fesses that vampires attacked her. The only way to get her
out is for Toni to prove that vampires exist. So Toni comes
up with a plan: make Ian lose control and beg him to make
her one of his kind . . .*

Ian felt ten degrees hotter in spite of the cold December air
that drifted through the open window and over his white
undershirt. The lamp between the two wingback chairs was
turned on low, and it cast a golden glow across the room to
outline her form with a shimmering aura.

She made a stunning cat burglar, dressed entirely in black
spandex that molded to her waist and sweetly curved hips.
Her golden hair hung in a ponytail down her back. The ends
swished gently across her shoulder blades, as she moved her
head from side to side, scanning the bookshelf.

She stepped to the side, silent in her black socks. She must
have left her shoes outside the window, thinking she'd move

more quietly without them. He noted her slim ankles, then let his gaze wander back up to golden hair. He would have to be careful capturing her. Like any Vamp, he had super strength, and she looked a bit fragile.

He moved silently past the wingback chairs to the window. It made a swooshing sound as he shut it.

With a gasp, she turned toward him. Her eyes widened. Eyes green as the hills surrounding his home in Scotland.

A surge of desire left him speechless for a moment. She seemed equally speechless. No doubt she was busily contemplating an escape route.

He moved slowly toward her. "Ye willna escape through the window. And ye canna reach the door before me."

She stepped back. "Who are you? Do you live here?"

"I'll be asking the questions, once I have ye restrained." He could hear her heart beating faster. Her face remained expressionless, except for her eyes. They flashed with defiance. They were beautiful.

She plucked a heavy book off a nearby shelf. "Did you come here to test my abilities?"

An odd question. Was he misinterpreting the situation? "Who—?" He dodged to the side when she suddenly hurled the book at his face. Bugger, he'd suffered too much to get his older, more manly face, and she'd nearly smacked it.

The book flew past him and knocked over the lamp. The light flickered and went out. With his superior vision, he could see her dark form running for the door.

He zoomed after her. Just before he could grab her, she spun and landed a kick against his chest. He stumbled back. Damn, she was stronger than he'd thought. And he'd suffered too much to get his broader, more manly chest.

She advanced with a series of punches and kicks, and he blocked them all. With a desperate move, she aimed a kick at his groin. Dammit, he'd suffered too much to get his bigger, more manly balls. He jumped back, but her toes caught the hem of his kilt. Without his sporran to weigh the kilt down, it flew up past his waist.

Her gaze flitted south and stuck. Her mouth fell open. Aye, those twelve years of growth had been kind. He lunged forward and slammed her onto the carpet. She punched at him, so he caught her wrists and pinned her to the floor.

She twisted, attempting to knee him. With a growl, he blocked her with his own knee. Then slowly, he lowered himself on top of her to keep her still. Her body was gloriously hot, flushed with blood and throbbing with a life force that made his body tremble with desire.

"Stop wiggling, lass." His bigger, more manly groin was reacting in an even bigger way. "Have mercy on me."

"Mercy?" She continued to wriggle beneath him. "I'm the one who's captured."

"Cease." He pressed more heavily on her.

Her eyes widened. He had no doubt she was feeling it.

Her gaze flickered down, then back to his face. "Get off. Now."

"I'm halfway there already," he muttered.

"Let me go!" She strained at his grip on her wrists.

"If I release you, ye'll knee me. And I'm rather fond of my balls."

"The feeling isn't mutual."

He smiled slowly. "Ye took a long look. Ye must have liked what ye saw."

"Ha! You made such a *small* impression on me, I can barely remember."

He chuckled. She was as quick mentally as she was physically.

She looked at him curiously. "You smell like beer."

"I've had a few." He noted her dubious expression. "Okay, more than a few, but I was still able to beat you."

"If you drink beer, then that means you're not . . ."

"No' what?"

She looked at him, her eyes wide. He had a sinking feeling that she thought he was mortal. She wanted him to be mortal. And that meant she knew about Vamps.

He studied her lovely face—the high cheekbones, delicate

jawline, and beguiling green eyes. Some Vamps claimed mortals had no power whatsoever. They were wrong.

Their eyes met, and he forgot to breathe. There was something hidden in those green depths. A loneliness. A wound that seemed too old for her tender age. For a moment, he felt like he was seeing a reflection of his own soul.

"Ye're no' a thief, are you?" he whispered.

She shook her head slightly, still trapped in his gaze. Or maybe it was he who was trapped in hers.

Coming December 2008

To Sin With a Stranger

The first in the new *Seven Deadly Sins* series by *USA Today* bestselling author

KATHRYN CASKIE

The Sinclairs are one of the oldest, wealthiest, and wildest noble families in all of Scotland. The seven brothers and sisters of the clan enjoy a good time, know no boundaries, and have scandal follow in their wake. They are known amongst the ton as The Seven Deadly Sins. But now their father has declared they must become respectable married members of proper Society . . . This is Sterling, Marquess of Sinclair's, story of how greed and a young beauty, Miss Isobel Carington, almost became his downfall.

"**A**s the Sinclair children grew older, they seemed to embrace the sins Society had labeled them with. Lord Sterling is cursed with greed." Christiana turned her eyes toward the fighter and Isobel followed her gaze. "Lady Susan epitomizes sloth, and Lady Ivy, the copper-haired beauty, envy."

"This is nonsense."

"Is it?" Christiana continued. "Lord Lachlan is a wicked rake. No wonder his weakness is lust. Lord Grant, the one with the lace cuffs, is said to have a taste for luxury and indulgence. His sin is gluttony. The twins are said to be the worst of all." She raised her nose toward the Sinclair with a sheath of hair so dark that it almost appeared a deep blue. "Lord Killian's sin is wrath. Whispers suggest that he is the true fighter in the family, but his anger is too quick and fierce. Why, there is even one rumor that claims that he actually killed a man who merely looked at his twin sister! That's her, there. Lady Priscilla. Just look at her with her haughty chin turned toward the chandelier—here, in a room full of nobility! Her sin is, quite clearly, *pride*."

"Nonsense! I do not believe it," Isobel countered. "I do not believe any of the story. The tale is not but idle gossip."

"I believe it." Christiana set one hand on her hip and waved the other in the air as she spoke. "Why else would they have come to London, if not to leave their sinful reputations behind in Scotland?"

"I am sure I do not know." Isobel saw Christiana's jaw drop, then felt the presence of someone behind her.

"Perhaps I have come to London to ask you to dance with me, lassie." His rich Scottish brogue resonated in her ears, making her vibrate with his every word.

Isobel whirled around and stared up into none other than Lord Sterling's grinning face.

"I apologize, I would address you by name, but alas, I dinna know what it is. Only that you are easily the most beautiful woman in this assembly room." Before she could blink, he reached a hand, knuckles stitched with black threads, and brushed his fingers across her cheek—just as he'd done at the club. "English lasses dinna stir me the way you do. You must be a wee bit Scottish."

Isobel gasped, drew back her hand, and gave his cheek a stinging slap. "Sirrah, you humiliated me, made light of my charity and my attempts to help widows and orphans of war. Why would I ever agree to dance with an ill-mannered rogue like you?"

"Because I asked, and I saw the way you were lookin' at me." He lifted an eyebrow teasingly, bringing to the surface a rage Isobel could not rein in. She slapped his face with such force that his head wrenched to the left. He raised his hand to his cheek. "Not bad. Have you thought about pugilism as a profession?" He grinned at her again.

Isobel stepped around Sterling Sinclair and started for her father. But he was only two steps away. Staring at her. Aghast. She reached out for him, but he stepped back, out of her reach.

She glanced to her left, then her right. Everyone was staring. Everyone.

Isobel covered her face with her trembling hands and shoved her way through the crowd of amused onlookers. She dashed out the door and down the steps to the liveried footman who opened the outer door for her to the street.

She ran outside and rested her hands on her knees as she gasped for breath. Her father would cast her to the street for embarrassing him this night.

No matter what punishment he chose for her, Isobel was certain he would never allow her to show her face in Town again.

And Lord Sterling, the wicked Marquess of Sinclair, was wholly to blame.